DESHI

Also by John Donohue...

Novels (Connor Burke Martial Arts Thrillers)
Sensei

Tengu

Kage

Nonfiction
The Overlook Martial Arts Reader

Complete Kendo

Herding the Ox: The Martial Arts as Moral Metaphor

Warrior Dreams: The Martial Arts and the American Imagination

The Human Condition in the Modern Age

The Forge of the Spirit: Structure, Motion, and Meaning in the Japanese Martial Tradition

JOHN DONOHUE

DESHI

YMAA Publication Center
Wolfeboro, NH USA

YMAA Publication Center, Inc.
PO Box 480
Wolfeboro, NH 03894
1-800-669-8892 • www.ymaa.com • info@ymaa.com

ISBN Paperback edition	ISBN Ebook
978-1-59439-249-8	978-1-59439-248-1

Cover Design: Axie Breen

20210624

Publisher's Cataloging in Publication

Donohue, John J., 1956-

    Deshi / John Donohue. -- Wolfeboro, NH : YMAA Publication Center, c2013.

      p. ; cm.

      ISBN: 978-1-59439-249-8 (pbk.) ; 978-1-59439-248-1 (ebook)
      "A Connor Burke martial arts thriller"--Cover.
      First published by Thomas Dunne Books in 2005.
      Summary: Asian scholar and black belt artist Connor Burke labors as a deshi (a disciple) under the tutelage of a master warrior-- a practice that draws him into the murder of a Japanese businessman in Brooklyn. An enigmatic message left at the murder scene leads Connor to the lethal samurai heritage of a mysterious martial arts sensei, a Tibetan clairvoyant, and finally to an elite mountain temple in Tibet, where his deadliest challenge awaits.--Publisher.

      1. Burke, Connor (Fictitious character) 2. Americans--China--Fiction. 3. New Age movement--Fiction. 4. Martial artists--Fiction. 5. Tibet Autonomous Region (China)--Fiction. 6. Martial arts fiction. 7. Suspense fiction. I. Title.

PS3604.O565 D264 2013	2013945345
813/.6--dc23	1308

Printed in USA.

To Kitty, with love,
for gently holding a writer's heart

Deshi
(The disciple)

The deshi believes he learns from the master
And moves on
The sensei knows
In truth, they are linked
Along the same Path
In separate places
A yoke of flesh and steel, bound together
Like two wheels on the same cart
—Yamashita Rinsuke

Prologue: Path

Everyone wants something: it's one of the few points of philosophy my brother Micky and I agree on. Desires shape the arc of life's trajectories, leading us to unimagined destinations.

The Buddhists say desire creates illusion, which is the source of all suffering. In the Catholic Church I was raised in, desire was equally disparaged. There are few things in life really worth wanting, but we are cursed with an almost limitless capacity for imagination and need. The truly wise know that what we really need are those things that permit our true natures to emerge. We're born with that knowledge, then quickly forget it and spend a lifetime trying to remember it again.

The path a life takes is the product of that remembering. We wander along in search of the selves we once knew. The way isn't easy: it's stony, studded with obstacles. And we're not alone on the lurching journey: there are forms crumpled in the brambles by the wayside, markers to those who've lost their way. And, when the path dips, there are others, still watchers waiting in the dim woods. Ghosts hungry to snatch us. The way winds and dips. There are times when the path is unclear. Faint tracks lead the unwary off to their doom. But, high up ahead, we can all glimpse the hint of something beautiful. It's faint and hard to see, but it pulls us nonetheless.

A good teacher tells you to keep looking at that gossamer image. I don't know whether it's kindness or cruelty. But it keeps the yearning alive; it makes you stay on the right path. And it prevents you from looking down. Because when you do, you see that there is blood on the rocks.

1
SPRING WIND

*You think about them so much—the victims and
the murderers. You go over and over the details
you string together until, after a while, the reality
of a stranger's experience becomes your own. And
then, the facts come alive and echo in your brain.
It's a vivid and painful resonance.*

The breeze was warm that day and the air felt soft and laden
with moisture. It was the time of year when a few good sunny
hours could make the plants seem to explode with buds and
blossoms. You could feel it: after a time of tense waiting, something was about to happen.

Edward Sakura knew about waiting. The people I spoke
with told me that. He had learned to check the urge to act
quickly with a calm, methodical discipline. The excitement
and anticipation that were part of putting together a good deal
never faded, of course. It was why he was in the business he was
in. But he had mastered his impulses through years of trial and
error. And it had paid off handsomely.

Shodo, the Way of the Brush, had been a constant teacher
for over three decades in his quest for patience. It was one of
life's little ironies. As a young man, he had learned from his parents' experience in Manzinar that safety in America was based
on conforming to American culture. In retrospect, people of
Sakura's generation were puzzled as to why their folks did not

grasp that one fact about America. After all, the Japanese themselves had a saying that the nail that sticks out gets banged down.

He had looked at the photos from the camps the American government had shunted his parents and other Japanese-Americans off to. The rows of slapdash wooden barracks, geometrically arranged in the desolation of the high American desert, would have been enough to drive the lesson home to even the dimmest of observers. And by the end of the war, Americans of Japanese descent had learned to look forward into the future, simply because the past was too painful. And, in so doing, they turned their gaze away from Japan.

Sakura had been a bright kid and he turned into an even brighter adult. After getting his MBA he had developed a taste for the high-octane deals increasingly being cut in the entertainment industry. And, over time, he succeeded quite well for himself. But with middle age, he had come to yearn for some sense of connection to his past. A high-energy man in a fast-paced business, he chose an endeavor diametrically opposed to the normal pace of his days.

For thirty years, every day, no matter where he was, Sakura surrendered part of his life to the Discipline of the Brush. As his teachers directed, he would set aside his worries. Enter a realm of a quiet focus. Then, kneeling before the purity of white paper, he would slowly, methodically prepare. The cake of dried ink would whir faintly against the stone as he ground it into powder. He would carefully add water to the mix, gazing intently at the liquid, thick with promise, dense and black with potential.

Then he would breathe, calming his hand, centering himself before picking up the brush. And, when spirit and brush were one, the ink trail would spool across the paper, leaving something of Sakura frozen in time, made manifest in the stark contrast of black ink and white background.

He had carried his art with him when he relocated to New York. The growing presence of Japanese companies like Sony in the entertainment industry meant that there were opportunities for a dealmaker like Sakura on two coasts. He worked in Manhattan and went home each night to a quiet, upscale neighborhood in the Fort Hamilton section of Brooklyn. It was a community that seemed tidy and green after the sprawling concrete of Manhattan. You could smell the sea in the breeze that blew in from the Atlantic. And best of all, amid the blush of life in a spring garden, it contained Sakura's small Shodo hut.

He had built it as far back away from the house as he could. The property lines in his neighborhood were set with high walls for privacy and thickly cushioned with trees. It made for a small island of tranquility. He felt drawn to it now more than ever, a stone that sat, still and isolated, in the rushing current of his life.

The hut's location was why he didn't hear his killer approach.

In this part of Brooklyn, people value their privacy. The streets are relatively narrow, the houses old and well established, their faces closed to the street. The lots that the houses sit on are irregular, with occasional backyards of surprising depth. The hum of traffic from the more congested avenues to the east is never absent. And one more Lexus tooling sedately through the late afternoon streets would not have excited much comment.

People think of hunting as essentially a chase. But professional hunters, the really successful ones, get that way by wasting very little energy and planning ahead. They can chase if they have to, but they much prefer to stalk. And, if possible, they would rather use the techniques of ambush. Know your prey. Know his patterns. Know where he will be. And wait there.

Did the killer sneak up on Sakura or was he already there, lurking in the undergrowth? It doesn't really matter. He knew where to find his victim. And with the pitiless certainty of all killers, he moved in.

The old masters, the real *sensei*, say that any Way leads to the same point. Whether you pick up the brush or the sword, the focus and training changes you. It's imperceptible at first. But it is cumulative. I later studied Sakura's calligraphy, and it told me that his three decades of training had not been wasted.

The whole point of calligraphy is to lose yourself in it, not dwell on distractions. It's probable that he picked up on the sensations swirling around him, because mastering stillness means you can also vibrate like a tuning fork when conditions are right. I know. And I'll bet Sakura did, too.

Professionals don't leak much emotion. The Japanese warriors of old talked about the concept of remaining in *kage*, within the shadow or shade. You don't give anything of yourself to your opponent. You don't let enemies see what you think or feel or intend. The killer that day was probably as quiet and self-contained as they come. Yet we all leak some psychic energy, no matter how hard we try.

The atmosphere was charged with tension that day, and the victim sensed it. I work in a discipline with different tools, but the methods are the same. My teachers say that the mind can be distracted and "stick" to some extraneous thing. It creates a gap in your concentration. And you can see it revealed in subtle ways in your technique.

And that's what I see when I look at that sheet of calligraphy from Edward Sakura. An intrusion. A change in focus.

The killer parked his car on the next block and walked back to the side gate that led to the rear of the property. He eventually had to leave the concrete and stone surface to get to his target, so he left a trace. His footprints through the rich, dark, spring earth suggested a big man. He walked slowly and quietly—the imprints are deeper on the toe and not much dirt was thrown backwards. There was no need for haste and no need to make noise. He obviously knew where he was going and knew what he would find there.

Sakura's head probably came up as he sensed the killer's approach. He remained seated in the formal position, legs tucked under him, insteps flat on the floor. The awareness must have come on him with an overwhelming finality. Not a thrill of panic or an electric jolt, but a deep-seated settling, like something at the body's very core shifting down toward the earth, where it lodged, unmistakable and immovable.

There was no forced entry and none of the smashed door-jamb theatrics you might expect. There was no wasted motion. It was economical and efficient. You would almost call it civilized. Except for the end result.

The killer entered the hut from the door to the calligrapher's left. Sakura shifted slightly to view the intruder, but remained oriented toward the low table that held his paper and brush. Did his eyes get wide as the attacker loomed there? I would have been scrambling around like mad. But there was none of that either.

Sakura knew about deals. He understood how they worked and how you could work them. But people who knew him also said he had the knack of analyzing things and predicting the outcome way before most other people. He knew when you could still negotiate and knew when the deal was done. So between the phenomenon the Japanese call *haragei*—a type of intuition common among masters of the arts—and his years of business acumen, Sakura pretty much knew what was about to happen. There was no way out.

There may have been some conversation. Not much. The killer was not in a line of work that did much to develop verbal skills. Messages got delivered in more elemental ways. Sakura, turned slightly to gaze on the hulking reminder of mortality that glided into the hut, would want to know why. It's probably the most common last question there is. But even then, despite the elevated heart rate and the sweat that sprung out in cold, oily drops on his forehead, Sakura was thinking. So his question wasn't just futile rhetoric. It was part of his last deal. Whether the killer picked up on it or not, Sakura was bargaining for the time he needed. To give us a clue.

He slid a fresh sheet of paper in front of him on the table. With a last look at the killer, Sakura rolled his brush in ink and sought the center one last time. It's a hard thing to do with the respiration going crazy and fear trying to hammer in through the barrier of discipline.

The brush rustled across the paper. The intruder's arm arced up as if it were an echo of the action.

The bullet punched in through the thin bone at the temple. The soft slug flattened out and gouged its way through Sakura's head. When it blew out the other side, his hand spasmed and his last work of calligraphy tailed off without control as the body collapsed.

The killer stepped over Sakura and poked the sheet of paper in inquiry. He grunted with contempt as he read the strokes. This calligraphy before him could tell people nothing. In the distance, a car door slammed and his head jerked toward the sound, alive to the possible threat. He moved toward the door to check and, vaguely uneasy, left without a backwards glance. What was there to see? A small refuge violated. A copy of the Platform Scripture. Rice paper with some meaningless brush strokes. A small huddled figure in a spreading pool of fluid. And, on the delicate *shoji* screens of the room, a pattern of small crimson dots, blown there like raindrops driven before a strong wind.

2

DEAD ANGLE

I wasn't thinking about a murder. I was thinking about killing.

The Japanese martial *dojo* is a training hall remarkable for its beauty. Clean lines. A lack of clutter. The warmth of wood and the stateliness of ritual. Don't be fooled. Look closely at us as we move in that space. We watch each other warily, alive to the sudden rush of attack. We're controlled and focused. But there's a murderous ferocity running like a deep current in us all. It gets exposed in many small ways.

Most dojo are big spaces. Sound bounces around in them in a jumble of shouts and thuds. But if you have enough experience, you can hear things distinctly. Asa Sensei was a kendo teacher of the old school. When you find a really good group of swordsmen training together, you can hear things in the quality of the noise they make. We were in Asa Sensei's dojo, and the chant of the swordsmen was fierce, a pulse of sound generated in a circle of swordsmen that rang throughout the cavern of a room. It created an energy that I could feel as I swung my sword and shouted along with them.

Out of the corner of my eye, I could see both Asa and Yamashita standing and watching us. Their dark eyes glittered, but beyond that, they could have been carved in stone. My teacher's shaven head sat on his thick body like an artillery shell. Asa was thinner and had gray hair swept back from a wide forehead. But the way they held themselves—the thick, muscled forearms that were visible beneath the sleeves of their indigo training tops; the dense, rooted silence of both men—made them seem almost identical.

They were watchers, those two. It's how you must get after a while. They drink in their surroundings until they can feel it on their skin, taste it in their mouths. Until the breath flows in and out in the rhythm of what surrounds them. And then, when ready, they strike.

When you see them as they truly are, these men are frightening. They hold so much back, measuring you, judging you. They dole out knowledge in grudging bits, forcing you to struggle for each morsel. Looking back, you reluctantly admit that maybe it was necessary. But while you eventually come to trust them, it makes you wary.

I struggle with this. Yamashita is my teacher and I had once thought him perfect. I knew better now. He was still my sensei, but the relationship had changed. He looks at me with flat, emotionless eyes. And sometimes, I look back in the same way. I've learned a great deal. Not all of it is good.

The first time I stood across from Yamashita, any confidence that a black belt in two different arts had given me vaporized in the blast furnace of his intensity. Yamashita knows what you are up to before the nerve flash of your latest bright idea leaps across a synapse. As far as I can tell, he is without technical flaw. And without remorse. With Yamashita, every time you step onto the training floor, you are being tested. Over the years you accommodate yourself to it, but it's still a reality that hovers just out of sight, like a prowling animal, both feared and resented.

Today, the animal was out in the open.

Yamashita and Asa had gleefully discussed their plans with me. They told me how the great swordsman Tesshu would test his pupils through something called *seigan,* or vow training. There were different levels, but each level required a certain period of practice—one year, two years, three—after which the trainee would face a set number of opponents, one after another. You could fight fifty people. Or a hundred. Or more. The idea was to exhaust the trainee until all conscious thought was burned away and only pure spirit animated the sword. This, they believe, is a type of *seishin tanren,* spiritual forging.

Yamashita related to me how one trainee, on his third consecutive day of fighting, had to be helped to stand up. His fencing gloves were so encrusted with blood that they made it hard to grip the sword. There was literally nothing left of the poor guy.

They love to curl your hair with these sorts of stories. Yamashita and his friend watched me carefully. I shrugged. "That's why I'm here," I said. They both looked at me with the contained yet satisfied look of cats. I stared back.

Deep down, of course, my nerves jangled. Yamashita would watch me struggle under the pressure to perform well in an unfamiliar style. Deep down, resentment churned within me.

Don't let anybody fool you. Underneath all the Zen window dressing, there's still a great deal of ego involved here. You don't devote your life to something as demanding as this without developing a certain amount of pride. There is humility, sure. But students measure themselves as much against each other as they do against the more demanding standards that we generate from deep inside ourselves. The sense of being tested again in a new way, of having to prove myself again to Yamashita and his crony, was exasperating. I expected something different after all this time. To have the two teachers watching me like pitiless judges made the subtle competitive vibrations that were always present when you fought people feel almost unbearable.

So you don't think about it. You focus on the fight. You take the churning and spin it into ferocity. All the blood spilled today would be symbolic, but it doesn't change the mindset: you strive to kill your opponent or die trying.

The boom of the great drum of the dojo called the group to order. We lined up and knelt in the formal kneeling posture. The bamboo sword called a *shinai* is placed to the left side. The silent row of swordsmen was garbed in the body armor and the midnight blue uniform traditional in this art. We sat and waited. At a command, we placed our hands in the meditation posture and closed our eyes. The effort of centering began for me.

Control the breath. A measured pace of being that slows the heart. Focus on the present. Set aside resentment. Distraction. Fear. There is no line of swordsmen. No teachers watching your every move. Only the Art of the Sword, a sea of experience in which the separate drops of our individual selves merge together.

At least that's the theory.

I had run through fifteen opponents in the first hour. They were all testing for the last rank before black belt level. Some were smoother than others, some quicker, but they had the intense energy and unconventional mindsets of novices and it made them a little dangerous. I was glad when the sensei called a break. They didn't let me take off my helmet: part of the whole idea was to create an ordeal. They were succeeding. The leather palms of my gloves were soaked with sweat, however, and they let me change them.

Now I faced the black belts. My awareness of time began to slip. These fighters were far more skilled. The psychic tension of fighting is as big a factor as mere matters of technique. I could exert a type of mental force against my opponents, but now they were capable of pushing back. It meant that the pace of the matches was different: a wary circling, a flurry of attacks. Manipulation of the tips of the swords. Deflections, feints. And pushing against me like a force field, I felt the psychic pressure known as *seme*, communicated through posture and the weapon itself.

After a time, you feel as if you inhabit a world where only heat, sweat, and the fury of the opponent exist. The rest of the world has fallen away. Which is what the sensei want. Total focus on the art. Nothing else. When my focus slipped, or I let fatigue begin to seep in, the sensei made the matches go longer. The message was clear: perfection was my only escape.

At the end of this section of the contest, they let me take my helmet off. It was soaked by this time, with the white wavy patterns of dried sweat forming in spots. I sat formally, put the sword down, and removed my mitts. I was permitted a sip of water. Yamashita glided up to my side and sat down in one smooth, flowing motion. He picked up my sword and began to inspect it, not looking directly at me, but speaking quietly.

"So Professor. I think that your technique is not completely orthodox by kendo standards but you have managed your opponents relatively well."

It was typical, the grudging compliment that hinted that you were still lacking. My response wasn't immediate; I was intent on just breathing. When you get tired, or excited, the breathing is the first thing to go. You lose the rhythm and then everything else just collapses. So I sat there. A big bead of sweat shook loose from my nose. I wiped my face on my sleeve.

Yamashita leaned his thick torso in across my front and picked up my gloves to examine them as well. "What is important about this exercise is the stress it creates and how you react to it. How well you maintain your…" he thought for a minute, "… composure. This is important. Now you will face a student Asa thinks has some promise… And… we will see." He set the gloves down again, placing them palm down on the floor and resting the helmet carefully upon them.

"So who's being tested, him or me?" I said.

His head swiveled slowly toward me. "It is enough that there is to be a test. I did not say of whom…" His voice was cold in dismissal.

I don't know whether he saw the annoyed look on my face. After a moment, Yamashita nodded, as if in response to some interior discussion. Oblivious to my feelings. "I think this should be most instructive for you. But remember," he held up a thick finger, "in terms of pure kendo *waza,* sheer technique, this opponent will surely be superior to you." I took a breath to say something, but he reached out. For a moment I thought he was going to touch me. It would be an unusual gesture for my teacher. Then he stopped, as if halted by a troubling thought. We looked at each other in silence. Then, with an effort, he went on. "Be aware, Burke. The man you will face has trained for years in just this narrow band of swordsmanship. He will be faster. And more accurate." His head swiveled up to take in the students milling about. He didn't seem to be looking at anything in particular.

"But you must move beyond a focus on technique. And this is where things of the heart come in, Burke. You must keep your spirit strong. And open to things… And, if you cannot best this one using kendo techniques you must use what you know." I grunted in acknowledgement. My teacher looked at me. "The understanding is here," he said forcefully, clapping his hand on his stomach. "Consider: every art specializes in something. Which means it neglects something else. This is like *shikaku*."

Shikaku. The dead angle. Just behind and to one side of an opponent. Out of the range of vision. In the blind spot. And, for a fighter, the dead angle. If you could get there, you dominated your enemy.

A call from across the room notified us that the last match was about to begin. Yamashita gazed at me once, the look flat and without encouragement, and then flowed up and away like smoke. He was like an idol with dead eyes, demanding worship but giving little in return.

If it was a familiar feeling, it was irrelevant. I pushed it down and away, checked the knots that fastened my armor to me. Put on my helmet and gloves. Picked up my sword and waded in.

There really wasn't time to think. I parried and evaded, counterattacked and tried to hold on to the center. But it was difficult. My teacher was right. This man was well on his way to mastering the art. He drove in relentlessly, seeking a gap in my concentration, waiting to lash out with a decisive stroke. My opponent used the small, snapping jerks designed to score points in kendo. It was blindingly fast and evading it made me sweat even more—if such a thing were possible.

He was pressing me. I could feel it. Is this what Yamashita had wanted me to sense? The feints were designed to get me off guard, to break my posture. I used my sword to parry his gambits, watching for the telltale signs that warned of a lunging attack.

Everyone telegraphs something of their intentions before they come at you. But the better they are, the more subtle it is. With novice swordsmen, you can see the attack forming in the tilt of the head, a rocking back as if gathering momentum. The tip of the sword dips slightly. For this man, there was none of that. That I could see. There was just a sensed pressure. The knowledge of imminent danger.

The next attack didn't explode at me so much as it flowed in an accelerating continuum, a smooth, highly compressed generation of force and intent. My hands rose up slightly to cover the unfolding technique. It wasn't a conscious action on my part. But it was as if there were a wire linking his sword to mine: as his rose, mine rose with it. It made his strike less than perfect: he hit me, but not without the clattering of swords as I parried. Then he whipped his sword down, pushing mine with it. It was a subtle, tight force and it caught me by surprise. His sword tip made a small circle, and as it levered against my weapon, it broke my grasp. My sword went flying from my hands. I was unarmed and at his mercy.

But here is where the killing fury comes in. You just never give up. Rationally, I was through. But I was operating with something else. I saw his sword wind up for the finishing blow and a strange part of me welcomed it. I shot in on a tangent. His attack took place simultaneously. We were moving so quickly that he was still focused on the mental image of me as a target. But he was focused on a place where I was no longer standing.

Because I had slid into his dead angle. I grabbed his collar with my left hand. I had stretched my right hand across his throat. His forward momentum carried his legs forward; my arm jerked his chin back and to one side. I pivoted and sent him crashing to the floor. He lay there stunned for a second, and I stood above him, panting. The he scrambled to his feet and came at me. And I was ready.

"*Yame!*" The order came to stop.

We backed warily away from each other, but the sensei had seen enough. At the command, we all lined up again to bow out. I took my helmet off and I'll bet you could see steam rising off my head. After the formal ending, I got to thank each person I had crossed swords with, sitting and bowing to everyone in turn. There was a faint roaring in my ears.

With his helmet off, I saw that my last opponent was a young man. His blonde hair was dark with sweat, but he had the square jaw and pale eyes, the good looks that I associated with high school athletes and actors. He smiled, and his teeth looked even and white. But the expression didn't touch his eyes. They were still burning with the desire to take the match to a real finish.

The hold of discipline is strong, however. We bowed, hands flat on the floor, torsos lowered over them. "Burke," I said.

He sat up from his bow and looked at me silently for a few seconds, without expression. Then the smile came again. It had a hard edge to it, tinged with a curious type of self-satisfaction.

"Stark," he said. "Travis Stark."

I watched him get up and move away. Slowly, the room and its details began to swim back into my awareness. Students were tying up their armor and congratulating each other. Asa and Yamashita were inking promotion certificates at a table.

By the door, two men entered and spoke to a student. They flashed police badges and looked around in that universally suspicious way policemen have. Both had bristly mustaches. The one with sandy hair was bigger and thicker. The other cop was smaller, thinner, and crankier looking, although they both had their professional cop faces on.

My teacher saw them and stood up quickly. He made a gesture at the cops as if trying to shoo them away. They paused. Then the two swordsmen came out from behind the table.

Yamashita and Asa sat down in the formal position and gestured for me to do the same. Then, Asa formally promoted me to the fourth dan—black belt rank—in kendo. I received the certificate he proffered, taking it in both hands as a sign of respect. Asa bowed to me and to my teacher, then rose and left without another word. Yamashita looked at me and then glanced at the cops, who were heading our way.

I held the certificate in my lap, silent. My hands trembled slightly. You might think it was muscle fatigue; in reality, it takes a while to bleed off the psychic energy of a match like that.

Yamashita nodded slightly to me. "So. An interesting performance. But it was not decisive. Perhaps if we had let it go on... one of you certainly would have won."

"It would have been me," I said. My voice was flat, but I gave him a look that said there wasn't any argument.

"So?" he said, and broke into a smile. "I would expect no less. And now you see the point of the exercise." He bowed in dismissal and left me in a smooth, silent glide.

I could hear bits of the quiet conversation the two cops were having as they approached me. "I'm telling you," the bigger one was saying, "there's a stylistic link here. These costumes make these guys look like Darth Vader."

His partner didn't reply. He had a white streak in his hair and a disgusted look on his face. They hovered about me and I got up to meet them.

"Well?" I asked them expectantly. My tone wasn't the friendliest. This guy with the streak in his hair had bugged me way before he had started to go gray. He was my older brother Micky.

He smirked at me. "You look like shit," my brother the cop said. "But I think we need you."

I held a hand up to my ear. "What was that?"

"Stop dickin' around," Micky said.

I gestured with my hand at my ear again. "Huh?"

"We need you," he said, biting the words off one by one.

His partner, Art, was a bigger man. He smiled at me. He also enjoyed needling Micky. It was part of a very complex relationship.

"I'll bet it hurt you to say that," I commented to my brother, and winked at Art.

"Oh, yeah," Art said happily, nodding. Micky was silent.

I gathered up my gear and changed. My muscles felt loose and disconnected. People talk about a "runner's high" after exercise. But in the martial arts world of Yamashita Sensei, you often just emerged stunned, bruised, and trembling. I've been at this for a while, however. Aside from the distant ache of new bruises I just felt slightly relaxed.

But I wasn't going to stay that way. When I came outside, the two policemen were waiting for me. We were heading for a place where the violence was less contained and all the blood-shed was real.

3
SPLATTER

They argued about who would drive. "You sure you're up to it?" my brother Micky asked.

His partner, Art, is pretty good-natured, but questions like this bother him. "Hey, get off my case," he snapped. "What, you think I'm not up to it?"

Micky held up his hands in mock surrender. "Just asking. You don't want to tax things." He went to the passenger door. Art moved past him, grumbling, and got behind the wheel.

I sat in silence in the back and let the flow of the trip calm them down. This crabby exchange was typical and the tense atmosphere didn't last long. Eventually, Art started to talk again. "So we say to ourselves," he began saying to me as we drove crosstown toward the East River, "why not share the wealth?"

"Hey, asshole," my brother Micky said, "you want to drive so badly, how about using two hands?" Now he was cranky.

Art was driving with his right hand and waving the other one around. It made me worry. Not too long ago, someone had sliced his right hand off with a sword. They had bagged it in ice and stuck it on the gurney when they wheeled Art away. No one paid much attention. The guy with the sword had done other damage and everyone expected Art to die.

He hung on. Micky and I tracked the swordsman down. Eventually, it came to a head on a steamy night in midtown Manhattan. I don't like to think about it too much. The only good thing was that, at the end of it all, I didn't die.

Neither did Art.

He spent quite a bit of time in ICU, hooked up to machines. I wonder if the doctors felt left out from the start and reattached the hand immediately just to have something to do. It turned out to be a good thing. Art got better and Micky would have refused to work with a partner that looked like Captain Hook.

Now we were rocking along the FDR drive with a cop's casual disregard for speed limits. He swerved around other motorists in long swooping moves that would have induced motion sickness in the less stalwart.

I was sitting in the back of their car. The shocks were mushy. The back was awash in clipboards and old newspapers. A paper coffee cup rolled wetly around on the floor. I inched the window down a bit and sipped at the air in quiet desperation.

"I gotta say, Connor," Micky commented, watching the scenery whiz by, "I thought, 'no way' when this call came through. I mean, come on."

"Strange," Art said in a thick, choked up weird voice.

"Let me get this straight," I said, and tried to focus on something other than Art's atrocious driving. "The Brooklyn cops called you in on a homicide because some bright light had read about what happened to us last time?"

"Famous, we are," Art said in that same voice.

"Yeah, well," my brother responded. "We got some Japanese guy. Apparent homicide victim. The only clue? Some calligraphy."

"Come on!" I protested.

"Mystery, there is. And danger," Art intoned.

"Art, I swear to God if you don't cut that Master Yoda shit out right now I'm gonna go insane!" my brother yelled.

Art just chortled and swung around a slow-moving vehicle. "Yeah," he said in his normal voice, "so we thought we'd bring you with us to take a look."

"Great," I said.

"You bet." Art smiled as he glanced up at me in the rearview mirror. We coasted onto the ramp for the Brooklyn Bridge. "Only one change in plans," he said, looking at my brother.

"Oh, yeah?" Micky asked skeptically.

"Yeah. If there's a guy with a sword, you go after him this time." Then Art put both hands on the wheel, as if suddenly remembering something disturbing. Micky looked at the side window, his face a mask.

There was a variety of uniformed types milling about the house when we arrived. Cops have a herding instinct. Most of the workday is indescribably boring. So when something big happens, they're drawn to it. From all over. There were marked and unmarked cars sitting at various angles along the street. The nicely tended trees tended to break things up, but you could hear the chatter from a number of radios, like the sound of nasty insects. There were a few plainclothes guys smoking on the sidewalk and a few patrolmen in the traditional blue uniforms of the NYPD milling about. They all seemed to have large, square automatics riding on their gunbelts.

I looked at Art and Micky. They wear rumpled sportcoats and pants whose manufacturers claim never need ironing. This is not true. I, for one, had left my shinai in the trunk of the car and, bereft of a belt loaded with cop hardware, I felt conspicuously under-dressed.

How Art and my brother got sent from Manhattan on this call was anyone's guess, but they threaded their way through a variety of suspicious uniformed people. We stopped briefly to ask questions at numerous points, getting shunted farther and farther back through the house and eventually into the yard at the rear.

Where the total crime scene experience was in full swing.

A guy in his early fifties was standing outside the hut and talking with a woman from the forensics squad. His suit was a stylish olive three-button number, but it was slightly wrinkled at the thighs. His hair, which was a speckled iron gray, looked freshly cut. Various people kept coming up to him to give brief reports. He didn't say much. His face looked tired.

"Lieutenant Strakowski?" Art asked. The man turned to look at us with a "what now" expression.

"You the guys from Manhattan?" he asked. Micky and Art flashed their shields, introduced themselves, and shook hands. All part of one big happy club.

Strakowski turned to look at me. "You are?" Cops don't waste much energy with the niceties. Micky and Art tried to explain my presence as if subtly conscious of my shameful lack of an appropriate firearm.

The Lieutenant nodded. "Oh, yeah. You're the guy I read about. With the swords and all." He turned to Micky. "He doesn't look that dangerous."

My brother shrugged.

"The Burkes are tricky that way," Art chimed in. "I speak from experience."

You could see Strakowski making connections as we talked. He was the one who had asked for us to come over. I saw him glance once at Art's hand. The one that had been reattached. But that was it. Strakowski was not easily distracted.

"Lemme show you what we got," he said and motioned us toward the hut. He trudged through the grass and we followed. "I gotta say," he commented, "your Lieutenant was awful cooperative. Almost eager to send you here."

"That's easily explained," Art answered.

"Yeah," Micky concluded. "Lieutenant Colletti hates us."

Strakowski paused and turned his head slightly in our direction. But he didn't say a word.

I was pretty clear about my role in the crime scene investigation, since I've done this before. I was to avoid touching anything. To speak only when spoken to. In short, I was expected to avoid annoying the adults.

It's just as well. Crime scenes give me the creeps.

First, there are all these cops stomping around with the heavy reinforced shoes they wear. You'd think a death scene would be quiet, reverential. It's not. The little cop radios that are clipped to their shoulders squawk intermittently. The officers call loudly to one another about various things. The forensics people are quieter, but they add a sense of bustle to the whole thing that is unseemly. Particularly if the dead guy is present.

Fortunately, he wasn't.

It was a relief. There's something about the undignified postures and often messy conditions that are the frequent accompaniment to violent death that get to me. Besides, I was still feeling faintly nauseated from the car ride.

The calligraphy hut wasn't a large place. It was meant to be a solitary refuge. Now, it was crowded with cops. Life is full of irony. Strakowski paused at the door and took a deep breath. A Hispanic plainclothes detective was lounging against the doorjamb, watching the forensics team working intently inside, but he looked up almost immediately at the Lieutenant. "Pete, give us a minute, here, would ya?" Strakowski said.

He gestured at the man with a thumb. "Sergeant Pete Ramirez." Then he pointed at each of us in turn. "Detectives Burke, Pedersen from Manhattan PD. The other Burke."

"The sword guy?" Ramirez asked.

I let out a long sigh. Some things are not worth getting into. Micky smirked. "Hey, Connor. You're famous."

"Everyone's famous for fifteen minutes, Mick," I told him.

"Yeah, well, time's up," Strakowski said. He was not a man with a high tolerance for banter. He gestured the forensics team out. "Give us a few minutes, people, OK?" Then he looked at Ramirez. "Fill us in, Pete."

Ramirez snapped back into focus and took a notepad from his jacket pocket. "Victim is Edward Sakura, fifty-eight. Works for Three Diamonds Productions, an entertainment agency or something."

We moved into the hut as he spoke. A taped outline was on the floor, showing the points of Sakura's last living contact with the earth. It was well done and you got a good sense of the arrangement of limbs. The area where the head lay was a dark, smudgy stain. You could smell the blood in the close confines of the room.

Art and Micky stopped once they were inside. They did it together, almost automatically, and slowly scanned the room as if imprinting it in their minds. Ramirez continued his briefing.

"Victim was alone at the time of the shooting."

"You got a fix on the time of death, yet?" Art interrupted.

Ramirez shook his head no. "Just a rough estimate from the coroner's guys. I haven't seen the paperwork yet."

"Get it as soon as you can, Pete," Strakowski said tersely.

"Wife?" Micky asked.

"Yep," Ramirez answered. "Gone all day. We're checking it out."

"Where is she now?" Art asked.

"She's inside," the Lieutenant said, "doped to the eyeballs. The doctor just left."

Ramirez went back to reading his notes. "Apparent cause of death was a large caliber bullet wound. Entered the left temple and blew out the other side of the head."

"Powder burns?" my brother asked.

"None visible. No weapon at the scene. Suicide is probably out. We'll do a paraffin check on the corpse anyway."

Micky and Art nodded their approval. "Do the wife, too," Micky murmured.

Then he turned to look around, and I did, too. It was a typical layout for Shodo practice. White walls, with natural wood trim. A low, wooden table where the paper, ink, and brushes were arranged. A small cushion for sitting on. There were some bookshelves and drawers behind the spot where Sakura had sat. It looked fairly tidy in there. But the white outline with the stain ruined the effect.

A few calligraphy brushes lay on the floor, close to the tape outline of an arm. The cushion looked like it had been shoved around, probably by the movements of the body as Sakura took his last trip to the floor. Other than that, most things looked normal.

"No sign of a struggle," Art said, as if reading my mind.

"Right," Ramirez responded. "No real struggle. No evidence of forced entry."

"Anything disturbed at the house?"

Strakowski let out a stream of air as if impatient with going over old ground. "No apparent break-in. Nothing taken. None of the neighbors saw anything. We're checking the wife's alibi. Looking for girlfriend trouble. Boyfriend trouble. Business trouble."

Art and Micky looked at him without expression as Strakowski went on. "Look, we know what we're doing. We know what we've got on our hands here."

"Ya do, huh?" Micky asked.

"Sure," Ramirez said. "It's a homicide, pure and simple. Clean, efficient. In and out. No fuss, no muss, no bother."

"Well, except for the floor…" Art commented. Strakowski looked pained.

"OK, if you're all so smart, then why are we here?" Micky asked.

Strakowski looked at him, hard. My brother didn't flinch. He saw the same look every morning in the mirror when he shaved. The only difference was that Strakowski had gray eyes and Micky had blue ones.

"Here's the deal," the man from Brooklyn said, puffing out his cheeks like he was bleeding off tension. "You looked at the crime stats for the sixty-eighth precinct?" We shook our heads no. "We had a total of two homicides here last year. Neat and tidy. No big mystery."

"We mostly work larceny cases," Ramirez added.

His boss glared at him. "And now I have Mr. Sakura meeting his maker in my nice, quiet community. It looks to me like a professional job."

"Oh, definitely," Ramirez commented.

Strakowski grimaced as if in pain, then continued. "And in the few precious moments he has left in this vale of tears, what does the victim do?"

"Scream. Cry?" Art suggested.

"Wet his pants?" said Micky. The rhetorical nature of questions is often lost on cops.

Strakowski lowered his chin and looked at the two detectives from Manhattan wearily. "I'm beginning to understand your lieutenant." He held out a hand and Ramirez put a manila envelope in it. Then Strakowski slipped out a sheet of paper encased in plastic.

"It appears that Mr. Sakura's last action on earth was an act of calligraphy. Now what are we to make of that?"

"Pretty cool customer," Ramirez offered.

His boss shrugged. "Maybe. And anybody that cool is gonna be doing what he does for a good reason." It looked like Art was about to say something, so Strakowski held up a hand. "Maybe, I thought in my own feeble cop way, maybe this is a message for us. I mean, we're no experts here in Fort Hamilton. Not like you pros from across the river. But maybe, just maybe it's a…" he paused in sarcastic emphasis "… clue! But surely I am out of my element. Then I thought, hmmm. Calligraphy. Murder. Exotic Asian culture. Who can help me with this puzzle?" He looked pointedly from Ramirez to Micky to Art. Then he turned to me and stood there, waiting.

"Can I see the paper?" I asked.

It was Sakura's last piece of calligraphy. A single sheet of fine paper, holding the black swirls of a dead man's brush strokes.

"This was found on the desk?" I asked. It was a stupid question, but I often sound that way while I think.

"There was a sequence of different sheets lying on the table. This one was on top," Ramirez answered.

"Ya think he got popped while doing this?" Art asked.

I didn't respond. I was scanning the record of his calligraphy from his last session. Conjuring a mental image of Sakura in the Shodo hut, totally focused on his art in the last few moments he had to live. I spread the sheets out on a side table and arranged them in the sequence I thought made the most sense. I stepped back and nodded to myself. Ranged the way I had placed them, you could almost see something happen. The first warm-up exercises, the testing of ink consistency and brush conditions, reveal an artist forging a tactile link with his tools. Then Sakura had started a quote from the Platform Scripture. The characters were classic Chinese, like many of the old Zen documents, and they revealed balance and poise and a fidelity to discipline. The characters flow across the page for four lines before something happens.

There's a break in the esthetic structure. It's hard to describe. You need to look at a lot of this material to get a sense of the balance and rhythm. And you need to experience something of the focused concentration that facilitates it. The victim and I practiced different arts, but shared a common tradition.

I could see the cops fidgeting around me. I shook my head. "Sure," I told them. "The murderer broke in while the victim was writing." I pointed to different sheets as I spoke, so they could follow me. "This was a man of great focus and calm," I told them. I sighed inwardly. The more we know of crime victims, the greater the sadness. The stronger the outrage. "The brush strokes don't show any sign of interruption. Until the final moment." I pointed some features out on the last page. "You can see that the balance of the calligraphy was done in one smooth motion. Even the final sheet. But there's this slight squiggle at the tail end. If he were shot while doing it, I'm assuming it would make his hand jerk."

"Micky rolled his eyes." Uh, yeah, ya could say that."

"And it would show up on the paper," I finished, pointing at the echo of the bullet's impact laid down in ink for us.

"What's it say?" Strakowski asked. I hesitated. "You can read it, right?" He looked alarmed.

I shrugged. "Sure. But it's not that simple." Art looked pleased. Micky wagged his eyebrows at Ramirez.

Strakowski held out his hand for the paper. "How so?"

"We done in here?" I asked. "I could use some air." It was getting a little thick in the hut. It may have been my imagination, but I thought that the smell of blood was getting stronger.

We ambled out toward the front of the house. Behind us, the technicians gleefully scurried back into the hut. Strakowski eventually turned and leaned his rump against a police cruiser, his arms crossed over his chest. He looked at me, then at the younger cop.

"Look, Burke," Ramirez began, and licked his lips. "We know what we're looking for, but we really don't know what we're looking for. Know what I mean? And the fact that it's in Japanese doesn't help."

"I understand, Ramirez, but look, some of this stuff is pretty obscure. There have to be people more qualified than me to do this."

I wasn't trying to be humble. When I started my studies years ago, I thought of myself as an academic with an interest in the martial arts. Then I met Yamashita. Now I've come to the awareness that I'm a martial artist with some advanced academic credentials.

"We know there are people more qualified, Burke," the Lieutenant groused. "We even spoke to one."

The younger cop eyed me. "You know a guy at Columbia named Cook? James Cook."

I got a mental image of Cook: tall, with long thin hair brushed back from a wide forehead. He wore wire-rimmed glasses and a bowtie. We had crossed paths in grad school. Mentally, he never really left. I went for different lessons in Yamashita's dojo.

"The Fujitsu Professor of Asian Studies," I answered. "Quite the expert."

Strakowski raised his eyebrows. "So he told us. Very impressed with himself."

"He sniffs a lot," Ramirez added.

I thought Cook was an insufferable snob, but I feel that way about a good many academics. So I kept quiet.

"Professor Cook, and here I'm quoting," the Lieutenant said, "had neither the time nor the inclination to assist us in our... what did he call it Ramirez?"

"Colorful."

"... colorful little problem."

Ramirez looked at me significantly. "The guy's an asshole," he murmured.

"So it was our thought, since you appear to know something about things Asian, that we bring you on as a consultant," Strakowski concluded.

I nodded in understanding.

"You read Japanese," Ramirez said, tallying off the points on his fingers. "You're familiar with the history and culture. You've worked with a police investigation before..."

"And I'm not an asshole," I added helpfully.

Strakowski gave me a look and pushed himself off the car with a grunt "That," he said, "remains to be seen."

"What's the calligraphy say?" Ramirez persisted.

I looked at them. "There's a Japanese tradition about leaving a poem or a piece of calligraphy behind when you're dying.

It's supposed to be a life statement. So these things are pretty elliptical." I could tell from the looks I was getting that my explanation was not helping any.

"OK," I tried again, "you have to understand that what this man wrote may be a clue. But it may not. If he knew he was going to be killed…"

"Hard not to notice," Art said.

I nodded at that. "If he really knew what was about to happen, he might have had time to compose himself. But then again, who knows what goes through your mind at a time like that?" I gestured at the paper in Strakowski's hand. "This could just be a random thought."

"But you can read it, right?" Strakowski repeated.

"Of course he can read it," Micky said. "He's just bein' a know-it-all."

I shrugged. In some lines of work, you get to carry large caliber automatics. In my line, you get to be pedantic.

I held the paper up and the four cops looked at me. They were different people but, for a moment, they all had the same look: like dogs catching a distant scent and hoping it would be something to chase. "It says," and I paused for effect, "*Shumpu.*"

"Is it a name?" the Lieutenant asked.

I shook my head no. "It means 'spring wind.'"

Strakowski puffed his cheeks out and let out a long breath. He glanced, up at the gray sky, where thin rain clouds were getting blown in from the ocean, just out of sight.

Ramirez was incredulous. "His last words are a weather report?"

"This mean anything you can think of, Burke?" Strakowski asked me.

"Nothing specific right now. Let me think about it," I said. You could tell he was disappointed, but I wasn't going to rush this. Strakowski's head swiveled toward Micky.

"Anything you want to add?"

Micky shrugged in my direction. "He's the expert."

"Some expert. So far, I gotta say," the Lieutenant looked off into the street and then back at us, one by one, "I am not impressed by you guys."

Art narrowed his eyes and said, slowly and ominously, in his best Master Yoda voice, "You will be."

4

Rumble

Different things are important to different people, but we're all searching for something. I spend a lot of time training with people who seem like they're interested in the give and take of fighting. But it's more complex than that. Scratch the surface, and most are also seeking some ill-defined mystic dimension to existence. I'm no different. But it's hard to admit out loud.

We come to the dojo looking for magic of a sort. The lucky ones who stay long enough find it. But it's a subtle thing, almost too fragile to bear direct examination. You glimpse it in the elegance of movement, the beauty of the sword's arc. Sometimes it's brought home to you by the subtle, warm buzz of integration you can get while doing a move correctly. Other times, it's just in the feeling you get on entering into the training hall after a hard day in the world. The dojo is stark and bare and quiet. You set your gear bag down, a soft weight of uniforms and pads, and think: *Home, this is home.* And you forget for just a little while about the rest of the things pressing down on your life.

But with Yamashita, there's more to it than that. It's not about comfort. If anything the experience is an exercise in constant strain, of having the horizon of your own potential stretched further and further until you can hear the fibers scream. In Sensei's training hall, the students have all been studying the arts for years, so on some level we all know that this is what's in store for us. Most karate students, for instance, start out practicing a series of fundamental exercises, *kata*. As time passes, there are new kata, greater challenges to be met on the path to black belt. And when you finally stand there, with a black belt tied around your waist for the first time, you think you've really arrived somewhere.

And you have, of course—right back at the beginning. Because the first thing they make you do when you get promoted to the *dan* level of black belt is start on the novice kata all over again. Only now, the sensei say, are you really ready to begin practice. And you sigh and get to work as the horizon seems to grow a little more distant again.

Yamashita no longer spends much time watching my form or correcting technique. In that, at least, I have won his confidence and a measure of approval. He now has me pursue more intangible things.

Sometimes the Japanese discuss *ri*, the quality of mastery that sets the truly great apart from the merely competent. It's the combination of many things: experience, practice, skill. And insight. You can analyze it all you want. I have. The subtle melding of perception and sensitivity with the lightning spark of muscle synapse. Easily described, but hard to reach. I've spent years with Yamashita, laboring at honing the technical details of my art to a razor's precision. And the process had made me feel changed, altered in a significant way that seemed to me to be at the heart of why I did what I did. But now my teacher appeared to take this as a given, and is focused instead on a completely new set of challenges. He wishes me to develop ri. I understand the quality, but pursuing it is tricky. Every time I sense the approach of ri's clarity, it slips away again. Skill isn't enough. And skill is what I've worked on for so long. For me, it's like arriving to play in the major leagues after years of apprenticeship, only to find that they've changed the rules of the game.

Why this surprises me is a mystery. You think I'd be experienced enough to know that with Yamashita, like life in general, what you tend to get is less than you hoped but more than you bargained for.

Yamashita's hands are thick and savage looking, better suited to grasp a weapon than to hold a book. He met me at the dojo entrance as I came in before the evening class. Students were scattered throughout the cavernous room, going through the small personal warm-ups we all do before class. I bowed at the door and to my teacher. He held up a hand.

"Wait," he ordered.

I stood and looked at him expectantly. Cast a glance around. There didn't seem to be anything significant going on. The light was fading outside and the fluorescent lights pulsed faintly. The wooden floor shone from a recent cleaning.

"What do you sense?" Yamashita asked.

The usual, I thought. But I made myself very still in the door's threshold and tried to focus. The wash of traffic from the street was a faint underlying murmur. Lights buzzed high up in the ceiling of the training hall. Students talked quietly to each other, but watched us surreptitiously. "Anticipation," I finally told him.

"So?" Yamashita responded. "Hardly surprising. Is that all?" He sounded let down. "We should work more on your capacity for greater sensitivity..." he said.

"Haragei," I sighed in response. The Japanese use the term to cover a wide variety of non-verbal communications. In the world Yamashita and I inhabit, it's a bit more of a focused concept. The more advanced sensei believe that there are emotional and psychic vibrations dancing in the air—invisible, but real despite that fact. And you can, with proper training, learn to sense these things. I've experienced haragei, usually at moments of great stress. But Yamashita's sensitivity is vastly more subtle. And he thinks mine should be, too.

I'm working on it, but I'm still a Westerner. My ability to access haragei comes and goes, and the harder I grab at it, the more it slips away. Yamashita must have seen some hint of the feeling of frustration in my expression. "We will talk more about this later," he told me.

Which was when he handed me the book. I looked at it, puzzled.

"Changpa Rinpoche," my teacher said.

I saw the name on the cover and perked up. "Oh, sure. There was an article about him in the *Times*, oh, maybe two or three Sundays ago."

"Indeed. He runs an institution called the Dharma Center in Manhattan. He speaks to many different groups on the internal dimension of existence."

I grinned ruefully. "They say he's prescient. That's why he's so popular. For every ten people interested in Tibetan Buddhism, there are about a thousand who'll come to see a mind reader."

Yamashita waved the irrelevant detail away and continued. "You are unfair. This man has been making quite remarkable presentations across the country."

"Does he bend spoons with his mind?" I asked.

"Burke, please. Behave yourself. I have known this man for many years and I respect him greatly. He could be an interesting resource for you…"

"For me?"

Yamashita sighed. "You have accomplished much with me, Professor. But now you struggle on another level. And sometimes, the very familiarity of a teacher's voice makes it hard to hear…"

"I'm paying attention Sensei," I protested.

"Of course you are. But…" One eyebrow arched up.

"Some of the more esoteric stuff is hard for me to get a handle on," I admitted.

"Surely you do not doubt the reality of the things I speak of? After all these years?"

I nodded slowly. "I've seen some remarkable things…"

"You have done more than see these things, Burke." He saw me fidget. "Yet?" he prodded.

"Look," I said, "when I see stuff in dojo that looks amazing, I remind myself that it's like any magic. Most of it's sleight of hand. Good technique. The laws of physics. It's complicated, maybe, but not mystical."

Yamashita smiled. "So… even after all this time?"

I shrugged. Yamashita looked at me for a moment. His eyes can be hard and unfathomable. In the quiet of the evening, with the dojo not yet active, his eyes were wide and questioning. Then he seemed to make a decision. He took the book and looked at the author's blurb on the back. Then he handed it to me. "Perhaps another teacher's voice, *neh*?" He turned then to the practice floor and I followed.

So I sat at lunch the next day reading the book called *Warrior Ways to Power: Entering the Mystic City*. The thoughts of a Tibetan lama thrust on me by a Japanese martial arts sensei.

The weather had slipped back into the clammy grayness of a Long Island spring. The temperature had dropped since that day in Edward Sakura's backyard. And the sun seemed too weak to burn through the constant cloud cover. The cafeteria at Dorian University was steamy and thin rivulets of rain ran down the plate glass windows that opened onto the quadrangle. I sat alone at lunch, hunkered down in the gloom.

Any university is an odd place. Dorian University was a bit odder than most. Inside the buildings, overeducated professors with wet, shifty eyes and little or no coping skills skitter down the halls. They labor with inept delivery and dated scholarship, sure that their personal magnetism alone keeps Western Civilization afloat. The students sit in the classrooms and eye their teachers with bovine tolerance and dream of the weekend. Each party to the ordeal tolerates the other, secure in the knowledge that classes run for only fifty minutes and the semesters are only fifteen weeks long. It's the *Classics Illustrated* version of higher education.

A few years ago, I had hoped to get a teaching job here. They could have used me. Dorian's faculty have all the depth of a silted-up drainage ditch, particularly in Asian Studies. There's a noodley philosophy professor who spent some time in Thailand, chanting in temples but secretly dreaming of the red light districts. An overweight woman sociologist concerned with gender issues is still trying to get a manuscript called "Coming of Age in Singapore" published, and a hypertensive historian who wants to be the Stephen Ambrose of the Korean War shows *The Bridges of Toko-Ri* a lot. But that's it.

I worked as a lowly administrator, since the faculty felt I was unworthy to be involved in anything remotely academic. They meant it to be insulting, but by now the sentiment was only faintly unpleasant, like the memory of an old toothache.

Tucked away in upscale suburban Long Island, from the outside Dorian looks like a real school. Its buildings are ivy covered and the brick blushes in the morning sun on clear days. The playing fields stretch away into the distance, and the bustle of fall and spring made it look like a place where something of significance occurs. I'm no longer really sure. Maybe it was Yamashita's ramped up training demands. Maybe it was the Sakura murder, but I found myself more and more frequently thinking about things other than the university. Increasingly, I just do my job and at the end of the day leave for the dojo, where more important things happen.

I found Tibetan Buddhism interesting. It's colorful and elaborate. There are all those stories of levitation and mystical powers. The Third Eye. Clairvoyance. But, mostly, the teachers were strict and their followers did what they were told. It was an experience I could relate to. The book wasn't bad, actually. The mystic city angle has been pretty well used since St. Augustine, but I was interested in the warrior aspect of things. The Tibetans aren't all sitting around in the lotus position. Life is pretty tough there on the Roof of the World, and they had a warrior heritage of their own. In the old days, they were pretty good archers.

The cadence of the lama's written words was soothing in a way that I hadn't expected. The prose was clear. I wondered what he was like in person. The picture on the book jacket didn't tell you much: a bespectacled man past middle age in the robes of a monk. I wondered how he had met Yamashita.

I tried to focus once more on reading the book my teacher had given me. But my attention wandered from mystic cities to the cryptic clue left by a murdered calligrapher. To the possibility of a type of experience that was unseen and yet nonetheless real. And to the increasingly conflicting demands of the different worlds I seemed to inhabit. It was like a low, distracting murmur. A rumble that, while still faint, would eventually grow in significance. I struggled hard against the idea that I would someday have to make a choice, and made another attempt to concentrate on the here and now. Develop some sensitivity. But the location wasn't much help. Just within the range of my peripheral vision, a young coed sitting at a nearby table was getting up and wiggling away. Her slim middle was exposed by a short shirt and her navel was pierced. I forced myself not to watch.

Training, as my sensei says, is never ending.

5
TARGET

The birds complained during the lulls. Off in the distance the trees were hazy with green buds. The weather had cleared and it was spring again. But the targets came at you fast, and there wasn't much time to stop and appreciate the weather.

My brother Micky set himself with arms outstretched. The pistol shots snapped out with a quick, machine-like pace. Micky's eyes were wide and focused on the human silhouette that raced toward him along the cable. The slide on the Glock rammed back and stayed open. The target was shredded in two spots. Micky stepped back away from the firing line and grinned.

"It's like everything else, buddy boy," he said to me. "You work the heart and the head." I nodded in appreciation.

Micky's shooting stance was all intensity. It wasn't that he was stiff. It was a quality that gave you a sense, for the brief moment between the thought and the pull on the trigger, that all of Micky's energy was focused on that one thing. I believe, if he could, that my brother would race along with the bullets he shot so he could pound them into the target by hand.

His partner Art stepped up to the line. The interesting thing about watching different people do any sort of similar physical activity is the degree to which their idiosyncrasies are revealed in the act. I see it all the time in the dojo. The same technique is rendered unique in different people by the ball of quirks that make up our personalities.

Art's a lefty, so there's a certain awkward appearance to his shooting. It's an illusion caused by the dominance of the right-handed perspective. He took his time placing his shots. His pistol let off a slow series of cracks, and Art's mouth tightened occasionally as he monitored his performance. It took a while. The Glock Seventeen is aptly named: the clip holds seventeen 9 mm bullets. And one in the chamber.

But I wasn't thinking about the technical details of the firearm. The most deadly thing about a pistol is the person who holds it. I was watching Art struggle with his marksmanship.

Cops qualify a few times a year with their pistols. Art's microsurgery had repaired his right hand, but I knew he was still going to therapy to regain a full range of use. In the two-handed shooter's stance, one hand grips the butt of the pistol; the other is cupped underneath to steady the aim. The lingering awkwardness of the right hand was bothering Art. You could tell.

There's a focus and a connection between all the parts of the body when you're doing something right. The head gives you away. If you're too overly conscious of what you're doing, if you're nervous or scattered, the head looks like it's rising up and losing connection with the rest of you. In training we say that you "float." People who float are easily identified in the dojo. They're usually the people getting knocked down.

I saw the telltale signs of floating in Art's posture. It wasn't just the grimace on his face or the obvious hesitation in his right hand as it scrabbled for a grip at the base of the pistol. He was thinking about it too much. Worrying. It created a break in his stance and his coordination. And when the target reached him, the shots were mostly scattered outside the primary target zones.

Art grimaced as he took off his ear protectors. "Shit."

I was standing next to Micky. "It's gonna take a while for him to get full control back," I murmured.

My brother bristled. "Hey, you put enough rounds into anyone, they're goin' down." Micky moved toward his partner and shrugged. "Don't worry about it, Art."

Art's face was twisted in annoyance, and it washed over us as he looked up. Cops take pride in their abilities. I could understand that. In many ways, Micky and Art lived in a very different world than I did. But we shared things.

I'd come along with these two to the pistol range as a lark. I spend my time with simpler weapons. But I was also there because we found something in each other's company that was deeply reassuring.

Danger shared creates its own odd connections. Sometimes, I still dreamed about the wash of blood and fear, a swirl of shadows and faces and struggle. We three had come through that ordeal, hoping that things would be like they were before. But it was a vain hope. Events had changed us in ways that were both good and bad. And there were reminders of the fact in the most unexpected places.

The two men cleared their weapons, taking refuge in the familiar actions. They picked up the spent shell casings and dropped them in a plastic bucket. Farther down the range, a marksman with a scoped revolver the size of an elephant gun blasted away. He wore a swank shooter's vest and had yellow tinted aviator sunglasses. He was very serious. Probably had seen too many Clint Eastwood movies. I swear you could feel the concussive blast of his weapon from where we stood.

I walked up to the counter where Art and Micky worked in an awkward silence. "Can I try?"

The two men looked at each other in surprise. I had never asked to shoot before. There was an unspoken agreement that each of us had different areas of expertise. We tried not to step on each other's toes. But, I owed them a great deal. I thought maybe I could help.

Art shrugged. "Couldn't hurt. Hard to be much worse than me."

Micky looked like he was going to say something to his partner, then thought better of it and prepared his pistol for me. "OK, Deadeye," he said to me. "You've seen it done often enough. But one important safety tip." He held the squat, black pistol in front of me, turned to one side. Then he pointed at the muzzle and smirked. "The bullets come out this end."

He slotted a clip into the handle and placed it down on the shelf that marked the firing line. Then Micky stepped away. "The safety is on." I picked the pistol up and slid the receiver back to run a shell into the chamber. I took off the safety off. The target was fifteen yards away: a long shot for a pistol.

"You want it closer, Connor?" Micky asked. He wasn't being a wise guy. Cops train for relatively close shooting scenarios. I shook my head no.

I held the weapon and pointed it out toward the target, getting a sense of balance. I slowed my breathing down. Then I fired a shot off. I wasn't too interested in where the bullet hit the target; I wanted to get a feel for the recoil, the weight, the tension in the hands as you squeezed the weapon into life. I slowly went through the clip. Then I placed the pistol down and Micky hit the switch that brought the target to us. There were holes all over the place. And there weren't even seventeen of them.

"Well," my brother said. "Not bad for a rookie, but I wouldn't give up my day job."

I picked up the pistol again, getting a sense of its heft. Wooden weapons feel different. There's a special type of connection forged with primitive arms. The whole process feels more integrated. With the Glock, you got the sense that you were trying to control something that had a life of its own. But still…

"All weapons are the same in some ways," I said. "They're extensions of us. Of our power. Or our will. Know what I mean?" The two men looked blankly at me for minute. I plowed on anyway. "When you use something like this, you know what you want to happen. The trick is to somehow get the tool to obey your will."

I reached over and clipped a new silhouette target to the wire. I ran it back out. Then I hit the button and ran the target toward us a few times. Watching.

"Seems to me, though, that if you worry too much about how to use the tool, you end up losing sight of the target. Know what I mean?"

The two men saw I was serious and nodded.

"I mean, *you* shoot the target. Not your hands. Or even the gun."

My brother's face brightened. "Like the bumper sticker. Guns don't kill people…"

Art smiled at us, his left hand on his hip, the right curled slightly at his side.

"So," I said, and I held out my hand to Micky for another clip, "you need to know what you're doing with your hands, but you've got to look beyond it. To the target. It's not a question of the hands being strong or skilled." I tried not to look at Art as I said it. I put the clip in and let the target run back out. "They are simply there to help you meet the target."

I nodded and Micky hit the button. The target ran in toward us. I fired the Glock until it locked back empty.

My shots were pretty nicely grouped above the neck. Micky took the shredded paper off the clip and both men looked at the target. And then at me.

"Yamashita says you get the head and the rest follows," I commented.

Micky looked at the target again. "You," he said, spacing the words out for emphasis, "are… one… weird… dude."

"I gotta agree," Art said. "But if you've got a secret handshake, I'd like to learn that, too."

We talked a little about breathing and muscle control. Focus. For the most part, these two guys thought that the training I did was an exercise in delusion. Years ago, my brother had come to a dojo and taken one look at the exotic costumes and odd movements. He called it a pajama party.

That was before Yamashita.

Now we were on common ground, talking about weapons and the skill that lets you use them. Cops are a clannish bunch—they have experiences and perspectives most of us are fortunate to escape. It means that it's hard for them to let you in. Even when you're a brother. Or a friend. But, for a while at the pistol range, I got the feeling that the barriers had broken down a little bit.

As we wadded up the paper targets, Micky looked at mine. "Sort of reminds me of that Sakura guy," he said. "How's that mystery clue thing going?"

I shrugged. "Eh. I met with Sakura's calligraphy teacher. Tried to get a sense of whether the phrase shumpu had any significance." I could still see the diminutive shodo sensei in my mind. She sat sadly, an old woman who had seen too many lives pass away. She answered what questions she could in a listless voice. The bold strokes of her brushwork were in odd contrast to her physical presence. She was a fragile and faint presence in the quiet of her studio, like a ghost slowly fading from sight. Nothing she said seemed to offer any insight into Sakura's final testament. I summarized it for Micky and Art. "I'll keep at it," I told them.

"We're working what we can from our end, too," Art said. "The guy from Brooklyn, Strakoswki, would like to keep us on a nice short leash." He grinned at me. "But it doesn't quite fit our unique genius."

"That's an understatement," I answered.

"It's killin' him that he has to use us," Micky observed. He knew he was right about Strakowski: it would have killed Micky if their positions were reversed.

"The calligraphy doesn't tell us anything?" Art looked at me.

I shrugged.

"We've taken a look at the guy's life," Art continued. "His business dealings…"

"It's why Strakowski needs us. Sakura's office was in Manhattan. So we're poking around."

I could tell from the tone of Micky's voice that they had something. "And?" I prompted.

"There's something hinky there," Micky added, and looked at Art for confirmation.

"Oh, yeah."

"How so?" I asked. I was used to this. These men thought in very linear patterns. They were methodical and went from point A to point B to point C. They built a conversation in the same way they developed a case file: a piece at a time.

"Most murders," Art explained as we walked off the range and away from Dirty Harry's blast zone, "get fueled by love or money."

"Feelings or finances," my brother chimed in. He had an unconscious appreciation of alliteration.

"Sakura's personal life seemed pretty stable. We checked the usual angles: lovers, office affairs, marital strain. Nothing there." Art sounded wistful.

Micky popped the trunk of the car. They placed the pistols in small locked cases for the ride home. I knew Micky had a .32 automatic strapped to his ankle. On a spring day in suburbia, going armed seemed a bit paranoid. Then again, Edward Sakura got his brains blown out amid the well-manicured splendor of a Brooklyn backyard. Cops see things differently from most of us. For good reason.

We settled in for the ride and Micky continued. "So, we're still double-checking on things, but the feelings angle seems out of the picture."

I sat in the back seat and Art twisted around to talk. "At one time in his life, Sakura was up to his eyeballs with all sorts of money deals. He was a show-biz specialist."

"An agent?" I asked.

Art thought for a minute. "Not really. He was more like a fixer, a guy who put different people together."

"For a price," my brother added.

"So how's that relevant? How's it fit in?"

"We're not sure just yet," Art admitted. "These days, he was semi-retired, spent most of his time doing calligraphy. Consulting with art dealers. But we wonder about things…"

"Like…" I prompted.

"Sakura had Asian connections," Micky began.

"Mick," I said, "he was a second generation Japanese American. His Asian connection was his grandparents."

Micky shot a wicked look at me over his shoulder, then swerved forward to steer the car. "Connor, I'm not a complete asshole, ya know? I mean that, over time, Sakura had put deals together at a lot of different levels. Some were big. Some were not so big. And a lot of times, you got people from overseas wanting to break into the business who are maybe not so legit."

"Movie industry is a money launderer's dream," Art added. "From what we can tell, Sakura had all sorts of people wanting in. Some he played with. Some he didn't. What we've gotta ask is whether there was something in the past, a deal that went sour. Maybe money was lost. Or feelings hurt."

"Feelings hurt?" I asked incredulously.

"Feelings," my brother repeated. "And you know what these types of people feel most deeply about? Money."

"You think there was something in his past? That Sakura was involved in something and he ticked somebody off?"

"Based on the condition of his head, I'd say someone was pretty pissed at him," Micky concluded.

"Not the action of a happy camper," Art said in support.

"Yeah. OK. But what do you think Sakura was involved in?" I persisted.

Art held up a finger in admonishment. "Our powers, while mighty, are not without limit."

"I'm shocked," I said.

Micky drove in silence, taking the turns to his house with easy familiarity. His wife Dee had taken the kids off for a day at one of our sisters' houses. The Burkes are a numerous clan, rapidly growing more so. I had a bewildering number of nieces and nephews. Some were dark. Some light. There were fat little Burkes and leaner, more agile models. But they all had the subtle underlying familial resemblance that marked them as Americans of Irish extraction. And they would all play together, which gave their parents an opportunity to relax. Which is what I hoped Dee was doing. Life with my brother was not an adventure in calm.

As we pulled up in front of the house, Art murmured to Micky, "Blue sedan. This side of the street. Motor running. Recognize the car? Looks like he's got himself parked so he can watch things."

"I got it," Micky answered.

The two men stepped out of the car and I followed. We went to the trunk, where Micky opened the lid, then put his foot up on the bumper, pretending to tie his sneaker. He took the small automatic out of his ankle holster. Art took a Glock out of the case and loaded it. Then they drifted slowly to the curb side of the car, using it to block them from the man in the blue sedan. I noticed that Micky edged forward a little, as if shielding his partner.

"Connor, you head up to the house," Micky directed. They both held their pistols down along their legs, not making a show of it. I started to move and heard the sedan's door open. I felt the muscles across the top of my shoulders tense up. Then I heard my brother.

"Oh, fer Christ's sake," he said disgustedly. A slim girl with long blonde hair bounded out of a neighboring house, and gave the driver of the car a hug. "That girl's got 'em coming and going. I can't keep track."

"Show them your guns," I said. "I bet it'll cut down on the dating traffic." Art and Micky looked slightly sheepish.

Micky opened up the trunk again and took out the pistol cases.

A kid on a skateboard growled by. He had on hugely baggy pants and a black knit hat that made him look like a moron. But he spotted the guns easily enough. Micky saw him gawk and gestured to the house with his head.

"Let's go inside."

Any house with kids in it is littered with things big and small. Inside Micky's, it looked like the footage you see of neighborhoods where tornadoes have touched down. It was dim in the entryway, and we skirted cautiously around the toys. Micky made a false step and we heard a loud crunching sound. He cursed under his breath.

The kitchen had some cups in the sink. A few Cheerios dried sadly on the table. Micky wiped it off with a ratty sponge and we sat down. My brother rummaged around in the refrigerator and found some cans of beer. I opened a series of cabinets, looking for snacks. I found Baggies, Pop-Tarts, Band-Aids, and other essential ammunition in the war for successful parenting. I finally located an open bag of pretzels on top of the refrigerator. Simple fare, but manly.

I looked at the two detectives. "You guys a little on edge for any reason?"

Micky shrugged. "Some guys are back on the street. It's been years, but ya never know when someone with a grudge will show up."

"Hell of a way to make a living, Mick,"

My brother took a sip of beer and closed one eye as he looked at me. "It's a wonderful world."

The two detectives drank silently. I knew that they had found something, but they didn't seem particularly eager to share it. Yet I could pick up that sense of suppressed emotion cops have: men who had been disappointed too often to show much excitement, but it was there anyway.

I couldn't stand it. "So what else have you found out?"

Art licked beer foam off his lips. "Well. We're looking at Sakura's business dealings, but there's not much there. So we went back yesterday and worked some angles."

"Angles?" I said.

He nodded. "We went back and spoke with the secretaries."

I nodded back in appreciation. From my perspective at the university, these were the people who really knew what was going on.

"I thought you questioned them pretty good first time around," I said.

"Yeah, we did," Micky admitted. "But we mostly asked them about Sakura. His schedule. His day. So we went back."

"And?" I said.

"OK," brother said, warming to his topic. "The guy wasn't really dong much at work anymore. Showed up one or two days a week. Mostly, the secretaries said, he was using the office to make calls, mail stuff. Things like that."

"Can't blame him," Art said, remembering the place. "You should have seen the offices Sakura had, Connor. Nice. Corporate. And the people who show up there tend to fit that mold, too."

"Riffraff tend to be kept down in the streets," Micky agreed.

"How'd we get in?" Art wondered out loud.

Micky ignored him. "Well, anyway, I asked the receptionists if Sakura was up to anything else. You know, while he used the office." He took another sip of beer and went on. "Now get this. He was obviously pretty well known for his skill in," he looked up at me, "… you know…"

"Shodo," I said.

"Yeah. He had started doing things with that. Appraisals. Some museum consulting. The day before the murder, he had sent some calligraphy off to another appraiser for a second opinion. I got the name and address from the FedEx receipt."

"So what's so special about it?" I asked. Micky didn't react for a minute.

Then he looked at Art triumphantly, and held up a hand. "Same day as the murder, someone came to Sakura's office. An Asian. Asking about some calligraphy he claimed the old man was looking at. You had to hear the receptionist describe this guy. She said he was spooky."

"He have an accent?" I asked.

Micky nodded. "Yeah. His English was fluent, but accented. A big guy, she said. Huge. The guy said that the stuff was his property and he wanted it back. He got all worked up, she said. She got flustered and mentioned the FedEx. He told her that Sakura wasn't authorized to send the document anywhere else. He almost blew a gasket."

"So?" I said again.

"So," Micky replied, "they gave him a Xerox of the receipt so he could track it down. To get rid of him."

"Notice that he didn't ask to call Sakura," Art pointed out to me.

"Yeah. Like maybe he knew he wasn't gonna be answering the phone anymore," Micky concluded.

"Did he leave a name?"

"Wong," Micky said.

"It's a common name. Like Smith," I said.

"And probably fake," Art grunted.

"If I could get a look at this calligraphy, it might give us a motive," I said.

"Ooh, good point. Sherlock," Micky cracked. "So what's the next question you're gonna ask?"

"Well… where'd the package go?" I said.

"It got sent to Georgia," Micky said.

The two cops talked for a while about the possibility of lifting some latent prints from the office that could match the crime scene. The dim likelihood of getting a positive ID. The mysterious Asian visitor. And the fact that someone would probably get to take a trip below the Mason-Dixon line to try to find the missing calligraphy.

"The South," Micky complained.

"They say it's gonna rise again," Art offered.

"More than I can say for Sakura," my brother concluded.

6
HOLY MAN

Yamashita hates crowds. He has trained for a long time to be able to spot the subtle muscular shifts that signal murderous intent. But if you put him in a room with a crowd of people, he gets antsy. The Japanese say that everything has *ki*, a type of energy that can be sensed if you're good enough. And Yamashita certainly was. The more mystically minded would say he is so sensitive to the energy force people give off that he's overwhelmed.

I was trying to be open to the whole invisible-world stuff, so I asked him about this issue with crowds and tried out the ki explanation. We were standing around after a training session. The students had bowed and shuffled away. Some nursed bruises. All were worn out. I held a wooden training sword in my hand. It was made of white oak and the handle was discolored from the sweat and grime that had been ground into it over the years. After a good workout, Yamashita seems pleased with the world, and is often more talkative than usual. As his senior student, he's also a bit more forthcoming with me. So I brought up the issue.

His bald, bullet head swiveled to look at me. The brown eyes glittered faintly. You can never tell whether it's amusement or the excitement of the hunt that does it. My master let me squirm for a moment and then replied.

"I like it. It is a colorful explanation. The intense ki of crowds." He made a slight rumbling noise deep in his chest. It's his version of a chortle. "If I were writing for one of the cheap magazines

American martial artists consume so avidly, I would use your explanation, Professor." He always calls me that, even though he knows I'm not a faculty member at the university. Sometimes I think it's a mark of respect. Other days, I can't be sure.

We walked over to the weapons rack, where I placed the *bokken* down. He smiled a little at me. "I assume your question is sincere?" It was a rhetorical question. He knew that I had learned a long time ago not to waste his time.

"So…" he began in the characteristic Japanese way. "It is true that crowds present a mix of sensations. Noise. Heat. Smell. Even, I suppose, ki. But ki is like smoke, Burke. When you try to grab hold, it eludes you."

"Do you mean you can't sense ki in crowds, Sensei?" I am a plodding student, but I persevere.

"Oh, the ki can be sensed. Certainly. It is there. Always. In crowds, there is ki in great abundance."

"And is this upsetting to you?"

He looked at me sharply. "Upsetting?" As if the idea had never occurred to him. "I think, no. The problem with crowds has nothing to do with ki."

"Then what is it, Sensei?"

"Burke," he said as if to a child, "too many people, too many intentions. It has nothing to do with ki," A student bowed as he left the training hall floor and Yamashita bowed forward a fraction in acknowledgement. "Crowds," he said to me finally, "make it hard to see someone coming at you with a short weapon."

My master is a mystic with unique perspectives.

Changpa Rinpoche was scheduled to speak at the American Museum of Natural History as part of the opening for a traveling display of Himalayan artifacts. I should have been struck by the coincidence, but then it dawned on me that Yamashita probably knew this before he gave me the lama's book. He's full of tricks.

What was interesting was my teacher's urge to see the Tibetan. I spent some time trying to figure this out. There were commonalities here. They were both probably about the same age. Both men were outcasts of a type—adherents of strange and foreign practices far from home. They labored in a foreign land to bring insights to people not always capable of understanding them. There must be a type of isolation in this kind of life. And loneliness. So maybe Sensei was drawn to him for this reason. It made me think of Yamashita in a different way. But then, again, they were old friends.

I wrangled some VIP tickets from a friend who worked in the research department there. His parents were farmers on Long Island's North Fork, past Riverhead: stocky, perpetually sunburned people who made an increasingly difficult living growing potatoes and flowers in the sandy soil of Long Island. Their son, the archaeologist, labored indoors, digging in different ways.

Yamashita and I arrived the night of the holy man's lecture and, if Sensei were a child, he would have been bouncing up and down on his toes. He looked, of course, totally placid when we got off the B train at the 81st Street subway station, but I had been with him too long to be fooled. We made our way up to the first floor toward the theater they were using for Changpa's lecture.

I love this museum. I'd been there countless times and never get tired of it. We walked through the Theodore Roosevelt Memorial Hall—TR shot and donated much of the big game trophies here. Part of it may have been guilt, but maybe not. TR didn't strike me as a guy with much self-doubt. Besides, his father had been one of the founders of the museum in the first place—a well-connected philanthropist probably responsible for getting Ulysses S. Grant to lay the cornerstone for the first museum building on the West Side.

But I could tell that Yamashita wasn't really interested in the trivia I was sharing with him about the museum. He was anxious to see the Tibetan. And this revelation heightened my own curiosity about Changpa. So I guided him quickly through the exhibit halls. As we sat down in the packed auditorium, I began to ask Yamashita something. His hand came up. "Hush." He was focused on his anticipation, enjoying it with a deep focus. Like a predator drowsing in the sun.

So I watched the crowd.

There was the usual mix of people: senior officials from the museum, a smattering of academics and graduate students. It was even rumored that the local real estate magnate who had largely funded the exhibit would attend. I wondered how a Tibetan monk would relate to that old gangster. The event had also drawn many people from the community: aficionados of things Asian. And others, some looking eager for enlightenment, others just looking for entertainment. It's the lifelong bipolar condition of many Americans.

We sat on the end of one row toward the rear of the big room. Yamashita would put up with only so much, and he liked to be in a position that gave him some defensive options.

Changpa Rinpoche was ushered in with all the fuss of any prestigious visitor. He had been in the news lately, advocating for greater freedom for occupied Tibet and appearing at rallies outside the U.N. I suspected that the Chinese were not crazy about him. So I wasn't surprised to notice that there were uniformed security guards as well as plainclothes people scanning the crowd. The audience was a typical jumble of voices and gestures, but I watched the mass of people with a seriousness not too different from that of the guards. My sensei's habits are rubbing off on me.

Changpa was a teacher, a lama, dressed in the saffron and deep red robes of a Tibetan Buddhist monk. His title, *Rinpoche,* was an honorific meaning "Precious Jewel." He was thicker than I had imagined, more energetic looking. It's a bias, but I tend to picture noodley, pale bodies when I think about the effects of long periods of seated meditation. I'm sure I wasn't alone—everyone expects him to be a clone of the Dalai Lama. But he wasn't. He looked more like a wrestler—solid and competent. But he had the same calm, gentle look as his more famous colleague.

He mounted the stage to applause. A small platform with cushions had been set up for him to sit upon. A simple vase filled with flowers stood next to it, echoing the yellow and crimson of his robes. Behind him, a large banner with calligraphy hung down against the stage's curtain.

"Can you read that?" I murmured to Yamashita. It looked like Sanskrit, with curves and angles and diacritical marks.

He shook his head. "No. I believe it is Tibetan script."

A young guy with a scraggly beard next to me leaned forward. "It's the mantra, *Om Mane Padme Hung,*" he said with smug self-satisfaction. He had the bright-eyed look of a true believer.

"Ah," I said.

The Rinpoche stayed standing and began speaking. His voice had a clipped, British accent to it. It wasn't a surprise.

Most of the lamas abroad today had made the tough hike across the Himalayas to India, the Chinese hot on their trail, and the cadences of the Raj still lived on in their English.

He was an engaging speaker; I'll give him that. Changpa seemed comfortable on the stage, with the audience. I had studied enough about Buddhism and its varieties—Theravada, Mahayana—and had been exposed to enough over-informed enthusiasts to know, however, that it was anyone's guess how the night might turn out. Especially with all the hype about Changpa's "powers."

I was really dreading an evening of mystic mumbo jumbo. I knew, deep down, that most people here hungered for a revelation of the powers of the mysterious East. But I thought they were doomed to disappointment. Revelation for me has always been a subtle thing, and as an object of desire is much like trying to grasp smoke. There are probably better ways to spend your time.

As the evening progressed, however, my fears were quieted. Changpa was pretty much what he appeared. Instead of a hyped-up mystic, what you came away with was the impression of a sincere man advocating the teachings of the Buddha and the benefits of belief and compassion. His voice was calm and clear. It had a cadence to it that gathered the audience in. You could almost feel the heightened intimacy, the sensation of the room growing physically closer, and of being gently drawn in upon a still center. Where Changpa stood.

I had experienced this before, with my own teacher Yamashita, when he chanted the warrior's mantra and showed me the ways to draw an ancient grid of power. Now I could sense a similar event unfolding. On one level, I was observant enough to see this. But the knowledge of what was happening did not prevent it from affecting me. What we were experiencing was a type of autohypnosis. Any good ritual contains it. But the astounding thing was to see the ease with which Changpa created the mesmerizing effect with such a large crowd.

The lama finished his presentation, and the crowd sat motionless for a moment, still held in the power of his words. Then the applause began.

I looked at Yamashita. He sat there, quietly intent, his eyes slightly narrowed as he watched the Rinpoche. "Wow," I said. My teacher nodded.

Then there was a period of question and answer.

I sat up a little straighter. This could be interesting. Personally, I find the prospect of fielding random questions from strangers tremendously unsettling. Like waiting for multiple attackers in a darkened room. I've done it, of course, but I would never volunteer to repeat the experience.

Fortunately, most of the people who spoke up were tremendously respectful. I suspected that the museum staff had arranged it. There were would-be Buddhists asking questions about the Dharma. The Sangha. Prayer wheels. You knew, deep down, that everyone was interested in the Rinpoche's reputed clairvoyance. And some people sort of hinted at possible connections between meditation and "higher powers." But no one broached the subject directly. Until the scraggly guy next to me stood up.

He had a brittle, intense voice that matched his looks. "Changpa Lama," he started, making a point of avoiding the Rinpoche title, "I wonder if you could comment on the allegations of your psychic abilities." There was a note of skepticism in the young man's voice. "And how this is consistent with the Buddha's teachings." A murmur, half expectation, half hostility, grew in the crowd. But the man wasn't deterred. He seemed, if anything, to be energized by the anger he was creating. He stood there, his chin pointing aggressively at the stage.

At the head of the room, Changpa looked placidly into the audience and held up a hand to quiet them. The lama smiled sheepishly. It was, I thought, the most genuine moment of the night. He had a good smile. A human face. I liked him.

"This is, I know, a thing of intense interest for people." He looked around the room. "There is, even in a place like America, where science is so powerful… there is this need for mystery."

I nodded to myself. I had seen the same hunger in the dojo. Many trainees worked long to get behind the veil of technique and effort and practice, hoping to find a mystery. Each student had his or her own idea of what the mystery should be, of course. And what many found depended on what they had set off to see in the first place. If you stayed long enough, however, I thought that what you discovered after hard training and discipline was simply more discipline. And maybe a small, tiny voice, whispering that the human spirit's ability to endure was the greatest mystery of all.

"There is no mystery here," the Rinpoche continued. "No magic. Please. I have no desire to appear on the cover of your supermarket tabloids." He grinned at the appreciative laughs from the audience.

"And I do not know what to call the… experiences I sometimes have." Changpa looked around. "You cannot turn it on and off like a light switch. It is not a conjurer's trick." Again, the smile. "So I will read your minds just once tonight and add that, no, I will not be able to demonstrate this experience to you further." There was some laughter again and a smattering of applause. Then he grew more serious. "But I have thought long and hard on a question very much like yours."

Changpa looked into the rear of the room, toward his questioner. For a brief moment, I saw the flash of focus in his eyes. It transmitted a sense of power and perception that was almost frightening in its directness. It was similar to what I often glimpsed in my own teacher: a revelation of an ability as intriguing as it was scary. I could see the young man standing next to me almost sag at the impact of Changpa's gaze. I don't know what he had hoped to achieve through his question. I only know that he got more than he bargained for. He sat down then, slowly, collapsing like a deflated balloon.

The lama continued his explanation as if nothing had occurred. But I noticed the tilt of Yamashita's head: he had seen it, too.

The holy man's words grabbed my attention again. "Certainly Chenzerig, the Buddha of Compassion, provides people with an awareness of many different things in different ways. Some people hear the beauty of music more clearly than others. Artists are more attuned to the subtlety of color. These are sometimes vehicles to lead us to dharma, to truth."

The room grew quieter as people listened intently. For the first time that evening, Changpa sat on the platform provided him. His hand reached into his robes and drew forth a string of prayer beads. He gestured with the beads. "But sensation often can serve as an impediment. Each bead on this *mala* represents four obstacles to truth. There are twenty-seven beads here, and four times twenty seven is one hundred and eight." I saw a number of heads nodding in recognition of the point. Changpa smiled again. "We believe that there are one hundred and eight basic obstacles that need to be removed or purified to reach the

True Way." His fingers worked the beads almost automatically. "In our daily lives, the endless details of existence can sometimes obscure the dharma, the true path. It is like the old saying you have: a man cannot see the forest for the trees." He looked around the room.

"My gift is that I can sometimes be elevated to a place where I can see the forest. Or even beyond it. I do not think it a mystery. Perhaps it is that, for a brief time, the Way is less…" he struggled for a word, his eyes remote. Then he finished. "… less occluded." He smiled sadly. "It is, I believe, what the Lord Buddha seeks for us all."

Out of the corner of my eye I had noticed Yamashita leaning forward, as if to better catch Changpa's explanation. As the lama finished, my teacher sat back, slowly exhaling in a sound that telegraphed a release of tension and a sense of deep satisfaction.

There was a reception for Changpa after the lecture. It was an invitation-only deal, but Yamashita's name and mine were on the list. It was held in a special exhibition gallery near the auditorium—not because the space was conducive to crowds, but, I suspected, because there was no furniture to move.

Even so, it was packed. The audience streamed out of the theater, setting up currents of movement, eddies of conversation. I tried to work our way through the crowd, but gave up and took my teacher around to the gallery's back entrance. A few people had the same idea. And they were being screened by a large guy with a clipboard. He wasn't wearing a museum staff uniform. And there was a subtle undercurrent in the air around him, a hint of barely suppressed anger. Or fear.

As we moved closer, I got a better look. He was in his mid-twenties, and had the easy stance of an athlete. Maybe six-two or three. Not huge by NFL standards, but big enough. He certainly loomed over me. I don't think Yamashita, who's even smaller, noticed. He's not even concerned, with these things. Size to him is merely part of an equation of angles, distances, and lines of attack. It's certainly not an element of intimidation.

But you could see that this guy liked to use his bulk that way. He was dressed all in black; an affectation that I vaguely associated with show biz or the art world. The dark clothes hid the musculature, but you could see the hint of power in the neck that swelled from his stylish little turtleneck. The guy was a people-handler. He seemed an odd companion for the Rinpoche.

We got to the head of the line.

"Hi," I said, giving the man my card. "I'm Dr. Burke. My guest and I should be on the list of invitees."

He took the card and didn't look at it. He looked down at his clipboard, flicking back and forth among the pages. His face took on a hard look. "No. Uh-uh. I don't see it."

I glanced at Yamashita. My job as his student is to pave the way for him. He is, after all, my sensei. It was embarrassing to have this sort of snag pop up. But I stayed calm.

"Sure, I understand," I told the man guarding the door. "Arrangements were made through the Office of Special Events." I could see that none of this made the slightest impact.

The man shook his head. "Yeah, well look. I don't know about that." You could see him make his final decision: it was like watching a shade roll down behind his eyes. His hard look got harder. "I'm gonna have to ask you to move along, now."

"Maybe we should talk to your supervisor…" I offered. "I'm sure the head of security can clear this up."

The man moved closer to us, trying to use his body to reinforce his request. Yamashita watched dispassionately, like a scientist viewing an interesting, yet routine, experiment performed by a colleague. But he didn't budge. And I got the subtle message: this problem was mine to deal with.

"I'm telling you once," the guard said tightly. "You're not on the list. You don't get in. Now beat it."

You could sense the shove coming. It was in the way his tone of voice began to cycle upward. A slight adjustment of his feet. I think his nostrils even flared slightly. In Yamashita Sensei's dojo we call it telegraphing. So I wasn't surprised when he tried to move me.

He shoved, and I could see his eyes narrow with anger when I stayed rooted to the spot. It's a pretty basic skill, once you get the hang of it. Without balance, my teacher says, nothing can be achieved. The naive think he's waxing philosophical. In reality, he thinks fighters should avoid falling down.

"I want you out of here," the big man hissed at me. He was getting ready to do something else. This was not the place for a shoving match. And I got the sense my friend here was getting ready to take things to the next level. It worried me. Not in terms of the physical stuff. But I could see the headlines in the paper: *Museum Mayhem: Martial Artist Crashes Party*.

"Is there a problem?" a woman's voice asked from the room beyond the door. I got the initial impression of an attractive, fit form with dark hair. She had a list on a clipboard, too. But I was mostly focused on the guy at the door. The man glared at me as I went through my explanation again to her. Presented my card. She looked at an index card clipped to her papers, and then put a hand on the arm of my wrestling partner. "It's OK. They were a late addition to the list." She said it in a calming way. But it was a firm tone, and not apologetic. The guard looked at us with resentment, but he stood aside. You could tell that deep down he wanted another go at me. And part of me was annoyed enough to oblige. For the first time, my teacher spoke. "Come, Burke. Let us go in." It was a mild command, but an order nonetheless.

"I'm sorry, Dr. Burke," the woman said as she started to lead us inside.

"There have been some changes in Changpa Rinpoche's arrangements. Different staff..." She smiled.

I smiled back at her and gestured for Yamashita to go in ahead of me. The man in black looked at us like we were reptiles.

I waited until she was out of earshot. "You think I'm hard to move," I murmured to the guard as I passed him, "you ought to try the Japanese guy." I grinned wickedly and entered the reception.

7

DISCIPLES

Yamashita and I made our way through the crowd with the woman who had brought us in.

"I'm so sorry about the fuss," she apologized again. She had dark brown, almost black hair that danced around her shoulders, and white teeth that glittered when she smiled.

"Is he with the museum?" I asked, nodding toward the man at the door who'd tried to bounce us.

"Oh, no." Again, the glitter of teeth. "Changpa Rinpoche prefers things simple, but his security advisors sometimes bring on added people for some events."

"Uh-huh ,"I nodded. "Is that where you come in…"

"Oh, I'm sorry." She paused and turned to face us. "I'm Sarah Klein." Her hair swung around and a few fine strands brushed across her forehead. She pushed them back absent-mindedly. Then laughed. "And no, I'm not part of the security. I spend some time at the Dharma Center in Manhattan and I volunteered to help out tonight."

We introduced ourselves. I watched with amusement as Yamashita gingerly shook hands with her. He doesn't like to do it, but he is invariably polite to non-students, especially if he likes you. I got the feeling he liked Sarah.

The action gave me a minute to look at her more carefully. She wasn't a small woman, but she had a lithe, graceful way about her. She looked fit. Mid-thirties, maybe. A good face, heart-shaped, with a lean jawline and brown eyes. She had the look of an adult about her—someone who knew enough about herself and the world to be relatively comfortable in it.

"Are you a Buddhist, Ms. Klein?" Yamashita asked. I was right. He did like her. Otherwise he never would have made the effort at conversation.

The flash of a smile. "Well, no. I study archery at the Center."

"Tibetan archery?" I asked.

"Oh, No." She hesitated for a second. "Actually it's a meditative form of archery from Japan called *kyudo*." She shrugged. "The Buddhists say there are lots of paths in life. These days, mine seems to include arrows."

"How interesting." My teacher smiled. I smiled, too. This was a woman I could grow to like.

Then she seemed to remember herself. "But you want to meet the Rinpoche, don't you? And here I am, keeping you from him." She gestured us toward the crowd and went off in another direction.

"A *kyudoka*, Burke," Yamashita said to me.

"You don't see one of those every day," I admitted.

"She is attractive." My teacher eyed me speculatively, but I said nothing. "She has good presence," he continued. "I liked her." Yamashita moved toward the Rinpoche, going slowly so I could worm my way through the crowd and stay next to him. "I had heard of this group practicing the Way of the Bow," he said as an aside. "It would be interesting to visit them…"

In general, I don't enjoy receptions of this type, so I distract myself by using them to train. I study people in motion: their patterns of movement and focus. At these events, there are typically a few spots where people concentrated their energies. It gave you a clue as to who was present and what was happening.

I try to see how good I am at figuring this out by sensing the patterns.

You discount activity at the bar and food areas, of course. That's a given. People cling to these sites like limpets, trying to look sophisticated while simultaneously consuming as much free stuff as possible. That night, there were a few other zones of activity I picked up on. The Real Estate Tycoon was there, natty and yet somehow feral at the same time. Various flunkies hovered nervously around him. He was trying to appear subdued in honor of his guest. It was obviously a strain—as you looked at him, you got the impression of a seething instability.

There was another major center of activity around Changpa Rinpoche himself, of course. He was hemmed in by the curious, by gushing student-Buddhists, and members of the museum's PR department. But he didn't seem overwhelmed. The Rinpoche was not a small man, and he had a certain presence. Even people who didn't consciously sense anything spiritual were obviously affected by him. He stood there, smiling and making pleasant small talk, his head canted to one side in amusement, holding a cup of tea.

He was the main focal point, but I was also picking up something else. Close by, but with a slightly different feel, there was another swirl of people.

The person at the center of that group of admirers was big and broad-shouldered, square-jawed and dashing. He had bright blue eyes and a full mane of brownish-blonde hair. It took a minute to place him, then I did: Travis Stark. He stood there, smiling pleasantly at people, like an actor beaming at an audience. He was holding forth about something that obviously engaged the attention of his listeners.

My attention was redirected. Yamashita was gently prodding me with a finger toward Changpa Rinpoche. At least he meant it to be gentle. It was like being jabbed by an iron pipe.

And that's when the really interesting thing happened. The room was filled with people, some clustered in the areas I had noted, but most circulating randomly. They spoke with each other, but their awareness wasn't focused on anything beyond that. Conversation swirled through the air. Laughter bubbled here and there and glasses and plates clicked with the usual cocktail party noise. The crowd churned, coming together in odd spots, then breaking up and drifting on. In all that, I doubt very much that it was possible for anyone to notice my master's approach to the guest of honor.

But the lama himself did.

I saw his head swivel around and those eyes look toward us. It was as if he heard something no one else did—a signal beyond the normal limen of human awareness. His body shifted slightly, facing fully toward Yamashita. A receiver turning toward a signal source. He raised his hand in a classic gesture, a *mudra*, or meditation posture that I had seen on countless statues of the Buddha: have no fear.

Some of the people he was with turned to see what Changpa was looking at. Simultaneously, I sensed a different type of activity from a few discrete spots in the room. A pattern was emerging. The Tycoon and his attendants began to approach. From another corner, Stark was listening, head down, as the bouncer we had encountered whispered in his ear. In the aimless swirl of party movement, the currents began to converge.

My friend Steve from the museum was with Changpa, and you could see his face brighten as he caught sight of me.

He touched the Rinpoche lightly on the arm as he prepared to introduce us. Stark and the bodyguard vectored in on our location at the same time, both sets of jaws set in photogenic determination. And Real Estate Man moved toward us as well, churning through the crowd with the unconscious momentum of an abandoned ocean liner.

The lama broke into a broad smile. "Sensei," he said, and bowed toward Yamashita. "How good to see you again."

Yamashita bowed in turn, more deeply than I had ever seen him do before. "It has been too long, Rinpoche," he answered. "Let me introduce Dr. Connor Burke."

The holy man tore his pleased attention away from Yamashita and turned that clear, deep expression on me. Some of the intensity of his gaze bled away. His face settled into a look of contentment after a second, and he extended a hand. I reached for it as I sensed the looming presence of the Tycoon.

"Dr. Burke," the lama said. "Your teacher has spoken of you. How nice to finally meet you…"

Real Estate's Big Man broke in, and his formal prose couldn't hide the accents of a New Yorker. "An extraordinary event, sir. We are honored by your presence." He edged closer to Changpa, and the signal was clearly that I should disappear.

But monks, for all their introspection, are sometimes made of sterner stuff. Changpa smoothly shifted himself a foot to his left and turned so that Yamashita and I were still in his view. Then the bodyguard and Travis Stark appeared on the other side of us, and tried to edge us away as well. Changpa was placid, but not unaware.

"The room is so crowded, Dr. Burke. I am sorry." He looked at the two men impassively, but the message was clear. They stepped back slightly, but you could see that they didn't like it.

In the small void left by moving bodies, Yamashita and Changpa stood regarding each other. Their eyes were wide and unblinking, dark pools that hinted at depths of knowledge that were simultaneously the same and yet vastly different. Neither man moved a muscle, but stood, content in each other's presence. It was an odd moment of quiet in the bustle that surrounded us.

An aide interjected himself. "Rinpoche," he said, gesturing toward other well-dressed types who were eager to meet the lama, "please…"

Changpa smiled tightly at us. "Even in little things, we see how tightly we are strapped to life's wheel. Please excuse me, gentlemen. Until the next time…" He turned to give the newcomers his full attention.

I thought at the time that the Rinpoche had an odd way of saying good-bye. I had forgotten that this was a man who saw things that had yet to come.

The bodyguard's bulk blocked off Changpa and the Real Estate guy. I was a little disappointed that I wouldn't get to watch the two of them talk. Would Changpa touch the Tycoon? I kept getting mental images of a vampire hissing as contact with a holy object burned his flesh.

"What are you doing here?" a voice demanded, breaking my reverie. I looked. It was Stark.

"What are *you* doing here?" I responded, ever the clever conversationalist and master of the quick comeback.

He gave me a hard look. "I'm helping with security."

"I came to see the Rinpoche."

"Andy tells me you gave him a hard time," Stark accused. His jaw muscles worked dramatically. I suspected he had been watching old Charlton Heston movies.

"Andy?"

"Part of my security detail."

Ah. The bouncer.

"He said he couldn't move you." Stark looked at me with frank disbelief. The last time we met, I had knocked him down. You could tell he thought it was a fluke. At six-three or -four he had about half a foot on me. So did Andy.

"I didn't want to be moved," I said. "Besides, he was being a pain."

Stark squinted at me. Very Redford-esque. Part of me thought he was silly. But he was still a pretty good size. And not very happy with me. The tension of our unfinished match still lingered.

Yamashita came up to us. Stark performed a pretty good bow toward Yamashita. "Sensei," he said. My teacher gave a slight nod, the briefest movement that satisfied etiquette.

"What's the problem here?" I asked. "Why's that guy Andy so jumpy?"

Stark waved a hand and gave me flash of those even white teeth. "The Rinpoche doesn't pay any attention, but there are always security issues. I try to be a little proactive about them."

"Were you expecting anything in particular tonight?" I asked him. "I mean, why roust us?"

He looked off into the distance with narrowed eyes. Man of action, seeing things no one else does. "Let's just say we had indications…" and he let it dangle in the air, as if mystery were the ultimate justification.

Yamashita lost interest, wandered over to a table and ate a piece of fruit. He watched the crowd impassively.

There was an awkward pause. Stark nodded toward him. "So. Old-style swordsmanship, huh?" I nodded. He flexed his hands in front of me. They looked like he could crack a coconut with them. "I always preferred the arts where there's a lot of actual sparring," he said with satisfaction. "Black belts in *jujutsu* and *kendo.*" Stark said the names like they were part of a magic spell. Was I supposed to swoon?

"But," he continued, "I've just completed a seminar with a teacher who believes you should master the whole spectrum of systems. It's very intense," he told me.

I'll bet, I thought. But I was polite "Who's the teacher?" I asked.

"Kita Takenobu," he answered. It was obvious from his tone of voice that I was supposed to be impressed.

"The Yamaji," I said. Stark nodded significantly and seemed gratified at my response.

I don't know whether I was impressed, but I had heard of Kita Takenobu. The story went that he left Japan as a young black belt and had spent years wandering Asia in search of the ultimate martial art. He had been heavily influenced by experiences on the mainland. They said he had studied with masters in Korea, China, and Tibet. And, at some point in his search, he had come to America to teach what he had learned.

Kita was something of an outcast to the mainstream Japanese martial arts community. Japan is a tremendously conservative place, and the sensei there are real chauvinists. Kita's synthesis of various Asian styles would not sit well with them, and from what I had heard, Kita was a maverick bent on doing things his own way. It didn't surprise me that he ended up in this country. Yamashita had, too.

The last I heard, Kita had established a monastic training center high in the California mountains, called Yamaji, the Mountain Temple. He was setting up a huge martial arts organization based on his new system, giving seminars and attracting students. The word was that he had tremendous pull with the show business community, and had a number of wealthy patrons. I suppose that's how you afford a mountain retreat. My teacher held lessons in a warehouse.

"How'd you hook up with him, Stark?"

He rolled his big shoulders, as if his muscles were too developed and needed to occasionally be bled of excess strength. "I was doing some stunt work in L.A. and met him out there."

Mentally, I nodded. Stark's looks had "aspiring actor" written all over them.

"And when I met him," Stark continued, "and saw some of what he could do, I was just blown away. I'm hoping to be accepted as one of his *uchi deshi*."

I arched my eyebrows in comment. An uchi deshi, an inner disciple, was someone who lived and studied with a teacher. It was an honor reserved for promising students. When I looked at Stark, I didn't see someone who was serious enough to merit that sort of distinction. He seemed too self-absorbed.

"What brings you to New York?" I asked.

He shrugged his big shoulders. "I've got interests here," he said vaguely.

"And I thought that before I go with Kita I'd study with some other people for a time. Sort of round my skills out. I thought that Asa Sensei might have something to show me… Now I'm wondering whether Yamashita might take me on for a while. Might be fun."

Now he was really annoying me. You don't shop for a martial arts teacher like Yamashita like you would buy a suit of clothes. Mostly, you hope you're good enough for him to even notice you.

"Sensei has very high standards," I said woodenly.

"Please." He waved his hand. "I've been around a bit. And I've seen a real master, Burke," Stark continued. "Kita's incredible. Even the Rinpoche would be impressed by him."

I shrugged. Every martial artist I know has some teacher he thinks is the ultimate authority. It's part of the dynamics of studying with someone. There's an emotional link created between a sensei and his trainees. It's part respect, part admiration, and part fear. Stark felt it with Kita, but that didn't mean much to me.

He must have read that on my face, because it became obvious that he realized that his enthusiasm was lost on me. I got the impression that he loomed large in his own imagination and it grated on him that I wasn't impressed with him or Kita. His voice got a little meaner, showed a bit of the fang hidden by those white caps on his teeth.

He nodded toward Yamashita. "I hear that he's some kind of master, too, Burke. But I'll bet he's not at Kita's level. Maybe second class, huh?" He paused. "What's that make you?" It was supposed to needle me.

"His student," I said simply. Then I walked away.

Stark was a jerk. He worked in a business where humility was a personality flaw and surface appearances were the ultimate reality. I was probably something of a mystery to him. I have the tubular build and strong legs of a martial artist. There is over-developed musculature in my hands and forearms and back, but it's not very noticeable. It probably confused him that I had fought him to a standstill that day in Asa's dojo. Stark might hope to study with Kita, but it might be something very different from what his L.A. perspective anticipated. Life out there made for a very different set of expectations.

I went over and stood by Yamashita. He had a toothpick in his hand. One end was covered in red colored cellophane. My sensei was eyeing it as if measuring its offensive capabilities.

"Have you seen enough, Sensei?"

He nodded. "Oh, yes. As always, Professor, excursions with you are quite interesting."

"Sorry we didn't get more time with Changpa."

Yamashita blinked. "He is a remarkable man. It was good merely to see him again." He blinked. "I recognized that man Stark, of course, from Asa Sensei's dojo. He may have promise…"

"I can't believe Changpa uses that joker for security," I said. I told him about the connection with Kita.

"Have you considered, Burke, that the Rinpoche tolerates Stark not because there is a need for security, but because Stark himself needs to guard something? It is, perhaps, an act of compassion on the lama's part." It was an insightful comment from a man who was my taskmaster. He's a strange blend of brutal energy and subtle insight. Yamashita placed the toothpick down on the table. "We may go now."

"You know they thought we were after Changpa," I commented as we made our way through the reception.

"I am not surprised. We reek of danger," he said. I snorted appreciatively. Yamashita's humor is extremely low key.

"As far as I can tell," I said, "none of the guys Stark's got working security know what they're doing."

"True," my master said. "But they are dangerous nonetheless."

"These guys?" I asked skeptically.

"Oh yes. Were you to fight them, it is highly probable they would lose their balance. And they are so large… if they fell on you, I am afraid you would be crushed."

"That would be bad," I agreed.

The museum itself was not open for browsing that night, but we were lucky that the reception gallery was located right next to one of my favorite exhibitions—the Northwest Coast Indians. I don't know what it is. I had first seen this place when I was maybe eight years old, and I never lost the feeling I got then. Maybe it was the sheer dense mass of the heavy wooden totem poles, the intricate, stylized art in red and black, but the testimony of the vividness and imagination of a people from another place and time struck me most forcibly here.

And there was the canoe.

A huge wooden Haida canoe dominated a hallway. It had to be thirty feet long, filled with life-size rowers wielding intricately carved paddles, all of them frozen in time as they labored over an imaginary sea toward 77th street. In the bow stood the chief, cloaked in a straw rain cape. The mannequins were Asian-looking, and something about the stout, remote figure standing there and looking off into the distance reminded me of Yamashita.

You had to admire these people. When you really got up close to the boat, it struck you just how gutsy they were. They would take vessels like this out into the churning waters of the Northwest coast to hunt whales. I could imagine them, scanning the dark surface of the heaving sea on a foggy day, listening for the telltale sigh of a whale breathing in the murk. Watching for the glimpse of slick skin as something humped up, just below the surface. Alert for the dorsal fins of a pod of Orcas. For all its size, the boat was a fragile thing against the immensity of the sea and its creatures. For me, it captured the essence of human life: an enterprise composed of equal parts daring and desperation.

I wondered what the lama would think.

Yamashita and I walked out of the light and noise of the reception, down the main entrance to the street. I thought some more about the relationship between Yamashita and Changpa, but said nothing as I followed my sensei down the street. I thought of the Haida chief, scanning the dark waters. What we can see is often not what is really there. I thought of Micky and Art and the Sakura murder. Sometimes things are hidden.

I glanced over the looming darkness of Central Park and into the sky. The ambient light of cities tends to obscure the view. But I knew, overhead, that stars dusted the night sky. They wheeled in patterns, made manifest only in silence and patience.

8

SEEKER

In the morning light of rural Georgia, the mist in the valleys was gray and cold-looking, shreds pulled through the wet tops of trees. Slowly, the cloud cover was burned away, and the hills humped up like waves, stretching to the horizon. There were small sounds. The rustle of squirrels. Wind in tree limbs. The door to the cabin stood ajar, like a mouth open in silent surprise. Everything was hushed in the aftermath. From within, there was a faint rustling sound that grew slowly fainter as the morning breeze died.

It had been cool at dawn this high up, the night's cold still laying in the hollows like the memory of a dream. You could smell the damp of pine needles in the air. Dogwoods flowered ghostly white in spots along the slopes. The scholar was an early riser who liked to watch day come to his retreat. But he was an old man used to comfort. He had watched for a moment, then turned to his cabin, the scent of coffee hurrying him back inside.

He turned the lights off as the sun grew stronger. The rays slanted across the old wooden table, washing golden bars across the papers that lay there. He carefully cleared a spot for his coffee mug and picked up a pencil, slowly editing last night's work. He moved hesitantly at first, then warmed to his task like an athlete who feels his muscles working themselves once more into readiness.

The sabbatical was drawing to a close. He had used the time off from his university post to come up here, away from the distractions of daily life, and write. The cabin was littered with reference books, notes, and photocopies of manuscripts. He came down from the lonely country cabin only for supplies and to pick up the important mail that his departmental secretary bundled together for him, but the months had been a quiet time that he treasured.

The birds had been calling since well before first light. Their noise came and went, pushed by the wind. But it was never really silent up here. You could hear the odd car or truck winding down the blacktop down by the river, tires whining faintly into the distance. It was a vaguely comforting sound. It was only during the last few days that he had grown increasingly apprehensive at his isolation. Yet he didn't hear the intruder approach—the carpet of pine needles muffled his steps.

It must have been the birds that alerted the scholar. He had grown used to their noise. And when they stopped, shocked mute by something, the awareness of their silence grew slowly in him until he got up, curious as to why the morning song had ended.

The door wasn't locked, but the intruder kicked it open anyway. He must have come upon the older man like a storm, all motion and unexpected violence. A force that could not be opposed.

The intruder slammed him down to the floor. Then the questioning began. There was not much in the way of conversation. The scholar had something of the ability to read a situation well. He played the game of Go for years and he had what the Japanese referred to as "a quick read of the board": the scholar could see where the stones lay and come to an intuitive grasp of things. The telephone warning now made some sense: he knew why the intruder was here. And the scholar was equally certain that he would not divulge what the intruder wanted.

It all seemed so remote to the old man. All this anger over what amounted to a point of pride, hardly worth pursuing. Maybe it was age: things that seemed sharp and clear to others began to soften for him, like objects viewed through mist. In the cool morning light, the blossoms on the trees outside still heavy with dew, the intruder's urgency seemed out of place to the old man. The scholar wondered whether he should just tell the man what he wanted.

Years ago, the scholar had been a soldier. And he had learned in the long slog through Normandy something about stubborn pride and the limits of what could be endured. So he set himself in silence.

The intruder almost pleaded for the information from the scholar. But the scholar was hard and stubborn. He lay, frightened, but flushed with pride in his fight. He believed himself set like stone against any persuasion. But he was wrong.

His master had given the intruder a hard apprenticeship; the student learned to see things with a cold clarity. The bulky form of the scholar, still so stubborn in old age, was filled with weakness.

The intruder wrapped a wire around the scholar's neck, twisting it tightly and jerking the old man to his feet. He yanked one of the old man's arms around, torqueing the joints and forcing compliance as he directed him toward the stove where the coffeepot simmered.

The intruder's voice took on some of the coaxing nature of a teacher leading a wayward pupil. He asked the scholar calmly, patiently, for the information. Such a simple thing. An address.

A location. Then, with each refusal, he brought the old man's hand closer to the stove.

The scholar bucked as the heat began to sear him. But the intruder held him tight, coaxing him, promising relief. But insisting on an answer.

There was just a scream. And deep down, the old man realized that he could not supply all of what the intruder wanted. He simply did not know some of the answers. Up to that point, despite his fierce determination to resist, the old man knew he could agree to talk. Now, with a jolt of deep, despairing insight, the old man realized that even full cooperation would not be met with mercy.

The intruder withdrew the scholar's hand and began again. This time more slowly. He sensed that he was close to getting a response. The trick, he came to learn, was not to rush the process. Torture is a squeamish business. But to be done correctly, it can't be rushed. To do so just short-circuits the whole process. And all you get are screams.

The intruder wanted information. So he learned to go slowly. He confused the scholar's ignorance for endurance and, as he pressed him once again with questions, the intruder was the source of his own undoing. The pain shot up the old man's arm to the jaw, and the wave of nausea engulfed him as his heart began to flutter. He collapsed to the floor, and the intruder realized that something had gone wrong. And that the information he thought that the old man had was quickly receding beyond his grasp.

The intruder looked at the old one lying on the cool ground, clutched up tight into a ball of agony. He tried to think of his next step, to envision another way to get what he sought. But he couldn't hold the image: it was blurred by the frustration of once more failing in his appointed task.

The old man was moaning quietly. The intruder felt a fleeting type of contempt for him: old, broken, humiliated. But then a curious compassion came over the intruder. So he reached down and tightened the wire that was still wrapped around the scholar's neck. The intruder's hands were strong, and the sudden tension cut off almost all but the beginning of the scholar's sudden gasp. The wire cut into the flesh and muscle of the neck, cutting off the old man's air. Then the blood flow stopped to the brain, diverted as the wire cut the artery. The scholar finally lapsed into unconsciousness and the blood pooled, faintly steamy in the cool cabin.

The killer finished the job and then stood up, curiously calm in the golden wash of morning. He looked out over the rolling hills that stretched away from him, the valleys still churning with mist. As always, the mountains offered a promise of serenity. He would wait and watch. The diligent seeker would be shown the way.

9

DARK VALLEY

There are different types of pain. My sensei has shown me that. Is there a benefit to the insight? Sometimes I wonder. Years ago, I had once protested, but Yamashita looked coldly at me. "What did you expect when you took up the sword?" he asked. It was something I tried to remember daily. It tends to put things in perspective.

Yamashita called me that evening with a cryptic request: we were to meet in Midtown. He gave me the time and the location, but there wasn't even the hint of explanation. I've grown used to it: the teacher-student relationship is pretty cut and dry in Japanese culture. Yamashita wasn't asking me to meet him. He was telling me.

"Do I need anything?" I asked. Sometimes he takes me to other dojos and we put the locals through their paces. I wanted to know whether I needed a uniform. Weapons.

"Your presence will be adequate," Yamashita replied. Then, as an afterthought, "Bring your credit card. Perhaps we can have dinner." On my end, the phone went dead.

He was standing at the address he'd given me, but he wasn't alone. Seeing Yamashita in street clothes was slightly disorienting: I always pictured him in the dojo, a solid, grounded figure swathed in the ritual robes of the martial arts. But now my teacher stood there amid the less hurried crowds of Sunday Manhattan with another Asian, a somewhat larger man draped in a tan raincoat against the intermittent drizzle. It was Changpa Rinpoche.

"Hello, Dr. Burke," the lama said. He didn't shake hands, just inclined his head and torso slightly forward. His eyes crinkled from the half-smile he gave me.

"I didn't recognize you for a moment," I admitted to him.

He held his arms up slightly at his sides, displaying the coat. "My robes of office can sometimes be a distraction for people. I thought this would be better."

I nodded.

"Besides," the Rinpoche continued, "it made it easier to slip away from my assistants." He looked at Yamashita. "It was like the old days, Sensei. I'm glad that you reminded me."

My teacher nodded and closed his eyes briefly in acknowledgement. The light, misty rain caught on the stubble of his shaven head. Dark spots peppered the Rinpoche's raincoat as well. My teacher gestured toward a restaurant door. "Tea?" he suggested.

I followed the two men inside, totally clueless as to what was going on. It was a familiar sensation: time spent with my sensei was routinely composed of confusion. Or terror. So far, the evening was shaping up nicely.

The Rinpoche sat there, his hands wrapped appreciatively around a teacup, comfortable with the silence. I merely watched. We had gotten tea, but the waitress came by again to ask if we needed anything else. I saw Changpa's face cloud over, as if he felt an unexpected stab of pain. The waitress went away. He watched her with a sad look, and then caught me staring at him.

He shrugged. "The Buddha's compassion at times seems inadequate for all the pain in the world."

I turned to watch the woman as she worked the room. I saw nothing out of the ordinary and my face must have shown it.

"Sporadically, Dr. Burke, I am sensitized to the inner state of other people," he said. "When it happens it is sometimes quite unexpected."

Yamashita regarded me for a moment and then spoke. "Burke has some experience of this, Rinpoche. But he is just beginning to develop that sense…"

Haragei again. But what the Rinpoche experienced seemed pretty vivid. For me, it's a subtle phenomenon: a wash of certainty or insight that creeps up over you. You can feel it in the electric tension rippling along your skin. It usually happens to me during periods of great danger. I'm in no rush to feel it again anytime soon.

Changpa brightened and looked interested in Yamashita's comment. "I have found this ability to be an extremely difficult one to develop in my pupils," he said. My sensei nodded in agreement. "How do you go about it?" the lama asked.

Yamashita sipped his tea. "Ah, Rinpoche. I have found it… challenging… to even begin to anticipate who will and who will not develop it." He looked at me pointedly, as if to illustrate the bewildering vagaries of fate. Yamashita's hands were not as large as Changpa's, but they were thick and powerful-looking. He held out a hand, palm up and continued. "I try to create opportunities for the experience through training. But it is difficult." Again, the significant glance at me.

It was a curious thing, sitting there as both a spectator and an object of discussion. It was like being a child in the company of adults.

The Rinpoche nodded in sympathy for my teacher. "Just so. These sensibilities seem to fascinate many people." He sipped some tea. "They are useful, of course, but too intent a focus on them obscures, I believe, the True Path."

"Yet ability is sometimes what moves us along the Way," Yamashita continued, "even if it is not the Way itself."

They both looked extremely gratified by the exchange. I thought it was interesting to see two people come at the same idea from diametrically opposed positions. An eavesdropper would have thought that they were writers for a fortune cookie business.

Changpa smiled at me then. "It sounds like the cryptic messages in Chinese cookies, does it not Dr. Burke?" I smiled back, but felt suddenly cold, unbalanced. Could he really get inside my mind?

The Tibetan very carefully pushed his tea away and to one side. He looked directly at me, and the clarity of those eyes was silent acknowledgment of what he had just done. "But I am being rude," he continued in an apologetic voice. "Has Yamashita Sensei told you of our conversations?" He looked across the table.

My teacher shook his head. "No, Rinpoche. I only told him that he was needed."

The lama regarded me carefully. "And that was enough?" he asked. I said nothing. "I have found Americans so… talkative," Changpa continued. There was almost a tone of wonder in his voice. Then he bowed slightly toward Yamashita. "You are to be congratulated. It is rare to find a disciple who knows the value of silence. And obedience."

Sensei bowed back and smiled as well. Then he nodded slightly in my direction. "He is a good student," he commented modestly. Which was the closest he ever came to giving me a public compliment.

Changpa adjusted his glasses. The lenses caught the light and, for a moment, his eyes were flat, silver slashes. "Students," he sighed, and turned his head to face me. "That is part of why we are here today. To be a teacher, Dr. Burke, is not really about showing people new things. It seems rather to consist of repeatedly trying to steer them away from old mistakes."

I was familiar with this idea. The Japanese masters spend years making you do things in a way that seems totally at odds with your instincts. That, they tell you, is because what they are showing you is the natural way to do things. The reason it is so hard is that you have developed bad habits. When my sensei twists your joints until they scream, he says that he is just clearing the dust from them. You nod and think about it later, but mostly are just glad when he stops.

"Illusion is the enemy of the Buddha nature," the lama continued. "And we manufacture so much of it for ourselves." He drew spirals on the table with a blunt finger, watching the pattern emerge and fade in the white tablecloth as he spoke, then suddenly looked up. "There are patterns in each life. We are drawn to repeat them over and over again. It is understandable…" and here his voice took on a dreamy, sad tone. "The future is so uncertain. And the familiar is such a comfort…"

His head moved and his glasses flashed and then were once again clear. "People ask me about my prescient abilities." He smiled suddenly at a thought. "They want to know, of course, who will win the next championship game. Things of that sort. I try to explain that looking into the future is like standing on a high mountain. You can see far. But only the peaks. The valleys are in shadow."

He stopped drawing and played with his teacup for a moment, making the fluid slosh around before going on. "And the landscape moves. It heaves and reforms… it is, I suppose, much like the sea," Again the smile. "But I come from the Himalayas. Mountains are a more appropriate metaphor."

I tried to imagine what the experience of prescience would be like: the sight of things to come and the taunting awareness that this vision was incomplete and transient.

"But some things I do know," Changpa continued after a while, gathering himself and using a stronger voice. "Some peaks jut up too high to be discounted. And then I must act on them." He seemed like he was looking for agreement.

"Knowledge without right action is futile," Yamashita said in sympathy. I kept quiet.

"And yet the correct response to that knowledge is difficult to see," the holy man murmured. "Can we really shape the future?" He said it almost to himself. Then the Rinpoche picked up his cup and sipped at the tea like a man searching for an anchor in the familiar and solid. He looked at us both, one after the other. "When I see a distant future… the path leading to an event is difficult to make out. But we must try nonetheless…"

"Is there something you need done for you, Rinpoche?" I finally asked quietly.

He straightened in his seat. Unconsciously, one hand dug into the pocket of his coat and emerged with his prayer beads. He fingered them as he spoke. "A teacher's duty is to point out the Right Path. And to protect his students from taking wrong ones. What I see… is unclear as yet. But there is danger there, Burke. A high peak. And a path that descends into shadows. I would…" he took a breath, as if the mere act of recalling his vision was painful. "I would steer someone from this valley."

Yamashita had watched him intently and now leaned forward to speak. I got the sense he did it to spare Changpa further pain.

"This ability of the Rinpoche, Burke," my teacher began, "is without question real. His perception is incomplete," he bobbed his head in apology toward the lama, "but that is the flaw we all share. All the advanced disciplines speak of this ability. The transfer of consciousness to another plane…"

"We call it *powa*," Changpa commented.

"But it is of limited utility," Yamashita continued. "It is much like the ability to sense an attack. It does not relieve you from the need to be ready for the many variations that the attack may come in. You must act, even if you are uncertain." I nodded.

"The Rinpoche has asked for our help in a specific matter. As a friend, I can do no less." Yamashita smiled modestly. "Action, after all, is what we do best."

I wondered again about this friendship.

Changpa sat back in his chair and smiled at me. "You wonder, of course, Dr. Burke, about our relationship." I just nodded in response. "It is of long standing and we were much younger then…"

My teacher gave an uncharacteristic smile. "Even then, you were a serious man, despite your years."

Changpa's eyes crinkled in acknowledgment. "But not, I fear, always as wise as I should have been."

I worried for a split second that we were getting off the track.

"But I digress," the lama told me. "I was fortunate enough to meet your teacher when he was still attached to the bodyguards for the Imperial Family."

I knew of my teacher's affiliation with the Imperial Household Guards of Japan. It was an experience in his past that had come back to haunt the both of us before. And now here was another aspect of Yamashita's past intruding once again on the present.

Sensei waved a hand. "The details are not particularly interesting, Burke. I was attached to a diplomatic mission with members of the Royal Family as they toured India. In the north, near Dharamsala, there were, as there are today, various elements intent on seeking independence from the government. They seek any means to draw attention to themselves and their causes…"

"The human wish for self-determination is a universal one," Changpa commented. "My own countrymen struggle for it even now. But the methods some groups choose for their causes sometimes create more suffering than they seek to alleviate, Dr. Burke. Such was the case when a separatist group plotted to kidnap a member of the Imperial family."

"The Rinpoche learned through his contacts of this plot, Burke," Yamashita blinked. "I was able to… neutralize… the threat in a way that satisfied all parties. And I have always remained grateful for his assistance."

The lama nodded in acknowledgment of the statement. After thinking a minute, he spoke. "Your teacher and I have discovered over time that we share much in common. It is a joy of a kind to discover another seeker in this world…" he glanced out the restaurant window at the concrete and cars, bluing in the waning light of evening Manhattan. Changpa seemed once again caught in the grip of some powerful internal experience. Then he brightened. "And it appears that each of us has a pupil in need of more than we are capable of providing…"

The lama let the statement hang in the air and began again. "Within each of us, there is a time when we feel the urge to seek the Buddha Nature. Indeed, it is within us always. But illusion cloaks its presence. It is as if..." and here his voice took on the tones of a teacher, speaking of things at once familiar and remote "... as if each of us is outside a beautiful walled city. We burn to enter, yet the walls—the illusions—keep us out. So we build ladders.

"Each person's ladder is made from a different design." The mala beads clicked faintly as he continued. "In reality the appearance of the ladder is not important. Only its ability to breach the wall."

I nodded sagely, but was not sure where this was going. Again I got that piercing look from the lama. It wasn't threatening, but it gave you the feeling that you were totally exposed to him.

Changpa smiled. I thought of the way he had greeted Yamashita the first time they met: a hand gesture, *have no fear.* The smile had the same impact. "But I am being obscure. People grow attached to their ladders, Dr. Burke. They understand the climb over the wall only in terms of the rungs on the ladder they have built." He smiled ruefully. "The climb is difficult enough without removing that small comfort."

My sensei broke in. "There is a disciple in danger, Burke. A martial artist," Yamashita said. He obviously felt I was a little slow on the uptake. "Changpa Rinpoche has asked for our help. I have agreed that we would."

"Who is it?" I asked. When they told me Travis Stark, I wasn't particularly surprised. I had been preoccupied with the Sakura murder, but even so I must have been making connections at some unconscious level. Yamashita had brought me to two different places where Stark was present. He rarely does things without a purpose, although he doesn't often tell you what it is. I sat now and waited for an explanation.

"A brother lama worked with Stark on meditative techniques in California. And Stark eventually came to me seeking more advanced training. Personal issues have drawn him here as well…" He paused as if thinking of saying more, but didn't elaborate on that point. "I have attempted to guide him while he simultaneously pursues his interest in the martial arts. Stark has been a challenging pupil. But he is, I think, good at heart."

"He has studied with Asa Sensei," Yamashita commented.

The lama nodded. "Now he seeks another challenge."

"The Yamaji," Yamashita breathed.

"I know something of Stark's new interest in this master, Kita," Changpa confirmed.

"Why do you need us?" I persisted.

The lama picked up the teapot and poured us each more tea. I noticed his free hand touched the underside of the arm doing the pouring. It was a habit developed by people who wore robes with wide sleeves.

"Remember the ladder I spoke of, Dr. Burke. Stark is someone who is focused on the martial arts. I have attempted to lead him along more…" he smiled at me with those clear eyes "… gentle, what you might call 'noodley' paths. But he yearns for more active pursuits. Kendo satisfied him for a time." Changpa sighed. "He has volunteered to work as a security person, but really…" he looked at each of us in turn, then sighed again. "He creates more problems than he solves."

I looked at Yamashita. He was sitting very quietly, regarding Changpa with a look of patient expectation. The lama followed my gaze and saw the expression on his old friend's face. My teacher is comfortable with silence. He uses it like a tool. Or a weapon.

"After our meeting the other evening," the lama began, but seemed uncharacteristically at a loss for words and stopped talking.

"What troubles you, Rinpoche?" my master asked quietly.

The monk glanced around him as if to check for danger. "Of late, there have been disturbing events at the Dharma Center. Our offices were broken into. Staff members have been followed. There have been threatening phone calls…"

"So what did the cops say?" I asked. Maybe it was impertinent, but I was getting tired of sitting there like a lump.

The lama shrugged. "They were as helpful as possible, but were not particularly reassuring. I would hope that perhaps you, given your background and your contacts with the police, could help me in this matter."

Changpa's sense of what I was capable of seemed curiously at odds with what I had seen so far of his perceptive ability. I was an overeducated martial artist who had gotten into a scrape or two. And my brother was a cop. But that wasn't the kind of thing that would inspire confidence in most people.

I looked incredulously at Yamashita, but he stared back in all seriousness. "Well, sure," I said slowly, "I'll do what I can, but is that all you want?"

Again the flash of his eyeglasses. "No, Dr. Burke. There is much more. It is why I have sought both you and your master out."

Yamashita became very still.

"The search for knowledge sometimes brings with it the problem of power," Changpa said carefully to us both. "Your Way is a perilous path—the allure of strength and violence."

His voice took on a wondering, almost dreamy tone. "The temptation must be acute." He seemed to gather himself and sat back in his seat.

"I have known your teacher for years. And I assume that, as his pupil, you are capable of walking the knife edge of this Way without succumbing to temptation," he said firmly. "You know danger and fear and struggle, yet I do not sense the dark shadow of illusion around you."

We sat for a time. Changpa cleared his throat. "There are dark shadows surrounding the Dharma Center. And around Stark. They draw him down a pathway and I fear for him. And those whose lives he touches. I would ask that you attempt to guide him, for I can take him no further."

But there was more to it than that, I'd bet. Maybe my teacher wanted me to learn from this guy and was going to help out with Stark. But there was a dark urgency here. Maybe all my teacher's stress on haragei was having an impact on me. I pressed the lama for more.

"But why us?" I said slowly and distinctly to Changpa, an echo of my earlier question that indicated I wasn't satisfied. "Why seek your old friend out? Now?"

Changpa sighed. His eyes closed as he spoke. "I told you of my vision—high places and valleys… of danger." His lids fluttered and opened.

I nodded to encourage him.

"You and your teacher were in the vision as well."

10
PATHWAYS

I should have been at the office, but I had begged a few days off from my dean. He seemed relieved to see me go. He's the administrative version of those circus acts that spin plates on long sticks. My absence gave him one less unstable object to worry about. So instead I sat, legs folded under me, and waited. Yamashita and I faced a line of prospective students hoping to be admitted to his dojo. The room was silent, but the faint sounds of morning traffic vibrated through the walls. It's a cavernous building, an old renovated warehouse off the beaten path in the Red Hook section of Brooklyn. Merely getting there is an adventure, but it's just the beginning.

The students had been ordered into *seiza*, the formal seated posture used for meditation in the martial arts, and they had complied with a smooth and easy familiarity. Now my teacher and I waited. Anyone who has been around a dojo long enough can sit like this for a time. But twenty minutes or so of motionless sitting on a hard wood floor gets to even the best of us. And Yamashita watched for the telltale flickers across faces, for the minute shifts of body weight, that would telegraph discomfort.

Being accepted as Yamashita's student is not a cut and dried thing. He's always probing and testing. Judging. These novices had been recommended by some senior Japanese teachers, but Yamashita was a skeptic at heart. He would take the students grudgingly through the initial phases of training, but always with the unspoken, although obvious, expectation that they would not endure. And to test them, he would keep them off balance, physically and mentally. I should know: he's done it to me for years. I'm not sure whether the fact that I'm still around is a testament to my skill or my sheer persistence. But now I was on the giving end of the process, working with Yamashita on testing the novices.

So they would wait in discomfort for a time. Orders would be slow in coming. Or they would be delivered with a lightning rapidity. And, above all, Sensei would work to show the new pupils just how inadequate their individual skill levels were.

They came from a variety of backgrounds. There were karate black belts here. I recognized one of them. He had earned his ranking in a school where I once saw an unwary student have a finger literally snapped off by a front kick that unfolded like a whip. Basic rule in fighting: try to keep your hands clenched. And your fingers on.

There were a few compact judo players, thick muscled and big shouldered. One had cauliflowered ears from the rough experience of tournament play. And sitting at the end of a line was Travis Stark. I sighed inwardly at the sight of him, but tried to keep focused on the class as a whole.

Yamashita's combat system hearkens back to the old days, when fighters were expected to be competent with a variety of weapons. Modern styles tend to narrow the focus somewhat. As a result, one of the first things we do with novices is cross-training. Nobody gets in the door here unless they've got a few black belts to their credit, they're in good physical condition and know enough about various things to keep from being seriously injured. But they've all got a propensity to favor one type of technique over another. And Yamashita wants to break them of bad habits early.

So all the karate types get put through matwork—the ground techniques of grappling systems. The judo guys work on blocking and striking. And people who use the wooden sword known as the bokken are introduced to the basics of Yamashita's version of sword handling. Then they all rotate.

My teacher assumes that these students are generally competent and have a basic grounding in unarmed arts. The weapons skills are a bit more varied. Many martial artists start in the more mainstream styles and gradually gravitate toward the sword arts. But there's a great deal of variety out there and most of them have never seen anything like Yamashita Sensei. Over the next few weeks, all of these people would be tested in ways they had never expected.

But for now, the dojo was still. The active training had not yet begun.

Sensei's bullet head swiveled slightly toward me. I leaned forward to catch his quiet words.

"What do you think of them, Burke?"

I scanned the double line of students. Most of them had their eyes almost closed, using meditative techniques to deal with the waiting. It was hard to tell anything significant about them from just looking at their faces. Can you read something of a person's character so easily?

"I'll know more when I see them train," I said.

"Try to see without seeing," Yamashita urged me.

Oh boy, here we go. But I worked on slowing the breath and opening myself to whatever vibrations were supposed to be out there. There was perhaps a slight tension, an expectancy, in the air. But that wasn't a shocking insight. I regarded them all through half-closed eyes. Was there a certain resentment there? After all, these were the cream of the crop from another dojo. Maybe they didn't like waiting around.

I looked at Stark, just another form in a well-worn practice uniform. He was fit and tanned and good-looking, a poster boy for martial training. There was something wrong with him, however. The question was, did I sense it, or did I just dislike the guy?

"Some of these students will not make it," I told Yamashita. I sat back contentedly. Pretty cryptic of me. I almost smiled, but my teacher was looking at me and I thought better of it.

Then Yamashita grunted and rose. *"Hajime"* he said. Begin.

Two hours later, I was soaked with sweat. I looked around the room and took the measure of the students. They were looking equally worn. A few were rubbing their wrists at the spots where I'd cracked them (lightly) with my bokken. But they all looked game enough. And there was something more.

There was a difference in the way they thought about Yamashita. I could sense it. It was partially revealed in the wary tracking of his movements, the tense expectancy in the ways they watched him. If they had doubts about Sensei, they were gone. Burned away in the heat of this very basic introduction to the world of Yamashita Rinsuke.

He glided up to me. The skin of his face had a slight sheen to it that may have been caused by exertion, but his uniform was impeccable and he wasn't even breathing hard. At least one trainee was doubled over in the corner with cramps.

Yamashita looked at the group contentedly. "Now we are ready for some serious practice," he told me.

I smiled slightly. "What would you like me to do next?"

"You have other tasks to accomplish today, Professor. Your brother wishes you to call on him. And the Rinpoche's needs must not be neglected. I will take the class from here. You may go…"

In a way, I was relieved. Micky needed me. But I was also conflicted. Yamashita may have sensed my feelings and held up a hand. "You are needed here, Burke. But others have greater needs at this point. Return tomorrow morning. They have much to learn." And without waiting for my acknowledgment or agreement, he stalked off, sure in the fact that I would obey.

I got changed and made a call to my brother. When I left the dojo, the bark of Yamashita's commands could be heard even on the street. Pedestrians glanced warily at the building's walls, as if afraid that wild animals would break out. I shifted the shoulder strap on my bag to a more comfortable spot and headed to see Micky.

We've pursued different pathways in life, but we share a few things in common. One is that we both live in worlds that are seemingly awash in paper. When Art brought me into a conference room, Micky began taking some files out and arranging them on the tabletop. "I followed up on the name and address where Sakura sent the package. So did someone else."

He took out the pictures.

I've looked at crime scene photos before, but it's never pleasant. There was the body of an older man on the floor, the blood thick and black under him. Papers were strewn all around: on the table he lay near, across the floor. One had blown against the victim's face. The blood had made it stick there.

Micky picked up a sheet and read from it. "Cameron Hoddington, Cappy to his friends. Age seventy-six. Professor of Asian Culture at the University of Georgia. Heard of him?"

"C. G. Hoddington, sure," I said. "I probably read some of his stuff in grad school." I had a vague memory of old articles in *Monumenta Nipponica*. "I thought he was dead."

Micky grimaced. "He is now. He was on leave writing a book. He owned a vacation cabin up in the hills for years. That's where they found him."

"They?"

"We tried his office," Art explained. "Left a message. Finally spoke to a departmental secretary. She told us where he was, but that he didn't answer his phone. So I put a call in to the local cops."

I gestured at the pictures. "What's the deal? Robbery?"

He shook his head grimly. "No. Nothing of value up there to take. Except the car, and they left that."

I gingerly moved the photos around to see them better. "What's with the papers?"

Micky shrugged. "The door to the cabin was left open. Some of it's just from the wind. But I'd guess that someone was also looking for something."

I looked at the pictures again. "Knife wound?"

The two detectives looked at each other. Art wiggled his eyebrows. "Good guess, but no. It looks like he was garroted. Some kind of wire. The weapon hasn't been found yet."

"Anything else?"

"No. No prints that are useable. Pretty remote place. No one noticed anything. Killer could have driven in and out without being spotted. The state police are still following up."

"So how does this help us?" I asked.

Art shrugged. "The deceased was an expert on old Japanese scrolls of some sort. I don't really get it. Certificates. Things like that."

"Sure," I told him. "I've seen plenty. They call them *inka* in the martial arts." I looked closer at the crime scene shots. You could see that many of the papers had Japanese characters on them.

"Right," Micky said. "So we put two and two together. Sakura doing some sort of work on a scroll. The angry guy looking for it. The FedEx." He gestured at Hoddington's body, glued to the floor by his own dried blood. "Somebody's looking for something. And they want it badly enough to kill for it."

"What did the Georgia cops turn up at the murder scene?" This isn't my first time with these sorts of things. I at least knew enough to ask some questions.

Micky made a face. "They got a list of documents and stuff that nobody can read—they're all in Chinese or Japanese or something. Right up your alley, buddy boy."

"Can you get them sent up here?"

His look of displeasure deepened. "I've got a request for copies in, but between you and me, I don't think they're real inclined to move quick."

"Still sore at the Yankees," I said.

"Yeah, they told us that they're a bit shorthanded for clerks right now and that standing in front of a Xerox machine was not high on their list of law enforcement priorities."

"Nice attitude," I said.

Art nodded. "It's at least comforting to note that assholes appear to be widely dispersed across this great country of ours."

"Lieutenant's thinking of sending someone down there. Maybe speed things up a bit." Micky sounded skeptical.

"Who're you sending?" I asked.

Micky pointed at Art. Art pointed at Micky. They both said, "Him."

Sarah Klein ate delicately, but with a determination I admired. I had screwed up enough nerve to ask her out for dinner, and, to my surprise, she said yes.

They were piping piano music into the room, and the low-level murmur of other diners and the tinkle of silverware made a pleasant background noise. It was a place Sarah suggested, near where she worked. She directed the research department for a commercial publishing house, and she sometimes took clients there. It was nice.

Part of my enthusiasm was for her, of course. But restaurants are always exciting to the Burkes. We didn't go out much as kids: my parents had six children. They entertained at home and during those occasions all offspring were banished to the basement or the backyard, forbidden entry into adult territory. On the odd times we would go out, all the young Burkes pilfered the table, cramming their pockets with sugar packets. You could only eat so many, but they were free.

So aside from the sheer pleasure of being with an interesting woman, the little Burke deep inside me sighed with a visceral pleasure at the mere motion of opening the menu.

We had white wine, and you could see the glint of Sarah's teeth as she brought the glass up to her mouth. I yearned for beer, but sipped at the chardonnay with all the couth I could muster.

"How'd you end up in research?" I asked her. "You seem…" I thought about a good way to say it, "… such a people person."

She cocked her head and smiled. "I had a literature degree, but my parents made me minor in marketing. I spent a few years trying different things, living on the West Coast, but really mostly just hanging around the man I was with…" She waved a hand in dismissal.

"Oh," I said, ever the master of small talk.

Sarah looked at me very intently, her eyes slightly wide. "When that ended, I was sort of left to create my own life for myself. All over again."

"Hard work," I offered.

She shrugged and took a drink. "Yes."

"Most things worth doing are hard," I said.

She smiled at me then. She had broad cheekbones and a pointy chin, a heart-shaped face that seemed made for smiling. "Are you speaking from personal experience, Burke?"

I grinned in mute acknowledgment, then asked, "Is that when you started kyudo?"

I was curious about Sarah. The martial arts world is generally male-dominated. There are increasing numbers of women in some arts, like aikido and, these days, kendo, but, for the most part, skilled and devoted female students are a rarity. It's a shame—they make excellent students and learn faster than men. The most dangerous judo player I ever met was a woman. I can still remember the grim look of satisfaction in her eyes as she choked me into semi-consciousness when I was still a novice. Yamashita makes a real effort to encourage women students, but they're few and far between. And yet here was one.

She was working diligently at her salad, but managed to explain. "I think for women a real challenge is learning how to define yourself on your own terms, you know? I spent a number of years essentially thinking of myself as someone's partner… And when I left, there was this big hole to fill."

"How'd he feel about it? The guy you were..." I trailed off, unsure how to put it.

"I was with," she said. "Living with." I nodded. "He's not a bad guy. A little self-absorbed. He's not completely... reconciled, I guess, to my leaving."

"But you are?"

"Another hard thing in life, Burke." Her chin stuck out a bit in determination.

"Ah," I ate some salad.

The silence could have been awkward, but Sarah carried on. "So when I got my present job—you would not believe how poorly people write..." She saw me smirk and corrected herself. "OK, maybe you would—it was like starting over again. On being me. Alone." She smiled self-consciously. "You know, Burke, I have a hard time imagining you working at a college."

She was good at steering a conversation. I didn't mind that she wanted to avoid more discussion of a touchy subject.

I thought of my work at the university and how increasingly distant it seemed from the important things in my life. "You're not alone," I said.

"No, I mean... Travis has been talking to me about Yamashita's dojo and how it's really for elite students..."

"Travis? Stark? You see a lot of him at the Dharma Center?"

Her eyes dipped for a minute. "He's around a bit. They've got a residence floor for visiting students and he's been staying there. He comes down to watch kyudo sometimes."

Sarah was wearing an open-necked shirt. She had an elegant neck, but I noticed a slight flush rising on her skin. I figured maybe it was the wine. But I wasn't interested in discussing Stark, and she seemed happy to oblige. "We were talking about you," I prompted.

The waiter brought us our dinners and there was a pause as we arranged cutlery and passed things around. At one point, our fingers touched and I smiled into her brown eyes. She smiled back, but went to work on her steak.

"Well, anyway," she continued, "the job is OK, but it's just a job."

"If it were fun," I commented, "they wouldn't have to pay you."

"But, you know, it's not me," she said. "I mean, there's more to life... there's got to be more to life... more to yourself... than just that."

I nodded. Every day when I pick up a sword, I think the same thing. It's what keeps me coming back to Yamashita's dojo.

"Out in California, there is no shortage of exotic disciplines. I'd done some yoga and meditation. Once I left and came here, I heard about the archery from a friend of a friend," she continued. "Someone who had studied dance at NYU and got interested in Asian performance arts. And I went to watch. And... I liked it."

"What do you like?" I said.

She rolled her eyes in thought. "I like... the pace of it," she said slowly, reflectively. "The sense of calm and isolation. There's a grace to the art. Have you ever tried it?" I shook my head no. "It's really hard to do. And I like that as well. Something you can bury yourself in that also becomes a part of you."

I grinned in appreciation, hearing echoes of things that I had thought for years.

Sarah seemed surprised that she had said so much, and skillfully turned the conversation around to me. I told her a bit about Yamashita and my job at the university. She had dessert, of course, and as I watched her eat it was hard to figure out which of us was enjoying the meal more. I told her a little about the case I was working on.

"Strange mix of things, Burke. Did you ever imagine you'd end up doing what you're doing?" she asked. She cupped her face in her hands and her eyes were clear and wide.

I thought about what I had imagined for myself: a life of learning, surrounded by books. Teaching. Somehow, the image of Hoddington, a still form in a room full of paper, kept intruding. "No," I said ruefully, "I don't think I could ever have imagined something like this."

She put her hand out and touched mine. Her hand was small and delicate, but warm. "Life is full of surprises, isn't it Connor?"

We lingered for a while over coffee. I watched her stir her cup and smiled at a sudden realization. "I'll bet," I said, "that I know what you really like about kyudo."

"Oh yeah?" she said, and her hair brushed across one side of her face as she tilted her head in amusement.

"Sure," I told her. "I'll bet you like it when the arrow *thunks* into the target."

Sarah Klein raised her eyebrows. "Maybe," she smiled.

I took her home to her apartment in Chelsea. She didn't offer to have me come up. I didn't ask. But I did tell her I'd like to see her again and that I thought we had a lot in common.

"That," she said and made an amused expression with her mouth, "remains to be seen." There was a flash of her white teeth and a wave of her hand.

I smiled all the way back to Brooklyn.

11

SCRAMBLE

The next morning, I went to see Yamashita's Tibetan friend. It was a nice change of pace. I had slept badly, with jumbled dreams of calligraphy. I then spent the drizzly hours right after dawn serving as Yamashita's training dummy, taking spectacular falls on a hard wooden floor. There was a spot on my shoulder where the uniform seam had started to rub the skin raw from taking a few too many forward rolls. But I had watched some of the novices wince and rub their own shoulders that morning and so I acted as if I felt nothing out of the ordinary. Pride is an Irishman's anesthetic.

I made my way through the dense streams of city workers. They moved with tense, quick strides along invisible routes mapped out and refined through long practice, the issue of commuting reduced to a time/distance problem. I walked, loose-limbed and disconnected, along the sidewalk. They flowed around me like water. The air, too, was wet: the cloud cover had crept down into the spaces between the high-rises, and the upper floors of the city had been swallowed up in mist.

Changpa Rinpoche's Dharma Center was a three-story Manhattan brownstone, donated by an eccentric patron and converted into a cultural resource on things Buddhist. There was a martial arts center of the same type only a few blocks away. It had much the same layout and housed one of the nicest kendo dojos in New York. But the focus at DC, as people called it, was mostly on Tibetan Buddhism and meditation. On entering the main foyer, I was greeted by a tall young man with a long ponytail. He was watching the door, clearly on the lookout. For all I knew, the Buddha could be due back any minute. But his interest was obviously more practical. He was polite, but watched me intently while he called someone.

I got cleared and was directed down the hall to an office. I passed walls that were covered with Tibetan representations of the Big Guy. The droning gargle of Tibetan throat singing washed through the background from discretely placed speakers. And, on a banner, I read the calligraphy, *Om Mane Padme Om.* A prayer wheel was set into the office door's threshold. You could spin it as you entered.

It was odd to see a monk dressed in the robes of his office sitting at a computer keyboard, but Changpa's secretary was sitting placidly next to one, waiting. He peered myopically at me through glasses with dark, heavy rims. I looked around, half expecting Travis Stark and an army of bouncers to try to pin me to the wall and frisk me, but the office suite was quiet. It was an odd sort of concern for security they had here. But then it occurred to me that Stark was still training with Yamashita. I had to acknowledge the focused efficiency of my teacher at the same time that I wished he had let me in on the plan: he had arranged for me to visit Changpa while Stark was away, arranging it so both students could benefit from different masters without any possible tension.

I introduced myself. The Rinpoche heard my voice and emerged, beaming, from his inner office. "Dr. Burke," he said, gripping my hand. "How nice to see you." He ushered me into his room with a gentle, yet practiced authority. This was, after all, a man used to dealing with people. "Perhaps some tea?" he asked, and his assistant nodded and went off somewhere, probably to peer at a kettle while he waited for the water to boil.

Once we were alone, the lama's voice grew quieter and more confidential. "I appreciate your coming," he told me.

I nodded. "It's the least I could do. Yamashita Sensei is very fond of you."

He looked at me with a half smile. "He is a good man, your teacher. But I imagine his lessons are sometimes hard ones… in more ways than one."

Was he looking at my shoulder? I dismissed the thought. "You mentioned that you were having some problems here." I let the statement hang in the air. Changpa nodded and sat back in his chair, gathering his thoughts. The walls were dotted with photographs of lamaseries, the temple complexes of old Tibet that rose from the stark sides of mountain slopes, dwarfed by the immensity of sky and rock.

"I find myself in a curious position, Dr. Burke," the lama began. "I had imagined a life of reflection and quiet for myself." He looked around the office: a large desk, an old wooden bookcase filled with odd-shaped volumes marked in gold Tibetan script on the spines, an old brown phone with multiple lines and an intercom button. He smiled at me sadly. "I am, it seems, a long way from the monastery."

I nodded in acknowledgment. "Life is what happens while we're making other plans."

He sat forward. "I have been thrust, it seems, into the public eye for my support of my countrymen and my protests against the Chinese occupation of my homeland." There were a few newspaper clippings on the desk, and I spun them around to see. Changpa before a bank of microphones, his glasses glinting. Changpa, his robes making him conspicuous in a crowd of protesters outside the Chinese Embassy on 12th Avenue. He sighed. "I assume this is somehow the cause of things…"

"Things?" I asked, ever the trained investigator.

Changpa touched the surface of the desk lightly, drawing the clippings toward him, and spoke precisely, as if contact with the print summoned forth the words. "The Center was broken into recently and my office ransacked. We keep nothing of value here and the police did not think the intrusion was a casual thing."

"Why?"

"It seems that the security alarm for the building was very neatly bypassed. Nothing was taken that could have been sold on the street."

"They left the computers and stuff?"

"Yes. Although they accessed the computer files, they left the machines themselves alone."

I had to agree with NYPD on this one. "What else?"

"My assistant, Dogyam, has been followed to and from the post office on a regular basis." He saw my questioning look. "We maintain a post-office box. It is more secure in terms of fund-raising. That way any donations are not left in the building overnight." He described the not-for-profit agency he had begun to support Tibetan culture and religion and gave me an idea of his fund-raising activities.

"So your assistant has been followed? But just to and from the post office? And he's never stopped?" The lama nodded in agreement. "Does he also make bank deposits for you?" Again, the nod. "But he hasn't been followed there? To the bank?" I made a face. I suppose Micky has rubbed off on me: I was hoping that the easiest angle—money—might be at work here.

"No. Immediately following the break-in, we alerted the bank in case any attempts at fraud were made. But nothing has happened."

"Is your assistant…"

"Dogyam," he supplied.

"… Dogyam still being followed? Does whoever's trailing him ever do anything? What do the police say?"

His secretary returned with a tea tray, as if our discussion had summoned him. We moved to sit around a small coffee table. Changpa gestured to his secretary to join us with a nod and a smile and poured for both of us. He used the small actions of hospitality as a way to avoid responding immediately. Then he sat back with his own cup and the steam from the tea fogged his glasses for a moment, making his eyes hard to see.

"The police have not been informed of this ongoing situation…" he started.

"What!" I protested.

Changpa nodded. "You must understand, Dr. Burke, that they were not particularly encouraging about their ability to catch the people who broke in…"

"A thousand stories in the Naked City," I commented, but the reference was lost on him.

"And subsequently we were… warned… that involving the authorities in issues regarding Tibet would not help matters…"

"I don't get it," I told him.

The Rinpoche sighed as if thinking about something unpleasant. For the first time, his assistant spoke. He had a heavier accent than his master, and his voice was soft and hesitant. "Changpa Rinpoche is a voice for our imprisoned brothers in our home country, Dr. Burke," he began. "To the extent that he can keep the issue in the public eye, he benefits the cause of a free Tibet..."

"But I am also caught in a dilemma," Changpa added. "I seek both freedom for my people and mercy for my brother monks in custody. And publicity sometimes can help the one cause while harming the other." He smiled bitterly. "Or so we have been told."

I nodded. It was the oldest, truest form of leverage: find out who someone cares about and threaten them. "Do you have any idea who's making the threats?"

For once, the lama looked helpless, a man out of his element. "I suspect elements of the Chinese government..."

"The *Guoanbu*," Dogyam murmured.

I looked at Changpa.

"He refers to the Chinese Ministry of State Security, Dr. Burke. *Guojia Anquan Bu.*"

"You're being threatened by the Chinese Secret Service?" I asked incredulously.

The monk looked at me in complete stillness for a moment. "The skepticism is shared by your police force. Whoever it is, they have threatened harm to good men if my protests continue. And, I must confess, I am unsure how to proceed."

Dogyam looked at his teacher with a combination of deep affection and complete understanding. He was a younger man than the Rinpoche and, while his look didn't have that unnerving, piercing aspect to it yet, you could see its beginnings stirring way back in his eyes. "We struggle, all of us, with the seeming contradiction between mercy and wisdom." He made the comment quietly, hesitantly. He was a man devoted to the clarity of silence who was afraid that the sound of his voice would shatter his World.

The lama sat back and regarded us quietly. He shook his head ruefully.

"It is only the illusion of this life that makes us see any duality, any difference between the two things…"

The two monks nodded in satisfaction, and I understood the philosophy, but this was not getting us anywhere. I set my tea down and looked carefully at him. "What would you like me to do for you, Rinpoche?"

The phone rang and Dogyam left us to answer it. Changpa watched him leave as he said, "Official avenues are not open to us, Dr. Burke, but I would very much like to know with certainty who it is who watches us. And who threatens my brother monks."

There was a reception room in the front of the Dharma Center with large windows that opened onto the street. I sat there and listened to the faint patter of light rain on the glass. The phone rang occasionally. Hanging around, watching the street, comparing every passerby to the vague description Dogyam gave me: it was probably the most boring thing I've ever done.

I talked to Dogyam and learned what I could. His eyesight was not the best, and his tail always stayed far enough away to make it difficult to see him. But he was often there, drifting along the avenue as Dogyam made his way back and forth from the post office. It wouldn't have been too hard to do. The Rinpoche's assistant picked up mail at eleven every morning and returned at three to post the day's correspondence. He took the same route every time, heading west down the street to 8th Avenue and then north to the post office. He'd be easy enough to spot: New York is a melting pot, but how many fully robed Buddhist monks in bad glasses would be on the street like that?

I left a little earlier than eleven and took the long way around the block to 8th Avenue. Then I waited right near the post office and watched. Eventually Dogyam scuttled into view under a big black umbrella and went into the post office. I loitered around and watched the crowd—but not too intently. There's a trick to it: you try to get a sense of the flow of the movement of people and wait for something to stick out in the pattern.

But this is New York. There is more weirdness here per square mile than almost anyplace else. And the volume of pedestrian and motorized traffic makes it hard to pick things out right away. I figured it would take me a few times just to get a feel for the flow of the area. But you can never tell.

Dogyam informed me that he thought his tail was an Asian man, and fairly big. But he wasn't really sure. The tail's hair, he thought, was black. "That's it?" I had said in exasperation. "He's big and maybe Asian, and probably with dark hair?" But monks don't detect sarcasm well. He just nodded and blinked in agreement. So I sighed and left to watch the crowd, not sure what I was looking for. Maybe if a homicidal-looking Samoan tiptoed along after the monk, I could spot him. Otherwise, I could look forward to standing in the rain and listening to my stomach announce the imminence of lunch.

I didn't notice anything much. After tailing Dogyam back, I got some Chinese takeout, hoping no one would be offended, and sat some more in the front room of the Dharma House. I thought about Sakura and wondered what the import of his last message was. It was a clue, but it was meant to be hidden. But from whom? The murderer? What did that suggest? I itched to be moving, doing something.

I could feel the muscles in my legs getting tight with all the inactivity, so I got up and paced around. Then I drifted down the hall and looked at the notices on the bulletin board. There was a poster there for the kyudo classes, and I thought of Sarah Klein. It wasn't the first time that day. Then I wondered whether she was thinking of me. Which was pretty goofy. Probably the MSG talking.

The weather wasn't getting any better, but it wasn't getting any worse: a light, persistent drizzle that made it seem later than it really was. I shifted in my seat and leaned back, opening my eyes periodically to look at the street as three o'clock got closer. Nothing.

Dogyam came out and offered me tea. I got up and followed him to the kitchen. Tibetans put butter in their tea and I wanted mine black. I got back to my seat and sipped the hot, bitter drink. Scanned the street. Nothing.

I set the tea on the table next to me and leaned back again. My eyes closed.

A phone rang and I looked around the room. I sipped at the tea, but it had gone cold. Looked at the street.

Near the corner just in view of the window, someone stood by a public phone. I looked at my watch. Almost three.

I stood up and got a little closer to the glass, but was hesitant about being seen from the outside. The man stood there, but he wasn't using the phone. He was wearing some sort of hooded sweatshirt, so his face was hard to see. Dark clothes. But he looked big.

I told Dogyam to head out and that I would follow him. I wanted to watch and see what the man at the phone would do. Part of me thought the whole thing was coincidence, but that was thinking with my brain alone. Yamashita wanted something a bit more complex from me, and right now I had that visceral sense, deep down, that something was up.

The monk went down the steps of the Dharma Center, awkward with his packet of mail and the shaking out of his umbrella. But once he headed down the block, the man at the phone drifted along with him. I watched intently, but the rain blurred the image, and all I got was the sense of someone very powerful, very contained and yet intent, moving down the street in the monk's wake.

The nice thing about following someone in the city is that the surrounding noise swallows the sound of your steps and doesn't give you away. And I thought the general foot traffic would give me enough cover as well. But I was, after all, an amateur, and somewhere, somehow, he must have become aware of me.

I didn't realize that until it was too late, of course.

We walked along the avenue in an extended line. Dogyam's bright robes flashed occasionally through the crowd as I tried to keep him in sight. And the broad-shouldered, hooded form of his follower threaded a way through the crowds, brushing by cars as he made his way through moving traffic. I tried to stay close, but not too close.

The tail was talking into a cell phone. Then he began to move faster, getting closer to the monk and leaving me far behind. I sped up to keep them in sight. They were a block ahead of me, at least, and I got a little nervous. When I saw the hooded man take a sudden quick turn down a side street, I figured Dogyam was safe for the day and I took off at a run to see if I could catch the tail.

I rounded the corner and turned down the side street. No sign of him. Could he have gotten that far ahead? I began to move down the sidewalk, looking down the block for any sign of him, when a huge hand grabbed me and jerked me into an alley.

You could feel the strength of the man concentrated in the hand that yanked me by my jacket collar. He was whipping me around in an arc that was meant to slam me into the brick wall of a building. And he did, but it didn't have quite the impact he had hoped for. I'd like to say that it was my cat-like reflexes that saved me. Years of highly developed martial arts technique.

In point of fact, my collar ripped. I was saved by a bad sewing job. It bled just a little of the force out of things for me. But I still hit the wall pretty hard. You could taste the masonry. I'd gotten one arm up to try to absorb the shock, but it wasn't enough. And I had to keep the other hand free for whatever was going to come next.

He gave me a few hard, jabbing shots, trying to work the kidney. But I wasn't going to let him pin me there. I couldn't see much of him, but what there was looked big, and if he got the chance to work me against a hard surface I'd be spitting blood for a week. So I slid along the wall, parrying for all I was worth, trying to twist out of the trap.

He swept my legs and I went down. But not as hard as he wanted. I've had a lot of experience getting knocked down. I stayed on the ground, spun on my side and gave him a quick, snapping kick to the lower leg. It wasn't much, but sometimes if you catch things right you can damage the Achilles tendon.

I must have tagged him a bit—you could see it in the slight hitch in his movement. It wasn't a knockdown blow, but it was enough of a complication to make him break the attack off. He left because things were already taking too long. He had wanted to immobilize me. And the best way to do that is with as much force and as quickly as possible. But I wasn't quite as easy a mark as he expected. So he cut his losses. He gave me one hard look—a young Asian face, flat and expressionless in the depths of the hood, except for eyes that burned out at you. Then he was gone, headed back in the direction of the avenue.

"Shit," I gasped. I scrambled to my feet and shrugged my shoulders to check on things. I got back out to the street, but he was nowhere in sight. People looked at me strangely and I realized that my face must have been scraped up a bit. My left eye was swelling and I closed it in the vain hope that it would make me feel better.

"He get you, too?" a voice asked.

I was still staring stupidly down the block and hadn't really noticed the bike messenger. He was brushing himself off and checking his bike. "Huh?"

The messenger gestured down the avenue. "That big asshole. Came tearin' out from the side street and wiped me out." He was wearing bicycle shorts and a helmet that looked like the carapace of an over-intelligent alien life-form. A whistle hung from a cord around his neck. The messenger was long and wiry-looking, with a big bushy beard and fierce eyes. Lance Armstrong channeling John Brown.

"Big Asian guy?" I asked, finally putting things together. "Hooded sweatshirt? D'you see where he went?"

The messenger adjusted the shoulder strap on his dirty satchel and straddled his bike. "Car picked him up," he snorted.

"Get the plate?"

He whipped a pen out of a pocket on his bag and wrote the number on the back of my hand. "Knock yourself out, dude. Not that it'll do you any good."

"Thanks," I said.

He jerked his chin in acknowledgment, then launched himself back into traffic, the whistle clenched between his teeth. His spinning tires had shot a line of dark brown crud in a stripe up his back. I heard his whistle going long after he was swallowed up in the swelling press of another nascent rush hour.

12

DHARMA CENTER

I used to think mastery was revealed only in motion. I've gradually admitted that it can be seen in stillness as well. That evening, the Dharma Center was quiet, as befits a place devoted to meditation. There was no hint of intrigue, and the report I had given to the Rinpoche was accepted with silence. Tonight the faint scent of incense filled the air. Smoke rises, of course, toward Heaven. Yamashita and I were directed to the lower level, where the kyudo classes were held. I hoped Sarah Klein was there.

I had called Micky with the license plate number and told Sensei about my day. He, too, considered my performance in silence. Then he noted that although it was still drizzling, it would nonetheless be a nice night to see some arrow work.

A typical dojo for the Japanese art of archery has an outdoor shooting area. Kyudo's targets sit almost one hundred feet away, embedded in sloping banks of sand. Here in the heart of the city, outdoor ranges were non-existent. Seekers found different ways to follow their paths. At DC, the cavernous basement had been converted into a shooting range and bales of hay covered with dark cloth had been set up to stop the arrows. A rectangular grid of plywood flooring marked the shooting platform. It was big enough to hold three archers at one time. Small bull's-eye targets waited at the far end of the area, staring at us with blank expectancy.

The interesting thing about kyudo is that all the emphasis is placed on the method of shooting. Kyudoka like to hit the target, of course, but they are even more focused on the esthetic of the actions that lead up to the shot.

As we came down the stairs, I heard a noise. It was masked at first by a group of round-eyed Buddhists chanting in a big room on the main floor, but eventually it became clear. The sound of the chanting died away as we got closer to the lower level, and I picked up more familiar, percussive sounds. Somewhere down there, weapons were hitting things.

Japanese archers often practice by shooting at head-high targets placed about six feet in front of them. The thudding was the sound of arrow shafts burying themselves in round straw bales, sent there by intent archers firing at point-blank range.

There are as many Ways, it seems, as there are people.

I asked Yamashita about this on the subway ride from Brooklyn. I've spent years following what the Japanese call a *Do*, a Way. And, I watch Yamashita, who has walked the path of his particular Way for so long and with such conviction. But I know other people who cling to other paths with as much ferocity. Who was right?

My sensei looked calmly at me, his eyes slightly wide. It was an unusual expression—he usually gazes at the world through narrowed lids, all focus and intensity.

"That is an excellent question, Professor," he replied. "And I will have it answered, but not now."

"Then when, Sensei?"

He rocked back and regarded me. "Why, when I die, of course." He smiled a little and continued. "You ask something any intelligent and sincere person would ask. In so vast a world, which path should I take? Each of us makes a choice we hope is correct. But we have no way of knowing. I suspect that all true Ways lead to the same destination." He probably saw the disappointment on my face. He put out a hand and touched me. "Some Ways are more direct than others. Some take you through different terrain. And at different times, each of us is more receptive to the possibilities of some pathways than to others. It is what I hope for you with the Rinpoche." He saw my look of skepticism and held up a finger in admonition. "Do not be so closed to things. This way, that way. What is important, I think, is the goal."

It was a wise statement, but I was focusing a little more practically on things. I asked him about kyudo. When he responded, comparing it to our discipline, a tone of chauvinism crept into his voice. He was, after all, human. The martial arts stem from many of the same sources, but their modern expressions have evolved in different ways. Yamashita's training harkened back to a time when aesthetics and functionality were not considered inseparable. Kyudo had opted for different sensibilities. Yamashita valued not only the form of his art, but its utility. In this, he departed from the kyudo sensei. "The trick, after all, Burke," he had said quietly to me, "is not to look like a warrior. It is to be a warrior. You may find kyudo somewhat… different."

Sarah Klein met us as we came down. "Hey," I said. For someone who reads so much, I'm a disappointing conversationalist.

But she didn't seem to notice. "Hey yourself." She reached out to gently touch the side of my face where the scrapes were. Her eyes looked concerned. "What happened?"

I brushed it off as a collision involving a bike rider and laughed to show there was no real damage done. And then we stood, frozen for a minute, and looked at each other.

Sarah was pert in her neat uniform—a black *hakama*—and a white practice top. Her fine, dark hair danced around her shoulders and she smiled guiltily as she realized we were standing there saying nothing while Yamashita waited. She grinned and bowed to him, then introduced us to the head instructor.

"Hello," her teacher said, bowing to us. "Sarah told me you might drop by. Always a pleasure to have people from other arts come to watch." I gave Sarah a quick wink and then gave the kyudo sensei my attention.

Sarah's teacher pointed at the activity behind him. "Right now, a few of the students are warming up, checking equipment," he explained. "That kind of thing. The Dharma Center sponsors us, and I emphasize the meditative aspects of archery. We're expecting a visit from Changpa Rinpoche tonight—he's been very supportive of getting the kyudo classes going at the Center. You'll also get to see some distance shooting as well as the more usual activities."

I looked around. "I was wondering if the Rinpoche would be here."

"Oh, he'll be here," Sarah promised, "but he's at a meeting crosstown—visiting another Buddhist center. Well, I better get ready." She smiled and wiggled her fingers in farewell as she and her instructor headed back to the performance area. I watched her appreciatively. There was a sense of life to her that was engaging. She was a woman, and I surely responded to her in that way, but there was more to it than that. When I looked at Sarah Klein, I got the sense of a person who was truly comfortable with herself. And that was a rare thing. Part of what we all seek in a Way is a path to become more truly ourselves. It was a pleasure to see the hope made visible.

I sat silently during the practice, my head swiveling from one archer to the other, observing, trying to weigh competence. For me, seeing the archers move to and from their shooting positions was the most interesting thing. Stillness tells you much, but I train in an art where motion is also a central concern. Motion brings targets to you. And you to targets. The way you move determines how effectively you wield a weapon. Your opponent's movements telegraph intent. Expose weaknesses.

The kyudoka were not like the blue clad trainees in Yamashita's dojo. I suppose it was an unfair expectation. But it seemed to me that they didn't move like people who actually fought. The balance wasn't there, nor was the feeling of power driving out from the hips. The archers instead seemed focused on managing their weapon, and it wasn't until they settled into a shooting posture that they seemed grounded in any way.

Once there, however, their movements became elegant. The Japanese bow is asymmetrical: the bottom half is short and the top stretches out in a long, gentle curve above the archer's head. The arrows are long, too. It makes managing the whole thing complicated. Archers stand perpendicular to the target, the tip of the bow pointing to the floor in front of them and two arrows grasped in the right hand. Then, with a minute settling of the balance, they begin the sequence known as the *hassetsu*, the eight fundamental stages in shooting.

It takes less than a minute to do. As I sat and watched, accomplished archers made the sequence flow in a gentle, graceful series. The bow is brought up. The arrow nocked. They turn their heads left to regard the target and their rounded arms bring both bow and arrow up in front of them at head height. Then, the slow draw, apart and down to the chest. A moment of focus, then the release of the arrow. The *kiai*, or shout, rings out, the echoing merging with the slap as the arrow hits the practice target. Then the bow is brought down and the sequence begins again.

There was a hypnotic cadence to it. It's the psychic spin-off you feel when actions with high mind-body integration take place. There are subtle differences in quality depending on what art you're watching. But I've been in a lot of dojos and recognized the sensation in most of its manifestations. Yamashita would have picked up on it, too, of course. I saw an older Japanese man sitting on the sidelines, his tanned face creased with years, watching intently. He was deeply still, like a man basking in the heat of a wood fire.

At one point, Sarah Klein joined the other shooters before the hay bales. I had to admit, my focus on her was not driven entirely by curiosity about archery. I was sure she was aware of my presence, but there was no wink or a nod in my direction, and I liked that. Sarah was focused on her art. She slid forward to her space and set the bow, tipped forward by the left hand at her hip, before her in the prescribed manner. She wore a brown suede shooting glove on her right hand, with a long inch-wide purple strap that wound around her wrist. Then, in unison with the two other archers, she moved slowly through the hassetsu.

The arrow thudded into the target. She moved to it, gliding in an unhurried rhythm, and grasped the shaft. Sarah rotated it toward her in three measured twists, then pulled the arrow free. Then she set herself to shoot again.

I continued to observe them. There was a grace here, a thing of importance in the archers' action. But was it martial? Or was the doubt just because I was blinded by my own type of training?

After a time, Changpa arrived to a general murmur and beaming acknowledgment from the kyudoka. Then the most advanced practitioner there engaged in a ceremonial series of shots at the more distant targets. There were noises drifting down from upstairs: footsteps and voices calling, the murmur of chanting, and the constant faint hum of traffic that is present in any city. But as Sarah's instructor slipped one arm free from his top, baring the left shoulder as the ritual prescribes, the spell of his movements seemed to draw your attention, making other things seem faint and unreal.

Changpa watched the demonstration with lively interest and, when it was over, got up to speak briefly with each of the archers. His voice was low, and he touched each person gently as he spoke to them.

The lama turned to those of us watching. "We know that the path to enlightenment is eight-fold. It contains right view, right thinking, right speech, right action, right livelihood, right diligence, right mindfulness, and right concentration. How interesting," he smiled, "that kyudo has eight fundamental steps in its method as well. There are many paths, but often the same goal." He looked right at me and I got the increasingly familiar sensation that he was aware of things in my mind.

Sarah approached, carrying her long bow. "It's a lot of equipment to manage," I commented to her. "What's the bow made of?"

"The really good ones are bamboo," she said. "But they're very temperamental. Mine is fiberglass. It's a bit more resilient." She shrugged. "Appropriate for a beginner like me."

"I enjoyed the archery," I said. "The esthetic." I got a mental image of her, delicate yet intent, drawing the bow and arrow apart.

She bobbed her head in acknowledgment. "But it's different from what you do, isn't it?" I looked at her and she smiled. "I saw you watching us," she replied in explanation." The expression on your face told me a lot."

"Did it?" I asked. "What did it tell you?"

"You watch things very… intently," Sarah said.

"Only when I'm really interested," I replied and smiled.

Yamashita, too, seemed engaged and in a mood to talk. He was discussing the different approaches to the martial arts with a few of the archers. I had been so focused on Sarah that I hadn't really heard the first part of his comments.

"Consider this…" Yamashita was saying. He caught the motion of our approach out of the corner of his eye and turned. He smiled at Sarah Klein, dressed in hakama and carrying her bow and arrows. She bowed to him.

Yamashita smiled, as well. "Perhaps I can ask Ms. Klein to help me demonstrate something to you all." Her eyes got wide with surprise and she looked at me.

I made a little shooing motion with my hands. "It'll be fine," I assured her.

Sarah approached my teacher and bowed again. Yamashita bowed back and gently pried an arrow from her grasp. "Consider the arrow." He held it up to show us. "See its thinness. I could break it easily. Yet it is a fearsome weapon. Not because of the strength it possesses by itself, but because of the union with the bow. The unity of strength with technical refinement makes it a good weapon. But see."

Yamashita murmured quietly to Sarah, then gestured for her to place herself on the shooter's platform. She looked doubtful, but obeyed. Sensei motioned us all to the sidelines, then placed himself at the opposite end of the room. There was about ninety feet between them.

"This is the optimum range for this weapon," Yamashita said, and his voice carried easily across the open space. "But even so…" He set himself and you could see the breath flowing in and down, grounding him to the earth. Sarah, her left side facing Yamashita, began the hassetsu, and there was a mirror image of a type there, as another person began the small motions of integration. She raised the bow, drew the arrow, and held it, aimed directly at my teacher. You could see her eyes widen slowly as she faced him. There was a slight tremble in the arrow's tip.

Yamashita nodded, and, with a cry, Sarah released the arrow. It streaked toward Yamashita, a grayish blur shooting through the air. I saw Yamashita jerk his hips around as he reached out. I had involuntarily started forward, but there was no need. My master had caught the arrow. Beside me, someone grunted involuntarily.

I had seen pictures of arrow blocking, but always using arrows with padded tips. I had never seen anything like this before.

Yamashita seemed calm. "Even a good weapon can be countered," he said. "Even when used properly." He bowed toward Sarah.

"And once this has happened, the weapon becomes a liability... So," he said and gestured for Sarah to prepare to fire her second arrow.

But he didn't wait for it. Yamashita began to churn across the floor toward her. She saw him approach, and nocked the arrow as quickly as she could, but it was no use. Before she could draw the bow, he was upon her.

But there was no clash. He simply reached out and touched the arrow's shaft. Sarah lowered the bow, a rueful expression on her face.

"The weapon, so fearful in one situation, is not useful in another," He smiled at her and bowed. She bowed back.

He approached the group, thick and dense with power, his dark eyes focused intently upon us.

"We all study with different masters. And respect them. As it should be. But we all need to remain open to new things. New ways. You all have the physical capacity to be good students," my teacher continued. "But there is something more needed..."

Sensei was speaking to the group, but he looked toward the spot where I stood and watched me closely for a moment. "There is a need for *nyunanshin* here. Do you know the phrase?" He glanced around the room.

Heads shook: no.

Yamashita looked at me. "Professor?"

"Soft-heartedness," I said, sighing inwardly. "A receptivity of the mind and spirit to instruction."

"Precisely," Yamashita breathed. "To be a student is not just a matter of being capable of learning. It is being willing to do so. And acting on the lesson, no matter how difficult."

"*Hai*," I said.

That night when I got home, there was a message waiting for me from my brother.

"What's up? You get a lead on the big guy and his getaway car?" I asked over the phone. In the background, I could hear one of Micky's kids howling. It was late and the usual struggle to wrestle them into bed was taking place.

"I'm workin' on that," he grumbled. "Whatta you got going tomorrow?" my brother asked.

"Well... work," I said. My time off was up.

"Call in sick, it's Friday anyway. We're on to something."

A screaming child wailed like a banshee on Micky's end of

the phone. The screaming receded and I could hear his wife Deirdre following in hot pursuit.

"We checked out the records from Sakura's office," Micky explained in the lull. "Following up to see whether we could get anything that might fit in with the theory about the connections between the calligraphy job and the murder."

"Aha!" I said. "You still think it's lame?"

"Time will tell," he said, not admitting anything. "But we tried to run down Sakura's most recent contacts and see whether there was anything interesting about them…"

"And," I prompted.

"There were some calls from a journalism student from NYU. Korean kid from Queens named Kim. He seemed a little out of the ordinary from Sakura's usual clientele. We ran it down, even though it took a while." He sniffed.

"Students are slippery," I commented.

"Well this guy thought of himself as some hot-shot investigative reporter. He was off on some secret project according to his friends. Doing research. Ya know, generally pestering the life out of people."

"What did he want with Sakura?"

"Once we got his name and stuff, the secretaries remembered a little better. He wanted Sakura to look at some stuff for him. The time frame fits."

"Interesting," I said. "Did the kid tell you what he wanted Sakura to look at. And why?"

"Sort of hard to tell," Micky said. "The kid's not saying much."

"Why not?"

"He's in the morgue."

13

STARE

There are cultures in the world that believe that the eyes can project an invisible power. It's more than just the windows to the soul idea. Eyes are portals of a type: they let things in, but can also allow other things to leak out. Cops are sensitized to facial expressions, the shift of the eyes and the minute play of muscles along the jaw. They watch you while you talk. You control what you say, but sometimes other energies leak out in other ways, and send messages into the silent space between words.

The eyes I saw in the picture Micky showed me were hidden behind a flat surface that gleamed dully in the light from the camera's flash. Two hard pools of darkness that had pressed themselves into the victim's flesh. You got the urge to pull the stuff off the man's head, even just looking at it in a photograph. But at the same time you were afraid to see what was underneath.

That little adventure would be left for the coroner.

I met Micky and Art that next morning. The day started with the usual sights and sounds. I took the subway to Jamaica to meet them, since the NYU student had been found in Queens. Walking through the Long Island Railroad station was surreal: the usual background of my morning commute from Brooklyn to the university on Long Island, but now with a very different destination. I heard the familiar garbled announcements from platform loudspeakers and watched commuters slip through closing train doors to the trilling of warning bells. I could smell the usual scent of dirt and metal filings in the air, the ozone of electricity and the deep, dark smell of grease.

We walked out into the rail yard. It's an expanse of open land, cut by train rails and dotted with small, oddly placed shacks, squat brick structures with grimy windows, and industrial detritus. Piles of rusting iron rails sit among weeds. There are old train cars shunted off into dead ends. Pieces of wood and wire are scattered along with the track cinders. At one point, a dilapidated kitchen chair, its vinyl seat cracked and oozing foam padding, sat by a siding, a shiny Coke can set down beside it.

We were headed for an old warehouse on the north side of the train yard. It was a sagging building with broken windows showing like broken teeth. The crime scene had long been vacant, but Micky and Art insisted on seeing it. My brother would scoff at the idea that a location gives off vibrations of any type. And I'm usually in agreement. I think he and Art go to places like this to make the crime more real for them. They don't want the victim to be just a statistic, or a report, or even a photograph. They need to see the place where it actually happened. Because sometimes the things they investigate are hard to believe.

We walked the perimeter of the building first, not saying much. Art and Micky talked quietly about what they knew from the investigation. It freed me up to just look and drink in the surroundings. These places smell like rust and dirty water. It's now an odor I associate with other things.

When they got started on Kim, the screams must have bounced around the empty space like trapped birds, desperate to escape into the sky. We finally ducked under the crime scene tape and paced the empty space, silently taking the surroundings in and matching them to what the photographs had shown us.

Someone had strapped him down on an old wooden work-table in the center of the room. When things really got going, Kim had tugged and sawed at the bindings with the panicked desperation of an animal. In the pictures, you could see where the cords bit into his ankles and wrists as he rocked and convulsed in the aftershock of what was happening to him.

There was the dark residue of old blood all over the place—from a knife. Or at least that's what Micky thought after reading the coroner's report. Someone had sliced and hacked at Kim, and it must have gone on for some time. He had wood fragments under his nails that had been gouged up by his struggles.

He had numerous small wounds all over him. You can plot the sequence of events like this by the flow of blood, which oozes and spurts out to the rhythm of the crime. I wasn't there when the cops had found him, which was just as well. The smell clings to you and it takes a long time to dissipate. And even longer to forget.

Whoever did it saved the eyes for the end. It made you shudder when you thought too much about it. They dropped hot solder into Kim's eyes, one drop at a time. It hissed and bit into his flesh, pattering around the orbit of bone, blistering the eyelids while he must have rocked and screamed and tried to escape. And slowly, they sealed Kim's eyes off forever.

When you looked at the pictures, it was bad. You knew it was bad. That it had taken a long time for Kim to die. And that somebody had enjoyed the process.

"My God," I had breathed as I looked at the crime scene shots.

"God's got nothin' to do with this, buddy boy," my brother said.

"Whoever did this," Art said, "is one sick fuck."

"Does this have anything to do with Sakura?" I asked.

Art sighed. "Stuff like this has got its own weird logic. Could be directly connected…"

"Could be coincidence," my brother said. But he didn't sound like he believed it.

"He was tortured," I said. Micky nodded.

"And not just for the hell of it," Art added. I looked a question at him.

"They didn't cut his tongue out, Connor," he explained.

"They?"

He waved his hand. "Figure of speech. He. She. They."

"It," Micky said.

"Whoever did this wanted Kim to be able to talk," Art said. "He was tortured for information."

I looked around the warehouse. Dingy and empty now, the yellow crime scene tape an incongruous slash of color in the gray landscape. "I don't think I can imagine anything worse," I said. The smell in the air here was bitter and made me feel sick.

"I can," Micky told me. I squinted at him, waiting. "It would be worse to have someone working on you for something and not really knowing the information they were torturing you for."

We all looked at each other silently.

"Let's get out of here," Art said.

Kim's torture and murder was not exactly a well-kept secret. The crime was more than a week old and the word on the street was that the killing was done by a group called the Street

Ghosts. Micky and Art hooked up with a female officer named Roth, who worked the Queens North bureau for the NYPD and tried to keep up with groups like the Ghosts. She collected whatever intelligence the PD came up with from the patrol units, the occasional tidbits from the Organized Crime Investigation Division, sorted through rap sheets and aliases, and listed the depressing statistics. She wasn't a street cop. She experienced things at one remove. But it was probably just as well. Art said later that learning about the gangs was a lot like the experience of pulling up a flat rock and being appalled by the squirming variety of life that coiled just below the surface.

Roth was thick-waisted from desk life, with a short, frosted, no-nonsense hairdo and enough time on the force to know how to cut to the chase. Her desk was covered with files, neatly stacked and sorted in some arrangement only she could make sense of. She had an aging PC in one corner with yellow sticky notes stuck all around the perimeter of the screen. Her file cabinets were heavy with paper as well, and the drawers sagged when she hauled them open to look for things.

"Street Ghosts. Sure." She had continued filling out a form as she talked to my brother. "Whattaya wanna know?"

Art and Micky laid it out for her. The Sakura murder. The NYU kid. An informant's suggestion of the gang as the perpetrators. Roth didn't even blink.

"I read about that Kim thing. Could be one of the gangs. They'll kill anyone. Anytime. For any reason."

"Pretty good motto," Micky said to Art.

"Short, yet oh so descriptive," his partner answered.

Roth eyed them both suspiciously. She got up and yanked a file drawer open with a grunt. She removed a thick file and a black ring binder and they thudded onto the desk.

"But I haven't picked up anything that would connect to this Sakura thing locally." She opened the binder and consulted notes. "No rumble on the street so far. All you got right now is this clue from the victim Sakura?"

Micky and Art nodded.

Roth made a face like she had just eaten something that didn't taste good. "Kinda thin," she commented. "And the Ghosts... we haven't heard much from them lately. Besides, they were usually a bit messier when they hit someone."

"How so?" Micky prompted.

Roth looked up from her desk. "These guys are kids, mostly." She snorted at the thought. "Scary to say, but there ya are. So when they do a hit, there's usually a bit more excitement. Lots of hacking and chopping. Excess bullets. Usually, they'll kill someone for a reason, but, for them, there's also a bit of thrill in it."

Micky shrugged. "No surprise. Even most pros, deep down, are gettin' off on killing."

Roth nodded, and when she did it accentuated her growing double chin. "The Street Ghosts tend to use blades in their hits. They get in the occasional shoot-out with other gangs, but when they really want to make a point, they use these short Chinese swords." She paused and checked a note in another loose-leaf binder she had lugged out from beneath the desk. "Yeah," she nodded. "Butterfly knives, they're called."

"No knives with Sakura," Art said. "But this kid from NYU was a mess..."

"A few years ago I would have liked them for it," Roth said. Her eyes were brown. She looked from one man to the other, and then shrugged." The guy who led them was named Han. Local kid from the Korean-American community. A freak. In and out of juvenile detention for years. Sexual assault. Aggravated assault. Assault with a deadly weapon. Extortion. A few murders we were real suspicious about, but nothing we could pin on him."

The two detectives were unmoved. Most rap sheets they saw were long, sad lists of minor convictions and, in between the lines, big suspicions.

"He's about the size of a refrigerator," Roth commented, rooting around in a drawer and pulling out a binder of mug shots. "He was into all that kung fu stuff… ah, here he is." She turned the book around so we could see it. Han's narrow eyes glared out from the picture, the rest of his square face a rigid mask. The height markers on the wall behind him showed us he was about 6'3". I didn't need the help. I had seen him staring down at me as I lay in a rainy alley.

Micky saw the expression on my face. "Wha'?"

"It's the guy who jumped me near the Dharma Center," I said.

"You sure, Connor?" my brother asked.

"Oh yeah. That's him."

"Big guy," Art said softly.

"Angry Asian male," I added.

"What's he doin' off his turf?" Micky asked.

"Why's he following Tibetan monks around the city?" I added.

Roth looked confused. "He was sent upstate for a while," she continued. "Did some time and then disappeared onto the street. Haven't been able to pin anything on him for quite a while." She looked at my face. "He do that to you?" I nodded. "Word is, he's moved onto to bigger and better things. Hired muscle of some sort."

"Ah," Art nodded sagely, "a thug with ambition."

"Chasing the American dream in the Big Apple," Micky added.

But Roth wasn't distracted. She kept looking at me. "You walked away from him? Be thankful. This guy likes his work." Then she eyed the mountain of paperwork on her desk and made an expression of distaste. "Look you guys, I'll give you what I got. Han's an animal and I'd hate to see him back on the street. But at first glance, the Sakura killing doesn't seem like a Ghost kinda job. As for this kid in the train yard…" She shrugged again. It made her uniform blouse move in odd ways: her shield weighed part of the fabric down.

"We'd still like to pick Han up for questioning," Art said wistfully.

"Maybe make him pay for Connor's Band-Aids. Got a line on him? Even if it's old?"

Roth gave them her weirdly sad, yet hard-eyed look. "These guys are mostly teenagers. You two have kids?"

They nodded.

"Teenagers?"

They shook their heads no. Roth grimaced. "I got three. Even I can't keep track o' them. Add the whole gang culture to the problem… It's like a secret society. It's built to keep people like us far away. And Han, if he's back, he doesn't want to be found. Most people on the street know it. You'll have to shake some trees pretty hard."

She wasn't putting much energy into the words: just going through the motions. She sighed and wrote something down on a yellow sticky note. "This is Han's last known address."

"Thanks, Roth."

"Don't get your hopes up. Any gang is its own special world. Asian gangs are even worse. Chances are you won't get anywhere near him."

It was Micky's turn to shrug. "Guy's gotta try."

"You got a liaison with the local precinct we can work with?" Art asked. She did. And she agreed to send copies of her Street Ghost and Han files to them. Then Micky and Art left her, a squat form awash in paper.

When we got back into the car, Art was already on the cell phone. "Cusick?" he was saying to another detective at the precinct house, "you still working with Sakura's secretaries, looking at mug shots to ID the scary guy at the office that day?" Art nodded at the response.

"Tell him about Han," Micky whispered.

Art took the little phone away from his ear. "Will you leave me alone?" He rolled his eyes, then moved the phone back. "Cusick?" he continued, "here's a photo file number." He read it off. "You have them look at that guy and see if it rings any bells." Art pushed a button and hung up. The two men looked at each other.

"Interesting," Micky said.

"Life is full of surprises," his partner replied.

We hooked up with Roth's contact, a guy named Whalen out of the 109th Precinct, and cruised the streets of Queens looking for traces of Han. Parts of Flushing had grown into a thriving Japanese and Korean community. The streets were studded with small shops whose signs were in Japanese characters, or the more angular phonetic Korean writing known as Han-gul, told you that you were in a different world—an outsider looking in.

Which was pretty much the way we felt. The cops went through the motions. Checked out Han's last known address and got blank-faced denials. They asked on the street about the Ghosts. Local merchants all shook their heads no and smiled. Micky admitted he wasn't sure whether the people they questioned were nervous or secretly amused. Maybe both.

It was the typical response Round Eyes get. I could have told them that and saved us all some wasted time. I had looked into the flat, closed faces of Japanese sensei for years. In the end, they tell you only what they want you to know. It takes a long time to earn their trust. Two detectives from Manhattan without any ties to the local community were not going to be showered with secrets.

So Micky and Art worked the usual levers. All communities, anywhere, have people on the streets who know what's going on. And often enough these people are vulnerable. They're junkies or runaways. They need money. A place to hide. Medicine. Sometimes they're just people who leverage knowledge into a type of secret power. If you can find their weak spots and press hard, these people will tell you things. It's not particularly nice. Or pretty to see. Micky shrugs it off. "Big bad world out there, Connor," he tells me.

"Ya take things like ya find 'em," Art continues. "If you can, you figure a way to turn it to your advantage. And, at the end of the day, you go home and take a shower."

It's a reminder of the hard world these two men inhabit. All the joking and patter is their way of hiding it. But under the kidding around, they stoked a focused, fierce anger. Micky and Art never said it out loud, but they worked homicide because every case was like a personal insult they were on fire to redress.

If the streets of Flushing presented them with what seemed to be a wall of silence, Micky and Art knew that, if they looked hard enough, they'd spot cracks. And when they did, they'd hammer at them.

"It's going to be a long shot anyone up here gives us anything," Art finally said. Micky grimaced in agreement. You could see that he didn't want to let it go.

"Maybe we should work another angle," I suggested.

"Ah, the expert weighs in," my brother said sarcastically.

I had been watching the street action, but my mind kept flashing back to the pictures of Kim. Horror pulls at you with the piercing directness of its message.

"Let's think about it," I told them. "Kim's what?"

"A student," my brother said.

"He's a journalism student," I corrected. "Working on his master's thesis." It was a statement, but I looked the question at Art. He checked through his note pad and nodded in confirmation. "He sees himself as an investigative reporter," I continued, "and we assume he's dug something up. He doesn't quite understand it all, so he starts seeking help."

My brother nodded slowly as he thought about it. "OK. And he goes to Sakura. So there must be some calligraphy or something involved, right Connor?"

"Sure. And someone… maybe this guy Han…"

"Or the people he works for," Art added.

"… is pretty upset that Kim's got the stuff."

Art was rolling his head from one side to the other as he listened and thought the sequence through.

"So if Kim's the guy with the information Han wants, why's he bothering with Sakura?" I asked.

Micky squinted out through the car windshield, seeing his own private world. "Two sequences of events," he said, starting slowly and then picking up speed as he grew more certain.

"Kim was on the run and hard to find. In the meantime, he had contacted Sakura. And then the killer got ahold of Kim." I shuddered at the memory of the photos of Kim's murder. I don't imagine the journalism student held out much once the torture really got going.

"So the killer found out about Sakura and got to him…"

"But he was too late," Art added, "since the stuff had already been shipped off to Georgia."

"And the killer followed it," I said.

"Could be," Art said.

"What's the second thing, Mick?" I prompted.

He looked slyly at me, then at Art. "You wanna tell him?"

"He's your brother."

"You sure? I mean, it's OK if you want to…"

"Fellas!" I said.

Micky shrugged. "It's simple. Sort of. If Han's our guy, and the secretaries at Sakura's office can give us a positive ID, then why's he hanging around the Tibetans? Because he's looking for more than whatever information Sakura had. He wants that stuff, sure. But it's only a piece of the puzzle."

"I don't get it," I said.

"Don't worry, Connor," Art said sympathetically. "If this stuff were easy, anyone could do it."

14
PUZZLE

Sakura's secretaries made a positive ID on Han from the mug shot Roth had showed us and the cops were beating the bushes for him. They were hoping that forensics had gotten some prints from the Sakura crime scene, but my brother wasn't optimistic. It's a skepticism reinforced by his occupation. But he called me early Saturday morning to say that the stuff from Georgia had arrived and maybe we could try to find something there.

I sat outside on the stoop to my apartment, waiting for my brother to pick me up. The sky was getting brighter, with a faint blue trying to push through the thin cloud cover. There might be sun today, but this early in the morning, the street was still in shadow and the steps were still cool and damp from the night. The occasional neighbor walked by, dog in tow. A quiet start to the day. It was no surprise when my brother jerked the car to a halt in front of me: I had heard him accelerating when he made the turn onto the street. I think he watched too much *Kojak* in his younger years.

Micky was rumpled looking, like a man who hadn't gotten much sleep. His mood matched his looks. The car was already rolling as I slammed the car door. "Morning," I said.

He grunted. We whipped down the block and onto the avenue. Micky double-parked outside a delicatessen and jumped out with saying anything, leaving the motor running and his door ajar. He returned with two big cups of coffee.

"What," I said, "no donuts?" Micky glared at me. His left eye was bloodshot.

We rocked along the street, making most of the lights. When we hit the expressway, the weekend traffic was light. I sat and sipped my coffee, watching the scenery, reading billboards. On the bridge to Manhattan, I looked down into the East River. The water was dark and dense looking. You imagined that things floated unseen down there, suspended just below the murky surface. The thing with my brother is that you've got to know when to poke him and when not to. I figured he'd talk when he was good and ready.

They'd boxed Hoddington's life up in neat stacks, as if sheer neatness was a response to the chaos of his ending. The copies of documents completely covered the expanse of the conference table in the room Micky brought me to. Art was already there. He had a St. John's Redmen shirt on, but, unlike my brother, he looked pink and wide awake. He took one look at Micky and started talking to me.

"We weren't sure what we might need, so we asked for copies of stuff from both his office and the crime scene," Art told me. He shrugged. "Better to be a little over-thorough…"

I nodded, but thought their Lieutenant would hit the roof when he got the FedEx bill. It wasn't my problem, though, and I got to work. Pulling documentation together on a violent crime creates a type of surface order. Police reports are neatly clipped into folders. There are lists and catalogues and images of the crime scene. But the more you look, the more apparent the confusion of the event becomes. Sudden death blows in like a violent storm, scattering the pieces of a person to the four winds. What's left are ashes and the dead fragments of a life.

It wasn't complete, of course. The Georgia authorities made copies of reports and documents, but original evidence couldn't leave the jurisdiction. So we had to guess at some things. I read quickly through the crime scene report. I looked at the same crime scene pictures of Hoddington that they had shown me before. And then I began to go through the copies of Hoddington's papers. Micky didn't say much, but sat there and watched me quietly. I could tell his mind was elsewhere.

I knew Hoddington had been on sabbatical writing a monograph titled *War Tales of the Great Houses*. I was really interested in what he had received in the last month or so, but I knew how academics worked: something could have been crammed almost anywhere.

There were extensive notes in a spidery hand and Xeroxed copies of manuscripts in Japanese and English. In a bundle marked "correspondence" I found a record of letters from Sakura, seeking Hoddington's comment on various calligraphic manuscripts. But nothing recent.

Most of the Japanese documents the dead man had worked from were photocopies. Many of the scrolls he had consulted were in university or museum collections, and he had obviously been collecting duplicates for a few years.

The cops hadn't organized these papers in any way—they were a jumble of source material, handwritten notes, and typescript. Anything that had been in the cabin that could be of some use in solving the crime had been swept up. It took a while to go through it and get a sense of things. I started to sort items by type. I organized the manuscript pages and read through them to see whether there was anything out of the ordinary there. No luck.

I looked at the Xeroxes of the scrolls he had been consulting. They seemed to tie in with the research and there were reference notes linking the different documents with his writing. Again, no luck.

And then, tucked away in a file, a note. It was in Hoddington's spidery hand, jotted down on the top of a sheet listing references the dead man had intended to cite. It read "E.S.—consult on doc. Problem?" with the last word underlined.

I placed the sheet in front of me and pushed the other papers away. It was tenuous, but here was a link.

There was no date on the note, but it was found in the cabin. I got up and began looking through the files again.

I looked up. "Most of this stuff is copies of copies. Do you know whether there were any original documents in Japanese found at the crime scene?"

Art scanned through the reports and shook his head. "No. *Nada.*"

A dead end. So I tried again. "From the description of the scene," I told him, "it seems as if there was at least some attempt at a search at the time of the killing."

Micky stirred, and picked up a file with the crime scene report clipped in it and paged through it. "Yeah, looks like someone went through at least some of the stuff," he finally said. "They also got a shoe print." He gestured at the photos and you could see that the killer had tracked through some of the blood on the floor. "We'll try to match it from the print at Sakura's place."

"Time'll tell," I said. "Any other signs of a more extensive search than was reported?"

Art's eyes rolled up as if he were mentally reviewing the pile of stuff in front of us. Micky pawed through the paper.

"Was there a bookcase?" I prompted. "Anything seem moved?"

"No," my brother said, reading the reports and looking at the photos spread out before us. "The books look like they were in place."

"Drawers? Files?" Again he shook his head no.

"Not much of a search," I said.

"Not particularly thorough, no." He looked up. "I don't get the sense that this was a pro's handiwork." He looked at Art for confirmation, and his partner nodded.

"How come?"

"It seemed too… haphazard."

"Does the killing look like the work of someone who was haphazard?" I asked him.

Art looked down at the photos of Hoddington. "Oh, whoever did this had killing on his mind, that's for sure. But I don't think it played out the way it was planned."

"How so?"

Micky closed his red eye and squinted at me. He gave me a tight grimace of satisfaction. "Read the coroner's report…"

So I did, but it didn't tell me much. My brother's lips just got tighter and he put his finger on the paper. "Look. The victim had his hand burned. There were bruise marks on the wrist, too. Someone was torturing him."

"There's a familiar tune," Art commented.

"For information?" I said. It sounded stupid the minute it was out of my mouth.

Micky rolled his eyes. "Of course, for information. Just like the victim in Queens. But the blood toxicology on Hoddington shows that it all got cut short." He pointed to the relevant line, but I couldn't figure it out. "Come on, Connor," he said, and his voice betrayed a growing excitement. "Look! Hoddington had a heart attack. Probably induced by the torture. So, whatever the killer had planned got cut a little short."

"So chances are the killer didn't get what he came for?"

"Maybe." He eyed me.

Art chimed in. "The bigger question is, what was it that got sent to the victim that made someone do this to him?" He gestured at the photos of Hoddington.

"I don't know," I had to admit. "But look." I showed them the paper with the note written on it. "I think we're starting to firm up the links. We know that Hoddington got something from Sakura…"

Art continued. "We know Sakura sent it the day before he was killed. Hoddington had it for four days before he ended up dead."

Micky paused and looked at me with a glint in his good eye. "There's one way to check on whether there's really a link, though," he told me.

"Hey, great," I said.

"Sure," he smirked. "Find the package and see if someone tries to kill you." With my brother it's hard to tell whether the sarcasm is a genetic thing, or something they teach you at the police academy.

It was a plan, of course, but not one I was particularly interested in. We began to go through the evidence again. There was a photo envelope filled with copies of snapshots that were found with the other documents at the cabin. They showed Hoddington smiling with the benevolence of age at some younger people. They were lifting wine glasses and toasting each other. You could see enough of the background to know it wasn't the cabin where he died.

There were other pictures of Hoddington with the same group, standing outside. The trees were in bloom. In one shot, he stood with his arms around a man and a woman, off to one side of a structure. It had a wide, peaked roof supported by natural stone at either end. And under the roof, a dark bank with an archery target centered in it, staring at the camera like an eye.

I turned the pictures over. They were developed the day before the murder.

"Any idea who these people are?" I asked.

"Locals checked around," Art told me. "They're not family. Maybe people from the university? They're old enough to be former students."

I let it go.

Micky had been watching me during this process as if waiting to see whether I would notice something. So far he had been patient, but his eagerness finally prompted him to action.

"You want a stronger sense of a link? OK. Here's a record of Hoddington's phone calls." He held the sheet out to me.

There wasn't much activity. Hoddington came to his cabin to get away from things, and it showed. I scanned down the list. "I assume that these are calls in Georgia?"

"Sure," Art said. "Seven-seven-oh, four-oh-four, those are Georgia area codes. I checked."

"Yeah," Micky said, "but look at this." He snatched the paper back. "Here's a call to area code seven-one-eight on the evening that the FedEx was delivered. It's Sakura's house." You could hear the excitement in his voice. "And here, on the day Sakura was killed, Hoddington called a New York City number. It's Sakura's office."

Art looked over his shoulder at the list. "He tried the two-one-two number a bunch of times, but there's a day or so gap without activity. And then he was killed."

I scrambled around the pile and picked something up. "The gap corresponds to the days before these pictures were developed," I told them.

"So now do you see?" Micky asked.

"Sure. Hoddington got sent something from Sakura. There may have been something unusual about it. Hence the initial phone call. Then we see a flurry of subsequent attempts to contact Sakura…"

"But he was already dead," my brother added.

"And then Hoddington takes a road trip somewhere for a few days. He comes back…" I trailed off.

"And he takes the big trip," Art concluded. He looked at me with arched eyebrows. "That's what I think. We'll check some of this out. See if we can get a fix on where he went before the murder."

"Not too bad," I said. "Now all we have to do is connect the dots to Han, right?" I looked at my brother, who was moodily pushing reports around the tabletop. He didn't reply. "Right?" I prompted.

"So you didn't talk with him on the way over, Mick?" Art said.

I looked from one to the other. "What?"

Micky sighed. "There's a complication here."

My brother and I went to school with a guy named Charlie Wilcox. He was wiry, with a shock of spiky blonde hair and an explosive temper. Charlie was a permanent fixture on the detention rosters of principals, the bane of the nuns in our Catholic grade school, and an even more dangerous menace in high school. His family had attained local notoriety by the simple fact that his parents had produced fourteen kids. The Wilcox family had thirteen beds, which meant that bedtime during Charlie's childhood was an interesting lesson in Darwinism.

He had achieved fleeting fame and actually generated some sympathy in the summer after high school, when a car accident had propelled him through the windshield of a Ford Maverick and out into the greasy August night, shearing off his ears. Several operations and many months later, Charlie emerged looking like a slightly altered version of himself and acting very differently.

I had lost track of him, but my brother hadn't. Charlie had actually graduated from college and pursued, of all things, a career in law enforcement with the FBI.

I snickered. "You gotta be kiddin' me."

My brother shook his head as he took the three of us back to Brooklyn. "I shit you not. He's actually working in the counterintelligence section here in the city."

The thought of Charlie, armed and somehow associated with intelligence, was deeply alarming. But I said nothing about that. "What's he got to do with our little problem?"

"We ran the plate number you gave us from when Han jumped you," Art said, "and we got an interesting result."

"That's the understatement of the year," Micky said, and there was resentment in his voice.

"It's a diplomatic plate," Art continued quickly. He could sense that his partner's temper was on the rise and wanted to head off an explosion.

"Diplomatic immunity," I said, and I realized why Micky was so annoyed. But I was wrong.

Art waved it away. "It's a little more hinky than that, Connor. We also got a little 'cease and desist' advisory from the Feds."

Micky made a right turn a little fast. Art and I were used to it by now and we leaned into the turn, but the tires squealed a bit. "Fuckin' Feds," Micky murmured darkly.

"So what's that mean?" I pressed them.

My brother sighed. It sounded like something bleeding off from a high pressure valve. "Somewhere, someone's got something going and it involves whoever was driving that car."

"Did you find out who it was?"

"No," Art said, "but we got the next best thing."

"What?"

"Someone who can," Micky said, and for the first time that day, my brother seemed content.

We eventually parked on Fifth Avenue in Fort Hamilton. It's pretty upscale down there, with condos facing the water and any number of small restaurants to choose from. The day had developed into a bright and sunny one, and the trees that lined the avenue were filled with new leaves. The weekend streets were busy with yuppie couples wheeling toddlers around in expensive strollers. One white-haired fellow with a much younger wife pushed his kid along, wearing a fixed smile on his face that couldn't quite hide a look of stunned disbelief.

Micky steered us to a small Chinese place. I glanced at the menu taped to the window and felt a surge of relief, since I knew the lunch bill wouldn't destroy my budget. Micky reminded me that Art has a thing for egg rolls. We squeezed into a booth. Art sat next to me out of habit, like he was taking me into custody.

"Why here?" I asked.

"Waiting for someone," Art explained.

I looked at Micky. He was watching the street for something. He turned his head and looked significantly at me and waited.

"No!" I said.

"Sure," Art told me.

"Charlie Wilcox," my brother added with deep satisfaction. "He lives on Staten Island. It took a bit of arm twisting, but I got him to come over and see us."

Charlie arrived a few minutes later, looking older but still thin. And a lot more worried-looking. He smiled when we shook hands—old school chums—but the expression came and went on his face like a muscle spasm. The waiter darted over and we made our selections. Art ordered egg rolls.

Charlie Wilcox waited for the waiter to leave, then slid a large manila envelope onto the table. "I don't like this much, Burke," he began.

Micky wagged a finger at him. "You owe me, Charlie…" Wilcox nodded, but he looked like someone who had eaten something that tasted bad.

The FBI man slid out some pictures, surveillance shots of a vehicle and various people getting in and out of it. The license plate matched the one on the car that Han had escaped in. Micky went through them one by one. He slid one over to me. "Recognize him?"

The shot looked like it was taken in Battery Park, but I was more interested in the fact that the hulking figure of Han was clearly visible talking to a smaller Asian man. There were other shots of the car, of the smaller man talking to various people, entering and leaving buildings.

"So what do we have here, Charlie?" Micky asked. Out of the corner of his eye, Wilcox saw the waiter returning and he quietly slipped the pictures back out of sight. The food came and the duck sauce flowed. But Charlie didn't seem to have much of an appetite.

"The smaller man is on the consular staff at the Embassy for the People's Republic of China," he said in an extremely low voice. "Cultural attaché." We all nodded at the significance. It was the usual posting for intelligence agents. "Wu Tian. Career officer in the Chinese intelligence service."

"The *Guoanbu*," I said sagely. But no one seemed impressed by my vast store of knowledge.

Wilcox nodded. "He's had postings in the Western Chinese Provinces. Spent five years in Tibet, and now he's here."

Micky and Art looked at each other at the mention of Tibet. Art's eyebrows rose.

"That could have something to do with things," I said.

"Buddy boy," Micky began, "it may be connected to the murders or it may not…"

"That's the beauty of what we do," Art offered. "Lots of interesting things; some are connected, some aren't."

"Drives some people crazy," Micky added.

His partner gazed about the restaurant with a look of serene satisfaction. "Not us. It fits our eclectic nature."

Charlie didn't know what we were talking about, but he plowed on. Life with the FBI had made him very serious. "Wu's a pretty slick character. We suspect he's got a sideline going and has been smuggling out Asian art and antiques for years. Lots of good looting opportunities in Tibet. Nothing real concrete, but he's dirty in any number of ways. It's not an unusual thing with the military and intel people in the PRC. The big man we haven't been able to identify yet, but they've met on a number of occasions."

"What are they up to?" I said

Charlie Wilcox shook his head. "I just work the tags on this. Collect the surveillance footage. It gets passed on to higher levels, and I don't know what they're doing with it."

Micky made a skeptical sound deep down in his throat.

"I'm telling you, Burke. The bag around this thing is big and black." He looked apologetically at Micky. "Sorry, but that's all I've got."

Micky squinted at him for a moment, then nodded slowly. "OK, Charlie. We can keep the prints?" Wilcox nodded reluctantly. Micky slipped a piece of paper over to the FBI man. "Here's the info on the big guy. We're lookin' for him if he turns up again, OK?"

Wilcox nodded and slipped out of the booth. He glanced nervously toward the door. "I'm out of here," he said, nodding to the detectives. "And you didn't get those photos from me."

"Came in a fortune cookie," Art said. Charlie did not look reassured.

"Nice to see you again, Connor," he said. But he didn't seem to mean it.

We got down to more serious eating. "I'm having a hard time putting this all together," I admitted. "It seems like Han is involved in three murders but we still don't know why. I thought it had something to do with the inka. But is he also working for the Chinese?"

"Han's muscle for hire," Art said. "He could be working for lots of different people. The Chinese could have nothing to do with the killings. You also have to think of the possibility that each murder could have a distinct motive."

"Links between the killings seem pretty good, though, Art," Micky said. "Sakura gets something from Kim. Han wants it back. But Sakura's sent it off somewhere…"

"Why kill Sakura?" I asked.

"Whatever Kim sent to him is something no one's supposed to see," Art told me.

"So Hoddington must have had it then, and got killed, too," I added.

"Plus he got tortured, which tells me that the killer was doing two things: trying to find the missing document and eliminating people who had seen it. Same thing with Kim."

The two detectives nodded.

"But what's with Han's interest in Changpa?" I asked. "What's with the Chinese?"

My brother shrugged. "Art may be right. Han's out on the street for hire. The guy's like a one-man crime wave, but not everything he's doin' may be connected. You don't want to fall in love with any one theory too soon," Micky lectured.

"We're not real sure about the Han link to the Hoddington murder," Art said. "The timing could just be a coincidence."

"That's what I mean," Micky said and filled his mouth full of food. "There could be a link. Then again, it could just be a coincidence."

"Come on!" I protested. "Do you really believe that?"

"Murders happen every day, buddy boy. Everywhere. Even down south."

"There's danger in them thar hills," Art said, like a man revealing a subtle truth.

"Yeah, Connor," my brother added. "Didn't you ever see *Deliverance*?"

"You guys are not serious," I said.

"No, we're not," Micky answered. He had finished his food. My brother ate mechanically: fuel for the machine. Most meals were gulped down as if he were a fighter pilot waiting to scramble. "But," he continued, "we're waiting to see what sort of forensic stuff we finally get from the cops down in Dixie. Be good if we could get some useful DNA stuff and match it to the crimes up here. But we're not too hopeful."

"I keep thinking about the *Dukes of Hazzard*," Art said.

"*Smokey and the Bandit*," my brother offered.

"Fellas, please," I pleaded.

Art popped the end of an egg roll into his mouth and chewed thoughtfully. My brother eyed me speculatively. "How's your research going on the Big Clue at Sakura's?" He grinned wickedly.

I hung my head and described how I had been trying to hunt down significant Japanese literary references to "spring wind." I had piled up books in reading rooms and hunted through indexes. The Japanese are big nature lovers: consequently, there was no shortage of things to look at. Days ago, I had asked Yamashita's advice and he pointed me in a number of directions. I read various types of poetry—*tanka*, haiku. I pored over the works of poets like Bashō. I even came across a famous martial arts dojo named *Shumpukan*—Hall of the Spring Wind.

"Hmm," Art said.

"Ya know what you got?" Micky asked. I shook my head. "You got dick," he concluded with a perverse look of satisfaction.

His cell phone went off. He grunted into it a few times then looked at Art. "We gotta roll."

Art got very still for a moment. "You mean," he paused significantly, "we gotta... egg... roll."

Micky groaned and made as if to whack him on the arm. But I saw him pull the blow at the last minute when he realized it was Art's wounded side.

If Art noticed, he didn't show it. He scooped up the remains of his lunch and they began to move. The bill sat there unclaimed, Chinese writing on a green ticket with the dollar amount underlined twice. I sighed and picked it up. At least Charlie Wilcox hadn't eaten.

"If you can get a handle on what Sakura and Hoddington were working on, maybe we'd see the connection clearer," Micky offered on his way out. "Meanwhile, we'll continue to run things down on this end. And Connor?"

I looked at him. Micky has hard, pale eyes. He's seen a lot of things.

"What?"

"Don't dick around with this one. If there is a link between these murders, the guy who did it…"

"Han?" I asked.

My brother waved the name away. "Han or not. The killer's big," Micky said, nodding at Art. "He's not afraid of getting dirty. And he likes to use his hands."

"You get anywhere close on this one, you call us," Art said.

"For sure," my brother said. And then they were gone.

15

ARROW

The dojo was silent, and you could hear the whisper of fabric as Yamashita untied the ribbon on his inka. He unrolled it, placing it with reverence on a square of silk so dark and blue that it looked black against the wood of the low table he had set in the training area.

I had seen it before. Every New Year, my sensei holds the traditional dojo ceremony, honoring the art he serves and the memory of the masters that stretch behind him like a chain forged to link the past with the present.

The scroll is covered with calligraphy that details the history of the Yamashita-ha Itto Ryu, my master's style. And mine. The inka is long and old. When you reach a certain level of proficiency in Yamashita's art, you are given a certificate attesting to your training, but also bearing his seal and a hand print as a mark of authenticity. A *ryu* is a style of martial art, and the word literally refers to a flow of tradition through time. On assuming mastery of the ryu, Yamashita had received the historical document that bore calligraphy, seals, and hand marks that stretched back generations. It's not just one scroll, but many, each representing a stage in the art's propagation.

We were alone in the cavernous hall. We had discussed my attempts at unraveling the mystery of Sakura's last message and had agreed to set aside the nagging problem of the meaning of *shumpu* for now. I had told my sensei about the murders in Georgia and Queens and the growing idea I had that the inka Sakura sent was somehow the key to unraveling the murders. But the question lingered: what could have been contained in the document? It was not tremendously valuable in objective terms, but if I was right, it had spawned three murders.

He had sighed and motioned me to follow him. Now, we sat on our heels in the formal seiza position, looking at his scrolls. It felt good to be barefoot and in the dojo. Even the sensation of the wood floor on the tops of my feet was a familiar, welcoming one. They say that a younger generation of Japanese is losing the ability to sit like this: it's an anachronism in a world where people use chairs. But I had been sinking down to the floor to sit this way for years, and it felt right.

We looked at the scrolls quietly for a time. Then Yamashita spoke. "Why do people write things down, Professor?"

I looked at him, but his eyes told me nothing of what he was getting at. "Many reasons," I said. "It makes things... concrete. Visible. When you write things down, they are fixed on the page."

My teacher nodded. "This is true. A document such as this one, for instance," he held his hand palm up and gestured gently across the table, "is a way to fix a line of transmission. The writing makes it public. And immutable."

"It also tells something important about you," I added. "Historical documents show where we come from. And also suggest where we may go."

His eyes narrowed with pleasure. "I like that, Burke. Like the hassetsu of the archer. Stylized actions that have an impact on the arrow's flight. Something that is grounded in the past which also suggests something of what can happen in the future." He paused for a moment. "Your countrymen are fascinated by history at the same time that they seek to free themselves of it. I wonder if they know this."

I smiled then. I had written an article on American culture and its fascination with the martial arts where I discussed just this issue. It was published in an obscure but respectable journal, and Yamashita had never mentioned it, but it was nice to know that someone was paying attention.

Americans, I thought, craved the tradition of the arts at the same time that they yearned to break free from their strictures. This is why Americans loved the idea of wearing a black belt—the cachet of secret and ancient knowledge—while at the same time felt drawn to start new systems headed by thirty-year-old masters. It was Miyamoto Musashi meets Daniel Boone.

"To be comfortable with something like this scroll," I said, "you also have to be comfortable with who you are and where you're going."

"That is true," my master replied.

"And," I reminded him, "the possession of something like this also gives you a certain power." I saw him look at me quizzically, and I made myself clearer. "I mean it gives you a certain authority."

Yamashita looked down at the scrolls. "I understand your meaning, Professor, but in reality the authority I have is generated here on the dojo floor. This inka has no real power to confer anything."

He saw my skeptical look and continued. "I value the scrolls for the fact that they symbolize a link to my teachers. That is all."

"You mean…" I started, but he broke in. In a fight, Yamashita could tell what you were going to do before you did. It was often the same in conversation.

"Were I to lack this inka, Professor, would my skill be any less? Would you no longer be my student?"

I looked down. "No, Sensei."

"And why is that?" he gently prodded.

I looked up. "I have been with you too long... and seen too much to have any doubts." I struggled to sum it up. The frustration he sometimes brought me, the feelings of impatience. But also the moments of clarity, the experience of revelation that chills and warms simultaneously. Finally, I just shrugged. "You are my teacher."

He sat back on his heels and nodded, watching me carefully. "Of course," he concluded after a moment. And he placed his two large hands softly down on the scroll. "This is a symbol of the connection between master and disciple. Nothing more. Nothing less. Without the human link, it is merely ink and paper. Only the foolish would mistake it for more. Or the inexperienced."

"But it's possible that someone could think it was valuable," I persisted.

Yamashita made a doubtful face and nodded. When the Japanese nod like that, it doesn't mean they agree. They're just too polite to say no.

"Value," Sensei said, "is calculated in many ways. Different people place value on objects for different reasons. It is as I have often told you, Burke. The wonder of any person is in complexity. A man is not always what he appears. There are within him varying hopes and ideas. Things we would not suspect until they are finally revealed..."

He stood up and seemed to switch topics. He walked to the stand on a table where his swords nestled in a rack made of deer antlers. They were stored with the handles to the right, cutting edge up, as befits a warrior. Yamashita lightly touched the black sheen on the scabbards.

"I have found watching the kyudoka interesting, Burke," he said quietly. "Their art is so different from ours…"

"The intervals are so wide," I said. "A distant target seems to create a different… dynamic." After I said it, I realized that I had unconsciously mimicked the pace of my master's speech.

Yamashita looked up sharply at me. "This is so. They yearn to bridge the gap between archer and mark. It is an interesting exercise in the projection of ki."

"Can they do it?" I asked.

"Some… with time. Others not. Then again, it is often hard to say." He came back to his seat. "I think the Klein woman has promise."

I grinned at him. "Me, too."

He settled himself in the seiza. "I have accepted the invitation of Kita-san to join his students at a seminar in the mountains. Ms. Klein will go. I believe the Rinpoche also."

This was a surprise, but I said nothing. Talking with my teacher was like sparring: you tried not to react much to feints. But a small feeling of uneasiness began to buzz deep down in my gut.

"I will go and watch Kita's students. To see whether the art Stark boasts of is worthy of attention." But he said it evasively, as if hiding his real motives.

I looked at him. Anyone else would have hung their head under the power of that skeptical look. Finally, he closed his eyes. "Perhaps the art is so much smoke," he admitted. "But there is something there to see. We must remain open to these things, Professor."

"It seems like a waste of time," I said quietly.

"What we expect to see and what is in front of us are sometimes different," Yamashita chided me. "As it is with people, so it is with other things. Think on this, Burke."

Like many things with Yamashita, the comment did not make things immediately clear.

I lured Sarah Klein out from Manhattan to the wilds of Brooklyn for dinner that night. There was a Japanese place I saved for special occasions—all cedar posts and whitewashed walls. The waitresses were often Filipinos in kimono, but the cook was Japanese enough and they served those really big bottles of Kirin beer. When you added Sarah to the mix, it was a beautiful thing.

I'm sure I impressed her with my dexterity at dinner. I snapped apart the wooden chopsticks known as *hashi* and deftly plucked a *gyoza* dumpling off a platter, setting it down neatly on her plate. The aesthetics of Japanese dining include your surroundings, the plates and cups, and even your eating utensils. As a sop to Round Eyes, cutlery is provided. But traditional Japanese sensibilities recoil at their use. They prefer the wooden hashi. The metal implements of Western tableware strike the Japanese as uncouth: more like tools used on an operating table than something fit for civilized dining.

She raised an eyebrow as I set the dumpling before her. "You've done this before, I see."

I had dipped my own gyoza into the sauce and crammed it into my mouth, so it took a moment to reply. I nodded and swallowed. "One of the side benefits of a youth spent in the martial arts. You get to eat Japanese food a lot."

Sarah slipped her hashi out of their paper sleeve and experimented with them. She did a pretty good job. "What are the other benefits?" she asked me.

"Well," I began, "the usual: bad knees, calloused feet…"

"It doesn't seem to have scared you off." She smiled.

I grinned ruefully. I also cast a covert glance at the gyoza tray, mentally tallying how many I could eat and not appear like a hog. "It's an Irish-American trait," I told her. "We're stubborn. Once we get going on something, it's hard to make us stop."

Sarah sipped at her wine and looked at me. Her hands were slim and graceful and her nails were cut short and carefully shaped. She was an elegant woman. "I'll bet there's more to it than that," she said to me. "You write about these arts. You study them. They occupy a big part of your life…" She let the statements hang there to get me to say more.

"Different people find different things in the arts," I finally commented. It was something I had thought a great deal about. "Competence. Control. Balance. Belonging…"

"It is like a really specialized club," Sarah said, shaking her head as if in amazement. "Or a family…"

"Sure," I told her. "The people who stay in it are probably attracted for a constellation of reasons. The physical aspect is important…"

"It's almost addicting," she said. "I know that if I skip kyudo practice, I feel out of sorts for days."

"That's a good thing," I told her. "I knew that I was finally getting into training when I would go even when I was sick. And it would make me feel better." I saw her looking at me with a puzzled expression. "Well," I finished, "at least it feels good when it stops."

"But it's not just the physical stuff, is it Burke?" she pursued hopefully.

"No," I had to admit, "it's not. You were probably closer to the mark when you spoke about family and belonging."

"Is that important for you?" she said.

I shrugged in acknowledgment. "I come from a big family, so belonging to something like that comes natural."

"Belonging and approval," she said.

I looked at her. Her face was open and relaxed, and if she knew just how strong a chord she had struck, she gave no evidence of it. "Big family," I shrugged, "you learn to do things to get noticed."

"The same thing with college life, I bet," she commented. Sarah set her elbow on the table and rested her chin in a hand. Her eyes were wide and brown. She waited.

We had *miso* soup while I told her just how weird life at the university could be. Of how hard it is to be accepted there. People outside the academy are often surprised. I think they fantasize a red brick and ivy universe where nerdy people with bad glasses band together, lost in deep thoughts.

Many of my colleagues are lost, but in more profound ways. I sometimes think that advanced education is a bad thing. For many people, the effect of knowing so many different facts about life is that they are powerless to choose a path for themselves with any confidence. It makes them distracted and cranky. So the image I have of academia is one of a place filled with tremendously bright, insecure people. They do have bad glasses. And atrocious people skills. They are distracted, yet vicious when aroused. At Dorian, the nerds had filed teeth, like cannibals.

Sarah's eyes got wider. "I guess it must make going to the dojo a relief."

"Yeah, it is. At least until Yamashita starts putting you through your paces."

She brightened at the mention of his name. "I don't think I've ever met anyone like him." She paused and then added,

"OK, maybe with the exception of Changpa Rinpoche. Interesting that they knew each other before coming to New York."

"Sensei is a remarkable man," I said. "He's just full of surprises." And there must have been some expression on my face I wasn't aware of.

"You've got mixed feelings," she said with certainty. "You care for him a great deal, but there's also strain, right?" she asked.

I pushed my soup away. "We've been through… a lot."

"So I gather," Sarah said. "Changpa Rinpoche thinks very highly of your teacher. He also says that not all self-knowledge is pleasant to gain."

It was true enough, but I was pretty tired of hearing it. Sarah must have sensed that. She sipped her wine in the sudden awkward silence. She set her glass down and reached out with her hashi, setting the last dumpling carefully on my plate. She concentrated hard on managing the chopsticks, and a pink tip of tongue appeared in the corner of her mouth. "Good things come to those who wait," she told me. I smiled and she smiled back.

"How do you like working with Yamashita?" I asked, diverting the subject away from me. I knew that my sensei had taken her under his wing and was working to invest her archery with some of the contained ferocity he taught to those of us training with the sword.

Our entrees came, and the pause gave her some time to think. "Remarkable," she finally said. "You think you're finally getting the hang of something, and he peels back a layer and shows you something else. Something new…"

I grinned ruefully and nodded. "With Yamashita Sensei, there's always something more to learn. But," I said, "he seems to reveal things on his schedule, not yours."

"So you develop patience?"

I paused, and for a moment it was as if I were back in the dojo with my teacher, looking at his scrolls. "Sometimes he drives me crazy," I admitted. "But sometimes… you get a glimpse of something…" I trailed off. Sarah smiled and patted my hand.

We got down to serious eating then. I managed not to embarrass myself. I grew up in the same place where my brother Micky learned to eat. At times, we can exhibit something the really polite might call gustatory avidity.

Eventually, Sarah and I got back on the topic of the murder investigation.

"So what do you think is going on here?" she asked. "I mean, is it OK for you to tell me?"

I waved her concern away. "I've got to talk about it with someone. I keep coming up with dead ends when I try to see a motive. My brother the detective tends to favor some kind of direct motive. He thinks it's got to be something that's either a personal grudge or maybe connected with money…"

"The source of all evil," Sarah commented.

"Filthy lucre," I agreed. But they haven't been able to come up with anything."

"Could it have been valuable?"

"We don't think so. Sakura seems to have shipped it off for a second opinion to this guy Hoddington…"

"The second victim?"

I nodded. "Right. But the package wasn't insured like something that was valuable."

"Value is relative," Sarah said. "I mean, look at what you do with Yamashita. From a purely economic perspective, it's a waste of time." I took a breath to speak and she held up her hand. "I know, I know, I'm just making a point here." I settled down and she continued. "It's valuable to you for different reasons." I nodded. "So maybe it's the same with the calligraphy Sakura had."

"That's the thing I'm trying to figure out," I told her. "I know that the written word has tremendous significance in Asian culture. Partially, it's just the result of the effort it takes to master a non-phonetic system. You've got to memorize something like twenty thousand characters to be literate. Plus they've got this whole aesthetic dimension to handwritten documents."

"But that's not it, is it?" She said. Sarah was a pretty smart person.

"No," I admitted. "Sakura had found something in whatever he was examining that didn't seem right to him, so he wanted Hoddington's advice. From the phone records, it's obvious to me they also spoke about it. But I don't know what they were looking at and why it's so important to someone. And there aren't many people who spoke with Hoddington right before he was killed."

I told her about sifting through his papers. And the photographs that were taken during his last days. "From what you say about the background in the pictures, it sounds like he was at some kind of target range. I'd like to get a look at them," she said.

Which is how we ended up at my apartment. Micky had given me copies of some of the documents from Georgia that I needed to study. I had them spread out on the big banged-up wooden table I garbage-picked when Dorian re-did its library reading room. I'd been making a tally of items on a pad of long yellow legal paper, but hadn't made much headway. Micky drew the line at copying the crime scene report, but he had gotten the negatives of Hoddington's snapshots and made extra copies for me.

"Here," I said to Sarah.

She went through them quickly, nodding with certainty. "This is a *matoba*, she said, "the target house for an outdoor kyudo range."

"I couldn't be sure," I told her.

Sarah shook her head as she thought. "Sure. Really good dojos have outdoor shooting ranges like this one. Look," she said, tracing significant points with a slim finger, "you can see the *azuchi* behind the target—the clay bank that stops the arrows. And look at the target in the picture…" It was a white circular target, and the only mark was a red dot in the center. "This is a classic *hoshi mato*."

"A star target?" I asked, doing the translation.

"Yep, that's what they call them. The other type used is the *kasumi mato*. It looks like the standard bull's-eye. Anyway," she said, getting back to the matter at hand, "this snapshot was taken from the shooting hall of a pretty good archery dojo."

"Not many of them down South," I ventured.

"Not many anywhere in this country," she said. "It should narrow things down for you considerably." I made a note on my pad while she shuffled the pictures around. "As a matter of fact, at least one of these people looks vaguely familiar…" She thought for a minute. "I wish I had my book here."

"What book?"

She smiled. "*Fundamentals of Kyudo*. All the students have it."

I went over to a bookcase and pulled it out. "Here," I said sheepishly. Sarah looked at me in surprise.

"Branching out, Burke?"

I shrugged. "Well, it seems important to you, so I thought I'd take the time to learn about it." As I handed the book to her, Sarah gave me a wry smile.

"How nice," she said.

But she was still focused on the issue at hand. I guess for an archer, a target is hard to let go of. She found one of the snapshots that showed Hoddington with a group of people. Then she began paging through the book.

"Ha!" Sarah said. "I knew that face looked familiar." She opened the book to me and I saw a photo of a Caucasian archer working under the tutelage of an older Japanese man. "Hoddington knew the author of this book."

"Robert Marinaro? You're kidding," I said.

"The community of kyudoka is pretty small. Marinaro's pretty well known because of the book." She flipped to the back flap, where a brief blurb told you about the author. "You see?"

The blurb told me that, in addition to his mastery of Japanese archery, Marinaro had a master's degree in Asian Studies. From the University of Georgia.

"You are the best," I said. She smiled brightly. We were close together by the table, and I leaned forward and kissed her lightly on the lips.

She moved her hand, and the photos spilled to the floor. Sarah quickly bobbed down to get them, and the small motions of collecting the scattered pictures had a grace to them that was an echo of her actions in kyudo. She handed them over without a word, looking at me with a slight flush in her cheeks.

A warm tension hung in the air around us, the vibration of things left uncompleted. "Sarah," I started.

She swallowed. "I know," she said quietly, but with an odd hesitation in her voice. "Let's take things a little bit at a time, OK?"

The she touched me lightly on the chest, a gentle pressure, and looked significantly at the pictures in my hand. I let out a quiet sigh and turned for the phone. I needed to get in touch with Micky and Art before someone else made the same connection Sarah just had.

16

KIRI

It's not unusual in a dojo for a new student to seek out a more advanced person to guide him. The *sempai*, or senior, is supposed to look out for the new student, the *kyohai*. The relationship is typically one that forms spontaneously. It's rare that a teacher goes out of his way to create one. But Yamashita had made a promise to Changpa to assist with Stark's training. And, in turn, the lama would work with me in my spare time between trying to solve mysteries and getting jumped on city streets. But my teacher made it quite clear that I was responsible for Stark. A promise had been given to the Rinpoche. It was my obligation to see that it was fulfilled.

And I had to admit that Stark was good. He had the knack, the inborn kinesthetic sense of the natural athlete. It took years of hard training for me to get to where I was. Stark had an easy connection with his body that made his acquisition of technique seem almost effortless. You watched carefully in the first few lessons to see the potential in new students. It was clear from his style of movement, even at this relatively early stage in training, that Stark had tremendous potential.

Stark had told me that he was dan ranked in kendo and jujutsu, and that he hoped to study extensively with the elusive Kita. And what I saw as Stark practiced with us was an individual whose innate potential had permitted him to advance quickly. But if there was promise here, there was also imperfection. His training had lacked some of the subtleties I had come to expect from working with Yamashita. Stark was all excitement and power. He projected a spiky, unsettling energy. It was both impressive and vaguely troubling at the same time.

He also lacked humility.

Stark was fine when Yamashita was around, subdued and pliant, but he pulled no punches with me: "Look, Burke," he murmured at one point during the Sunday training session, "I've been around a while, you know? Yamashita's got a good reputation, but come on…" He was obviously skeptical. "The real reason I'm here is to keep an edge on while I wait for the call from Master Kita."

The real reason you're here is because the Rinpoche pleaded for you, I thought. His attitude would make for a tough time between the two of us. I was supposed to shepherd him through training, but I wondered whether he could learn. Someone like Stark was so focused on himself that he would be deaf to the lessons his teachers presented. And part of me was aware of the subtle parallels between the two of us in this regard. But you couldn't really make the comparison, I reassured myself. Then I swallowed my annoyance. I looked at Stark when he made the comment and said, "Well, stick around. You may learn something from Yamashita Sensei."

Stark smirked. "We'll see. So far, you guys don't seem to do much of the bang and crunch." He stretched his broad chest. "That's what I'm into."

I looked down at my hands and stretched them a little. When you tensed them just right, my muscles ache with the memory of old wounds. "You ever heard of humility, Stark?" I told him. "You may learn some here."

"Oh, come on, Burke," he said in a low voice. "You ought to look at things a bit more critically, man. You act like this guy walks on water." He snickered. "You should see yourself, following after Yamashita like some puppy dog, doing his bidding…"

"Stark, you don't even know what you're talking about," I said.

"You think what you want, man. But I'm going to be Kita's uchi deshi. You're more like Yamashita's…" Stark gave me a knowing, provocative smile as he searched for a description, "… house slave."

I held my temper. And my tongue. But his words were hard to forget.

Later, my teacher came to my side. "The Rinpoche was correct," he said. "I begin to see it now." Yamashita gestured with his head toward Stark, working alone in a corner. He was endlessly repeating the basics of the action of *kiri*, cutting with the sword. I myself had once been in the same place in this room, forging a type of link to my master that was ironically made through practicing the art of severance.

"He struggles with something," Yamashita said, "and searches…" His voice was somber and low. Then he looked at me and his tone brightened. "He has great potential, even so, Professor."

I shrugged. "We'll see."

"He trains at another school downtown. He has asked me for permission to take you. I have agreed."

"What if I don't want to go with him?" My thoughts were elsewhere, trying piece together the possible links between three murders. Han's interest in the Rinpoche. The Chinese. Working with Stark on personal development issues seemed tangential.

"Burke, we are obligated to the Rinpoche," Yamashita said dismissively. "Besides, the experience will be a good one for you."

Although I didn't like it, I went.

Stark seemed eager to get me to his other dojo. That alone should have tipped me off. But I think I was too focused on other things. So intent that I didn't notice the larger picture that was forming.

The school was tucked away in the lower level of a building near Washington Square. You walked down four dirty steps to a battered steel door. It was painted gray, and the lock was surrounded by scratches, as if small animals had been pawing at it. Stark grinned at me as he pushed it open, like a man sharing a secret.

The dojo was a long, rectangular space with a floor covered in battered mats. The pillars that supported the floors above had been wrapped in foam and duct tape. The ceiling was crisscrossed with pipes and jury-rigged fluorescent panels hung down on chains. You could smell wet cement, disinfectant, and sweat in the air.

I've been in places like this before. There's a range of martial arts schools in the world: they go from the strip mall clubs where legions of suburban kids kick and scream the afternoons away to more traditional places where serious-faced adults in expensive uniforms stretch assiduously, pull their punches because they've got an important meeting tomorrow, and worry about being centered. This place was nothing like that. It was part cage and part classroom, a feral combination of dojo and biker bar.

Stark had been sampling the martial arts universe of the Big Apple. While nothing would probably compare with Kita, he confided, he was interested in the range of possibilities out there. "Ya gotta absorb what is useful, Burke," he told me on the way down, his eyebrows arching with an attempt at sophistication.

"Gee, I wonder where I've heard that before?" I replied sarcastically. It had been one of the mottos of Bruce Lee.

"Don't knock it," he said, too self-involved to note my tone of voice. "Form is nice, but function is better." I didn't tell Stark, but my sensei agreed. Or rather, he didn't see a distinction between the two. Yamashita had a real appreciation of the useful, but he didn't let his students define that category. In the West, a student is an explorer, charged with discovering truths. In the East, the disciple is a receptacle to be filled by the master.

There was more to Stark's interest in different fighting styles than just trite philosophy, however. I also suspected, for all his seeming docility in Yamashita's presence, that Stark was finding the structure and discipline of my teacher's method difficult to endure. In some ways I could understand the feeling.

But the Japanese prize fidelity. They frown on students who wander from style to style, searching for something. The old masters believe that what is missing in such searchers is something within themselves, not the system. But Stark seemed impervious to this sentiment. You could see in the set of his shoulders that he was excited about something. At the time, I thought it was just the effect of being liberated from Yamashita's strictures, if only for the day.

When we entered that room, there were any number of fairly hard-looking cases warming up on the mats. Stark led me over to one and introduced him as the teacher.

He wore a black gi faded to gray and high-topped split-toed socks called *tabi*. A ragged black belt dangled from his waist. The breast of his gi was embroidered with something that looked like a ship's wheel. But, colored in red and gold, it was actually a mandala, the sacred wheel of esoteric Buddhism. I noticed it had eight spokes. All the other students were dressed the same way. That's when I knew I was in for trouble.

I had been lured to the lair of the *ninja*.

They claimed to study the ancient warrior arts of stealth—*ninjutsu*. The good schools practice an effective mix of unarmed and armed systems; the bad ones do a lot of cartwheels, roll around a great deal, and wax mystical. It's not that ninjutsu doesn't have a basis in real techniques. But practitioners of the more breathlessly acrobatic variants annoy me with the certainty that theirs is the only truly superior martial art. And there are harder versions of the art, as well. Darker systems. That's where I suspected I had ended up. And I wasn't surprised that Stark had led me there.

Their leader looked like a real hard case. His hands were square and you could see the calluses on the knuckles. He was broad-chested and solid-looking, with a big droopy mustache. Probably drove a Harley to ninja school.

They all eyed me suspiciously when Stark introduced me as Yamashita Sensei's senior pupil. If they were dogs, the hair on their necks would have risen. They had heard of Yamashita, I was sure. And, like many of the more non-traditional martial arts groups, they were both self-conscious about their identity and eager to prove their superiority.

So they invited me to join them in their workout. This was not a gesture of magnanimity. What it really meant was that they were going to be eye-balling me the whole time, critiquing my moves. I changed into my training gear with Stark. He kept glancing my way like a man enjoying a private joke he was nonetheless reluctant to share. But we didn't talk much.

I was a little out of place there—I had retained the dark blue uniform of my dojo, including the pleated hakama of the traditional arts. But I had decided to try to do this on my terms, not on theirs.

Every martial arts style is a little different—issues of stance and technique vary a great deal—but it's all based on similar principles. As a result, I could keep up with them without too much awkwardness. They ran through various warm-ups, strikes, kicks, and rolls.

After a while, the leader called out, "Circle up!" The students formed a ring with him in the center. What followed next was an exercise in dealing with multiple attackers. One student would stand in the ring and be attacked by a succession of fighters. The point was to learn to flow with the action, to demonstrate a variety of technical responses, and to defend against the attacks. It was difficult in any situation, and more so here.

Because these guys played for keeps. You could see it in the sweaty faces of the succession of people in the center of the ring. Hear it in the smack and deep thud of meat and bone as hard blows were parried with a mix of focus and desperation. And occasionally, a really well-focused blow would knock someone flat onto the mat, where he would lay stunned for a minute.

I stood watching this for a while, silent and apart from the action. Finally, Mr. Mustache faced me. He smiled grimly. "You see what we're up to here."

I wasn't sure whether this was a question. "Very impressive," I replied. I pitched my voice low and calm. I could sense something here, an invisible emotional charge building like static electricity. A situation felt like it was developing and I wanted to defuse whatever the situation was.

The big guy eyed me critically. "How about a demo, man?" He gestured with a hard-looking hand to Stark. "This guy's been shooting his mouth off about Yamashita and his stuff all week. Let's see what you got."

I looked a question at Stark. This was a guy who seemed skeptical about my sensei? Why the change of heart? The need to prove something about Yamashita to these guys? Stark shrugged at me, feigning innocence. "They seem pretty good, Burke." He gestured around the room at the watching group. Then his eyes narrowed, and things got a little clearer to me. "You seem so sure about your style. Why not test it out?"

I looked silently at him. There was a hard set to his face, a coldness that I hadn't seen before. It made me wonder for a fleeting second about how accurate the lama's read on Stark was. But I refocused on the issue at hand.

A few things shot through my head. One was maybe that I should have seen this coming. *I'll never live this down with Yamashita.* But then another idea followed immediately: *I'll bet he knew. Yamashita. And he sent me anyway.*

Which made me wonder. Was the point that my teacher wanted me to be put in a situation where I was supposed to *sense* coming danger? Was that it? Just another elaborate training exercise? Or did he send me here because he wanted to see how I would fare fighting these people? Or did he merely want me to keep tabs on Stark?

It was way too much to think about. And I had no desire to lock horns with these guys. It wasn't an issue of being reluctant to test my skill against them. I'd been watching them for a while and was pretty sure I could hold my own, no matter what. It was just that I like to think I'm beyond that. There's fighting and then there's *fighting*. These guys trained hard; there was no doubt about it. But I know what it's like to be rolling around on the floor with someone who is actually trying to kill you. You can feel the homicidal rage mixed in with the body heat and smell it in their breath. And I know what it feels like to stagger away from something like that, leaving the other guy in a still heap. It makes you think that everything else is so much play-acting and that you'd be wise to save your strength for the real thing.

So I sighed and explained to the ninja that I was just a visitor and probably wasn't worth the effort on their part. I worked the humble angle about as hard as I could. But it wasn't good enough. He looked around at his pals and said, "I told you they didn't have balls…" He gestured at my hakama. "Must be why they wear dresses." His audience snickered.

Oh boy, I thought. *Here we go.* The hakama is a standard part of the practice uniform in many traditional arts. It really is a pleated and divided skirt, but we like to think it lends dignity and elegance to our practice. The ninja, however, seemed immune to the power of esthetics.

Maybe the arrogant smirk on the ninja's face was what finally set me off. Maybe I've come to share the simmering anger that Micky had developed in the frustrating experience of investigating murders. Part of me wonders whether I was just trying to show Stark that I could cope with whatever he and his pals dished out. I could rationalize it as a useful lesson for him. But that wasn't true. Part of me was deeply angry. At the situation. At my inability to understand Sakura's last message. In any event, I let things get the better of me.

I glanced around at the class. Their faces were flat and hard, but with a slight gleam of anticipation showing here and there. "Well, look," I said quietly, beckoning the teacher closer. Again, he smirked. I looked up into his face. It looked like his nose had been broken more than once. "If you're really interested, I can probably show you some techniques."

He smiled at me like a carnivore sighting the distant motion of prey.

We walked out onto the mat and I suggested we use weapons. The *bo* is six feet long and probably one of the most common types of wooden staff used in many arts. I was trying to be nice to ninja boy. At least for the moment.

He grabbed one from a corner and twirled it around in whistling arcs as he made for the center of the mat. I was handed a staff as well. The class closed in around us, a living ring of flesh, tense with anticipation. I stood there with the bo's tip resting on the ground, a straight shaft going up through my right hand. The weapon was actually taller than I was.

The ninja adopted a ready posture, but I held up a hand. "We usually start with a seated bow," I told him.

He shot a disparaging look to his companions, but knelt down, the bo placed flat beside him. I knelt on my left knee, my right foot still flat on the ground and the bo erect in my hand. It's a type of battlefield salutation that lets you get up more quickly. We bowed tightly to each other, and, with a final smirk to his audience, he began to stand.

I'm not saying that what I did was fair. Fighting rarely is. Yamashita likes to tell us that what he teaches is *heiho*—strategy. It sounds elegant, but sometimes heiho is just brutally effective. That's what counts.

I had let him kneel first so I could gauge the distance, of course. As my opponent came up from kneeling, he raised his right leg and placed the foot flat on the ground in front of him. It was what I needed.

Still kneeling, I pushed the bo in my right hand down from the vertical with all the speed and force I could muster. It whipped in an arc, bridging the gap between us, and cracked its tip across the fragile bones on the top of his foot. Maybe the tabi absorbed some of the blow, but you could hear him gasp as the strike went home.

I wasn't letting it go at that, however. He looked a little too competent, and would probably fight through the pain.

And he did, rising up and starting to bring his weapon to bear. But he was a little slow and a little off balance. I grasped my bo like a spear and drove it deep into his solar plexus as hard as I could. When I jerked up, I felt the tip grind against his sternum.

His eyes bugged out and he backpedaled a bit, but I could see that he would keep coming. I reversed my handhold and brought the bottom of the staff around, cracking him across the head. It made a nice, deep sound when the wood hit the bone.

He had about had it by then, but amazingly enough he was still standing upright. I dropped my weapon, knocked his right arm down and grasped his bo. It came out of his hands easily: there wasn't much resistance left in him. Then I whipped a roundhouse kick into the back of his knee and down he went like a sack of meat.

I pointed the tip of his bo against his neck as he tried to recover. And pushed. He was pretty stunned, but the gag reflex still worked.

When you move this fast you don't start breathing heavily until things are all over. I looked around at the watching class. "The lesson…" I said as I took a breath, "is over."

I glowered at the circle of angry men that surrounded me. I projected as much force as I could, tensing my abdomen with the effort. They say your ki, your internal energy, can be projected this way. I'm not too sure, but I was hoping it would work. It was my big plan for escape. My angriest stare was reserved for Stark. No one said a word. No one moved. I dropped the staff onto the mat and went off to change.

When I got back to my dojo, Yamashita looked silently at me, and I don't know whether what I saw in his eyes was approval or disappointment.

"And your visit?" he finally prompted me. "Was it… instructive?"

I glared at him. I still hadn't cooled down. "It was a waste of time."

"Tell me about it," my teacher asked.

So I did. I described the trip and Stark's secret excitement. My dawning realization that I was being set up. And Stark's role in it. I briefly described the fight itself—a tight sequence of technical Japanese terms that serves as the shorthand of our system.

My teacher looked at me with those dark eyes. "Not too long ago, Burke, you would have talked more and acted less."

There didn't seem to be much to say about that. Was this good or bad? My teacher offered no clue. Yamashita considered me for a moment. "So you used the foot attack?"

I nodded tightly. "Yes."

"Well," he said, "there was at least some training value in the exchange." Then, almost to himself, "It is unfortunate that the match was not against Stark himself."

And it struck me. It wasn't just Stark who had set me up. My own teacher had been a part of it. I was momentarily stunned.

Looking back, I shouldn't have been. The martial arts world is filled with stories of the old days, when a style's master would be forced to choose between two promising students. Invariably, the method of selection would not be a humane one. And, in the final analysis, I was willing to undergo the ordeal. But against *Stark*? The very thought was insulting.

"Is that was this was all about, Sensei?" I demanded. "A trick? Another test?" Yamashita's face was closed, his eyes narrow slits. "Again?" I could feel myself getting worked up.

Yamashita turned away, but I wouldn't let it go. I moved to block his way, and he came up short, looking almost surprised. Affronted.

"I don't have time for these games anymore, Sensei," I told him. "We've been at this too long!" I thought of Sakura and Hoddington and Kim. Of Han stalking the city. Of the thousand and one other things that demanded attention in my life, and the way I neglected them to follow this man.

Yamashita stared at me in silence.

"I'm sick of it!" I told him. "I don't want to play these games with haragei anymore. I don't want to have to guess what you're up to. You want me to fight Stark, tell me. Give me a reason…"

"I am the sensei," he said stonily, "my reasons are my own." It seemed that the angrier I grew, the quieter he became.

"That's…" I suppressed the expletive, even as angry as I was, "… that's not good enough!" But he was immovable. Unyielding.

We stood staring at each other. You don't often look directly at your superior's eyes in Japan—decorum and sincerity demand an averted gaze. But I looked hard at him, hoping for some hint that I was getting through.

In the end, I broke away. "Fine." I moved to the wall rack and removed my bokken, the wooden sword battered from years of training with him. And then I headed for the door.

"When will you be back?" he asked quietly. But I kept moving. When I reached the door, he spoke again. His words were hard and tight, as if they hurt to say.

"Will you be back?"

I stepped through the door without replying. I had one last glimpse of him, squat and hard and alone. Yamashita stood there in the silence that swallowed his unanswered question, like a rock in a falling tide.

17

FLICKER

The room was dark, the air somber. Tapestries hung on the walls, dimly seen figures that danced and whirled in the grip of karma. A bank of thick, squat candles guttered in a nave, and in the occasional surge of light you could pick out the crimson and gold thread in the wall hangings. Incense burned: a faint scent hung in the air, almost nonexistent, like an item recently lost to memory. The lama's students chanted.

I had wanted to talk with someone. I thought immediately of Sarah Klein, but she was traveling on business for a few days and was then heading directly to Kita's seminar. I could imagine calling her, hoping that she'd come home sooner. Whining, essentially. But I thought of her clear eyes and the way she understood things and realized that she would expect more of me than that.

So I sat in the back of the meditation room, waiting to talk with the lama. In that cool, dark room, everyone else seemed lost in the rhythmic murmur of the mantra. I still burned.

At the close of the session, Changpa's students came to kneel before him. He gently placed gossamer-thin white scarves around their necks, a symbol of blessing stretched gently between his big hands, laid with delicacy upon his disciples. There was calm here, lapping against my anger, but I fought it.

He finally looked up at me. The light played on his glasses. He seemed composed and yet concerned.

"And," he breathed, "now you have come." He made a motion as if looking about the room. "Where is your teacher?"

I started to say something, to explain that I had left the dojo. But I couldn't get the words out. The Rinpoche looked at me, his eyes wide and sad as I floundered for words. Speech seemed inadequate at that moment. The lama reached out and placed a prayer scarf down across my shoulders. It fluttered there, light as a bird. My eyes burned with emotion.

"Come," he said, and led me out of the meditation chamber.

The Dharma Center had a library and reading room, a high ceilinged formal space that smelled of wood polish and old paper. Amid the books, I felt more at home. At intervals, small portraits of monks hung on the walls. Changpa walked slowly around the room, drawing me after him, pausing at each picture. "Teachers," he told me. "Disciples of the Lord Buddha in my homeland." His voice sounded sorrowful.

"You must miss them," I said.

"Some of my brother lama have gone into the Great Void before us. And now, since they are one with all things, they are with us here." He paused for a moment. "But for others, we know only that the authorities have taken them. I memorialize them here. I seek information about those in prison. I advocate with world governments." Merely reciting the litany of activities sounded as if it tired him. He sagged down within himself for a minute, then straightened. "But mostly, I hope that the resonance of our prayers reaches them in captivity."

I nodded. Since my run-in with Han, I had read up on this. The Chinese government has been waging a decades-long struggle to control the Tibetan Buddhists. And it's not just all that puritanical communist opium-of-the-masses stuff. In the Chinese drive to expand their hegemony in Asia, the unique hold of Buddhism in Tibet had to be broken in order to destroy the cultural distinctiveness of the Tibetan people. Protests in the West get some attention, but the Chinese are old hands at this: there's a relentless, single-minded, and persistent brutality that totalitarian regimes have mastered. The Rinpoche struggles against it, but we're probably incapable of stopping it. Most protesters are well meaning. But they think that if only we could all hold hands, the world will change. The Chinese don't want to hold the Tibetans' hands; they want to shackle them.

And, of course, the prominent lamas embody the persistence of Buddhism there and are the targets of Chinese repression. Monasteries have been dynamited. Monks killed. And slowly, ever so slowly, the Chinese occupiers of Tibet are putting the remaining religious leaders under their control. Those who resist are never seen again.

"I knew many of these men," Changpa told me, moving his hand in a gesture to encompass the portraits. "They were men of great compassion and wisdom. And some were gifted with powers that you would have a hard time accepting, Dr. Burke."

He knew, of course, about my struggles with Yamashita. How much of it had been told him and how much he just sensed seemed irrelevant at the moment.

"But perhaps the greatest gift and the heaviest burden to bear is to be a teacher," he told me in a voice heavy with significance.

He motioned me to a chair and set himself in a seat facing me. He arranged his robes with the unconscious efficiency of habit and reached within them for his prayer beads.

His fingers worked at the beads and they made soft clicking noises that lent rhythm to his words. "We are both in pursuit of the Way, Dr. Burke, albeit along different paths. As you progress, different challenges must be faced. Some of this, of course, you know.

"It is your teacher's job to prepare you for these challenges. And to make you face them." His voice had that calming, clear quality I had experienced the first time I saw him. I felt some of the tension leaving me.

"It creates a curious link between teacher and student, does it not, Burke?" He persisted. "So much achievement. So much struggle. And always, more struggle ahead." He sighed. "The Way stretches out before us with no end in sight. It is only the compassion of the Lord Buddha that sustains us.

"The duality of our nature, physical and spiritual, is, of course, an illusion. Your teacher seeks to destroy this illusion by helping you achieve a type of physical mastery that frees you to transcend its limitations." He looked right at me with those unsettling eyes. "This has been a hard path for you." I nodded in agreement.

Changpa closed his eyes briefly in acceptance of my silent response, then continued. "You are a man of books. There is a measure of control in the printed word, is there not?" He paused. Interesting to think that we say that a book is bound. It suggests something, don't you think?"

"A lot of the martial arts seems to me to be about control," I answered. "How to cope with the chaos of violence."

"Certainly," he smiled. "It is the thing we fear the most, chaos. It threatens our very... selves."

I listened to the measured, calm cadence of his voice. The clicking of the beads. His words seemed to occupy the entire space of the room we were sitting in.

His tone became gentler. "But in both my Way and yours, we are called to move beyond the discipline of the body. To grow in new ways. And this creates… challenges within you. It is not physical fear; it is something more profound."

"What is it?" My voice was raspy.

He smiled, but didn't answer the question. "It is elemental and potent this fear, is it not? We cannot put it into words, but it is there, deep within us." He stood up and once more moved along the portraits of teachers that dotted the walls. "And think of this: once the fear has been faced, the disciple moves to a different plane. He is changed forever. How does that make the master feel? When for years the bond between master and disciple is one based on… what?" He looked at me.

"Inequality," I ventured.

"Oh, Burke," he sighed, "you are unkind. The master knows his student. His flaws. His strengths." He was talking now of something he knew intimately. "Our disciples are our children. We guide them, protect them. And, when they are strong enough, we force them to grow beyond themselves…" I followed Changpa down the hall toward the meditation room, and his following comment was almost lost to me. He said it quietly, softly, and the words fluttered like a prayer scarf in the wind. "We help them outgrow… us. Students are not the only ones to struggle with the self."

But the anger was still with me. *A lecture on Tibetan tough love?* I thought.

He turned and his eyes flickered with that cold flash of knowing. "It is not love, Burke, but true compassion that is often difficult. Because it demands so much from us. To awaken this awareness in a student is the teacher's greatest task and perhaps the most daunting for both."

He gestured me to the floor. I sat in the Japanese style, while he adopted the lotus position. "You are angry," he told me. "And you fear…" He smiled wryly as I started to protest. "The point I wish to make is that often our emotions, our fears, our… insecurities sometimes cloud perception. We must learn to see through this fog of illusion if we are to follow the True Path."

"What is the illusion, Rinpoche?" I asked quietly.

But his answer was elliptical. "We struggle all our lives as individual actors, discrete drops of water. And our destiny is to seek a union with the great sea of unknowing. When we merge with that ocean, what becomes of the drops? To the individual self? We now are one with something greater and move to its tides.

"You doubt others because you doubt yourself, Burke. And you fear what will happen when you break through the barrier of perception. To a place where things are not always in your control. Where the very idea of *you* becomes blurred."

His words were simple and direct and spoken with utter conviction. They made the very core of my body go cold.

"And," he concluded, "because you fear so strongly, you hate the one who is pushing you to confront that fear."

Some of the anger was still there. I felt it stir, an ember being blown upon. The lama held up a calming hand. "Peace, Burke. Now you must learn something of the human capacity for the unexpected," he said.

"I don't understand, Rinpoche,"

"Hush. Chant with me." And, in that dark room, we sat in the candlelight, the murmur of words and the cadence of breathing slowly bringing us to that place where you both sink and rise at the same time.

My eyelids flickered. I felt suddenly nauseous and stirred uncomfortably. "I feel sick," I murmured.

Changpa smiled slightly. "You are not sick. Your conscious mind struggles against release. The power deep within you struggles for release. And your conscious self struggles to imprison it." He held up his hand in that familiar mudra, the open hand gesture that said *have no fear*. I concentrated on my breathing once more.

Your eyes start to close slightly. Shadows begin to swell and shift. The sound of chanting filled the room; the image of the lama before me grew faded, less distinct. And slowly, subtly, in a way that made the final apparition appear almost expected, Changpa's raised hand began to glow. It was as if heat and light was leaking through the folds and seams of his palm: warm red and yellow energy seeping out into the still air between us.

He rose then, still chanting, and touched his glowing palm to my forehead. The location of the third eye. Then, he gradually touched the other chakra, the power centers of the body. The throat, the solar plexus, the spot below the navel that Japanese call the *saika tanden*. The base of the spine. I felt a warmth envelop me as I sat motionless under his touch. It struggled against another fire that still smoldered, deep within me.

In time, the sensation faded. I rose, curiously tired and light-headed. Changpa held out his hands in benediction, offering a peace I could not yet accept. "Surrender is not defeat, Burke," he called out to me as I left. His voice had quiet resonance that stayed with me as I left the building.

"We gotta stop meeting like this," another voice said as I came down the steps from the Dharma Center onto the street. Micky and Art were standing there.

"A force larger than any of us, there is," Art said in his Master Yoda voice. Micky and I both glared at him, but my brother's partner seemed unperturbed.

"You guys following me around?" I said.

My brother gestured at me to come closer to him. "So we're running down things on this torture victim…"

"Kim," Art supplied.

"Somebody wants something from him. Is it whatever he sent to Sakura? Could be, but we gotta make sure." Micky squinted at me as he ran through their reasoning, like he was thinking about what to reveal and what to withhold.

"We checked out his apartment," Art said, consulting his notebook.

"Grad student housing at NYU," he sniffed. "Turns out someone had been there ahead of us."

"The place had been tossed," Micky added. "We spoke to the security people… Kim hadn't been seen on campus for a few weeks."

"So he'd been hiding out?" I asked.

My brother nodded. "Possibly. According to his professors he was working on some independent project."

"Did you look for fingerprints at the apartment… anything that might link up with the Sakura murder," I started.

Micky waved me off. "You been watching too much TV, Connor. Forensics is useful for firming up links, but it's hard to generate theories from it. Too many variables."

"Besides," Art told me, "unless the prints are in the local files, we end up sending stuff to the FBI for a check, and they seem a little preoccupied lately…"

"Ever since the Twin Towers came down," Micky told me, "the routine stuff has been moving slowly."

"The Feds have bigger fish to fry, these days, Connor. All sorts of suspicious folks around…"

"Cabbies from Bangladesh," Micky offered.

"Yemeni tobacconists," Art added wistfully. "Basically, ninety percent of the managers of convenience stores in the five boroughs…"

"OK, I got it," I told them.

"We knocked on some doors instead," Art told me. "It's what we do. Talk to people. Not fancy, but it sometimes gets results."

"And?"

"And eventually we ran into a buddy of Kim's. Told us that he'd stopped by briefly a while ago…" Art looked at Micky, who finished the sentence.

"He seemed agitated and asked his pal to hold onto some stuff for him."

"Such as?" I pressed.

"Computer files," Art said. "Kim hinted that they were part of some big investigative report he was working on…"

"These journalism students at NYU take themselves very seriously," Micky confided.

I nodded. "Woodward and Bernstein?"

Micky closed one eye and looked up into the sky. "After talking to his pal, I'm thinking more… what Art? Geraldo?"

"Definitely," his partner replied.

"What's in the files?" I said, worrying about where they could go with this.

"Hard to say, Connor. The files are password protected," Micky said. "What a pain. We got a guy back downtown who can deal with it…"

"Take a day or so, though," Art said thoughtfully.

"There may be another copy if Kim used the university's network to store files," I suggested. "He might not have encrypted it there because the school has its own security protections."

Micky looked thoughtful. "Whaddaya think, Art?"

His partner grimaced. "We'll need a different warrant. That, too, will take some time."

"Shit," my brother commented. "OK, we'll get that running. Thanks for the suggestion, buddy boy." Micky smiled at me. "But in the meantime, we're following up on some other loose ends."

I looked at him expectantly.

"Kim seemed like a pretty digital kind of guy, but even he wrote stuff down. Addresses, things like that. Sakura's was there. And so," he said nodding up the stairs toward the Dharma Center, "was this place."

"What's the link?"

My brother shrugged. "Beats me. That's why we're here."

"We knock on doors," Art confided to me. "Ask questions."

"But do you get answers?" I said to them. I had stumbled out of Changpa's meditation hall confused and disoriented. The sensation of calm warmth had started to fade as soon as I had left the lama's presence. I stepped into the clutter of a New York night, back into a world that hummed with disjointed activity. Pedestrians wandered by. The deep bass thudding of overpowered car stereos pulsed in the distance. Horns honked. Lights flashed on and off. And two cops followed the tangled ball of hint and possibility in any number of different directions. I felt numbed by it all.

I left them to their investigation and wandered off down the streets of Manhattan. Cars shot by in the darkness. Occasionally, faces would be revealed in the dark interiors, flashing by streetlights and flickering like the faint promise of meaning in a world built of questions.

18

FLASH

I threaded the gauntlet of various disgusted cop faces: front desk sergeant, tired-looking patrolmen, and plainclothes guys in rumpled suits as I made my way to Micky's desk. Their faces matched my mood. In its march to modernity the NYPD had been modifying the typical bullpen room, open and dotted with desks, to a brightly lit space with tasteful beige fabric partitions. But when you eavesdropped on conversations or looked at the paperwork, the esthetic effect faded somewhat.

My brother's cubicle was unoccupied. You couldn't say empty, since it was crammed full of paper. Dog-eared sheets spilled across his desk. Cardboard file boxes sagged in a corner. An old IBM Selectric typewriter stood on a small green metal table with wheels. A form of some sort was loaded in it, with spaces blotted by white-out. A Burke had been at work here.

A passing detective spotted me, checked my pass, and led me to a conference room, where Micky and Art sat sifting through documents with the excruciating patience of hungover forty-niners. My brother looked up when I opened the door.

"Unh," he said, and gestured me to a seat.

His partner was a little more talkative. "The computer guys have accessed some of Kim's files," he told me. "We've been going through the printouts most of the morning."

"What do you have?" I said.

"More shit than we know what to do with," Micky grumbled. He gestured at the papers. "Some of this is school stuff—term papers, notes. Other stuff was digital copies of photos."

"Stuff in Chinese," Art told me significantly.

"Calligraphy?" I asked. Maybe there was something here related to what Sakura had been sent. Whatever that was.

"Nah," Micky started, then corrected himself. "You tell me. Looks printed to me."

And it was. They were, in fact, official letters and documents of some sort. I didn't recognize the insignia on the letterhead, but the characters were easy enough to decipher: *Zhong-guo Renmin*, the People's Republic of China.

"So, what are you thinking?" I pressed. "That Kim took pictures of these documents for some reason? Part of whatever he was investigating?" I was disoriented. I hadn't shaken off the impact of my session with Changpa, as well as an irrational sense of impending danger. I had come to the precinct hoping to follow up on the links between Kim and the Dharma Center. What I got was more confusion.

"We figured out Kim's link with the Tibetan guy," Art said. "At least that's something." I looked up. "Yeah," he continued. "Kim was using the library at the Dharma Center to do research on Tibetan lamas."

I nodded, remembering the photos on the wall that the Rinpoche had shown me.

"As far as I can see," Micky said, "Kim was putting together a report on the fate of these guys…"

I was skeptical. "This is cutting edge journalism? The Chinese have been jailing these guys for years."

"Richard Gere seems to think it's important," Art offered.

Micky shrugged. "I didn't say I'd figured everything out. It's where we are right now..."

"Maybe you can take a look as well, Connor," Art prodded.

I hesitated. "This not really my area, you know. The shodo stuff is even a stretch..."

Art waved my protest away. "Come on. Asia is your thing..."

"Dig in, buddy boy," Micky said with grim determination. He pushed a pile of papers my way.

I sat back and got to work. After a while, I rubbed my eyes and told them, "Look, if I'm going to make heads or tails out of Kim's notes, I need some reference materials. The Tibetan stuff is confusing. Let me take copies over to the Dharma Center. They've probably got the best local collection in the area. And I can pick their brains if I get stuck."

They eyed each other. "Whaddaya think?" Micky asked Art.

His partner shrugged. "Why not? It's gotta be an improvement over where we are now..."

"Which is nowhere," my brother concluded.

They hovered for a while like mad wizards over a Xerox machine, then bundled up the copies and slipped them into a brown manila folder. They walked me to the door so I wouldn't get stopped.

"Technically," Art murmured, "we're not supposed to do this."

"That's half the fun," my brother told him.

I spent the day sorting through Kim's stuff and cross-referencing facts, looking for a pattern. A clue. By nightfall what I ended up with was a sad list of a bunch of Tibetan Buddhists who had been noted teachers and scholars. They still could be, for all anyone knew, but their fate seemed to be a mystery: after a long period of successfully avoiding notoriety, they had somehow run afoul of the Chinese authorities. I imagined the high, cold air of Tibet. Chinese prisons there would not be pleasant places.

I asked to see the Rinpoche, but was informed that he was traveling. I remembered that Yamashita had said they were going to visit Kita. It made me uneasy, but I figured the emotion was the result of a combination of residual anger, confusion, and frustration. My usual internal state. Then the skinny guy with the ponytail drifted in and told me there was someone on the telephone asking for me.

"They got it," Art told me, and you could hear the excitement even over the phone.

"Huh?" I had been reading all day and my brain was still engaged in the world of books.

"Sakura's scroll," he said. "You were right. Hoddington stashed it with his former students. The archery people." I knew that they had made a call to Georgia after Sarah had made the connection between Hoddington and his student, but it had been lost in everything else that had happened. Now, I felt a jolt of excitement.

"What's it say?" I asked.

"Damned if I know," Art admitted. "They sent a digital copy. It's calligraphy. Japanese, I guess. You need to translate it for us. Now." There was a scuffling noise and my brother came on the line.

"You stay put. We're on our way."

I was too anxious to continue reading. I wandered around the room and then went downstairs to watch the archers. Stark was there, hovering around with Andy, that same guy I had met at the museum. Stark's face clouded when he saw me, which wasn't surprising. I wondered whether Yamashita had said anything to him. Whether he was still training at the dojo. I ignored him, gave the teacher a bow, and watched.

The kyudo sensei was working with the archers—not on technique, but on the spiritual projection needed to use a weapon, any weapon, well. Sarah Klein was still away, but I could imagine what she would look like here, listening solemnly to everything he said, her eyes big with attention. I liked that about her. The sense of focus. Of paying attention to life's lessons. She seemed like someone who was alive to life's possibilities. And mature enough to appreciate them.

After a while, I went upstairs to wait. Soon the archers would bow out and it wouldn't be long before Micky and Art got there. I walked around the reception area, looking at the Tibetan art and killing time.

I checked my watch, went into the reading room and scooped up my file folder, then started down the five granite steps of the Dharma Center entrance. I figured I'd meet them on the street. As I came out into the night, I felt the change in air pressure and heard the faint rhythm of street sounds in Midtown. I looked down the block expectantly. It was dark, and the streetlights bled the color out of the world, while shadows clung at random spots in doorways and between cars.

I was eager to see what the Georgia police had turned up. The feeling I got as I came outside was from a different type of expectation, however. Behind me, I could hear the sounds of people preparing to leave the building. But that awareness was a distant one, muted by another sensation that was washing over me.

I felt a tightness on the skin. A visceral type of cognition that I had experienced before. But this was stronger, more immediate: the certainty of something out there, just beyond the threshold of consciousness.

It was the experience of *haragei*.

I moved downward like a man in a dream, one step at a time, feeling the stone surface with my feet while my whole attention was directed outward into the street.

Where something lurked.

There were pedestrians scattered up and down the block. I heard the murmur of traffic from Seventh Avenue. A car door slammed. They were the usual sights and sounds of a city night. But around the Dharma Center there was a shimmering sense of expectant tension.

The door at the top of the stairs opened and Stark and some other people came out. He looked uneasily at me. We hadn't spoken since the incident. A group of students was right behind him. Then Stark saw me, rooted to the pavement, and left the others on the stairs.

"What?" he asked quietly. At least Stark had the good sense to know something was up. It was the most genuine I had ever heard him. But I pushed the thought away and focused on the here and now. I held up a hand. Shook my head.

Other people began to crowd the entrance. As they did so, I heard the rubbery whisper of car tires. I looked up the block and a dark sedan, lights off, was slowly drifting our way.

There was laughter and good-natured conversation from people leaving the building. I was having a hard time concentrating.

I thought suddenly of the lama's vision—dark valleys where danger lurked.

"Get them back in," I told Stark. He was looking up the block, trying to see what I did. "Move," I hissed.

Stark jumped up the steps. I caught a look of bewilderment from one woman before she disappeared inside with the others.

Stark and Andy came back out and stood with me. They may not have been too bright, but they were willing.

Somewhere close by, a car engine whined into life. The noise sent a jet of alarm through me, an innocuous sound made sinister by my sense of fear. That darkened sedan was still rolling. As it approached, the driver's window whirred down. You got a glimpse of a pale face and dark shadows for eyes, looking us over. Andy's hand began to move toward his jacket.

"Don't!" I grunted.

The snout of a shotgun rode up over the door and toward us. I edged away from the two other men, hoping to space the target area out and reduce the impact of the blast. I was sure it was coming.

I could hear another car approaching down the block, but my attention was elsewhere, riveted to the shotgun's muzzle, which swayed back and forth, tracking each of us, like a snake seeking a victim. Most people aim a bit too high when they shoot. The rule is that you dive down and to your left. The movement can possibly take the shot off target and away from the left side of your body and the heart.

Then again, that little technique is predicated on the assumption that you're faster than a speeding bullet.

I knew Andy had the almost uncontrollable urge to go for what I was sure was his gun, but was also petrified he'd be the first one to be shot. I was not sure what Stark was thinking.

The man with the shotgun said something, loud and quick, and then the gun went off. I was down and rolling while my eyes were still blinded by the flash. I heard the whoop of a siren, a squeal of tires, and then a series of shots followed, handguns and shotgun mixed up. I could hear the sound of tinkling glass, a shout from my brother, and tires squealing as a car tore away.

Stark and Andy had thrown themselves down and were now slowly getting up. Micky and Art were crouched down behind the doors of their sedan. Its front grill was chewed up and leaked steam. Art was working the radio and you could hear distant sirens. To one side of us, a parked car had been mangled by the shotgun pellets as well. Its alarm system had been triggered and the horn bleated rhythmically into the night, like a wounded animal.

There had been a great deal of different noises compressed into a few seconds and my brain was trying to process things. I was still muddled with the flash and bang of the guns. I brushed myself off and took stock. Stark's face was pale even under the tan, and his mouth hung open. It didn't do good things for his jawline. Andy stood shakily, staring at the sidewalk.

By this time Micky was standing in the street, pistol up and facing the car as it sped away from him down the block. He was still hoping for a good target. "Shit!" he yelled, and the gun came down as the car sped around a corner.

We made statements to the NYPD. I tried to think coherently, but I just came up with images: the car and the face; a shotgun's snout and the cold, dispassionate review of victims; the electric thrill of fear as the gun went off; the smell of spent shells and concrete dust.

I tried to focus on relevant things. The man with the shotgun sounded Asian to me. It could have been Han, but in the dim light I couldn't tell. Yet his message had been very clear: *We want what's ours.*

I sighed. Don't we all.

The night wore on back at the precinct house. "Here's what I got for you," Micky told me as he put down the phone.

"Well, actually I made the calls," Art said. "Your brother wants to hog all the glory."

"There's glory?" I asked.

"Uh, no," he admitted. "But crime-stopping is a thankless business. You gotta take what little joy you can get."

"OK, we weren't as close to the shooter as you guys," Micky said. "Stark and his man Andy were not much help. The car windows were tinted and the shooter was hard to see."

"Yeah, I remember," I told him.

"Well, you weren't much help either," Micky protested. "From what you tell me, you were all too busy running for cover to notice much."

"True," I had to admit. "What about the car?"

My brother sighed. "Medium size, late model four-door sedan. Color could have been dark blue or green or black. Not much to go on, Connor."

"The taillights didn't look like a domestic model," I offered.

"Locals turned up a midnight blue Honda Accord coupla hours after the shooting. It had been boosted earlier from a pay lot."

"Well that's something."

Micky snickered at me. "Buddy boy, it's the most frequently stolen car in America. Could have no connection to you whatsoever."

But Art held up a hand. "It turned up on 11th Avenue." He looked at me significantly. "The West Side," he prompted. "Not too far from…"

"The Chinese Embassy," I finished.

"The freakin' Chinese again," my brother said. "We're running a test to see whether there's any gunpowder residue."

"How 'bout the gun?"

"Well, it's a shotgun," he started.

"Wow," I said, "you guys are really sharp." He didn't respond to my sarcasm, so I continued. "Can you get a make on the weapon?"

"Nah," Micky said. "It chewed up the cars pretty good, but all you can tell is what size load the shooter used. You can't do a ballistics match on a shotgun. We know that this is a pretty serious character though—he used 9mm pellets. Probably a combat shotgun."

"Great."

"Could be worse. Most of these things hold anywhere from five to nine rounds. If this guy really wanted you, there'd be nothing left but a grease spot on the pavement. Good thing we came along when he did. Probably scared him off."

I digested that piece of information while Micky went on philosophically. "So the shooter could've used any number of different weapons. Benellis, Mossbergs…"

Art said, "Did you notice a magazine on the weapon? Look kinda like an assault rifle? Or was it just sort of the usual configuration?"

"Guys," I said, "all I could see was that thing pointing at me. It looked as wide as a tunnel."

"OK, OK. Just asking. We're seeing some Saiga-12s on the street. Not many. They look like Kalashnikovs."

"Look," I said, "it was black and went boom."

My brother sighed. He questioned me for a while longer, but all we came away with was a sense of nighttime and noise and the bright flash of the combat load.

In my sleep, I trained, jerking restlessly in the vividness of the dream.

As the day died, the earth's breath grew cool and damp. Down in the hollow where the teahouse nestled, the light was blue. The small, rustic Japanese house was deserted. Just outside, water ran from a wide bamboo tube, falling into a stone basin. Small stones were arranged in the bottom to make the falling water gurgle. The blade of my sword was only a ghostly, shimmering silver presence as it sliced through arcs set down by masters long dead. A faint breeze rustled the top leaves of the surrounding trees, and it seemed like the murmuring of generations of teachers, watching me from a far place.

The sword of the samurai is a blade of razor sharpness and exquisite balance. The handle is wrapped in sharkskin and silk cords. The scabbard covered with a black lacquer so shiny as to faintly pick up the light from the emerging stars. Along the length of the blade, the wavy temper mark, or *hamon* seemed to glow.

I worked hard, alone in a clearing by the hut. Balance. Breath. Technique. Focus. The trick is not just to learn them; the challenge is rather to meld yourself with the sword and to create an elegance worthy of the weapon, to demonstrate the deadly esthetic my master demanded.

When I finally stopped, the moon was high and I was covered in sweat. I rinsed off at the stone basin, and savored the feel of the icy water sluicing down my back. I felt the heft of the blade and the play of night air across my wet body.

I brewed some mint tea over a small charcoal brazier kept in the house for just that purpose. I sat then, sipping tea, watching the coals in the hibachi glow and grow covered with ash. I could hear the small sounds of the woods at night. The errant whine of the occasional mosquito as it flitted by my ear. I felt worn out and yearned for sleep.

I closed my eyes in my dream and when they opened, the sun was setting once again, and shadows grew in the hollow where the Japanese hut stood, while the treetops on the hill above were washed in light the color of blood. I was walking, sword in hand, toward a clearing to train. And my dad was there.

My dad. Alive again. And he was Dad as I remembered him when I was a kid; not the way he was at the end. My father had fought cancer every step of the way. It was a retrograde advance of the type he had learned with the Marines in Korea, and he gave up each inch of territory stubbornly, waiting for us all to adjust to the inevitability of defeat.

But here he was, crouched by the clearing, squinting at me, and I felt like laughing and crying at the same time.

Dad! You're here! I began joyfully, then came up short. *But you're dead.*

He smiled at me and nodded, like it was a mild form of a joke. *Isn't that something?*

I wanted to laugh: it was just like the Old Man to treat coming back from the dead with such understatement.

I reached out to touch him with a yearning pent up over the years. He held up a hand and I stopped. He pointed off, up the hill toward the line of trees on the hilltop, silently commanding my attention there.

The clearing there was still well lit, but on the edges where the trees and brush stood, shadows were growing larger and deeper. From within a dark clump of foliage, Changpa drifted into sight. He looked toward us and the sun glinted on his eyeglasses. He reached up and removed them, showing eyes without pupils. His lids slowly closed and a spot in the middle of his forehead began to glow. He drifted backwards, fading into the shadows, and the light from his forehead shrunk into a small point, all but swallowed by the black.

Suddenly, Yamashita was there, peering after the lama. He paused to look down the slope toward me. As he turned his back on the darkness, something unseen dragged him slowly backwards into the inky spot where the lama had gone. There were screams from the depths of the shadows then, and the small point of light was suddenly snuffed out.

I felt as if I should race to my teacher's aid. But I also had an overpowering urge to be with my father. I began to weep with frustration, a small boy again, afraid of the dark and overwhelmed by the world.

I looked at my dad, seeking comfort, looking for direction, and asking a silent question. He smiled sadly at me, and the light around us began to fade until it was hard to see his face at all anymore. There was only the old, familiar sound of his voice.

Time to wake up now, Tiger.

I jerked into consciousness, wracked by sobs. They faded as I grew more and more awake, but the sheer emotional power of the dream didn't leave me. Tiger. It was what he had called me when, as a pudgy child, I had wrestled with him on the living room floor. I hadn't thought about that in years.

Dreams are things we shrug off, secure in the light of day and surrounded by the thousand things that both comfort and distract us. But when you strip away those distractions, life is revealed as more complex and more mysterious than you pretend. And then the messages in dreams linger, vivid and insistent.

In the half-light of dawn, birds began to call. I picked myself up, moving through the morning shadows, eager for light.

19

LINKS

Summer came down on the city suddenly, like the drop of a hammer. Parked cars cooked under a white-hot sun. Blinding light winked off the chrome and you could feel the heat steaming off the pavement. Merchants on the avenue wisely huddled behind plate glass storefronts, watching me impassively as I waded through the heat waves toward the Dharma Center.

The air was alive with more than heat. The imminence of danger danced around me as well. It was a logical conclusion—after all, someone had shot at me last night. But there was still the lingering experience of haragei. There was deep certainty here that went way beyond the results we in the West expect from reasoning.

The killings, the documents, the people. I was sure they all fit together somehow. But the more I reached out to connect them all, the more the elements scattered away, as if the effort at imposing order only created more chaos. I turned to the familiar world of written things in the hope that I would find a clue.

Copies of the inka that had been found in Georgia had been added to the growing pile of documents from Kim's computer files. I had worked through his research on the persecution of Tibetan monks, but came up with nothing more than an overwhelming sense of depression. The official documents in Chinese I left to one side, assuming they were source material for some of Kim's observations. I turned eagerly instead to the inka, figuring that its translation was something that I might actually have some success with. I'd fiddled with it on and off last night, but I wasn't very focused after the shooting. I hoped that the morning would bring more clarity.

The inka was a long document—a series of scrolls. I had flipped through the file quickly the night before, and today I had a growing feeling that there was a clue for me here. Someone had hunted for the inka with growing fury and urgency. Everywhere it went, people died. Surely, buried within the flowing lines of calligraphy, there was something important.

The inka was not only a certificate, but one connected with the martial arts. The carefully brushed characters sprawled down the page in the traditional format—top to bottom, columns reading from right to left. When you first start to read this stuff, it makes your head hurt because you want to scan it like an English-language document. But I had been at this long enough to know that the wisest course was to surrender to the dictates of the masters—Yamashita had taught me that, if nothing else.

I began with the premise that whatever was in the scroll was fairly convoluted, and that only someone with a certain expertise would be able to recognize it. Someone like Sakura could judge the quality of the calligrapher's hand, the authenticity of the ink and parchment, and all the technical dimensions of the inka. But he had sent it to another expert. Why?

Hoddington had probably read his share of scrolls, but he wasn't an expert in issues of provenance. He was a historian. I thought back to the book he was working on—a treatise on the war tales of the samurai. He was someone who knew that history backwards and forwards. Which made me suspect, as always, that the devil in this particular inka was in the details.

It was a long slog. A scroll of this type is not only a testimonial to the skill of its owner, but also a chronicle of transmission, listing names and dates of masters, each of whom forms a link in the chain. There are formulaic pronouncements interspersed, but they tend to be carbon copies of each other.

So I ignored the formula and concentrated on the names. In a few hours, I had a basic chronological listing with the associated details and dates. I stood up to stretch and decided to take a break.

I thought, for some reason, of Yamashita. Maybe he had never really been out of my mind. I was floundering around here, trying to make sense of things. Which was not very different from what I had done with Sensei. He had worked with me for years on methods for seeing clearly, for cutting through the fog of emotion and dealing with life. I thought about Changpa telling me of illusion and the challenges we faced along life's way. And what was my life? I'd been calling in sick to the university to spend more time on the investigation. Dorian was part of my life but, increasingly I realized it was not the important part. Yamashita and Changpa called me, it seemed, to a world where issues were both more vivid and more vital: where honor or disgrace, life and death, victory and defeat, ignorance and enlightenment were matters of paramount significance. And the difference between one or the other of these things was a matter not only of inches or split seconds, but of your fundamental response to crisis.

I thought of Sakura and Hoddington and Kim. About a sensei and a lama. I didn't come to any real conclusion, so I dismissed it with a favorite Japanese expression.

"*Shigata ga nai*," I muttered. It can't be helped. Then I took some deep breaths and focused once more on the inka.

The historical story the scroll told was a complex one. The transmission of traditional arts is done through lineages within the systems, so the identification of the people in that lineage is important. But it gets convoluted. The Japanese are big believers in family succession, but suitable heirs are not always produced. So individuals are adopted into lineages. This makes for a confusing mix of family names and titles. In addition, during the feudal period it was not unusual for samurai to change their names at different points in their lives. They could adopt a portion of a name bestowed on them by a lord as a token of esteem. Older swordsmen sometimes retired to a life of contemplation in their golden years, and often adopted Buddhist names in place of their former ones.

Then there's the dating method. Historical eras are dated by something called the *gengo* system. So years are expressed as "year 12 of a reign year X," named for the emperor who held office during that time.

The inka before me was the succession document for a martial ryu. It alleged to be an offshoot of the Yagyu Shinkage Ryu, one of Japan's most famous schools of swordsmanship. This was a surprise: there are two formally recognized branches to Yagyu, the Owari and the Edo schools, but I had never seen reference to this third variant. The more recent details of lineal transmission were a mystery to me: there are literally hundreds of these old ryu in Japan, even today. But I was interested in how this ryu, with such famous antecedents, had escaped most people's notice.

It told the tale of Yagyu Mitsuyoshi, the founding elder of the Yagyu Ryu, and how he invested a certificate of mastery on a promising warrior. I read it with interest, sure that there had to be an inconsistency somewhere. I had high hopes that it would be the name. Yagyu Mitsuyoshi is a well-known historical figure. But in his later years he adopted the Buddhist name Sekishusai. If the inka I was reading was somehow a fraud, it might show up in an inconsistency of naming. Depending on the date when the founding of the new ryu was supposed to have happened, the old master could have been using the name Mitsuyoshi or Sekishusai. But I knew most historical documents in the Yagyu tradition use both when speaking of him: he is identified as Yagyu Sekishusai Mitsuyoshi. Anything else would suggest a writer unfamiliar with the ryu's tradition.

My hopes were dashed. The scroll clearly stated that a certificate of mastery had been bestowed by Yagyu Sekishusai Mitsuyoshi in the twenty-third year of the reign of Emperor Go-Yozei. The era name checked out and I went on.

I worked through the lineage, but I realized after a time that this was way beyond my expertise. You would need access to records in Japan to go through it all I began to think it was a blind alley. Yet there had to be something here.

I took a walk around the block to clear my head. After the air-conditioned cool of the reading room, the stifling heat almost felt good. I glanced about for any sign of someone watching the building, of Han's hulking presence, but came up empty. Changpa was away with Yamashita and Sarah at a mountain retreat. I don't imagine that the place held much interest for Han now. The streets were fairly deserted, so I wandered without interruption, not thinking about anything in particular, just letting my brain rest.

The world danced in the summer heat, shimmering like an illusion, as if everything were flimsy and somehow not real. Like the sheets, I realized, that waited for me back in the Dharma Center. Documents lie.

And when I got back to my inka research, I looked again at the dates. The line of succession it detailed had a provenance that stretched back into the seventeenth century and connected to one of Japan's most famous swordsmen. All the way back to the twenty-third year of the reign of Go- Yozei. I did the mental arithmetic. It was 1609.

I rolled that idea around in my head and then it hit me. It was a very impressive pedigree. Except for the fact that Yagyu Mitsuyoshi died in 1606 and could not have bestowed the inka.

I ran for a phone. Because the person who was presenting this inka as a certificate of mastery was a fraud. And that person was identified at the very end of the document.

It was Kita Takenobu.

"That guy Kita's a fraud," I told Micky with a jet of venom in my voice. I thought with grim satisfaction about Stark's enthusiasm for Kita. His denigration of Yamashita. "I knew it all along. And Stark is probably involved somehow, too."

My brother seemed unconvinced. "How so?"

"C'mon," I urged him. "Think about the connections. He's Kita's student. He shows up in New York about the same time that Sakura gets killed. Then you've got him weaseling around Yamashita. And keeping tabs on Changpa." It all seemed obvious to me.

"Maybe," Micky said. "But your man Stark got shot at that night, didn't he? How's that fit?"

I thought about it for a minute. "Well," I stalled, "he didn't actually get shot, did he?"

"No," Micky admitted, "but he probably got the thrill of his life."

"How about this," I started, my brain jumping into high gear. "What if the shooting was just something staged to throw suspicion off Stark? Huh?" I was pretty proud of myself.

"I dunno, Connor," Micky replied, "it seems a bit elaborate, ya know?"

"I like him for it," I said.

"I know you do. Wait a sec." Micky cupped his hand over the phone and you could hear a muffled conversation take place. Then he was back. "OK, your instincts are good…"

"But…" I said, sensing what was coming.

"But there are a coupla things…" I waited and Micky continued. "We got no evidence that puts him at the murder scenes. Stark's shoe size doesn't match those found at either the Sakura or Hoddington killings. And we know he can be accounted for during the periods when Hoddington and Kim were murdered."

"How'dya know?" I asked, feeling a bit deflated.

"We checked, you dope," Micky said. "Whattaya think, our heads are made of wood?"

"Well," I said grudgingly, "I still think he's involved."

Art came on the line. "Connor, you gotta clear your head a bit about this one."

"How so?"

"There's something that bugs you about Stark. Maybe he's a creep. I dunno. But that doesn't make him a part of this. Trust me: the city's full of creeps. Some of them are murderers. Most are just pains in the ass." He said it wearily, as if it were a fact learned through hard personal experience.

"OK, Art. I hear you." I tried not to sound too skeptical.

"On the other hand," Art said brightly, "we have been making some major headway in getting Han tied to things."

"Like what?"

Micky broke in from the other extension. "We matched Han's prints to the partials we lifted from the Honda…"

"It's a partial match," Art noted.

"Not good enough for court…" my brother said.

"… but good enough for us to pull him in for questioning," Art finished.

"I still don't get the motive," I said.

My brother grunted. "Doesn't have to be one. Han's a psycho for hire from what I can see…"

"So who's doing the hiring?" I persisted. "You get any more on the Chinese connection?"

Micky snickered. "I called Charlie Wilcox. He says if he talks to me anymore, he'll end up reassigned to the Juneau office."

"We're getting close to having enough circumstantial stuff to pin the murders on Han," Art said thoughtfully. "Once we start questioning him the motivation will emerge."

"We know he flew to Atlanta the day before Hoddington was killed," Micky told me. "The word on the street locally is that he was the one who tortured Kim. Someone'll squeal."

"What about Sakura?" I asked.

Art recited the facts point by point. In my mind, I could see him holding up fingers one by one. "We got Han at Sakura's office looking for the inka. We got a shoe print at the murder scene that's consistent with the one found at Hoddington's cabin as well. And everywhere Kim's research material goes, Han shows up." He paused, then said, "And get this…"

"Sakura knew him," Micky blurted out.

"What!"

"Ran into him years ago," Art confirmed, sounding a bit annoyed that someone had stolen his thunder. "Some sort of community association for wayward youth."

"You know the drill," Micky continued. "Rich people donating their time so they don't feel so guilty about being rich."

"I wouldn't feel guilty," Art said.

"Me neither," Micky answered.

"That's because you're both so pure," I said sarcastically. It was lost on them.

"Anyway, as we know, Han was something of a bad boy early on, then got involved in martial arts. And he's kept up the interest."

Something went click in my head.

"He's about the size of a refrigerator," Micky added. "They nicknamed him 'the Mongol.'"

Another click.

I started to say something, then paused a minute, mentally lining up all the things I had found out and integrating them with the facts they were throwing at me. It's always hard for me to do this kind of thing, especially over the phone. But eventually I got it. Except for one thing.

"The thing I really wish we had is the motivation," Micky said. "For all of it. It'd be nice to have something a little more solid for the D.A. Something that gives us a reason for all the killing. That ties Han definitively into it."

Then it all started to come together and the answer flashed into my brain with a certainty that was startling. "I think you have that," I said.

They both answered together. One said "Huh?" The other said "What?"

"Something solid," I told them. It was my turn to stump them.

"Connor," Micky complained, "what the hell are you talking about?"

"A few things." And I told them about what I had learned from the files they had given me. The forged inka. And the clue in Sakura's last bit of calligraphy.

"I should have seen it sooner…" I told them.

My brother took a deep breath and pronounced his words slowly and separately. "Connor," he said. "What. Do. You. Mean?"

"Sakura's last calligraphy," I said.

"The death poem?" Art asked.

"It was more than a poem," I said. "He was also identifying the killer."

And I told them how.

20

KIMON

In old Japanese farmhouses, they would set an arrow into the eaves where the rooflines met in the center. It was mystically charged with protective powers to ward off evil and it was pointed north to *kimon*, the devil's direction. As my car pounded its way along the highway to the latest location for one of Kita's franchised mountain temples, I noted that I was heading north as well.

"How freakin' appropriate," I muttered under my breath.

Micky and Art wanted to take one last look in New York for the Mongol—" Most of these guys are morons, Connor," my brother had said. "We find them hiding at their girlfriends'." But they admitted that he had disappeared. When I heard that, I threw my gear into the car and took off. I had a sensation of lines flowing together, of Sarah, Yamashita and Changpa, and the Mongol converging at a point of intense danger. Micky and Art were working two angles, doing a last-minute sweep for the Mongol locally and getting clearance from their Lieutenant that would free them up to follow.

I didn't speak about my feelings to them. It didn't take much guesswork to figure out where the different threads in this thing led. The Yamaji East, Kita's newest training center, was sponsoring the seminar that Yamashita was attending. And he wasn't alone. As I thought about Changpa and Sarah Klein, in the clutches of Kita and probably Han the Mongol, the needle on the speedometer began to climb.

But cars have never been a high-priority item in my life, and after a while the vibration of excessive speed began to rattle the frame alarmingly. I eased off the gas pedal a bit, but it didn't make my stomach muscles relax any.

In summer, martial arts training camps known as *gasshuku* spring up all over the country. They're usually opportunities for people to engage in some concentrated, extended practice, train with new instructors, and get some R and R. Most martial artists are the equivalent of weekend warriors, and the chance to push their limits a bit is attractive, especially for black belts.

It's also not unusual to have different prominent sensei give seminars at these things. Martial artists have an insatiable hunger for new styles and techniques. The ninja I'd fought was the darker manifestation of that impulse. For most people, it's not so sinister. It's part enthusiasm and part American consumerism. Most people I know in the arts have trained in more than one system. For some of us, it's an evolutionary process of development. For others, it's an exercise in fickle delusion: when you hit the wall of hard training, you jump to another style. It's the martial arts equivalent of the hunt for the Holy Grail. It's not that the search isn't sometimes sincere. Just pointless.

Yamashita weeds these types out pretty quickly. I thought of the most recent group that had come to him, hoping to be accepted into his dojo. He has some mysterious criteria he uses for letting people in. You need some pretty good prior training, of course, that goes without saying. But that's not all.

A few days ago I had watched an applicant bow before him. Sensei sat and looked at the person. His eyes were dark slits and his face impassive. Sometimes you can feel the energy pulsing off him when he sits like that, and it's always interesting to see whether the aspirants pick up on it or not. Sometimes,

Yamashita asks questions. Other times, he lets silence wash over the room. And after a time, he makes a decision.

If the new student was looking for mysterious techniques and sudden revelations of hidden secrets, he was disappointed.

He stood expectantly, holding a wooden sword. My teacher glided toward him and simply said, "*Suburi*." The new student looked puzzled, so Yamashita added, "*shomen-uchi*." You hope that the new student is sharp, and he will begin the series of practice cuts to the head that Sensei just specified.

The new guy got the command to begin, but he hesitated. "How many times?" he asked the master.

Yamashita glared at him, and the look alone could pin you to a wall. "Until it is perfect," my teacher growled, and walked away.

It tends to quickly weed out the faint of heart.

Up in the Berkshires, the day was just as hot as it had been in New York, but the sky was bluer and cleaner-looking. Along the state road leading out of North Adams, the trees looked somewhat droopy along the roadway, but there was a small, rocky stream running along the side of the road that hinted at coolness in shaded places. The charm was lost on me.

Kita's Yamaji East was on the site of a failed recreation community—a few hundred acres perched on a hill studded with sugar maples and fir trees. At one time, this part of the Northeast had been almost totally clear-cut for timber—the stony slopes weren't good for much more. But you'd never guess it looking at the series of forested hills that stretched away into the distance as far as you could see, the green getting darker and bluer with distance. It made an ideal site for a summer training camp focusing on arts like aikido, *iaido,* and kyudo.

I thought about Kita: things I had heard, things I had learned recently. He was known as a maverick teacher, although supposedly quite a gifted martial artist. You'd see articles about him occasionally in some of the mass-market martial arts magazines, often appearing in action shots wielding a sword or spear, his long black hair flowing as the freeze-frame photography caught him in moments of posed ferocity. In interviews, he hinted at a personal history of esoteric training in various disciplines and seemed intent on creating a synthesis between the various Asian martial systems and meditation techniques. He spent a lot of time with Tibetan masters of one type or another. And his name had popped up in the notes of a dead journalism student.

They ate Kita up on the West Coast, where there was no shortage of martial arts freaks, celebrities looking for the cachet of a black belt, or lost souls seeking exotic salvation. That's how Stark met him, I was sure. Some Hollywood celebrities had been attracted as well. And their money followed. As a result, in the last ten years or so, Kita had slowly been building a little martial arts empire. There was a national organization, chains of schools, and a Web site that offered tantalizing yet incomplete glimpses of the hidden techniques of his system, fluff pieces on the great man himself, and an extensive retail outlet.

The Yamaji East was the latest installment in his franchise operation. The Mountain Temple was in reality not one place, but a series of locations. There was one in the Sere Hills above L.A., another in thinner air near Boulder, and even one in Florida. How he found a mountain there was anyone's guess. Maybe it was at Disneyworld. I thought that might be appropriate.

The latest acquisition was Yamaji East, here in Massachusetts. Kita was new to this part of the country and was hosting the summer seminar series as a way of establishing the Yamaji's presence, getting some respectability, and marketing himself to the martial artists in the region. I had wondered initially why Yamashita was bothering to attend, but my questions had gotten burned up in more immediate things. Now I thought about it again.

Perhaps, for all my skepticism, the complexity of haragei was greater than I suspected. Greater than just the cool electric thrill of approaching danger. If, for Changpa, the flow of time was a great heaving sea of future peaks, distant and hard to make out, did Yamashita share something of the same ability? And did he in some way sense that here, at this point and at this time, he would be needed?

He was right. He hadn't seen the inka, but even so, Yamashita's instinct was good. The scroll was a fraud, an attempt at making Kita's martial pedigree more respectable. It seemed that those who uncovered his secrets were killed. And Yamashita, a master of the deadly, close-quarters combat systems of the old warriors of Japan, knew that sometimes the best way to defeat an opponent was to get closer to danger, not to flee it.

I knew this as well. And more. But if it was initially an intellectual knowledge, it had an increasingly visceral feel to it. My stomach was in knots for the whole trip. I guided the car around the last few curves of the road and my tires made the bluestone that edged the roadway skitter off into the culverts on either side. I didn't know how I felt about my impulse to come to the Yamaji. Part of me avoided thinking about meeting my sensei again. But I knew I had to go. It wasn't just that I was worried about Changpa's safety. Or even Sarah Klein's. I was pulled along this path with the cords, invisible but strong as plaited silk, that had been woven over the years in the dojo. I thought ruefully about it: I could struggle against these things, but it was pointless. They were shackles I had helped weave myself.

A pupil, a deshi, follows in the footsteps of his master.

There was a pretty young woman at the compound's reception center. She had her blonde hair pulled back into the New Age version of a samurai topknot and wore a black polo shirt with the Yamaji crest embroidered on it in red. She was bright-eyed and greeted me pertly when I came in the door. The reception area was pleasant compared to the blazing parking lot, where my car sat, the engine pinging randomly as it cooled down.

"Good afternoon," she said. "Welcome to Yamaji. Are you here for the *gasshuku?*" She was already sliding a registration form across the desk toward me. "Things have been going on since the weekend, but I believe we have some room for late-comers." She smiled to let me know that she was willing to overlook my poor timing. A poster for the seminar stood on the counter, highlighting the activities we could all look forward to. There were some tasteful reproductions of old Japanese art-work around the room. And a Visa/MasterCard sticker prominently displayed in the front window.

"Actually," I told her, "I'm the assistant for one of the sensei at the seminar,"

She brightened a little at that. She'd been looking doubtfully at my car through the glass. Probably wondering whether my credit card would be rejected. I gave her Yamashita's name and she fingered her way through a bunch of registration forms. She frowned at me.

"I'm sorry, Mr. Burke, but I don't see a VIP registration for you." She didn't sound particularly sorry, but it didn't bother me. The Burkes rarely get VIP treatment anywhere.

"No problem," I told her. "Probably just a screwup. Let me register for the seminar and we'll straighten it out later."

She seemed happy at that, particularly after my credit card had passed muster. I got a packet of information with schedules, a map of the complex, and promotional material for many of the teachers running the seminar. She handed me my room key and gave me instructions on how to reach it. "Don't forget to stop by the Yamaji Gift Shop," she told me.

"I wouldn't miss it," I assured her.

She smiled artificially at me. Facetiousness is wasted on the young.

The complex sat on the crest of a wooded hill. The reception area was down on the lower end of the property. There was a good-sized parking lot filled with cars, many of them with martial arts bumper stickers and pretty embarrassing vanity plates like SAMUR-I. A five-foot-wide blacktop path led up the hill toward the meeting facilities and guest cabins. Cement stanchions at the beginning of the path served to prevent motor vehicles from using the path. The brochure noted that no cars were permitted beyond the reception area "to preserve the reflective aura of the Yamaji." There were a few local kids in short pants and Yamaji polo shirts waiting to give the infirm a lift up in electric golf carts, but I waved them away.

My schedule indicated the location of various seminars throughout the week. I knew Yamashita would be busy and I was still hesitant to see him, so I took the time to walk the grounds and get oriented.

The main path snaked up the hill, and different offshoots led to small cul-de-sacs where guest cabins were clustered. The terrain was well wooded, but you could see that the trees had been thinned somewhat to enhance a park-like appearance. There were jumbled slabs of rock back in the deeper woods, covered in moss. Birds chirped and a faint breeze rustled the leaves of the decorative white birch trees that were planted in small clumps at the points where new paths split off from the main road. My room was functional, one of four attached units in a cabin structure. It was predictably rustic and you got the faint damp whiff of the woods when you opened the window.

There was a large meeting building at the hill's crest. It also contained the restaurant. A built-in pool glinted in the sun, but there were few bathers. Off in various spots under the trees, open-air pavilions with wood-shingled roofs were scenes of intense practice by various groups of sweating, gi-clad people.

I consulted the guide that I had received when I registered. There was a great deal going on at the gasshuku—"Ten Days That Will Change Your Life," according to the brochure—but it was hard to see. The grounds of the Yamaji were laid out so that different areas were well screened by the curve of the land and foliage. In addition, different styles and sessions seemed to rotate around different locations. The only exceptions were the systems like jujutsu and aikido that needed mats, and kyudo, which required a hundred-foot-long field of fire.

I went by the archery area. A line of women archers moved in unison in preparation for shooting. They tipped the long arc of their bows forward and, with a focus and gravity that was almost magical, slowly sank into the seated position. They were impervious to the wash of strong light and heat, deaf to the whirring of insects in the distance. They gazed at their arrows in rapt attention, their energy building for the draw, the release, the cry of focused energy as their shafts sped across space, hungry for the target's heart.

From a distance, I saw Sarah among them, her white gi top almost blinding in the sun and her hair as dark as the shadows you glimpsed in the deep woods. I smiled at the sight of her and was relieved. My dream still haunted me, and I was glad to see that she was all right. I didn't let her see me: it seemed to me that whoever had actually read the inka was in danger. That included me, and I didn't want to drag her into it.

Finally, I found Yamashita working with a bunch of people from various aikido and jujutsu styles. They were dressed in blue or black hakama and white tops. You can often tell what style someone practices merely by looking at the type of knot someone has in the front of a hakama. Some iaido schools have elaborate systems for tying their hakama. My sensei uses a simple square knot: he's mostly concerned that the knot is properly placed and doesn't come undone. It's hard to be deadly while your pants are falling down.

When I finally saw him, I felt the currents of old anger mixed with something else. I remembered some of Changpa's advice. I had been trying to consciously avoid thinking about some of what he had said, but it must have been working on me subtly. Mostly, when I looked at Yamashita, I felt a type of comfort in glimpsing an important part of what had become my world.

Does absence soften the rough edges in people? If so, there was little indication here. The lesson that day made me feel as if I had never been away.

Yamashita was working with the students on variants of *tachi-dori*, the process of taking away someone's sword. *Aikidoka* work with many of the same types of weapons Yamashita uses, but I've come to see a difference. Whatever their level of practice, in most other arts, weapons training is ancillary to the heart of the system, and it shows in the technique.

I glided quietly to the edge of the practice area, nestled amid a grove of big pines. The wooden platform was open to the air, with a roof that was high enough to permit the use of swords. Trainees lined the periphery of the platform while my master demonstrated his latest point.

"No," Yamashita was saying forcefully. "You must focus!" He was letting a trainee try to disarm him. The guy seemed competent enough. He moved well and was obviously gliding in to set Yamashita up for a joint lock that would neutralize the older man's attack. But Yamashita wasn't budging. The guy moved in and made his move, but you could see my teacher set himself, extend energy, and refuse to be moved. It's a variant on the same technique I used on Andy the night we first saw the Rinpoche.

"What are you doing!" my teacher protested.

"I'm trying to control your center," his partner replied. I could see heads nod in agreement around the floor.

"My center!" Yamashita seemed puzzled. He looked at the man's hand as it gripped his right wrist. "Where is the danger here?" my master asked the man.

His partner looked puzzled. "Well the sword, of course."

"The sword," the sensei replied, sounding skeptical. "Then why do you attack my wrist? You say the sword is the danger, but you do not take it seriously. You grab—so," Yamashita glanced at his held wrist, "but the danger has moved." My teacher let go of his bokken with his right hand, pulled it away with his left, and brought the point to bear against the man's throat.

"Is the danger the sword or the man wielding it?" Yamashita asked.

"*Ki, ken. Tai,*" Yamashita reminded the group. "Energy, sword, body, all united as one." It was my turn to nod as I heard the familiar admonition. "All these things are together when we fight, yes?" I saw the respect being paid him reflected in the faces of the people around the training floor. "So when you attack, you must defeat all these things at once. You must break the link between them to defeat your opponent. The center..." My teacher almost sounded amused. "It is easy to talk of the center. But easy also to be distracted from it. Be sure you remember where the center is before you attack." He moved away from his opponent and brought his bokken up into the middle position. "Please," Yamashita invited the man.

His partner raised his own sword and came forward. The two men's weapons crossed at the tip as they met. They circled, regarding each other warily. As they rotated, Yamashita faced the edge of the floor where I stood. His eyes didn't even flicker in recognition, although I knew he saw me. His opponent stepped back and raised his bokken, the wooden sword held high overhead. Yamashita's response was subtle—he raised his sword a fraction and angled the blade portion to face his opponent's left fist. With real swords, it would have permitted Yamashita to slice his opponent's hand open if he struck down with his sword.

Other than that slight move, Yamashita was rock steady. The opponent sensed it and brought the sword down, bringing his leading left foot back behind him to increase the distance between them. I sighed quietly, knowing that it was all over.

In a flash, Yamashita shot forward, uttering a *kiai*, a shout that seemed to be generated from his hips. He came in on a tangent that would have allowed him to cut at the opponent's entire right side, but instead he attacked the bokken that the man held. The wooden weapons barked as they made contact, and the snapping authority of Yamashita's strike was so great that his opponent's sword was jerked from his hands and flew, end over end, into the bystanders.

There was a murmur of appreciation. But I wondered how many people had actually seen everything he was trying to show them. I had been with him for years, but even now I was still discovering new facets to old techniques.

Yamashita approached me and I thought of all the things I wanted to say—a swirl of emotions fighting to get out. But this is not the Japanese way. I knelt there on the edge of the platform, as any latecomer would, to formally request permission to join the group. I had done this thousands of times. The movements were so familiar as to be almost automatic, the sensations of kneeling, the feel of the careful placement of the hands on the floor before me, were old and unremarkable companions. Yet it was invested with a meaning that, while it may not have been noticed by the students standing around me, was real nonetheless.

Typically, when a student knelt to ask permission to enter a lesson in progress at his dojo, Yamashita would remain standing, give a quick jerking bow, and gesture impatiently for the student to join the group. Today was different. He glided toward me, weapon held formally in his right hand, the tip pointing to the floor and the cutting edge facing behind him. That was unusual. Most times, he gripped the bokken in his left hand, where it could be brought into action in a flash. This posture was one of unqualified greeting. Of respect.

Yamashita knelt down before me with the unconscious grace of a master. His face was fixed, impassive. I bowed deeply. He returned it. And as we straightened up we looked at each other for a moment. Then he smiled. "You are here," he said simply. And I felt an odd calmness wash over me. There is more than one way to disarm someone.

"I've seen the inka," I told him. "And more…"

Yamashita nodded. "And so?"

"I think there is danger, Sensei," I said quietly. I didn't want anyone to overhear me, but I also felt a bit self-conscious with the melodrama of the words.

"Think? I believe there is more to it than that, Burke…" He somehow seemed obscurely pleased. Then he continued. "Danger, yes. Of that, there is no doubt." He gazed at me and I thought I saw something like approval deep in his eyes. He looked about him reflectively at the waiting students. "I could have used you earlier, Burke," he said, raising his voice. "There is great danger here…" his eyes crinkled in amusement "… we are surrounded by hundreds of warriors. None of whom seem to know how to hold onto their weapons."

I understood that this was not the place to talk, and I nodded at the silent message he was sending me.

"Meet me here after the evening meal," my teacher suggested quietly. "We will walk and listen to the sounds of the forest at night."

"How's the food?" I asked him, trying to maintain the casual mood.

"The food is adequate. The coffee, on the other hand, is a disappointment." His words were sad, but his eyes twinkled.

21

TRUE BELIEVERS

Micky and Art had arrived late in the day, local cops in tow. My brother was fuming at how long it had taken to get the NYPD to react, and the technicalities of taking the investigation across state lines. The local cops politely questioned Kita's people, flashed pictures of Han the Mongol, and got the predictable shakes of the head. No one had seen him. Kita himself was in transit from L.A., so the cops would be back.

After the questioning, I had walked with them down the sloping black-top path to where their cars were parked.

"This is bullshit," my brother snarled. "Someone knows somethin' and they're not sayin'."

The local guy hooked a pair of aviator sunglasses over his ears and nodded without enthusiasm. He was broad-shouldered, but still young enough not to have gotten thick around the waist. "You're probably right." He had copper-colored hair in a buzz cut and light gray eyes. The name tag on his sharply creased uniform shirt said "Wallace."

"So where do we go from here?" Art asked thoughtfully. He rubbed the scar on his wrist absentmindedly. It was a new habit.

My brother eyed his partner and then looked away.

The local cop was talking. "We'll flash the picture of your suspect around some. Locals usually have a good handle on who's coming through these small towns," he said.

"Whaddaya think?" my brother asked his partner. "Hang around?"

"Sure. Why not?" Art said. He looked at Wallace. "You guys can back us up?" The cop nodded.

"Maybe you want to go with the locals down into town, Art?" Micky sounded hesitant. "You know, in case Han shows somewhere else. I can cover this end." It sounded lame, even to me.

Art flushed with annoyance. "So what are you sayin', Mick?" My brother held up his hands to calm his partner down, but Art continued. "What? You think I can't hack this?" Art turned away, hands on his hips, staring off down the road. "Shit," he said.

"OK, OK, forget it." Micky looked guiltily at the local cop. "We'll stake out the entrance here," Micky told him. "Wait for Kita."

Wallace looked from one to the other of the two men. He didn't say much, just thought about things for a minute, then nodded, although he didn't seem real sure. "OK. Anyone on the inside who can give us a heads-up if this fella appears?"

Micky nodded at me. "He can."

The local cop nodded slowly. "All right. The suspect shows up, Mr. Burke, you know what to do, right?"

"I'll call you," I said dutifully.

"And then run like hell," my brother added.

Later, as night approached, I found Yamashita. We sat on a park bench near a stream, facing into the woods. I wanted to tell him something of what I'd learned and he could sense the eagerness in me. It was just like him to force me into a moment of calm. But maybe it wasn't solely for me. Since my session with Changpa, I had tried to think about things from multiple perspectives. Yamashita could sense my agitation, but I was surprised to realize as I watched him react to passersby that he was on edge. The teacher-disciple bond cuts both ways: he could always read me, but increasingly I was able to read him as well. It made for silences alive with things unspoken. You could sense the faint tension in the air. It leaked off him like the buzz of a transformer. He was very careful with what he said and he kept his voice low when we spoke.

"So the police finally found the inka?" he asked. I nodded and he went on. "And what does it tell us? Does it provide what you had hoped for?"

"It's a fraud," I said. "Kita's pedigree is a fabrication."

He didn't act particularly surprised. *Did you know something all along?* I wondered. But I didn't ask.

Yamashita held a hand up, patting the air in a gesture meant to make me lower my voice. My teacher had changed his clothes and wore an old pair of khaki pants and a spotless white t-shirt. He's not a tall man, and seated on the bench he could wiggle his legs to and fro, his zori sandals lightly scuffing the dirt in front of us. He looked slowly about to check for people nearby. Then he peered deeply into the woods where the outlines of rocks and tree trunks were slowly fading in the dusk.

"Indeed," Sensei finally said. "He has built his world on a lie. Yet do not be fooled. Such a man is not without skill." My teacher looked at me. "You should take the time to observe his students, Professor. There is something to learn here."

I nodded, but knew he was seeking in some way to rebuild the links between us with the mundane issues of training. I dropped that thought for one more pressing. "Kita, Han… and Stark. They're up to something."

"Ahh, Stark," Yamashita said, nodding. "I sense… confusion, not evil in that one." Yamashita smiled to himself. "But each student is a different type of trouble."

"The Rinpoche thought Stark was going to be in some sort of danger," I reminded my teacher. "I don't think that he was seeing things clearly. I think that maybe Stark is part of the danger."

"Perhaps," Yamashita said, seeming to be unwilling to take it further. He got up and stepped down the slope to approach the stream. He skipped lightly across the rocks and entered the darkening wood. I followed and the gloom covered us like fog.

"Today when I was instructing the trainees," Yamashita began, "do you remember my admonition?"

"Sure. The need for focus. Controlling the center."

"I cautioned as well against being distracted," he told me. He heard me take a breath but began talking before I could respond. "I, too, am worried, Burke. But I think there are more important things to worry about than Stark. The police think that this man, Han, has murdered three people, *neh*? And yet from what you know of him, we would assume that his motives would be… mercenary."

"That's what Micky thinks," I told him.

"Indeed. And we must respect his insight in this. So… Han is a weapon. But he cuts only where directed. Who directs him?"

"Kita," I suggested.

"Perhaps," Yamashita answered. "I know that for a man like Kita, the secret of the inka is one that must be kept. His pride would demand it. And the pride of his followers…"

"But is it enough to make them kill to keep the secret?" I asked. I had to be honest. Even at this point I wasn't sure. You could hear the vestiges of disbelief in my voice.

"I do not know. An emotion like pride is a powerful force, certainly," Yamashita said quietly as he slowly moved along a faint path in the woods. "These are proud people." He looked at me. In the fading light his eyes were lost in dark shadow. "You know something of this. For Kita's disciples it is an immature pride, but it is powerful nonetheless."

"Like in Stark," I suggested.

He ignored the comment. "Pride can blind us to the truth," Yamashita told me. "Or make us unwilling to admit it. Emotion is like the darkness that makes a path hard to follow."

I made a misstep and a small rock clattered against another. Yamashita stopped and waited for me, a ghostly form in the gray light that was thickening into black.

"There may be more here than we understand," my teacher continued. "It seems as if violence follows those who have read the inka, but surely this journalist who was killed…"

"Kim," I supplied.

"… Kim was working on more than just this?"

Maybe it was the illusion of anonymity in the darkness, but it made it easier to talk with him. "There's the Chinese angle as well. What's Han up to with them?"

"Ah," he said significantly. "The Chinese. Do you know that a group of *Wu-shu* artists were invited to perform here at the last minute?"

Wu-shu is the modern, highly acrobatic martial performance art of mainland China. It's heavily subsidized by the central government. But I didn't see how it was relevant.

My teacher sighed in the darkness. "It seems to me that there are… minders… with these artists. People who do not seem particularly interested in the training here."

"This gets more tangled by the minute," I admitted. Then I realized something. "So here we are and all the loose ends are coming together. Kita, the Rinpoche, the Chinese. All that's missing is Han." In the gloom, I thought I could see a small smile crease his face. "You knew there was a connection some-how. That's why you came. To finally figure it out." I felt equal parts relief and exasperation. Yamashita sensed the danger, but was no clearer as to its ultimate source than I was. "You should have told me before you left," I said.

Yamashita hulked before me, almost indistinguishable in the gloom. "Burke, coming here was dangerous. It may even be a type of trap. I sensed it vaguely, but was unsure. Even the Rinpoche did not see the full extent of what we face…"

"Does he have any ideas about what's going on?"

"He arrived yesterday and has kept himself in isolation. I have been unable to see him."

I briefly wondered whether Changpa was hiding or whether Kita's people didn't want him communicating with Yamashita. But I couldn't let go of Yamashita's reluctance to tell me things.

"You should have told me," I said again. "I've earned your trust." It wasn't the first time I'd had to remind him, and we both knew it.

My teacher's voice was tight and hard. The words punched out at me through the darkness, their impact heightened by the night and the silence around us.

"Burke, I do what I do for good reasons. It is not your place to question me." The rebuke heightened the tension in the dark air. "I am your sensei. All these years you struggle. But with this above all things." And his tone was one that made me feel like I was a fool.

My ears burned. I started to say something, but he fore-stalled me. "Think! See! There is more to things than what is on the surface."

Then I heard him make a small sigh. "If I had told you what I suspected," he said, and his voice was gentler, more intimate, "you would have come with me without a second thought. Yes?"

"Yes, Sensei," I answered tightly.

"You would have had danger thrust upon you," he said quietly. "I know the toll that such things take on people… I know what it has done to you in the past," he added quietly. "It is not something undertaken lightly."

"But I'm here," I said to him, demanding recognition of the fact.

"Ye-e-s" he said slowly, letting out a long breath. "But you have chosen to do this of your own free will. I did not force it on you. You have chosen the path for yourself. It is as it should be. As a student, your choices are made for you. As a warrior, you must learn to make them on your own." He sighed, a soft sound in the darkness. "It is a difficult thing…"

I nodded, even though he couldn't see me. My stomach churned and I felt off-balance. My teacher has that knack: every time you think you've got him figured out, or that he's shown you all there is to show, he surprises you. And it forces you to look at things again, with new eyes. Even in the darkness.

I breathed slowly and listened to the sounds of the night. You could hear branches creaking in the faint evening breeze. Leaves fluttered high overhead in the canopy. A mosquito buzzed around my head. Somewhere farther up the slope, something hard struck a rock, making a deep thump. My heart, which had slowed down, leapt in alarm, echoing the noise from deep in the woods.

"The deer are on the move," my master said. "They hide from danger during the day and move when they think it is safe."

"It is not safe for us, Sensei," I ventured, with a certainty that surprised me.

"No. It is not. But we must wait and watch. Kita himself will not arrive until tomorrow. Nor has this man the Mongol appeared, as far as I can tell. You saw what I did this afternoon during the tachi dori lesson?"

"Part of *rippon-me* of the *kendo-no-kata*," I said. It was a basic lesson.

"*Hai.* I waited and used seme, pressure, to force his hand. We will do the same." I felt him brush against me as he moved back down the path.

We. I walked in his footsteps, heading out of the woods toward the faint distant lights of the Yamaji, which shone like a false hope through the trees.

Morning is a long time coming in the hills. The day seeps in with a wash of light and it is hours before sunlight pops over the rim of ridge tops and warms things up. In the woods, the green forest breathes cool vapor at night, and dew is everywhere. It's as if there's a reluctance to let go of the cover of darkness. Or maybe it was just me. I had a feeling that the day would bring hard revelations.

But you do what you have to, not what you always want.

Yamashita was right: the coffee was terrible. I'd wandered over to the cafeteria in the faint light before things got started. I ended up tossing the dregs of my cup into a bush. It wasn't a judgment call; it was time to run.

The gasshuku featured a dawn run every morning. Folks met at the conference center, straggling in by the twos and threes, jerking and bobbing around in an attempt to warm up. You could see that some people were a bit stiff from all the activity of the last few days. I saw more than one person gulp down a few Tylenol with their breakfast.

In keeping with the martial theme of the whole seminar, most folks wore some part of their training uniforms. Gi pants seemed popular, along with t-shirts with dojo logos. I opted for my running shorts, even though the air was still cool. I also wore a shirt that Micky had given me years ago. There was a big picture of a pint of dark, creamy stout on the back. And under it, the words, "it's not just for breakfast anymore." We all have statements of some sort to make, I suppose.

There were trails threading through the woods all over the mountain that the Yamaji stood on. The Appalachian Trail ran by here and the woods were also crisscrossed with old logging roads. We ran along some of them. After the first quarter mile I had warmed up and my breath matched my movements in an old, familiar rhythm. It let me think about what had happened and all the elements in play.

After the run, when people went off to their different classes, I wandered around. I noted the location for the wu-shu people and drifted by. They were wiry and compact, exploding across the performance space in single and paired forms. Some used swords. Others spears. They were tremendously flexible, and leapt and tumbled in actions that were as much shaped by the entertainment traditions of Chinese opera as they were by fighting arts. There were coaches around, older men in tracksuits, watching the performance with a stoic expression. But not all the watchers were focused on the action. I saw one man notice me as I came into view. I couldn't see him clearly, but I thought it better not to be too conspicuous. So I pretended not to be interested and wandered off in another direction.

I went hunting for the lama. It wasn't difficult: the Rinpoche traveled with a few other monks and their robes made them easy to find. I lurked around some of the meditation sessions and followed one of them back to where they were staying.

The Tibetans occupied a whole cabin complex of apartments, nestled in a cul-de-sac. I drifted by, watching from a distance, and saw a few Yamaji employees posted at strategic spots on the path leading to the cabin. From what I had seen, there were two broad classes of Yamaji people in the organization: attractive and fit-looking young women who handled the public relations aspects of things, and the other guys. Men tended to dominate the technical aspects of the operation. Some looked Asian, but many were Westerners. And they weren't particularly pert. I much preferred the women.

It was the non-pert segment that lurked near the Tibetans, however. They were big and brawny and were obviously not hanging around in the hopes of learning more about the wheel of karma. I knew muscle when I saw it.

So I slipped into the woods and made my way around back. There was a private patio that led off the largest of the cabin apartments. Sliding glass doors opened onto a wooden deck. A neatly kept lawn led off for another thirty feet before the trees took over. It made for a splash of warm light in the morning cool of the woods. I moved quietly through the trees, grateful for the muffling effect of pine needles, and waited. Changpa's gift of sight was something that made him peer into the darkness a lot. But I was betting that even he yearned for the sun at times.

I thought of Yamashita's admonition to wait, and I stood quietly, leaning against a pine tree. Birds called in the distance. I could smell the pine resin in the air. The sun rose and insects danced in the bright light that washed over the grassy clearing.

The glass doors to the cabin slid open and the Rinpoche emerged. He was dressed in his robes, yellow and red that exploded into more vibrant color as he moved out from the shadows. He held a cup and saucer in his hands and walked slowly around the deck. It seemed that he was alone.

He moved to the edge of the wooden platform. His face, which had clearly reflected a man thinking hard about something, gradually grew slack. He set the cup down on a table and, removing his glasses, stared off into the distance, motionless.

I stepped out of the woods and stood there watching him. I didn't say anything, just waited for him to notice me. His eyes looked unfocused and he gave a sort of sigh. The eyes began to roll up into his head. Then he closed his lids for a moment, and when he opened them, I had moved across the grass to stand in front of him.

He focused on me slowly, like someone whose attention was coming back from a great distance.

"It is really you," he said. He almost sounded frightened.

"In the flesh," I answered.

Changpa threw a hurried glance around and beckoned me into his apartment. He locked the door and listened carefully for a moment.

"Dr. Burke," he began, then seemed at a loss as to what to say.

"You're in danger, Rinpoche," I told him.

I explained about the material Kim was collecting: a history of persecuted monks. A profile on Kita Takenobu. The fabricated inka. "I don't have all the pieces put together," I said, "but the links are clear. There are secrets here that Kita wants hidden. And someone is doing the dirty work for him." I told him what I knew about Han. I went on, and asked him whether he thought Stark could be involved.

Changpa winced. "He is a troubled young man, Dr. Burke. And yet, even so, I cannot believe this of him…"

"You might have to believe it," I said. "Think about things… he arrives and starts sticking his nose into security issues with you. Works to screen access to you?" The lama nodded in affirmation. "Tries to keep people from bothering you?"

The monk sat down in a chair, wearily. "Dr. Burke… I sense… turmoil within him. Nothing more. I still have hopes that he will come to a type of clarity."

Clarity would be very nice, I thought. And something in the lama's voice gave me the sense he had something else to tell me.

"Rinpoche," I pleaded, trying to figure out a way to make him tell me things, "the darkness you saw… the valley. We are being drawn into it. And you saw that Stark was there, too."

He smiled sadly at me. "My visions. There are many ways of knowing, Burke. I am convinced that someone, perhaps the Chinese government, wants me silenced. And someone has silenced the poor men who were murdered. But are these things related? I cannot see how. If they are, why am I not dead as well?"

I shook my head in an inability to respond.

"I have no real links to this man Kita. Why should he be interested in me? It makes no sense."

I sat forward, eager to make a point. "But you have said there are other ways of knowing. I'm coming to understand that." He looked at me fondly, as you would at an apt pupil.

"There's something brewing here, Rinpoche," I told him with urgency. "Surely you must sense it? What does your inner eye tell you?"

He sighed. "I do not see everything, Dr. Burke. There is danger, yes. But there is always danger. I was drawn to seek help from an old friend and his student, but in my visions I never saw the roles you would play." He stopped for a second and looked out into the bright clearing, a splash of light at the end of a dark room. "Even now it is occluded."

"What do you see?" I asked in a small voice, still hopeful.

He squeezed his eyes tightly shut. Whether it was an attempt to see better or to block the vision out, I couldn't be sure. He sat heavily in a chair, his big hands in his lap. He said nothing.

"You should leave," I told him.

He shook his head. "If I may. They watch me, you know." Then he seemed to summon himself and sat up straighter. "No. I will not leave. I still hope for Stark…" He looked up at me and smiled sadly. "The Lord Buddha knows our understanding is feeble, but he wishes our compassion to be as boundless as the ocean."

What do you say to something like that? I left him, slipping out the glass doors and into the woods. The lama sat very still in his chair, focused on things only he could see.

Yamashita Sensei was waiting. He wanted me to lead a practice session of aspiring swordsmen, a mixed group of men and women who were clearly less than enthused to have me teaching them instead of Yamashita. My teacher had been somewhat cryptic about what he was going to be doing while I led the training, but his expressionless face told me volumes. He would prowl the Yamaji. Probing for weaknesses. Watching for danger. There was a restless vigilance to the man, even at the best of times. It was the mark of a survivor.

I stood before the class in a sunny clearing. The grass underfoot was well tended and short, but there was enough irregularity in the ground to make things challenging for all of us in bare feet. There were going to be some stubbed toes today.

I worked with the group on a distance exercise, one designed to keep the combat interval, *ma-ai*, at an optimum level. In practical terms, I tried to get the pairs of students to be able to keep their bokken in contact, the tips crossed two to three inches below the sword's point. When Yamashita crosses swords with you, it's like there's a magnet in his weapon and it sticks to you no matter what. It sounds easy, but when two people are moving around seeking an advantage, it's not. The trick is to relax and keep centered, but that's pretty much the trick for everything in life—easy to say, hard to do. I've gotten so that I can do it, but it's a strain, even after all these years.

Stark strode over, dressed in the black uniform of Kita's system. He carried a wooden sword. I called for a break and went over to him. Whatever comfort we had once developed with each other had evaporated. Stark's face seemed stiff. "You're here," he said simply. "You shouldn't have come."

"I know what's going on, Stark," I said with a low urgency. He looked startled for a moment, then confused.

"I don't know what you're talking about," he said. But his eyes looked like he was hiding something.

"What did you come to New York for?" I persisted.

"To study with other masters," he said simply. "The Rinpoche."

I almost believed him. "Changpa Rinpoche doesn't teach what you're interested in," I said. I saw his eyes shift a little and knew he was hiding something.

He shrugged. "Kita Shihan has respect for the lamas."

I looked hard into his face, but couldn't pierce the look of flat sincerity he had generated. He could have been telling the truth. Or at least part of it. But he was uneasy. Stark sensed my skepticism. He looked at me with narrowed eyes for a minute, then gestured with the sword. "I thought I'd help you give your people a run for their money."

The shift in topic clinched it for me: something was going on here. "Thanks," I told him. "You're just full of good deeds these days. How's Sarah Klein?"

Again, I got the sense of an emotional shift taking place just below the surface. "We spend some time together," he said evasively.

I wanted to choke him. Could he be so oblivious to the danger he was putting her in? I was convinced that contact with people involved with whatever Kita was up to was danger-ous. Was Stark really that oblivious? I wanted to think about it, but the students were looking at us and I called the class back into order.

Most of them had been at yesterday's session and had seen Yamashita disarm his opponent. They asked to see me demon-strate it again. Part of it was enthusiasm for the technique, but there was another, less innocent undercurrent. Martial artists, even the best of us, have a predatory urge. In time, with good training, it gets sublimated, but it's still there. There's always a subtle urge to gratify it. I caught the looks on some faces. They wanted to see whether Yamashita's senior pupil was up to the skill level of his master.

I looked reluctantly about for a partner and Stark spoke up. "Here you go," he said in a low voice as he took his place before me and brought his sword up.

We crossed swords and I felt the buzz of tension flowing off him like a current. I couldn't figure him out. Did he really know something and was here to keep tabs on me? Or was this something more basic, like simple rivalry? Out of the corner of my eye, I glimpsed a few of his black-clad friends drifting over to watch. There was a look of satisfaction on Stark's face, and I wondered whether there wasn't more than one motivation working in him.

We began to circle each other, looking for a *tsuki*, a gap in concentration, that would permit an attack. It was early afternoon, so the sun was still high. It was a good thing. A classic bit of strategy is to maneuver an opponent so that the sun is in his eyes. I was spared that, but I was a bit worried about the irregularity of the ground. Stark had on sandals. I was barefoot. It only takes a small pebble, unfortunately placed, to bruise a heel, and in the fleeting moment when you wince in pain, a flaw appears in your defenses.

I worried too much, and it must have showed. He used the distraction and struck out at my right wrist in a quick, tight snap. Stark had always had potential, and the short time with Yamashita had brought it out. I dropped my arm down to avoid the strike, pivoting away from his attack, but even so he caught my forearm and it buzzed a little bit from the blow.

I came back and tried to ride his sword blade down, but he swept it out and back behind him. It was nice technique, but the set up for the head strike he followed with took a shade too much time.

I parried the strike and countered, using the force of his strike to help me whip my sword around. I brought it down, reaching for his right clavicle. He backed away and I recovered, thrusting out at him and hoping that the jabbing sword point would send him reeling. But he had trained in my dojo and he knew the technique. He parried it with an easy movement and a twist of the hips. I circled away, out of range.

It was hot there in the sun. I felt the eyes of the onlookers measuring me. And as he came at me again, I realized that the ferocity of the attack made this something other than a training exercise. I had watched him in training these last few weeks. And training takes place at a high level of intensity, but it's not as high as a real fight. Now Stark was going full throttle, driving for the decisive result he had been seeking ever since we met at the kendo dojo.

The realization of what was happening meant that I had to shift mental gears. There is, after all, fighting. And then there is *fighting*. It's a point I continually try to bring home to people in Yamashita's dojo. They don't really get it—it's something you have to experience for yourself. But it's not something I wish on anyone.

In the next few minutes he had clipped me any number of times—I'd have welts by dinner—and I'd gotten a few good shots in myself. But I had been slow to focus on the seriousness of things, and the match was going on way too long. Any time you fight, time is your enemy. It saps your energy and exposes your weakness. The best strategy is a lightning attack, but you've got to be good. Or lucky.

Some days I'm neither. In my concern for the behind-the-scenes hunt for the killer, I had not taken the gasshuku itself seriously. Maybe I hadn't taken Stark seriously, either. And now I had to ramp myself up for the type of effort this fight was going to require.

He tripped me at one point, and I felt myself going down. Your instinct is to fight it, but there is a deeper, truer series of reflexes and Yamashita had worked to bring them to life in me. So I surrendered myself to the fall and rolled out of it, a split second ahead of my opponent's follow up blow. I rolled onto my knees and pivoted around to face him. My bokken was set between my outstretched hands to catch the force of his strike, coming straight down for my head.

"Enough!" The voice like thunder. Yamashita stood there, swelling with indignation.

I stood there, breathing hard. Stark reluctantly backed away, the energy slowly bleeding out of his form. Sensei dismissed the class. The students didn't say much, just milled around making muttered comments to each other.

Yamashita was tight-lipped. "What is the meaning of this? Burke, I left you in a position of responsibility. You were to teach these people. Not engage in… acrobatics." The unspoken message in his eyes was one of the need to avoid distraction. As far as he was concerned, I had failed.

Stark said to me, "You think that was tough, wait until Kita Shihan gets here with his advanced people." He was breathing deeply, but it was under control. Then, in a voice that was half warning, half insult, "You shouldn't have come, Burke."

"Idiot," my teacher barked, rounding on him. "There is more to this than you know." Stark blanched under Yamashita's anger, but was smart enough to stay silent. "You look at things, but do not *see*," Sensei hissed. "Go. Think carefully. A time is coming for you."

"A time for what?" Stark asked.

"Decisions," Yamashita said, then wheeled away from the two of us.

22
TANREN

Kita's arrival was marked with tremendous fanfare. There was a flurry of activity among the Yamaji staff and, although no one actually saw him, word of his presence spread. I snuck down to tell Micky, but it's true what they say about cops—they're never around when you need them. Then I tried to call my brother, but his cell phone didn't work in the mountains. I ended up phoning his precinct house and asking them to relay the message.

Late in the afternoon, there was a reception at the conference center. The senior instructors lined up to one side of a dais, Yamashita with them. I knelt behind him. Other advanced students sat on either side of me, each behind his or her own sensei. We looked across the floor to where Kita's disciples were, a mass of serious, yet excited people in black. The gasshuko participants formed an audience to our right, and their expectant hum filled the reception hall. As we waited, Changpa and his retinue walked slowly in and were seated in a place of honor on the dais.

I saw Sarah Klein enter and slipped over to see her. She was waiting expectantly with the other kyudoka for Kita's appearance and didn't spot me until the last minute. Her serious heart-shaped face broke into a smile. "Burke!" she said and reached out to touch me.

"Let's go outside," I murmured. It was dangerous for our connection to be too apparent, and I hoped it would get lost in the excitement. Sarah looked concerned, but nodded and followed me out through the crowd. It wasn't difficult: most people were focused on getting into the hall, not getting out.

I steered her around a corner where we'd be out of sight of the main entrance. "I didn't expect..." she started. But I cut her off.

"Listen, Sarah. I need you to be careful. Things are happening here."

Her eyes got wide. "Related to the murders?"

I nodded. "Kita's involved somehow."

"Kita!"

"Keep your voice down," I urged her, and cast a quick glance about for anyone watching. So far, so good. "I'm not sure what's really going on, but the mysterious inka shows that Kita's a fraud." Sarah had picked up enough of the tense urgency in my voice not to bother interrupting. She listened carefully as I gave her a quick description of Han and his probable involvement with the murders. "If you see this guy, get away and tell my brother Micky. He's around somewhere."

She reached out and touched me softly on the arm. "I've never met your brother, Connor." Her voice was quiet.

"He looks like me, only taller, thinner. Crankier. Mustache. White streak in his hair. He'll be down by the reception area."

She smiled a little and you could see the thought processes behind her eyes as she digested the description.

"I don't want to let anyone see me with you," I explained. "It might make things dangerous for you."

"What do I know?" she said.

"You know me. It might be enough." She hadn't broken off contact when she touched me, and now her hand slipped down to hold mine.

"It's that dangerous, Burke?" She swallowed as she said it, and you could see the neck muscles tense.

I didn't answer the question. "You just stay low and keep your eyes open. And Sarah," I pulled her gently a little closer to me and felt a curious tense fluttering in my stomach that was generated from her nearness. "Keep tabs on the Rinpoche. He may be in danger as well."

"Why me?" she asked. It's the classic response when people first get exposed to these sorts of situations. After a while, if you want to come out the other end, you stop wondering about things and just get on with it.

"I trust you," I said.

Something flickered in her eyes. "Oh, Connor," she said, and her voice sounded shaky, "I've got to let you know something..." She licked her lips as if summoning up nerve. "About Travis. And me."

I gave her a small, tight smile. I'd figured a few things out over the last few hours. "You don't have to explain." She did anyway. How she had met him in California and they had lived together. The breakup and her move to New York.

"And he just showed up," she said in a rush. "I never encouraged him in any way..."

I put a finger on her lips and smiled again. Explanations weren't necessary. Stark had ulterior motives in coming to the Dharma Center, all right. But they were much more basic: he just wanted his lover back. At least now I had figured that much out. Maybe I was becoming a sort of detective after all.

"It's OK," I said. "We'll talk about that later. Right now, I need you to make sure that the Rinpoche will be safe. With any luck, you're not on these people's radar screens yet. I've been watching. They don't tend to associate women with competence. All the power positions are dominated by men." Her eyes narrowed as she thought about it. "They don't know you," I explained, "and that gives us an advantage. You can do it."

"Can we just wait for the cops?" she asked.

"I think things are gonna play out too fast. And there are too many loose ends…"

"What will you do?" And she looked at me searchingly.

"I've got to follow Yamashita's lead," I explained. *Simple really. You blunder around until someone makes a move, and then you fight back.* But I didn't say it.

She saw it in my eyes. She gave my hand a squeeze. "We better get back in," I told her, and my voice was husky with all the other things I should have said. I sent her in ahead of me and I slipped in a side door. Then we were swept along in the flow of events. Kita had arrived.

He appeared like smoke. One minute the dais was empty, the next he was there.

Kita had long shoulder-length black hair, shot with gray, that swept back from a wide forehead. His eyes were dark and glittered in the light. His mouth was held in a tight line as he looked with a dramatic intensity at the audience. He held his hands together in the traditional gesture and bowed in respect to the Rinpoche and his monks. They responded in turn. Then Kita slowly turned his gaze toward the seated sensei.

There is a type of energy projection that can be done, even without much physical movement. It's usually associated with a shout—the famous kiai. The projection of ki is an elusive skill at the best of times, and it's rare to experience it in stillness and complete silence. But the energy poured out of Kita with an odd concussive force that was startling.

Yamashita sat stock still. He must have felt it, but he gave no sign. I saw a few of the other sensei turn to look at each other significantly: they had sensed something as well. Kita continued to stare at the teachers with that fierce, predatory look. Then he slowly bowed in the direction of the other instructors. They bowed back with equal precision, careful to match the degree of his courtesy. But only that. These were proud men.

It was a carefully orchestrated ceremony. Kita welcomed all the participants formally, acknowledged the presence of the master sensei participating, and beamed with pleasure at the presence of Chanpga and the other lamas. I wondered why he was so happy. It was odd to see him smile, because even when he was being pleasant, I experienced the disquieting sensation of an underlying power that pushed against you.

"We are honored to have the presence of these holy men," Kita told us all, gesturing at the monks. "So often, the martial path is seen as a way of force alone..." He sounded regretful. "We must remember that we are in the service of a higher purpose and that the ferocity of our training should be matched only by our diligence in pursuing spiritual ends. These seekers remind us that, while the Way is often difficult and presents us with challenge, we persevere in the belief that we serve something greater than ourselves."

It sounded great, but I had seen Kita's fake inka. I kept my face immobile as I listened. You may think it odd, but I was worried that this man, like Changpa, could sense something of my inner thoughts.

Kita spoke of his time in Tibet and of the lamas he had studied with. Of their remarkable insight and even more remarkable powers. It seemed vaguely familiar, and then I realized with a start that it mirrored in large part Kim's notes. Even the list of lama sounded familiar in some way I couldn't immediately place. It nagged at me, but I was being buffeted by many things. And I was on the lookout for Han. Most other things tended to fade into the background.

I remembered snippets of the rest of his speech. There was a pattern to it, a subtle intensification that progressed through the mundane to the more exotic, obviously designed to keep his martial arts audience in thrall.

"I have traveled through many lands seeking the secret ways to unlock human potential. Generations of masters have passed these skills on to select students in mountain refuges..." His English was polished and now there was a singsong cadence to his delivery. His followers sat, bright-eyed and rapt with attention. "I stand before you as a link in a chain that stretches back into the glorious past..." He held up his arms and the fine silk sleeves of his black kimono top fell back to reveal powerful forearms. "I am a conduit of wisdom that can lead the worthy to higher knowledge..."

I snickered mentally. Sort of an opportunity to kick butt with the Buddha. Or at least be an understudy. I glanced over at the group of lamas. Changpa's face was rigidly immobile, his eyes hard to read. But some of the other monks were clearly upset at the import of Kita's claims. The general audience seemed to be lapping it up, however.

At that point one of his acolytes began softly tolling a small, resonant handbell. The bell wove in and out of the background, and his words were fading in and out with the rhythm of the bell's clapper. The pulse drove the words home, deep down into the mind where they swirled and resonated, drawing energy and growing in force.

He spoke then of the *tanren*. The forging of the spirit that lies at the heart of the warrior's art. His disciples were subject to this ritual: a passage in pain and effort that brought them to new heights. To a spiritual home on the mountaintop. To the Yamaji...

Eventually he encouraged those present to see whether any were brave enough to endure the ritual. It was part exhortation and part challenge, an invitation to join his mystic inner circle. I thought this would have a real impact on his audience: the hunger for the esoteric lies buried deep in the heart of many martial artists. And I knew with a cold certainty what would happen next.

Yamashita put my name forward as representing one ready for the ordeal. His eyes locked with Kita's, and the flash of mutual awareness and challenge was instantaneous. A few other sensei nominated students as well. I saw a look of relief on some faces when they weren't selected. There is wisdom in knowing when to pass on something.

Yamashita had then been invited to speak with Kita individually. As they sat on the dais it was hard to get a sense of what was transpiring. The words they spoke were quiet ones, and while both men seeped energy even while still, they kept their real thoughts and emotions hidden from the world. But they understood each other perfectly.

When the ceremony was over, I shuffled out with Sensei. The days when I would have simply and mutely obeyed him were gone. I asked him directly why he had put my name forward. Yamashita steered me firmly out of the hall and we walked on the grass in the waning wash of the dying sun. "Burke," he said quietly. "Kita fears us for some reason. And the danger is growing. But as yet we have not seen the other..."

"Han, the Mongol," I supplied.

"Just so. The weapon of choice." Half my teacher's face was washed with light and his left eye squinted slightly. He was looking north into the blue hills that churned off to the horizon. "Your brother has not come back yet?" I shook my head. "So," my teacher acknowledged, "we must wait and see what happens. And be ready."

"So we're trying to draw him out somehow through this... thing?" I asked. I didn't mean to sound unwilling. But I've been through an ordeal or two. Real ones. I don't have a burning need to subject myself to these things unnecessarily. You've only got so many of these types of experiences in you.

"Indulge me, Professor," my teacher said. We moved off toward the trees, into the long shadows and further away from the people milling around the conference center. "I am confident," my teacher continued, "that you are capable of this thing, this tanren. Kita does not believe so, and part of me wishes to see him humbled."

"We don't have anything to prove to anyone," I told him. It was a realization I'd been a while coming to. And it was the difference, I felt, between people like Stark and myself.

Yamashita nodded slowly. *"Honto."* True. "But there is a value in demonstrating this for the others here. You must think more as a teacher now, Burke. The things we do are not always for ourselves." And he sounded sad for a moment.

Yamashita moved along the tree line. He placed a wide palm against the white, papery bark of a silver birch and stood there for a moment, as if he were feeling vibrations from deep within the tree.

"Something will happen soon, Burke. I have been closely watched during my time here. The fight you had with Stark..."

perhaps it was merely rivalry, but perhaps in some way he is being manipulated. They meant to disable you and isolate me. They are afraid of us."

"For what we know about the inka?" I asked.

"Yes. And no. It is not just the forgery, or what it reveals… there is more to this than we understand."

"Look, it's only a matter of time before Micky and the cops get up here," I began, but Yamashita waved me down.

"They would find nothing. And they are… limited… by the constraints of your laws, yes? Better we remain and permit Kita's people to show their hand. For I think they will attack soon. And then we will know…"

When I hear Yamashita talk about attacks, I worry. He doesn't use words like that lightly. "We could walk right into a trap," I observed.

"Professor," he sighed. "We are here. On a mountain. In a compound where access is tightly controlled. Surrounded by highly trained disciples of a man we suspect of great crimes. I would say that we are already in a trap."

He looked contentedly across a field that ran down behind the conference center. On the fringes, the grass was high and going to seed, the straw-colored heads moving faintly in the light air like soldiers stirring for battle. A hawk high above us whistled in the deep blue of a waning summer day. Yamashita seemed content.

"A trap is most effective only when the victim is unaware, Burke. It is as I have taught you: a distant interval is safest. But when confronted with an attacker…" He looked at me expectantly.

"… move in toward the blade," I finished.

His eyes crinkled with pleasure. "So… Kita wishes us to experience the tanren. We will do so."

I still don't know what all that *we* stuff was about.

The chanting beat like waves against the room, my breath rising and falling with a rhythm driven by the thud of a wooden bell, pulsing amid dancing candlelight and faint threads of incense. We had been at it for hours now, and the brain's rhythms had shifted. Even if you hadn't known the process, the culminating effect would have been the same. It's an autohypnotic experience.

I had done things like this before, however, and knew to surrender quickly to the pull of the meditation. Otherwise your joints begin to hurt too much. You're supposed to think of nothing, of course. Your eyes are half closed and unfocused. The breath is regulated. Thoughts are supposed to come and go, to bubble away until the surface of the mind is unruffled by conscious thought. But my mind has an unruly owner. The ancients used to compare the process of taming the mind to that of herding a large, stubborn ox. It takes a lot to make the beast of the mind move the way you want. And deep down, I did not want to go in the direction Kita was leading me.

I slipped in and out of the meditative state. Fragments of conversations replayed themselves in my head, then nothing. Then more conversations. It was analogous to the series of experiences a dreamer has during a long night of restless sleep. But I was, in a curious way, awake. Kita's recital of his Tibetan experiences echoed in my head and I sensed something significant, but every time I tried to focus, the sensation of importance faded.

The chanting droned on and I slipped away. My eyelids fluttered faintly.

The candles were burning lower in the meditation hall. A slight breeze wafted the smell of burning incense into my consciousness. Like all sensations during the meditative state, you don't focus on it, merely accept it. It is the images the mind throws up that seem more important.

Even through half-closed eyes, I could sense the coming of dawn. My body was way down in the ebb that comes before a new day. Soon, the candlelight would weaken as its strength was leached away by the gray wash of morning. I was caught in the swirl of the tanren's current. Dawn would bring the ritual's culmination.

When we finally stood after the long night of meditation, it was painful. It was dark, but birds high up in the trees had started to stir. I moved stiffly, trying to get my heart going and the blood circulating. I'd need it.

They had told us about the tanren. Before the meditation session, we had a few hours working with the wooden *yari* of Kita's initiates. Using any new weapon induces muscle strain—you don't know how to wield it, so you tend to over-compensate with strength. After hours of it, my shoulders and wrists and forearms burned. Then, the night of meditation. And now, in the dark before morning, the true ordeal began.

They called it the Warrior's Path. *Michi no bushi.* When they spoke of it, I had to smile a bit. But Kita's disciples didn't see the humor. They were a melodramatic bunch.

Each aspirant was to run up a trail on different hills surrounding the Yamaji. Alone. And, along the way, each would be tested. Until the summit, where the mere act of completion served as a kind of validation.

The other victims nodded sagely when they were told. I looked around and thought they were being way too docile.

"How long's the run?" I asked the guy in charge.

"Different slopes. Different trails. Each path varies," he said evasively. "It'll take a while, I can tell you that. And it's uphill." He was extremely somber. I was beginning to catch the mood.

The sponsoring sensei arrived to see us off. There was some food in a bowl for each of us. Yamashita looked at it. "The vegetables are pickled, Burke. Salty. Leave them and drink the *cha*."

The green tea was bitter and rapidly growing tepid in the cool of morning. But I would need the fluids and I did as Yamashita directed.

I changed into the gi he had brought me. It was made of heavy canvas. I figured a hakama would not be the thing to wear while running up the side of a mountain. The gi would be more practical and, I hoped, would offer some protection.

When he handed me the bundle of clothing, I felt a hard shape buried in the folds. Yamashita looked significantly at me, but said nothing. And when I dressed, I slipped the short knife he had smuggled to me into my waistband at the small of my back. The gi's long jacket and the black belt hid the weapon from view. I felt equal measures of reassurance and alarm. I was comforted that I had a weapon, but worried that Yamashita thought I might need one.

Each path was marked by colored tapes, tied to trees and bushes. My path was red. I was rolling my head around to loosen the neck muscles. The oak shaft of the yari they had given me was smooth to the touch. I could smell the deep dampness of the woods. Yamashita came close and whispered.

"In the night, the police questioned Kita. He gave them nothing, but now his people have been warned. Beware the trail, Burke. They will try again for you. You must persevere and reach the top. I will be waiting there. As will Kita."

"And then?" I said, part of my mind still lulled by the night's chanting. There was something dreamlike about the whole sequence. It seemed threatening, yet remote.

Yamashita's hands reached out, his fingers probing for nerve clusters. He worked my hands, my arms, my legs. The pressure was hard and insistent. Painful. But after a moment, he looked closely at me and nodded in satisfaction. "Good. Now you are fully with us." And I did, in fact, feel more alert. I rocked back and forth from one foot to the other, getting ready. Most of the foggy feeling had dissipated.

"When we get to the top…" I inquired again.

"Kita seems a man who enjoys the dramatic. This ritual…" He held out a strong hand and gestured around us. "I would be surprised if we were alone with Kita at the summit. He may bring some assistants." My teacher looked at me significantly. "It will be the culmination of the ritual, Professor. I will try to see that others join us as well."

Then they took our sandals away and sent each of the aspirants out onto the trails. We were enjoined to move as quickly as possible. To race the sun to the different summits in the hills. To prove our worth.

I thought of the knife nestled in my back. Yamashita looked at me, his eyes hard and betraying nothing. "*Gambatte*," he said, and turned away. Hold out. Endure.

I started out on the final section of tanren, the forging. I thought about the significance of the name. The Japanese say you forge your spirit through martial arts training. The image is one taken from the blacksmith's creation of a sword blade. The metal is shaped and reshaped in thousands of actions until it is refined and melded into a thing of fearsome purity.

I had seen the end result of such an action and had also glimpsed something of the forging itself. Whatever the beauty of the product, it was created by a brutally refined process.

They pound on the raw material.

23

WARRIOR'S PATH

I listened, hearing made keen with terror. There was not much wind. Somewhere out of sight, a stream flowed. Birds sounded from faraway perches. And I tried to control the ragged sound of breath. Because being quiet might give me a chance.

The first one had come at me within the first few minutes of the run, before my breathing had a chance to settle into its rhythm. It was a straight, hard *mae-geri* attack and it was all I could do to keep the front kick from smashing into my thigh.

The path they'd marked was narrow. It was studded with rocks, and fallen tree limbs had been crudely cut to mark the way. They looked like victims of bad butchery. The trail was cool to the touch in places where your feet hit the slick earth. Cloud cover had made the night linger, and the air in the woods was dank and still. You looked up toward the sky and thought a storm was coming.

Mostly, you looked down. Running barefoot in the woods is hard. And I didn't want to break any toes. I've snapped any number of them over the years and the nice thing is that you can set them yourself with a quick jerk and a little tape. But I knew I needed to be firing on all cylinders that day. God help me if I wasn't.

It was stupid of me, of course. They wanted you jogging along, head down. And I was so focused on getting to the end of the ordeal that I forgot that the journey is sometimes as critical as the destination. So when the first attacker came at me, a blur of motion exploding with a hiss of breath, I was caught unawares. It was only reflex action that kept me from going down. I jerked away just enough to rob the strike of its full impact. I turned toward him, expecting more, but he faded back into the underbrush. I backed slowly away and began running again. I kept looking over my shoulder, but he didn't follow. I went on.

After that, I watched. They waited in the shadows, like wraiths, although their blows were solid enough. At a twist in the trail, a dip or rise—anywhere your line of sight was obstructed—they'd spring at you. They took one shot apiece, giving it all they had, but not following up. A sudden jab, a hard shove, delivered with concentrated venom, but then I was free to go on.

The point, I came to see, was to keep me off balance. To disrupt the rhythm of breathing. Because breath centers us and gives us strength. And, I was sure, they wanted me weak by the end.

The blows were directed at my arms and legs, mostly. They wanted to damage the muscles just enough to slow me down. To make me vulnerable. So as they came at me, I knew what to expect. And after a while, you could predict the timing of attacks.

It was, after all, a ritual. It reminded me of the gauntlet the Iroquois would make captives run: contained cruelty driving victims on to what lay ahead. And that fate was always worse than what went before. But Yamashita was waiting for me somewhere up the hill. I flinched at the blows, but I settled into it. And kept running.

The path dipped and twisted, a living thing whose stony surface bit at your feet and whose branches whipped at you with a malevolence that was a pale echo of the lurking attackers. But the trail always trended upwards. You could feel the strain as you wound up the mountain. It was hard to tell how far I'd come, or where the summit was. The footpath was too narrow, the ground jumbled and choked with trees. But slowly, the sky lightened and the gray dawn began to spread.

I hit a level patch of good, soft earth and raced along. I could see no more attackers. I'd gone down a few times and knew my feet were cut, but I hadn't taken too much damage. Sweat clung to me in the close air of the woods. I could feel spittle in the corners of my mouth from the effort of breathing. I scanned the way ahead of me, alert for the next attacker, head up.

The path wound along a ledge. To the right, the hill fell away in a rocky shoulder studded here and there with trees. Laurel bushes clustered in places down slope, and you could see how far up the mountain the path had come. There was a glimpse of rushing water down there, all dark glitter and foam amid a rocky bed, and I probably would have heard it, but my ears were filled with the vibration of my running, the thudding of blood in my ears, and the sawing of breath.

I see now that the view of the drop was a distraction. The sensei would nod and talk about a tsuki, a gap in concentration. It's the point of dangerous vulnerability. I should have been looking up to detect an attack, but my eyes jumped to the slope, partially out of the novelty of the view after the miles of closed forest. So I didn't even see the final attack coming.

The tripwire he'd strung across the trail was thin, but strong. It sent me sprawling and I landed hard. Small pebbles ground into the palms of my hands. He moved quickly for such a big man, but even so I managed to scramble away on my hands and knees. The sweeping underhand strike from the butt of his yari gave my ribs a glancing blow, but he was strong and it was enough to make me gasp with pain.

I looked at him. It was the same flat face that had stared along a shotgun barrel as it tracked me on a New York street. That night his eyes were dark pools, his face pale in the shadows thrown by streetlamps. In the half-light of the woods you could see him clearly. Han. You got a sense of the force of him and knew why they called him the Mongol. He was dressed in the black uniform of Kita's disciples with a red belt around his waist that, for all the muted light that morning, was like a crimson splash of blood and heat in the still woods.

He was big and strong. And he knew it. His square face was set in a grim smile and his massive hands gripped the spear and waited for me to stand. I got up, my back to the drop-off, and knew I was in a bad spot. The yari's protective sheath was removed, and the long steel head was aimed right at me.

"Why?" I asked. Not that I was really interested: I was stalling for time to prepare for what was coming.

"You know too much." He had an oddly quiet voice. But his eyes were hard.

I kept stalling for time. "Others will know soon, too," I said, trying to get away from the edge and find some room to maneuver. But the lance's head tracked me without mercy.

The Mongol shook his head from side to side, jerking like a meaty machine. "Others will not know. It ends here. With you and the old men."

I had put out a hand in supplication even before I consciously registered the fact that he had begun to move. He drove the spear at me in a savage lunge made deadly by years of practice. His thrust was hard and precise, man and weapon welded together in one deadly urge. I'm sure, in his mind, that the spear had already ripped through me. You could see the glow of anticipation in his eyes.

But the rocks betrayed him. His footing slipped—just a little—and bled some of the accuracy out of his thrust. As quickly as I could, I closed with him, hoping to get inside the spear's offensive radius. I parried the shaft with my right hand and jabbed at his eyes with the rigid fingers of my left. For someone this big, you can't bludgeon them. There's too much muscle and bone. The sheer mass is too great. You have to go for selected targets. The soft tissue.

He swept the strike away with a grunt. He tried to bring the yari around, but it was too cramped—I could hear the shaft clack on wood and stone as he tried to bring it to bear on me. I drove into his solar plexus with my right fist—I would have dug into him and torn his lungs out if I could—but I couldn't get the angle right. And now he had dropped the spear.

I could sense the fight's balance tipping. He knew it, too, and saw the knowledge reflected in my eyes, because his savage grimace just got bigger. I knew if he got his arms around me that I was finished. I tried to spin away, out of his killing zone. But he moved in. A massive hand locked around each of my wrists and he held my arms out away from him. He looked at me and his eyes were deep, partially hidden behind the slope of the epicanthic fold, but still lit with a feral sense of triumph.

The Mongol's head reared back for a moment and I actually thought he was going to howl. Then he brought his forehead smashing down into my face. My head snapped back. I could feel my leg control fading away, but I tried to backpedal to stay upright. He let go of my wrists then. And his kick blew me off the ledge and down the slope like a leaf caught in a storm's vortex.

I was partially stunned, but Yamashita has worked for years to make my body responsive to events that flash upon you quicker than thought. I felt the first, sickening lunge into nothingness. My arms wheeled and my feet scrabbled for a purchase that had evaporated. What do you feel at a moment like this? Regret? Anger? It really happens too fast, to be frank. Training takes over. As a result, there was only a fleeting idea. And I swear it was in Yamashita's voice.

Do not hit your head. It would be bad.

The laurel bushes slowed me down some. The undergrowth and rocks on the slope meant you didn't fall for long in a straight line. It was more a punishing series of rolls: a bounce, some scraping, gravity twists the body and then the series starts all over again.

I stopped with a punishing thud, coming to rest on the limb of a downed tree. I was lucky. One jagged branch tore across my chest and out the front of my gi. I lay, pinned there, waiting for my sight to clear. I sagged, eyes closed, while distant birds shrieked alarm.

I was stunned, and that's probably what saved me. From the ledge, the Mongol looked down and saw me, inert. From his angle, I'll bet the tree limb looked like it went right through me. I should have been trying to move around, testing my limbs and probing for injuries. But if I had, he would have seen me moving and come down to finish me off. As it was, the Mongol figured his job was done. When I finally opened my eyes and peered up, he was gone.

I lay there and listened to the still sounds of the woods: birds in the distance, a rustle of dried leaves as something scampered through the underbrush, the whine of the mosquitoes as they found me, drawn by blood. I wanted to lie there for a while.

I knew that when I moved, it was going to hurt. And part of me didn't want to take the inventory of damage.

But the ordeal wasn't done. I could see that. Yamashita was waiting for me somewhere at the summit. The old men, Han had said. First they'd take Sensei. Then they'd go for Changpa. And I had to get to them because the Mongol was heading there as well. I knew that this wouldn't be the last time that the Mongol would try to send a victim spinning off into the void.

I moved gingerly downhill. The trail was a trap and I wasn't about to get caught again. In the ravine, I splashed down into the cold water of the stream. In a flat space, silt swirled around my feet and I collapsed to my knees, then dunked my head to clear it. The water was like ice. I gasped and looked up the streambed, a jumble of mossy rocks, and dark water swirling along. The Chinese philosopher Mencius said that human nature tends toward good the way water runs downhill. I was headed up, against the current.

My feet were a mess. Even covered with mud I could see that. My left elbow felt sprung and my nose was broken. Again. I had been mostly worried that Yamashita's tanto would have broken through its wooden sheath during the fall and cut me. I hurt so much allover that I held my breath when I felt around in the small of my back: I could have been cut to ribbons and not known it. But the fall must have shaken it loose, and the knife lay buried somewhere along the slope.

My gi top was ripped in a number of places. I tore the lower part up into strips—the material is thinner there. My elbow got wrapped up in a primitive brace. I would like to have done the same for my hands, but I wanted them free for whatever was coming. It was the same with my feet. Some kind of protection would have been nice, but I was afraid that it would make my footing unsteady when the time came. Over the years, I had learned that the wise thing to do is not always the easy thing. I would bleed a little longer. *Gambatte*, Yamashita had told me. Hold out. I started to move up the hill. It hurt, but I kept moving. I would endure.

I wondered how much time I had. Whatever the reality of the whole tanren ritual, it was clear that Kita had arranged a special reception for me. That's why I was on a special trail. I knew too much, the Mongol had said. And it was clear what happened to those who knew. Sakura. Hoddington. Kim. And perhaps Yamashita and Changpa as well.

But was the guilty little secret embedded in the inka something that Kita was willing to kill for? Part of me couldn't believe it. A forged certificate of mastery seemed like such little thing. It was clear that Kita had skill: his ki projection alone was astounding. And from what I had seen of his students, they seemed competent enough. Why even bother with the inka?

But the need for legitimacy is a powerful thing. Especially among the masters of the martial arts. They are conduits of wisdom, of the experience of master warriors, compiled over centuries. It's gathered into a curious treasure of insight and technique that they hoard jealously. Possession of a thing like the inka is almost mystical in its bestowal of prestige.

If Kita were building an empire, legitimacy would be an important thing. You'd think this would only be true in Asia, but American students are funny that way. In some ways, they're even worse. Maybe it's that most of our roots are so shallow here: we tend to stand in awe of genealogies that stretch back into time. And in the martial arts world students seem to hunger for a connection to the old times, the ancient warrior ways.

You can argue that it's a psychological need and it has nothing to do with technique. Which is true. But the need is a powerful one nonetheless. Everything I saw of the Yamaji told me Kita was working hard to exploit this need. And to be revealed as a fraud would threaten everything he had worked for.

But there was more. Most of my recent energy had been focused on bodywork, but the mind churns on despite us sometimes. And it had been working all night, just below the threshold of consciousness. I had been making connections.

Kim had suspected something about Kita. The kid might have turned out to be a real journalist—he had a good nose and smelled something, even if he couldn't nail it down. And he'd done his homework as well. The background on Kita's travels in Tibet. The list of Buddhist masters he'd studied with. And the sad roster of executed or imprisoned lamas. He had collected it all and was probably still trying to make the pieces fit when he somehow got hold of Kita's inka. When alarm bells went off, Kim had scrambled to what he thought was safety and tried to find people to help him make sense of things. And the killing began.

But I think too much.

I tried to use the streambed as much as I could, vaulting from rock to rock. It was better than winding through the brush along the sides. I'd been torn at enough for one day. But it was tough going in spots, the rocks jagged and tilted at crazy angles. And the sound of water masked any other noises. I looked frequently up to my left, to the ridge line where I knew the trail was. I dreaded seeing him looking down at me, the Mongol, looming there. It made me scramble faster, afraid to be at a disadvantage. But at the same time, part of me was simultaneously worrying about what I would find at the top.

The air was soaked with moisture, and the light was a sickly grayish green. The sun never burned through the cloud cover that morning. If anything, it got thicker and the air only grew stiller. It seemed like the only things moving were the water, tumbling downhill, and me, gasping and scratching my way up.

You set your mind to it. You ignore the pain. It's going to be with you anyway, so you just try to accept it. My skin burned in spots. But I had burned before. The breath scraped up and down my throat and the sweat stung my eyes and the cuts on my head. I must have had a few broken ribs. At one point, my stomach heaved and I retched painfully. But there wasn't much in there to come out. It left a thick, bitter taste in my mouth. I leaned down and scooped some water up to my lips at one point. I was moving too fast and whacked my nose accidentally: my eyes teared up again.

On either side of me, my way was bound by rocks and dark, silent trees. It was a hard, unforgiving path that I moved along. To most people, it would not have looked like much of a way to anywhere. It depends, I suppose, on where you're heading and how badly you want to get there. I struggled through the terrain, accompanied by a jerky interior dialogue.

Again. You're in one of those weird situations again. The moss on rock is fragile: my foot slipped and tore the green away. Down I went. *Shuddup.*

I hope Sarah called Micky. I hope she's all right. A tree trunk three feet thick lay across the stream like a dam. I started to lean my stomach on it so I could pivot my legs up and down onto the other side. The sharp pain reminded me of my ribs. *Yeah, well, she's tougher than she looks. And it can't be helped. Gotta deal with things.* There was a hard rationality to the thought. It was almost Yamashita-like. I wasn't sure I liked it.

I knew I didn't like the tree. Most days I would have simply jumped up on the trunk. I was learning caution, however. And saving my strength.

You better hurry. I made a misstep and came down hard on my backside, sliding down waist-deep into the current. *Yamashita's waiting for you.* I surged forward. *You better hope he's got a plan.* More rocks. Jagged tree limbs set like old weapons. The water, dark and cold and uncaring, moving away from me.

No, I thought grimly. *Get your own plan.*

The forest changed as I climbed. Pines took over, and their needles carpeted the forest floor. I left the stream, heading off to my left to find the trail. I looked down the long chute of the streambed for a minute, feeling a dull sense of accomplishment, then jogged off into the woods. The ground was softer here. Or my feet were simply numb. After a while, the rhythm of movement returned, the well-known cadence of breath and body, spiced with pain. The sensations were at least a bit familiar; a comfort in a strange place.

I pounded along, ragged and muddy. I watched the woods and although my eyes were busy in the here and now, my brain began chanting. It was an odd snippet of prayer, part of an old psalm, written by someone who knew about life's hard edges:

> *Blessed be the Lord, my rock,*
> *Who trains my arms for battle,*
> *Who prepares my hands for war.*

I thought of what might be laying ahead at the end of the gauntlet. The way to live life is not to let your imagination rob you of courage. You need to prepare for what lies ahead, but you can't focus on that alone and let fear bleed your spirit away. It's the same with dwelling on the past. It can serve as an anchor. But you need to be fully present in the here and now. Changpa would like that idea. And Yamashita would support him, but quietly remind me that you also need to plan to endure.

I smiled grimly. I've learned that, above all.

24

STEEL RAIN

The flat ceiling of cloud cover had begun to churn. You could sense it growing denser, a restive blanket of water and wind. As the clouds thickened, moving with increased energy, the surface of the sky began to coil and twist, as if huge serpents lurked just beneath the surface. The light, dim and green in the forest, was pink in the clearing on the mountain, as if everything you saw was tinged with blood.

They were clustered around an area nearest the trailhead. Kita was there, dressed in jet-black robes. He seemed to swell in the air's turbulence, drawing energy from the gathering storm. His retinue of spear-carrying followers was with him. One ceremoniously held a bow and a quiver of arrows. Another held up a long sword. It was the type of formal weapons display common years ago in feudal Japan for individuals of high rank. I thought it was a little over the top, even for the Yamaji. It was a fleeting insight that might have been useful a while ago. But things had spun too far out of control.

Yamashita was there with them as well. I checked my first impulse to go to him and moved stealthily through the undergrowth instead, biding my time. Because the Mongol was nowhere in sight.

I circled the clearing, noting that there were other paths leading to the oblong slash in the trees where Kita and Yamashita waited. I glimpsed a gravel access road across the clearing. A few cars parked there explained how the bunch of them got there. There was also the path I was to have completed. And an old logging trail, narrowed so much by the resurgent forest that it appeared like a dark shaft, a tunnel leading down into the woods.

The wind stirred, and leaves hissed like the sound of distant fires. It covered the noise of my movement as I circled warily, just out of sight in the underbrush. I moved closer, watching. There was a certain fascination to Kita. He lifted his head into the wind and his long hair began to dance. His eyes closed, as if he were feeling the currents of pressure and temperature that swirled around us with senses calibrated in a different way from the rest of us. I shuddered: you try not to look too much at someone like that. Even normal people are sometimes sensitized to the energy given off by someone watching you intently. I was afraid that, at any moment, Kita's eyes would snap open and his head would swivel toward me, pinning me with an invisible force.

Yamashita regarded the sky and then looked down the mountain trail that I was expected to arrive on. It was difficult to hear everything they said—the wind was starting to whip old leaves around the clearing, and it snatched their words as well. But there was concern from Yamashita about the delay in my arrival.

The Mongol slipped into view at the trailhead. One minute the dark hole in the forest was empty, the next it was filled with his presence. He trotted easily to Kita, bowing and reporting to him in a low voice.

"My student shares your concern for your pupil, Yamashita-san," Kita said. "He fears that perhaps an accident has occurred…"

Yamashita looked around, at Kita and his impassive students. At the woods, where leaves were showing their light undersides and the tops of trees were beginning to whip around. His eyes were narrowed into slits as he measured the situation. He, too, sensed invisible currents.

"I will go," my teacher said, and turned toward the trail.

I had drawn breath and was beginning to move out into the open when a shout stopped me.

"Don't!" a voice called.

"Don't go," another added. "It's a trap!"

They must have come on foot along the gravel road. Sarah Klein, Stark, and the Rinpoche. I didn't know whether to be glad to see her, or just worried that she was now closer than ever to danger. All their faces were dark with concern and effort. And, at their cry, Kita's students began to move. There were six of them in addition to the Mongol, and there was a smooth, deliberate flow to what they did. The ceremonial bow and sword were dropped and the spears were leveled in a protective ring around Kita, long black shafts tipped with steel that gleamed dully in the weird light. The Mongol stood close to Kita, gripping the shaft of his weapon with huge hands.

Stark hurried across the grass. Changpa laid a restraining hand on Sarah and they remained near the cars at the road's end. At least he had some sense. But not Stark. "Please, Shihan," he called as he approached and bowed to his master, "this is not necessary."

The energy crackled out of Kita. The air was already humming with electricity as the storm approached, but his anger brought it up another notch. Stark flinched as if he had been struck.

"*Bakka*," Kita hissed. Idiot. "How dare you interfere with the ceremony?" Even at this point, Kita was maintaining a façade. Later, when I thought about it, I realized that I shouldn't have been surprised. He had labored so long and hard on creating it. And as it began to shatter, he grew defensive.

Stark was clearly afraid, but he held his ground. I'll give him that. Kita's arm shot out, a black blur driving into the nerve plexus in Stark's chest. He collapsed almost silently to the ground.

The sudden, unexpected brutality of it made me move involuntarily. "Sensei!" I called and stepped into view so Yamashita could see me. The Mongol growled at the sight of me and Kita shot a look at him that was filled with equal parts venom and confusion. The ritual was not following the script he had developed.

"It's over, Kita," I called to him. "The secret is out. I know, and others will, too."

His eyes bore into me, his form still despite the force of the wind whipping around us. You could see the effort it took to compose himself, but he pulled it off. "What can you know?" he asked, and he made his voice sound intrigued, not threatened. But his eyes darted around the expectant faces in the clearing.

I gestured at the Mongol, a hulking, angry presence whose mood seemed to be part of the increasingly violent air around us. "He's a murderer," I said. "I don't know whether he did it alone or had help. But he killed Sakura."

"Ridiculous!" Kita scoffed. "We are seekers of wisdom here. My disciples would never…"

"How nice. All here together." Another voice broke in as someone else emerged from the undergrowth. He was one of the Chinese coaches, his navy blue tracksuit making him look plain and small in contrast to Kita. But there was an energy to him that was more than a match for the master of the Yamaji. Kita looked at him with something like fear in his eyes. Han relaxed a little: you could see it in the set of his shoulders. The look that passed between the Mongol and the man in the track-suit was enough to spark a memory of where I had seen the face before: in the FBI surveillance photos Charlie Wilcox had given us. It was Wu Tian.

Wu had a small automatic pistol in his hand. One of his eyes was closing and it looked like he had been hit pretty hard on the side of the head. He didn't seem happy, no matter what he was saying.

"Yes," he went on, "how nice. All of our concerns tied up in one little package." He looked at me, then Yamashita. It was like being sized up by a viper. The he turned on Kita and Han. "I am not happy with the sloppiness here, Han. Now we will have to adapt to a new plan." The Mongol hung his head slightly, a giant, murderous child cowed by some power I couldn't quite fathom. "And you," whipping around to let Kita feel the full power of his anger. "I told you I wanted any and all links eliminated!" His English was excellent, but he still had trouble with the "l's." "When you are no longer of use, Kita, you merely become a liability."

Wu said it almost matter-of-factly, but you could see some of Kita's spearmen bristle at the import. Han turned to face them. Wu glanced over to Sarah and the Rinpoche and his voice changed. It was casual, almost friendly.

"You led me on a merry chase," he called, and rubbed his injured head gently with his gun hand. "But there is no need for more hide and seek." He gestured at them. "Come here."

Sarah looked at me, silently pleading for advice. Changpa seemed calm, almost resigned to things.

"Oh, I get it now," I said. My brain had been racing as I put things together. Unfortunately, I didn't have a plan to get out of this mess. When in doubt, stall. "You're a seeker all right, Kita," It was finally coming clear in my mind. I spoke loudly enough so everyone could hear me. "Traveling all over Tibet, getting access to all these holy men with weird powers." I glanced at Changpa, who drifted toward us as if pulled by a force not under his control. "Did anybody ever wonder how it was that you were able to do this? A foreign national in Tibet? Getting access to people the Chinese government didn't want anyone to see?"

Kita made a calming gesture at me. "Please. Your imagination has gotten the better of you. I was fortunate in being able to study with the lama, to be able to preserve a rapidly disappearing body of wisdom…"

"Oh, save it!" I spat. "It took me a while to piece it together. You weren't fortunate. You had help." I looked at Wu, remembering what Wilcox had told us of him. His time in Tibet. His probable involvement with smuggling. The man from the Chinese embassy looked at me, his eyes intent behind hooded lids. "That's how you two met. The seeker and the secret agent. I'll bet he could arrange access for you. But it came at a price."

Wu's casual stance grew more rigid. The gun hand, waving casually a minute ago, slowly rose into place, cocked at his hip. "This is what happens from leaving loose ends," Wu spat to Kita.

Kita's face was pale. I couldn't tell whether it was a trick of the storm's light or the reaction as a realization set in.

I looked around at his followers. "You've all heard the list of holy men he studied with," I told them. "Teachers with mystic powers. It's part of his PR." They stood there like stone pillars, deaf to reason. But I kept at it. "It's interesting that when you track Kita's progress across Tibet, a series of unfortunate events seems to follow." I gestured at Changpa. "Ask the Rinpoche. He monitors the fate of prominent monks in his country."

"The allegation…" Kita's face grew hard and his eyes narrowed "… is false. You have no idea of the complexity of the situation there." He was facing me, but the words were for his students.

"I know that in every case, after you finished studying with a lama, he was arrested by the Chinese authorities." I saw Changpa's eyes close in sorrow. Or in sudden pain. "What was the deal, Wu? Kita'd pump them for information, you'd loot whatever artifacts you could find, and then arrest them? Career advancement and some extra money in one fell swoop?"

"The government keeps a close watch on the religious in Tibet," Kita protested. "The Interior Ministry controls all access to the holy men… I had no choice but to comply with their rules…"

"It wasn't a rule," I said. "You two cut a deal. And sold the monks down the river!"

Now Kita glanced at Wu, as if for help. The man from the consulate was watching me intently with pursed lips, obviously trying to figure out what I really knew and what I was guessing at. But he said nothing.

Kita licked his thin lips. "You fool!" he said to me. "This is all conjecture! I went to the Roof of the World to save the last remnants of esoteric knowledge. To preserve it for generations to come! The authorities were slowly smothering the old ways. It would happen with or without me." He gestured with a jerk of his hand at Changpa. "None of us can alter that fact. So I chose to save what I could. In any way I could…"

I snorted with contempt. "You used them for your own gain. To create a reputation. And it's as fake as the inka you had created for yourself."

He rocked back as if struck. There probably wasn't much talking back at the Mountain Temple. I pressed him. "The irony of it is that Kim wasn't even sure what he really had in his hands. All kinds of facts but precious few connections. Maybe the inka was fake, but that was just the tip of the iceberg." I turned to Wu.

"It's not about Kita, is it? Not really, I mean. He's just one of the loose ends that lead to you. No one really cares about the calligraphy." And I had to shake my head at how stupid I had been. "Maybe some of the Hollywood people who bankroll Kita wouldn't be happy to hear that he was an informant for the Chinese. But that's not why all those people were killed."

Wu was very still, and although the weather was whipping around us, it was as if things got very quiet there for a minute.

"I don't know how Kim got the stuff he did," I continued, "but once it was out, it was only a matter of time until someone started digging through it and making connections. So you turned Han loose." "Ridiculous," Wu scoffed. "How can you know this?"

"Sakura told me," I replied.

"The dead tell us nothing," he replied with certainty. There was a grim satisfaction to his tone, and he seemed to relax slightly.

It was my turn to give a hard smile. "You're wrong. Sakura left us a clue. A message in his last piece of calligraphy. Don't you know what he wrote before he was killed?" Wu looked at Han, but the giant said nothing. Kita's eyes were lit with a jumpy energy.

"He wrote *shumpu*," I told them. "Spring wind."

"You waste my time, Burke," Kita spat, finally coming to life. "This is of no interest to me."

"And yet it should be," Yamashita interrupted. He had been nothing but a stout figure, pushed at by a hard wind. Immobile. But now he spoke. "It comes from a poem by a Zen monk…"

"Bunkko Kakushi," I added.

"His monastery was raided by barbarians," Sensei said, then gestured at me to continue.

"As they broke in on his meditation and threatened him," I said, "he composed this poem:

> *In heaven and earth no place to hide;*
>
> *Bliss belongs to one who knows that things are empty and that man too is nothing.*
>
> *Splendid indeed is the Mongol long sword*
>
> *Slashing the spring wind like a flash of lightning."*

I looked at the Mongol. He stared back at me with no apparent emotion—a homicidal robot waiting for someone to punch the "on" button. "Sakura fingered your man, Wu," I told him.

"Absurd!" he protested haughtily.

"Maybe," I said, "but we've got Kim's notes to suggest a motive. And once the cops start digging, I'll bet they can pin it on him. And on you, too."

I turned to Kita. "Now you're not only a fraud, you're an accomplice to murder." The wind dragged his long hair across his face and Kita clawed it away from his eyes, his demeanor altered. He looked at my teacher and me with pure hatred, stepping back as if to avoid contamination. He reached out with his hands, the fingers like talons, straining toward us. Then he jerked his hands closed into fists and made a motion as if dashing us to the ground. The order was silent, yet unmistakable. The spearmen began to move.

Events became as swirled and jumbled as the air. Yamashita glanced at me, sending silent messages and simultaneously moving to intercept some of the attackers. Stark, still gasping on the ground, rose shakily and lunged to try to stop the Mongol. The killer knocked him back over with easy contempt and the spear drove down with an almost casual brutality. Stark's choked gasp of pain was masked by the sound of the wind and the distant scream from Sarah. Kita's robes swirled in the wind as he whirled away. The spearmen closed on Yamashita and me. And a pistol shot boomed through the clearing.

"Police!" a familiar voice shouted. The spearmen hesitated for a moment, unsure as to what to do next. Another shot punched through the air. "Freeze! I'll shoot the next asshole that moves!" Micky yelled as he and Art, guns drawn, moved into the clearing from the access road. Wallace brought up the rear, carrying a shotgun at high port. I sighed in relief.

Art leveled his pistol at Kita, who was edging closer to Sarah and the Rinpoche. "That includes you, too, Johnny Cash," he said.

An enormous boom shook the mountaintop. It was as if the air had been rent apart in a powerful convulsion, a flash of pink light and the concussive blast of the thunder. It stunned us, freezing us in our tracks for a moment. But Kita recovered first.

"Han!" he called. Kita drew a short sword, the *wakizashi*, from his sash and slipped behind Sarah with the fluid, predatory moves of a snake. The long blade was at her throat before we could do anything. The Mongol left his spear buried in his victim and drew an automatic pistol from under his gi top.

Stark, pinned to the ground, had stopped making noises. His legs moved in faint, aimless jerks, spreading the blood that pooled under him. Wu sidled along, using the spearmen as cover, toward the trees.

"Do not move!" Kita screamed. Han pointed the pistol at my head. Micky and Art stood, guns up, but frozen into stillness. Wallace looked at them quizzically.

"Do what the man says, Wallace," Art told him. We all knew that this was a standoff.

Kita smiled tightly in triumph. "We are leaving," he told us. "Move away from the cars."

"Won't do you any good," Micky told him. "State troopers were on their way when we came up. The roadblock's probably already set."

"You're trapped, Kita," I shouted. I was watching Han, looking down the barrel of his pistol and trying to see Wu out of the corner of my eye. I heard Kita cackle.

"Trapped? We will see…" Sarah gave a little shriek and I half turned away from the Mongol to see what was happening. Kita was dragging her backwards, using her as cover, heading toward the old logging trail. Rain began to slant down.

"Wait!" the Rinpoche commanded, and his voice had an odd, powerful resonance, even in the midst of the rain and wind. It was the first overt action he had taken since preventing Sarah from following Stark into the killing zone. The lama walked slowly toward Kita. He was dressed in his full robes, the deep crimson of his sash looking even darker in the storm. He stood and faced Kita. Their eyes locked.

"I will go with you as a guarantee of safe passage," Changpa told him. Kita grimaced and jerked at Sarah as if to resume his retreat. "Do not!" Changpa said in that quiet, compelling voice. "Think. This one is an innocent, but she will fight you." Wu had made it to their side. The lama gestured at him. "You know this already. I will go willingly. As a hostage." He turned to look at us all. His eyes behind his rain-spotted glasses were sad as he took in the men with guns, the men with spears. His gaze lingered on Stark's body. "There has been enough suffering here. These men do not wish me harmed. It will be your guarantee of safe passage." He held out a hand in supplication and slowly, Kita's blade came down from Sarah's throat. The lama took her hand and passed her to Art, then crossed to Kita's side.

Kita barked a command and the spearmen trotted into the forest ahead of their master. Wu was already fading into the brush. The Mongol gave me one last deadly look and turned to him. Kita dragged Changpa along to the trail's entrance. It was like a dark mouth in a green wall that hissed and moved with the storm. I felt sick with a mixture of dread and an odd sense of the familiar, a horrible experience of déjà vu. Changpa paused, framed by the trail's darkness and a lightning flash made his glasses go opaque for a moment. Then he turned and was dragged down the trail, vanishing from our sight along with the others.

We all stood without moving for a minute, then Yamashita shot across the clearing. He, too, paused at the trail's mouth, like someone taking one last look at the world before entering the cave to hell. The rain was cold, but that wasn't why I shivered. It struck me. My dream. I had seen this before.

"*Hakka yoi*, Burke," Yamashita called to me. Hang in there. Stay ready. Then he, too, was gone.

Sarah Klein looked at me with big, sad eyes. Then she knelt down, rocking silently in the rain as she cradled Stark's head in her lap. Wallace came over and checked for a pulse. It was something to do. He looked up at us, blinking in the downpour, and shook his head no.

"What a clusterfuck," Micky said as he came up to me on the run.

"What took ya?" I protested.

Micky squinted at me. It wasn't just the rain. At first he looked like he was going to say something cranky, but he got a good look at my condition and said in quiet voice, "Lucky your lady friend got ahold of me. All hell's breaking loose. The Feds are down there, screwing everything up."

"The Feds!"

"Later," Micky said tersely. Then he looked at me again. "Can you hold it together a bit longer, Connor?" He was, after all, my brother.

I nodded. "What now?"

Micky jerked his head and we all moved to the trailhead. The trees offered some shelter from the storm. "The troopers will be all over this hill soon. So Kita can forget his car. Maybe they can get back to the resort thingy…"

"The Yamaji," I corrected.

"… but there'll be units there as well. So they'll run wherever this path leads them and hope that they can find a car or something when they get down."

"What about Changpa?"

"Hostages are a pain when you're on the run," Art told me. "They'll keep him long enough to make sure they can get away…"

"And then?" I pressed him. Art shrugged.

"They'll toss him," Micky said, and it was clear from his tone of voice what he meant.

I thought about Kita, scrambling to keep things together. Of Wu, obsessed with loose ends. And the Chinese had no love for Changpa. "We gotta go after them," I said.

"We're goin'," Micky said, "but us, not you."

"Eight, maybe nine guys," I told him. "And you and Art." I nodded at Wallace. "And him. You like the odds?"

"I don't like anything about this," Micky said tightly. All three men were checking their weapons and looking down the trail. The rain fell steadily, and the earth was dark.

Micky looked at Art and Wallace. Both men nodded at the unspoken question. I went and spoke with Sarah.

"We're going after the Rinpoche," I told her quietly. She nodded as if she were taking it in, but I wasn't so sure. "You hang tight. The cops will be up here soon." I gave her shoulder a squeeze and she smiled tightly as I left.

"OK," Micky said to no one in particular and let out a long, tense breath. "Wallace, give him the shotgun." He showed me how to work the pump while Wallace took out his pistol and made sure that there was a round in the chamber. "You bring up the rear, Connor," my brother instructed. "Keep the muzzle pointed away from everybody. Anything happens, get off the trail. Get down. Don't fire that thing unless you have to. Got it?" His voice was tight and his eyes were serious, but there was a type of wild energy that mimicked the storm, a weird light dancing way back in there as well.

I nodded and we headed down the green tunnel.

The trail was uneven, studded with rocks and fallen timber, an obstacle course that twisted and turned down the mountain. Under the canopy of trees, the force of the rain had lessened, but the humidity closed around you like a blanket. We moved at a tense half-run, crouching in anticipation at every blind turn. The foliage here was thick, closing in on the path to cut off your view of things in the distance.

The run was taking its toll on Micky: you could see his chest working hard. He stopped, bent half over as his spleen started to squeeze a bit. Art stopped with him, watching dispassionately as my brother hawked up something and spit. Wallace, younger and in better shape, continued to move ahead. Art shot a worried glance toward him.

"I'll go with him," I told them.

"I'm comin', I'm comin'," Micky protested. You could hear a slight wheeze and he spit thickly, shaking his head.

Art jerked his head. "We're right behind you Connor. Don't get too far ahead of us."

I nodded and headed after Wallace. Two minutes down the slope, he paused, peering out of the shelter of the trees as the trail entered a clearing. Out there, the rain drummed on the exposed ground. The trail ran straight across the top of the clearing. And it ended there. To the right, the open space was dominated by a pond, a dark round pool some hundred feet in diameter. Cattails rustled anxiously in the rain. A culvert ran along the left hand of the trail, turning about halfway across the clearing and disappearing into a rusted drainage pipe that ran under the old logging road to the pond.

"Where're the others?" Wallace asked me, peering back down the trail.

"On their way." I gestured toward the clearing. "Whaddaya think?" I looked out and had the sudden premonition of danger.

Wallace shrugged. "That's where the trail ends. I don't see anything. They're probably heading cross-country downslope.

Let's move." I started to say something, to delay him, but he had already stepped out, moving fast in the clearer space.

I hesitated. "Wallace!" I hissed. I cast a glance back up the trail for Micky and Art, but couldn't see them yet. I looked into the dark spaces under the trees across the clearing and knew that something wasn't right. There was wind and noise. My ribs hurt and the shotgun felt heavy and foreign in my hands. But deep down inside me there was a quiet place, where I could feel an old familiar experience of certainty. And dread.

Wallace had almost reached the spot where the culvert cut under the trail when the tree line exploded with noise.

You could see stone fragments shooting up from the ground around him as the bullets hit. Almost too fast for sight to register, his right leg below the knee jerked violently away, bending out to the side. There was a faint spray of fluids, mingled with the rain. Wallace screamed and went down. His pistol flew out of his hand and skimmed into the pond. I looked around for help, but there was just me.

I ran as fast as I could, out along the trail to where he lay. I fumbled the shotgun up and pulled the trigger, aiming in the general direction I had seen the initial muzzle flash come from. I heard the answering pop of the pistol and I worked the mechanism like Micky had shown me and fired again, a jerky reflex shot. Then I dropped the weapon, grabbed Wallace by the shoulders and pulled back, desperate to get him into the ditch and out of the line of fire. As we slithered down into the muck at the bottom of the culvert, he shrieked as his wounded leg, attached mostly by some gristle, bounced over the rim.

Now there was an explosion of shots and Micky and Art pounded out of the woods, laying down some covering fire. They thudded into the ditch behind me, breathless.

"Jesus H. fuckin'…" my brother gasped. A shot whipped across the top of the culvert as I peeked out, and small pieces of rock stung my face.

"Christ," Art finished. "Wha' happened?" They were both panting. He gestured at Wallace, who had passed out.

"They caught him out in the open," I said.

Micky squinted at me. "Didn't I tell you not to do anything stupid?"

"You didn't tell me anything," I started, my voice shrill.

He waved that point away in disgust. "Great. This is classic…"

"Never use the trail," Art intoned. "Never cross a clearing without covering fire…"

"Where's your gun?" Micky said. I pointed out on the path where it lay, just out of reach.

"Never lose your gun," Art finished.

They both slithered up along the edge of the ditch, taking stock, guns pointed up to the trail's end where I assumed our attackers waited. The rain pelted down, the woods drinking it in and growing darker. The pond churned like a cauldron.

"Here's another fine mess you've got me into," Art said. He grinned to take the sting out of the words.

But Micky looked down. "Yeah," he said. My brother squinted up at his partner through the rain. He seemed like he wanted to say more, but didn't. The two cops looked away, almost as if embarrassed. A rumble of thunder seemed to bring them back into the here and now. Micky and Art silently checked their pistol clips, counting rounds. They looked into each other's eyes.

"Pretty thin, Mick," his partner said. "You better take it all." He gestured with the pistol. "I'm no good with this thing anymore."

Micky looked at him silently, then gave a wicked grin. "Like hell. We do this together." Art said nothing, but they divided their ammunition equally.

I looked from one to the other and knew what they were thinking. Kita had counted on the trail leading somewhere, but it dead-ended here. These guys were not woodsmen; faced with the option, they'd prefer to head back up the trail and find another escape route. Which meant coming through us. They wanted us dead anyway.

Another shot made us duck down.

"OK," Micky said. "Two pistols that we know of…"

"They're probably running low on ammo, too," Art commented.

My brother eyed the tree line to the left of the culvert. "Trees are what, thirty feet away? They're not comin' across the pond."

Art slid up along one side of the ditch, peering toward the place we thought the gunman was hiding. "One guy will keep us occupied. The rest'll sneak around our flank in the trees and make a quick dash for us with the spears."

"You think?" I was incredulous.

"If they had more firepower, they would have finished us off way before this, buddy boy." Micky was squinting into the woods. Way back there, you got a hint of movement, a faint blur as shapes flitted from tree to tree.

Art put a tourniquet on Wallace's leg to slow the bleeding. I tried not to look at the damage. Thunder rolled across the sky.

They came at us all at once. The Mongol moved out from the trail's end, firing his pistol as he came. A spearman ran alongside him. But they were a distant threat, thirty yards away. On our left flank, screaming attackers plunged through the scrub along the tree line, trying to cover the open ground between us quickly. Their spear points raced out ahead of them, hungry for targets.

"Get up! Get up!" I remember Micky screaming. If they caught us immobile in the ditch, the spears could do their work. Art started shooting, spacing his shots carefully, like a man unsure of his marksmanship. Back in the trees, I heard someone scream; maybe a bullet went home. Micky ripped off a string of shots in the Mongol's direction, then jumped out onto the trail and scooped up the shotgun where I had dropped it.

They didn't get to us all at once. It's probably what saved us. I collided with the first attacker, knocking the yari to one side, then scooping low and sending him somersaulting over me. Another swarmed up, spear at the ready and I heard Micky's scream of warning: "Connor!" I ducked down again and felt the breath of the shotgun blast as it blew by me. It caught the guy in the midsection, shattering the yari's shaft and chewing his chest up.

A spearman rocketed across the clearing, weapon driving in toward my brother. I remember how his mouth was locked open in a feral scream. Micky was still looking my way and the attacker was in his dead angle. I tried to get over to him, but slipped in the mud. The first guy I had knocked down started to get up and tripped me.

"NO!" I screamed in frustration.

Art's head whipped around. He ran toward Micky, barreling into him and knocking him away. His hand came up and he waited, watching the tip of the spear drive closer and closer behind the screaming lunge of the attacker. I saw Art swallow with tension and then fire. Once: a hard flat bark of an explosion in the driving rain.

The spearman was blown flat.

I picked up the two halves of the yari and went to work. You spin in multiple attacker situations, trying not to present too stable a target. It's a matter of odds really: you move as quickly as you can—strike, dodge, spin, block—and hope you don't spin onto an unseen opponent's blade. Or into the line of fire of your friends.

Art's gun went off a few more times nearby, but I was busy. I used the bottom of the yari shaft in my left hand, parrying attacks. But I drove the attack home with the spear point in my right. It was all thrust work: hard and mean. You get close to people when you kill with blades. You can feel their body heat, smell their breath. It's a perverse intimacy.

I heard a shout and even through all the noise—thunder and water, gunfire, and the deep thud of bodies in motion—it pierced my awareness. It was a kiai of immense power.

Kita had emerged into the clearing and Yamashita stood before him, offering a challenge. Kita was armed with a sword, and it traced a ghostly arc through the storm. My teacher stood empty-handed, immobile for a split second. Then, with another cry, he was upon Kita.

They were locked together, eyes narrow and noses flaring with effort. Sensei had immobilized the sword blade, but Kita snaked a leg around him and they fell, grunting, to the ground.

Micky shot the Mongol's companion. Han kept coming. He was alone, but even so, he was formidable. And now we were all out of bullets. The giant's handgun clicked empty, but he never even slowed down: he threw his pistol at us, snatched up a spear, and came for Micky. In the distance, Kita and Yamashita rolled through the mud. An arm raised up high, a knife flashing before it took a thrusting descent.

I cried out in echo of the weapon's impact. I couldn't see who had won. And, simultaneously, the Mongol reached my brother. I tried to lunge at them. I had the sickening fear that I was going to be too slow. Too late. Lightning crackled, and I thought it was a trick of the light when something flashed by the Mongol's head. He jerked slightly, his full attention diverted from my brother. Even so, the Mongol parried Micky's lunging attack away and clubbed him down to the ground with tremendous force. You could see Micky's mouth open as he grunted in pain, but the sound of thunder, the hissing rain, swallowed up all other noise.

Kita rose from the ground, eyes fierce and dark. His hair was wet and matted down across his shoulders. He reached out as if to direct his disciple. But Yamashita rose with him and, driving hard once more with the knife, severed the last of the life force that held Kita upright.

The Mongol saw him fall. Alone now, he howled in rage and went for my brother. As I scrambled toward them, desperate to save Micky, I saw the flash again.

The Mongol stopped in his tracks and looked across the clearing. In the flicker of a lightning strike, Sarah Klein stood there, bow bent in the classic shooter's posture of kyudo, drawing another arrow. The Mongol grinned savagely and set himself in readiness. I saw Sarah's mouth open for the kiai. The snap of the bowstring and the streak of the arrow as it shot across the rain-soaked space.

In one fluid motion, the Mongol reached out with a giant hand, trying to snatch the arrow in mid flight. His mouth opened in a cruel laugh as he reached out, but he missed and the shaft transfixed his hand.

I drove the yari's point into his throat with all the force I had. He rocked back and stood there for a moment as the blood began to spurt. I was still hanging on to the shaft, working the blade back and forth in his neck; he was so big that the step he took actually pulled me along with him. His eyes focused on me, then faded, then focused again.

Micky drove the butt of the empty shotgun against the Mongol's head. The three of us slipped and collapsed in the mud on the trail. I could feel the flow of the Mongol's blood hitting me, strangely warm in the cold rain. Micky hammered at him some more.

I rolled to my feet, frantic to anticipate the next attacker, but it was over. The rain slackened and the noise suddenly subsided. Yamashita approached. The blade and his arm were both soaked in blood. Changpa drifted out as well, silently moving across the landscape, pausing to look at each still form in the mud. It was hard to tell whether the marks on his face were from rain or tears.

Sarah moved toward us, dragging the bow on the ground, a useless appendage. She was staring at the Mongol, his body covered in a coating of mud and dark blood, slowly being washed by rain. I reached out for her and touched her lightly on the arm. She turned her head slowly, away from the sight.

"You were... amazing," I told her quietly.

She didn't respond. She started to shiver and I held her close, but it seemed a gesture out of place. Sarah stood there, her shoulders hunched up and tense. I wanted to offer her some comfort, but there was precious little to go around.

I could hear the little things that had seemed to fall away during the fight: the rasp of my panting breath, the plop of individual raindrops hitting the pond. In the killing ground between the ditch and the woods, someone gave out a faint, wavering moan.

The lama reached us. "So much suffering," he said quietly. He seemed stunned.

Yamashita came close and gestured with the bloody blade. "There is another in the trees." His voice was cold and matter-of-fact.

I closed my eyes for a second. I could smell the faint scent of Sarah's hair. But the scene had a power all its own and I opened my eyes again. Micky sat in the mud and looked at the sky, squinting with my father's expression, looking for a sign of clearing.

Art sunk down heavily, legs dangling into the culvert. He still held his pistol, the slide locked back on an open chamber. He put it down into his lap and looked at his hands. "Michael," he said quietly, emphasizing each word, "I am getting way too old for this."

For a moment, I thought I heard the sound of help coming—footfalls on rock and the crackle of radios. But then the heavens opened up again, soaking us with water and noise. In that dark space it was hard to tell who was colder, the living or the dead.

25
Far Mountain

It rained for the next few weeks as if heaven was trying to soak the blood from that clearing. The rainy days, where you wandered around with hunched shoulders and wished you had stayed in bed, were a pretty good match to our moods—we were all hunkered down and hoping that things would blow over.

The Massachusetts State Police weren't too pleased with us. The woods were a mess and the fact that some New York cops had jumped jurisdictions and made a bloody ending to a homicide investigation didn't seem to mollify them one bit. Probably just jealous. Micky told me that there was a great deal of yelling and screaming over phone lines. Letters of reprimand were written on official letterhead. Even more alarming, higher-ups were involved, hammering out new rules for "modalities for inter-state law enforcement cooperation." Whatever that was.

And the Feds were even more furious. They murmured darkly about national security. The Patriot Act. They were dying to tell us what we had done. But they couldn't, and that made them even madder. It didn't stop Micky and Art from getting hosed down pretty good by some suit from headquarters. The word on the street was that we had screwed something up. Imagine.

Wallace was finished as a cop: the high velocity rounds had wrecked his tibia. His wife was angry beyond words when we met her at the hospital. She was a thin, diminutive blonde woman who eyed us as if we were roaches when we came into the hospital room. She didn't say a word, all hard looks and lips pressed together into a tight line from the effort of self-control. I think she wanted to bite us.

But Wallace seemed philosophical at the prospect of retiring on long-term disability. "Hey," he shrugged, sipping at some apple juice through a straw, "more time for fishing." The color was back in his skin, which was nice to see. When they had trundled him off the mountain, he was the color of putty.

I'd been alarmed when Wu had not been among the bodies on the mountain. My brother shrugged. "A Chinese guy in a tracksuit is not gonna last long out here, Connor. They'll pick him up soon." And they did, the Feds whisking him away without a word. But it didn't cheer me up. Once we got over the relief of coming out alive, not one of us felt particularly happy.

I had looked at the Rinpoche in the immediate aftermath of the fight, and he seemed overwhelmed with sadness. Each still form in the woods seemed to affect him the same way, his grief as great for the Mongol as it was for Stark. I don't know whether that was a measure of his greatness or just the fact that he was fundamentally different from the rest of us. When someone tries to impale me with a spear, my supply of compassion tends to run out quickly.

Together, he and I watched the coroner's people put someone into a black rubber bag. Changpa touched the gurney lightly as it began to move, the attendants bouncing it over the rough stones with the callousness of routine. He looked at me.

"I'm sorry," I told him quietly. "I failed you." I wasn't thinking about the mystery of who was watching the Dharma Center, or whether the Chinese were involved. I was thinking about Stark. The lama's look told me that he knew that.

He smiled, but it wasn't an expression that gave me comfort. Changpa gazed off over my shoulder. The trees were dark with rain and the mountain vista was obscured with a rising mist. What did he glimpse on those far mountains?

"I once spoke to you about the ability to see… about prescience," he said quietly.

"The dark valley," I nodded.

Again the grim smile. "Some people think it is a gift. And perhaps it is so…" He took a ragged breath. "But not in the way they think. To see only partially is to be reminded that the thinking mind is still clouded with illusion. I let myself be deluded into thinking I could steer Stark onto a different path." He sighed and the wind echoed him.

We were silent for a while. Micky and Art, wrapped in space blankets, were talking quietly with the cops who were taping off the scene, marking the placement of spent shells and broken spears. The medical people had bundled Sarah away. Occasionally, one of them tried to dab at my cuts, but I fended them off for a while. Yamashita stood silently, waiting his turn to take the detectives into the woods to mark the place where he had left a body in his wake. He had cleaned his hands off, but a streak of gore had spurted across his temple, a dark mark of someone's passing.

"Maybe you did steer him," I finally told Changpa. His eyes focused back on me, away from the soft hint of ridge lines in the distance. He was puzzled, clearly waiting for an explanation.

"Maybe, in some way, you did help Stark. Each person chooses a path for himself," I explained. "Maybe, when it came down to it, Stark chose to do the right thing. He didn't let Yamashita walk into a trap. He didn't go along with Kita's scheme…"

The lama nodded slowly. I'm sure it wasn't a new thought to him. But it was hard to feel comforted in the clearing that day. The air was thick and pungent with moisture and the smell of blood. He turned from me and began to walk down the mountain, his mala beads clicking, the tiny percussive sounds of a man trying to hammer a good lesson out of the callous school of experience.

The weather cleared in time for the Burke family. Every year, the whole clan gets together for what's known as the Memorial Golf Outing. My dad died late in June and rather than mope around on the anniversary, we've created this Outing. Why golf was selected is anyone's guess: my father had spent a year in Korea with the First Marine Division and that had cured him of the desire for any outdoor activities whatsoever. But there's a small public course in Robert Moses State Park off the South Shore of Long Island. The beaches stretch for miles, part of the barrier that creates the Great South Bay. You can barbecue there and spend the day on the sand if your Bourgeois Sport Skills are not what they should be. No one takes the game seriously, but there's a chintzy trophy awarded and we spend some nice time together.

After the ritual toast to Dad at the end of the game, the solemnity of the mood was overwhelmed by picnic logistics. Folding chairs pinched fingers; blankets were spread; immense coolers, awash in melting ice, food, and drink were lugged into place.

My sisters had packed the usual buffet specialties: casseroles heavily dependent on mayonnaise or unlikely recipes culled from the side panels of cracker boxes. What was a "mock" apple pie, anyway? I had learned long ago not to inquire too deeply.

My brothers-in-law sipped surreptitiously at beers. After the sham golf game the ever-expanding tribe of Burke kids were turned loose on the wide expanse of fine white beach. Later on, someone would fall from a swing set in the nearby playground and run, screams muffled by a mouthful of bloody sand, back to the adults. But for now, we sat under umbrellas or stood in the early summer warmth, squinting at the ocean, content.

"Well, you played your usual crappy game," Micky said to me. We were standing by the cooler, a little bit away from everyone.

"I use you as my role model," I told him. He handed me a can of beer, decently hidden from the Park Police by an insulating tube that wraps around the can to keep it cool. Sometimes technology is our friend.

Micky sipped the foam out of his newly opened beer. "Yeah, well. I don't know about you, but I'm still a bit sore."

I flexed my fingers almost unconsciously, testing for the stiffness that had just begun to dissipate. The joints made little cracking sounds. "How're things going with the girl?" my brother asked.

I shrugged. Sarah and I had sat in the conference center in the Yamaji, almost forgotten in the bustle and confusion of a crime scene investigation. Rain dripped down the windows—fat drops striking the glass in gusts, like the surf beating against the shore.

She was draped in a blanket and her hair was wet and plastered against her head. She shivered. "I'm sorry, Burke," she said to me.

"There's nothing to be sorry about," I said. "You got through to Micky, which ended up saving all our necks. And I talked to the Rinpoche. He tells me that when that guy Wu came to get him, you clocked him pretty good."

She smiled very slightly, waving the things I said away. "No," she said. "I'm sorry I missed with the arrows." But her eyes filled with tears at the memory of things. Her voice thickened. "I'm sorry I didn't tell you earlier about Travis…"

I reached out on impulse to touch her face. My hand was streaked with dirt and dried blood. She saw it and shied away from my touch. I wiped my hand self-consciously and set it down gently on her hand instead.

"It's OK," I said. She gave me a small, sad smile.

I looked at Micky now. "We're working on it," I said.

"And?" he pressed.

I shrugged. "It's hard, ya know. Sometimes when I'm around, all she can remember is the blood and stuff…"

Micky grunted. "Ya gotta make her see *you*, Connor."

"Easier said than done."

He snorted. "Is she worth it?"

I got an image of her, small and strong and determined, shooting arrows like arcs of lightning across that clearing. "Oh, yeah," I said.

"So what's that thing that Yamashita's always telling you? Ya know, keep at it?"

"Gambatte," I told him.

Micky nodded. "OK. So, *gambatte.*"

The adults had settled in a semicircle, talking to each other while keeping an eye on the kids. Micky and I joined them. "I still don't know why on earth you two went up that mountain in the first place," my mom said to us. When Dad died she got very thin. She's better now, but increasingly birdlike in her fragility. She sat, swathed in a windbreaker, looking smaller than I remembered. But she was still feisty.

Micky didn't talk much with Mom about what he did: for a woman who had experienced so much of life she was still remarkably naive. "Well," he told her judiciously, "it's like I said to the Internal Affairs guys—it seemed like a good idea at the time."

Micky's wife, Deirdre, made a "humph" noise and got up to tend the kids. Somebody was going to get brained with a seesaw at any moment. I could feel it, and so could Dee.

I nodded in support of Micky. "Ya had to be there, Mom." She, too, made a dissatisfied noise way back in her throat.

Micky watched the playground as his wife pushed their son, Tom, higher and higher on the swings. At the apex of the swing, Tom escaped gravity for a moment and shrieked with delight before the breathless fall backwards. When you're a kid, danger is the brief electric swoop of a swing, kept under control with a tether.

From what he could piece together—Charlie Wilcox had slammed the phone down when called and that was the nicest response Micky had gotten—my brother knew that there wasn't going to be any legal action against Wu. He was still at the consulate.

"Diplomatic immunity, buddy boy," he told me.

"But you'd think the Chinese would pull him once they found out about this stuff…"

"Who's to say they're gonna find out?" He looked at me archly.

"I don't get it, Mick."

"Ya don't, huh?" My brother dug a hole in the fine sand with his toe. There are deep purple grains mixed in with the white on Long Island's beaches, the minute fragments of clam shells that the Indians used to turn into wampum centuries ago. Micky concentrated on the hole, not looking up as he explained.

"The best spies are the ones you've already identified," he told me. "And the ones you own…"

"But the guy's a killer," I protested.

Micky shrugged. "Far as I can figure it, the Feds had their eye on Wu for a while. They knew he was dirty in Tibet. Probably still was. And they wanted to turn him. But the evidence was not all that great and Wu's a pretty slick character. So they figured that they've got to somehow… encourage him to do something."

"Isn't that entrapment?"

Micky filled the hole in and began another. "Intelligence has sort of different rules. Besides, they weren't going to take him to court, they were going to blackmail him. Make him into a double agent."

"So they got him to kill someone!" It sounded far-fetched to me.

Micky laughed, but it wasn't a happy sound. "I think this got away from them, Connor. They arranged for Kim to get access to the documents and start investigating. When Kita got wind of it, he freaked. Never mind the inka, he knew that the documents he'd saved would implicate Wu in art smuggling. So Kita had to contact Wu and ask for help in getting things back."

"But it didn't go as they planned, did it?" I said.

Micky shook his head. "Didn't go as planned for anyone. Wu probably told Kita to deal with it, so he could keep things at arm's length. But Kim gave Kita the slip and farmed stuff out to Sakura. He encrypted his files and stashed them. So Wu had to get involved, but he used hired muscle…"

"Just to stay out of it," I said.

"Sure. And the FBI was so busy watching Wu, they didn't bother to keep tabs on that psycho Han, which is when things really started to spin out of control for all concerned. Han followed the links from Sakura to Hoddington to Kim, but he couldn't find the documents."

I nodded. "So they watched Changpa, figuring they'd turn up there?"

"That's my guess. Best place to hide something is in the mail. So Han waited around to see if it would turn up. In the meantime, Wu's pressuring Changpa to keep a low profile. Beijing doesn't want bad PR when they're negotiating trade deals, and Wu doesn't want anything coming out about what he was up to in Tibet. Kills two birds with one stone."

"What a mess," I said. "More than two birds got killed."

Micky nodded. "Be more than a few Feds reassigned to North Dakota sometime soon," he said. Then he looked up at me. "Makes straightforward police work look appealing doesn't it?"

"Where's Art today?" I asked him. I'd had enough of the whole thing.

He snorted. "He might be by later. Claimed his sister-in-law was having a christening, but he also mentioned something about being afraid of beach ninjas."

I snickered. "Weenie." But we both knew I was kidding: Art had been one of the few people left standing in the clearing that day. Micky got up and went over to help Deirdre with the swings.

Later I made my way through the crowds that were settled on blankets nearer to the shore. The fine, grainy sand was hot and it growled as my feet rubbed against it. I reached the water's edge and stood watching the ocean. The water's color went from a translucent champagne where it slid up the shoreline to a deep blue out beyond the breakers. The wind came in off the ocean and I could feel the salt on my lips.

I watched the water churn and heave against the distant horizon and thought of Changpa's description of what it was like to see into the future: a surface in continual motion with peaks and valleys that formed and reformed before your eyes. You marked a spot or got a sense of shape only to watch it shift a moment later. Out in the distance on the water, fishing boats were pushed up by waves and then slid down into the troughs. They bobbed uneasily, frail-looking against the immense breadth of the sea. Sometimes the water was kind, but it could turn on you, whipped into surges where the valleys were deeper and darker than anything you could imagine. And then it could swallow you.

It's a realization we try to keep buried way down deep. I wondered how someone like the lama dealt with it, because the awareness seemed always to be upon him. I had spoken with Yamashita about this.

"There are many types of strength," he said. "If we are lucky, we each find our own before we pass out of this life."

We were talking about Changpa, but I knew that he was thinking of Stark.

"He was drawn to a bad teacher," I said. It was ungenerous of me, but true.

"In the end, he chose well," my teacher reminded me.

"It killed him," I said.

Yamashita had looked at me with that powerful look that is the combination of deep calm and the potential for sudden ferocity. "To live well is to hold onto life loosely, Burke, and to surrender it to something greater than yourself."

I nodded slowly in acknowledgment. Stark had come to the Dharma Center following after Sarah Klein. He was probably more interested in her than in anything that Changpa or Yamashita could teach him. And what I had thought was a sinister motive of some sort on his part was really nothing more than jealousy. It was because he resented the relationship that was developing between me and the woman he once lived with. He could have left me up there in the clearing with Han. But he didn't: eventually, he came to the Rinpoche and Sarah Klein and they took that fateful hike up the mountain.

Kita and Wu hadn't counted on the power of men like Changpa and Yamashita. They root through the world, seeing people as rough stones. They polish and shape us, and if there is heat and pain, at the end they leave us more brilliant than at the start.

I like to think that's what happened to Stark. That something of what Changpa had hoped for him came to pass. I don't know. Maybe we just see the world through a perspective shaped by our own individual experience.

The water was still cold this early in the season; not many people were swimming. The surf washed up across my feet, an icy surge that was a strange contrast to the heat of the sun. My wounds had healed and I was almost back to full speed in the dojo. I'd have plenty of time there. The flap with the state and federal authorities, as well as the high body count, did not enhance my popularity at Dorian. The university did not want me back. But I didn't dwell on the thought.

It was just as well. The university was like an ocean liner whose passengers turned resolutely inward, never trying to glimpse the ocean that surrounds them. A journey, I suppose, but an ironic one. Yamashita keeps yanking me out into the larger world. Sometimes it's a scary place, but on days like today the expanse of light only hurts your eyes, not your heart.

The wind bounced around my ears, and the rush of sea sound on that bright blue day pulled me out and away, far from mundane things. I watched the heaving sea and imagined a swimmer, fighting through the swells.

We each carve a path for ourselves through a field of time and space that remains forever fluid. For the most part we look down, alert for imminent dips and unexpected surges. It's probably just as well. We fight through one experience in the hopes of smoother seas ahead. If we lifted our eyes to the horizon, we might despair of ever finding rest. Or certainty.

But Yamashita has taught me something of the dignity of perseverance. In the end, it may be that all paths lead down to the dark valley. That we may never reach the far mountain. It may be the manner of the journey that's important. And the people you travel with.

A small voice nagged at me as I stood, eyes wide and gazing into the distant ocean. It persisted, and eventually I looked down.

Meghan, my sister Irene's kid, was standing there.

"Whaddaya lookin' at, Uncle Connor?" she asked. Meghan was a moon-faced nine-year-old, and her stomach was giving the elastic material in her one-piece bathing suit a run for its money. Like most Burkes, she would grow steadily chubbier through adolescence, and then suddenly slim down in a rush of hormones just before adulthood. Her Long Island accent was heavy, and when she said my name, it came out as "Kahnah."

"Wha'?" I asked, not fully focused. I was still far away.

"Whaddaya lookin' at?" Meghan said again. The expression on her face was concerned. I smiled and ruffled her hair in reassurance. She smiled back. "Mommy says we're gonna have cake soon and that you should come back."

Meghan squinted up at me and it was the same quirky expression as my dad's, alive in a new generation. For a moment, I heard the voice from my dream.

Time to wake up now, Tiger.

"She did!" I said, and smiled at the child standing next to me.

Meghan nodded solemnly at the power of cake. "Come on!" she urged, taking my hand and tugging me away from the water.

I looked up into the distance and saw Micky watching me. Art was with him, having come after all. And in between them, I saw the squat bullet shape of Yamashita, who was waiting as well.

Meghan and I threaded our way across the beach, her small feet leaving a trail that my larger ones followed. Later, the winds would send the sand skittering across our tracks. The seasons would scour them away. In the end, we wander across an uncertain world, and if it is hard to see the path, or to tell masters from disciples, it may be because who leads and who follows is not as important as the journey.

I held Meghan's small hand and we went together to our destination.

About the Author

John Donohue is a nationally known expert on the culture and practice of the martial arts and has been banging around the *dojo* for more than 30 years. He has trained in the martial disciplines of aikido, iaido, judo, karatedo, kendo, and taiji. He has *dan* (black belt) ranks in both karatedo and kendo.

John has a Ph.D. in Anthropology from the State University of New York at Stony Brook. His doctoral dissertation on the cultural aspects of the Japanese martial arts formed the basis for his first book, *The Forge of the Spirit*. Fiction became a way to combine his interests and *Sensei*, the first Connor Burke thriller was published in 2003. John Donohue resides in Hamden, CT.

CPSIA information can be obtained
at www.ICGtesting.com
Printed in the USA
JSHW020207280122
22337JS00001B/88